Headwind

Christopher Hudson

Aerial Productions, ©2010

Published by Aerial Productions

ESBN: 1453744533
EAN-13: 9781453744536

For Cheryl, Linda and Carol

1

A cloud of dust followed the Cadillac as it sped along a country road west of Miami. The driver winced at every rough patch that threatened to shake the car apart. A gold chain bounced against his chest under a Hawaiian-print shirt. In spite of the air-conditioning going full-blast, his olive forehead glistened with perspiration and he ran his hand over it and through dark, slicked back pre-maturely balding hair.

Suddenly he grabbed the wheel with both hands and slammed on the brakes, his sunglasses slipping down his nose as the car skidded to a stop.

"Goddamnit."

He threw the barely stopped vehicle into reverse, throwing a cloud of dust in the opposite direction. Slamming on the brakes again, he jammed the Caddy back into drive and swung it onto a barely visible two-track.

He eased the car a quarter-mile down the primitive driveway, stopping in front of a gate in a ten-foot high chain-link fence. A sign proclaimed, RODRIQUEZ BROS. AUTO SALVAGE. He stepped out of the Caddy into the blazing Florida sun, walked to the intercom mounted on the gate and pressed a button.

A barely recognizable, "Yeah?" filtered through the static.

"It's Tony," he said just as two snarling Dobermans reached the gate from the inside, barking frantically and pressing at the fence to get at the sweating man. "Give me a sec to get back in my car before you …"

The gate began to slide open, the dogs nosing at the quickly widening opening.

"Sonofabitch," Tony yelled as he scrambled back to the car and dove through the open door.

He slammed the door shut as the lead dog reached the car and leaped on the window. "Christ," he said, breathing hard and trying to compose himself as the dogs bounced off the car, snarling and snapping. "Damn mangy hounds."

He slipped the car into drive and pulled through the gate, flipping off the dogs as they followed, continuing their vicious attack on the car. Once inside he sped up and watched them in his mirror as they disappeared in the dust.

Bouncing another quarter mile past rusting hulks of cars and piles of parts, he pulled up to a small building, its corrugated tin roof brown and dented and weather-beaten cement-block walls flaking green paint. Stepping out of the car he shook his head in disbelief at the oppressive heat, but on hearing the dogs gaining ground up the driveway he stepped quickly to the front door.

He stepped inside to blessedly conditioned air. "Thank God," he said, then walked down a dimly lit hallway to a grease-stained door marked LUNCH ROOM and pushed it open.

The air in the small room was surprisingly fresh, but the sunlight that filtered through dirty windows barely competed with the two bare bulbs that hung from the low ceiling. Sheldon Isaacs and Vince Jackson sat across from each other at a picnic-style table. Vince munched a sandwich while Sheldon idly flipped through the channels of a television mounted on a wall on the other side of the room.

"Tony!" Vince said, a toothy smile splitting his handsome dark face. Thirty-years old, his six-foot-two pudgy frame hid the well-muscled body of a former college wide receiver. Sheldon glanced at Tony briefly then back to the TV.

"Will you keep those goddamn dogs chained up?" asked Tony.

"Hey, Caesar and Anthony are friendly pups. They wouldn't hurt a flea," replied Vince.

"Those two land sharks nearly got me this time."

"Nobody else seems to have a problem with them. Must be you. They probably smell fear." Vince laughed and slapped the table.

"I'm going to shoot those sonsabitches next time."

"Johnny and Fred wouldn't like that," said Vince.

"What the hell would they care? They're never here."

"So do you have the trucks and drivers lined up or what?" Sheldon asked as he continued to idly flip through the channels.

"That's what I wanted to talk to you about."

Sheldon clicked off the TV and swung his heavy body around, his dark brown eyes quickly focusing on Tony. "Now what?"

Tony returned Sheldon's glare. "Look, I had no problem with the drivers … plenty of guys out there looking to moonlight. But the trucks are a little trickier."

"How so?" asked Sheldon.

"They all have their own rigs, but I have to provide the car haulers."

"Why is this *our* problem?" said Vince. "You have the contract for the transportation."

Tony shifted his gaze over to Vince. "Yeah, I know, but I had to have the trailers moved down from New Jersey. It's going to take me two more days."

"Two days! We've got a barn full of hot metal that is getting hotter by the second," said Sheldon. "We've got to get it out of here by tomorrow."

Tony held is ground. "Sorry boys. No can do. Wednesday night is the earliest we can do it."

Sheldon frowned and looked at Vince. "Johnny and Fred are not going to be happy about this." He looked back at Tony. "They were depending on you."

"Don't give me that bullshit. They asked if I could help them move the merchandise by mid-week, and I can. They never specified a day."

"Maybe not to you, but they told us that they expected the cars to be outta here by Tuesday."

"Well, now, that's your problem. I'll be ready to go by Wednesday … that's as good as I can do."

Sheldon ran his hand through his close-cropped curly hair. "Goddamnit, Vince, I told you that we couldn't depend on this guy. His old man shipped him to Miami because he screws up everything he touches."

Tony blushed slightly. "You don't know shit. Why don't you find your own trucks?"

"I didn't tell Johnny that I had the best connections for drivers on the East Coast," said Vince.

"Well, I do. And if I say that Wednesday is the earliest that the cars can be moved, I guarantee that no one else can move them sooner."

Sheldon sighed. "You're the big shooter, Tony. But I can tell you that Johnny ain't gonna be happy."

"Then tell him to find somebody else."

"Hey, hey, relax Tony." Sheldon's tone suddenly became friendlier. "If you say it's going to be Wednesday, then Wednesday it is."

Vince smiled broadly. "See Tony, we ain't hard to do business with."

Tony nodded slightly. "Now, if you don't mind, I'd like to look over the merchandise."

"Sure thing. It's out in the barn." Vince waved toward a door that led outside.

Tony started to walk toward it then stopped. "Those miserable hounds are still on the loose out there."

"Tony, you're such a pussy." Vince got up, walked over to the door and pushed it open and yelled, "Caesar. Anthony."

The Dobermans raced around the side of the building and bounded up to the door. Vince stepped outside and the dogs jumped with glee, licking his hands and face. "See? Friendliest damn pups you ever saw."

Tony watched through the window. "Just get them goddamn things out of here."

Vince herded the dogs to a large kennel that stood amidst piles of car engines and put them in. Then he yelled back toward the building. "Come on ya pussy."

Tony pushed open the door and walked across the dusty yard. The dogs started barking madly as soon as they saw him.

"I told you them things are vicious." Tony gave the kennel a wide berth. "Where are the cars?"

Vince laughed. "Right over here, pal." He led Tony to a huge pole barn. It was newer than any of the other buildings in the yard, but still weathered and suffering from lack of maintenance.

Parked on the side was a brand-new, thirty-five foot Winnebago Journey diesel motor home. Tony stopped and looked up at it.

"Jesus, what's that thing?"

"Oh, that's Sheldon's new toy."

"What the hell is he going to do with that?"

"Sheldon don't want to fly no more."

"He doesn't want to fly any more?"

"Yeah, he hates it."

"I didn't know he hated to fly."

"Yeah. Can't stand it. Like that football guy … what's his name … he wants to keep his feet on the ground."

"John Madden?"

"Yeah, that's the guy."

"That's nuts."

"I don't know. It might be fun."

Tony stood shaking his head.

Vince walked around the RV to the large sliding doors in the front of the barn. He pulled out a key and opened the heavy padlock that secured the doors and pushed one open far enough to pass through and Tony followed him inside. Faint sunlight filtered through holes in the walls and a few windows high on the walls. Vince found a switch and turned on the overhead lighting system, the light bouncing off the shiny bodies of late model Cadillacs, Lincolns, Lexuses, Mercedes and Porches.

"What a sight, eh Tony? All late models and clean as a whistle."

The cars were lined up in seven rows of six. "I thought there were thirty-five? I count thirty-seven," said Tony.

"Yeah, there was a last minute delivery from Tampa," replied Vince.

"But the car haulers I have lined up can only handle seven full-sized cars … that's thirty-five, Vince. I can't take the last two."

"You have to, Pard. The boys are expecting all thirty-seven to be shipped. Besides, half of them are Porsches … they ain't full-sized."

"I don't have to do shit, Vince. I don't have time to get another trailer and driver lined up and if I can't get the last two cars loaded then I'm not responsible for them, understand?"

"Well, I sure don't want to be the guy that has to tell Johnny two red-hot items aren't going to be moved."

"You just might have to."

"You'll get 'er done, Pard. I've got faith in you."

"Well, if I don't, it's your problem."

"Get that damn thing outta here," said Tony.

The driver looked down at Tony for a long second and touched the bill of his greasy cap in a mock salute. He started the diesel and cloud of black smoke belched from the stack. Gears ground and the rig lurched forward, the headlights glancing off piles of junk as the loaded trailer swayed precariously on the rough ground of the yard.

"If we can get eight more on the last trailer I'll have 'em all, Johnny," Tony said to the taller man standing next to him. Compared to Tony, who was nervous and sweating profusely in the muggy Florida night, Juan Rodriguez was cool and calm, his thick, wavy hair graying at the temples giving him a distinguished air.

"That is good, Tony." said Johnny.

They stepped to the side of the building and watched the last truck pull up in front of the big door of the barn, the driver skillfully maneuvering the trailer into position. A stocky, balding man descended from the cab and prepared the trailer to begin loading the cars. As he did, a Cadillac Escalade pulled out of the barn, gleaming white under the flood lights, a stark contrast to the piles of rusting hulks all around.

"Hold it right there," said the truck driver as the car nosed up to the trailer. He adjusted the ramps to receive the car.

A boy, no more than eighteen, wearing a baseball cap backward on his head, sat behind the wheel of the Escalade. He looked out of place in the luxury vehicle, but seemed to be enjoying the moment.

"Alright, ease it up, son."

The car began to ascend the ramp.

Tony shook his head. "Goddamn, that's a big mother."

"That's the last Escalade," said Johnny. "There are five Porsches, a Lexus and C-Class left.

Tony peered around the corner of the open barn doors to see for himself. Vince Jackson was getting in a 911, the next car in line. Sheldon Isaacs and Federico Rodriguez stood in the back of the barn watching the operation. Sheldon held a clipboard in his hands. Fred was a younger image of Johnny, except that his disheveled black hair was more in line with a pop-culture attitude.

"Damn, this is one fine automobile," Vince said through the open window of the Porsche. "You sure I can't keep this one for myself, Fred?"

"Just get that goddamn thing loaded, will ya?" Sheldon answered for Federico.

Vince put the car into gear and pulled up to the ramp of the truck. The Lincoln was still being eased into position on the top rack.

"Come on, hurry it up Melton," Vince yelled.

Vince's nephew, hated to be called Melton. He stuck his arm out of the Lincoln's window and flipped Vince the bird.

"You little punk, I'll whip your ass," said Vince, even though he had no intention of doing so. Melton, who preferred to be called by his street name, Shuggy, was Vince's sister's oldest kid.

Twenty minutes later the S-Class was aboard.

"That's it, Johnny," said Vince as Shuggy clambered down off the trailer.

Johnny nodded.

Tony watched the driver button up the ramp. "I'll be by to pick up my money tomorrow, okay Johnny?"

"Sure. As we agreed."

"You shouldn't run up your gambling debts, Tony. Then you wouldn't be so desperate for money," said Vince.

"Who asked you?" said Tony.

Vince laughed.

"Vince is right, Tony," said Johnny. "You ought to be more careful who you do business with.

Tony flushed briefly. "So I can pick up my money tomorrow."

"Sheldon will have it."

2

Tony pressed the TALK button on the intercom. "It's Tony," he said over the din of barking dogs. "Don't open …"

The gate began to move.

"Goddamn it," Tony yelled as he scrambled to the car.

A few minutes later he pulled up to the green building that served as the headquarters for Rodrequez Bros. Auto Salvage. He parked and walked briskly to the door as the dogs raced up the driveway behind.

"I swear I'm gonna shoot them sonsabitches," he mumbled as he walked through the front door. He blessed the cool air inside as he walked to the lunchroom.

Shuggy sat alone, watching a rap music video on the TV.

"Where're Sheldon and Vince?" Tony asked.

"They're gone." Shuggy's eyes never left the screen.

"They left you with my money?"

"I don't know nothin' 'bout no money."

"What?"

Shuggy ignored him.

Tony reached over and grabbed the remote off the table and clicked off the television.

"Hey!"

"Where's my goddamn money?" Tony demanded.

Shuggy grabbed for the remote. "I told you. I don't know nothin' 'bout no fuckin' money."

Tony threw the control on the floor and stomped on it. Then he grabbed Shuggy by the shirtfront and jerked him across the table. "Look, you little punk. You tell me where my money is or I'm gonna stomp *you*."

Shuggy ripped away from Tony's grasp. "Get your fuckin' hands off me."

The dogs were barking madly just outside.   Shuggy moved toward the back door. Tony raced around the table and grabbed him from behind and spun him around.

"I want my money. Where the hell is it?"

Shuggy struggled in his grip, reaching vainly for the door. "I told you I don't know."

"Where're Vince and Sheldon?"

"I don't know. They took off this morning."

"Where?"

"How the hell should I know? Let me go, ya faggot."

Tony pulled Shuggy around so he was standing between Shuggy and the door. Then he let him go and pushed him toward the table. "Sit down."

Shuggy straightened himself up and stood defiantly. He looked down at the pile of plastic shards and computer chips that was the remote control only seconds ago. "You're gonna pay for that."

"Shut up." Tony stood staring at the blank TV screen and rubbed his forehead. Then he pulled out his cell phone and punched up Vince's number. Shuggy tried to move but Tony pushed him into his seat.

"Vince, it's Tony."

"Tony who?" said Vince over the phone.

"Tony Boccaccio … you know goddamn well who it is. Where the hell are you?"

"Orlando, I think … yep, it's Orlando."

"Orlando? What are you doing there?"

"We're on our way to …" Vince paused. "What the hell is it to you?"

"You're supposed to be giving me my money … how am I supposed to get it if you're in fucking Orlando?"

"Well," said Vince, "funny damn thing about that, but you aren't."

"What! What are talking about?"

"Your money … seems it ain't your money after all. Here, talk to Shelly, I'm getting into some heavy traffic."

"Wait, just a second …" said Tony, but Vince was gone.

Shuggy was grinning mockingly. Tony remembered the RV that was parked in the yard. He went to the window. The dogs saw him and started barking and leaping toward him. He looked over toward the barn and it was gone. *Sonofabitch*.

"Tony, my friend." Sheldon Issac's nasal tones came over the phone.

"Don't *friend* me. Where the hell is my money?"

"Like Vince told you, it ain't your money anymore."

"Yeah, he said that. But it is my goddamn money and I want it right now."

"That just ain't the case, Tony. Seems this money belongs to Max Burke"

Tony dropped the phone away from his ear. *Burke. Oh Christ.* He put the phone back to his ear. "How the hell did Burke get in on this?"

"He's an associate of ours. I thought you'd have known that."

"So what?" he said. "What does that have to do with me?"

"Burke called this morning and said he had the authority to … ah … garnishee your wages."

"Garnishee?"

"Yeah, you know. Like what Uncle Sam does when you don't pay your taxes."

"I know what garnishee means, dipshit. What gives you the right to give Burke my money?"

"Seems you owe him a pile of money."

"Did that goddamn mick tell you that?"

"You really shouldn't run up your gambling debts, Tony."

"Goddamn it, Sheldon, it's my money and you know it."

"Well, I suppose technically you might be correct, but Burke convinced us that you owe it to him … how did you manage to rack up a debt like that with him?"

"Burke is full of shit. I don't owe him anywhere near that much."

"Guess you'll have to take that up with him. As far as we're concerned the money belongs to him and we're gonna deliver it to him in California … that is all but the cut we have coming."

"California? I thought you said you were in Orlando?"

"That's on the way to California, isn't it?"

"You're driving to California?"

"Beats the hell out of flyin' as far as I'm concerned."

Tony dropped the phone again. *Goddamn it*. Shuggy laughed again. Tony turned around and glared at him. He put the phone back to his ear. "That's my money you goddamn welcher. You bring it back here or so help me …"

"So help you what, Tony? What are you gonna do?"

Sheldon was right. Tony had no real muscle. He changed his tone. "How much is Burke paying you?"

"I believe the agreed upon amount was ten percent. It was ten percent, wasn't it Vince? Yes that was it. Ten percent."

"I'll give you twenty."

"That's very generous of you Tony, but you don't have any money to give us twenty percent of," said Sheldon.

"I've got a hundred and fifty large coming to me."

"Had, Tony. The word is *had*."

"But you made a deal with me first."

"No. Johnny and Fred made a deal with you."

Tony decided to try another tack. "Look you sonofabitch, I'm going to see Johnny about this."

"You do that, Slick. Hey, I gotta go." Tony heard Sheldon yelling at Vince, "Where the hell are you going? You just missed our exit!" The phone went dead.

Tony dropped his hand away from his ear and ran his hand through his hair. "Goddamn it," he said to no one.

Shuggy laughed more.

"Put them goddamn hounds away you little prick."

"Hey, I don't have to do shit …"

Tony took a couple of steps toward him and Shuggy recoiled slightly.

"Put them away now."

"Yeah, yeah."

Tony started to walk toward the hall door. Then he turned toward Shuggy. "I said put them goddamn hounds away … now."

"Yeah, yeah, ya faggot." He went out the back door, just barely managing to keep the dogs outside.

Tony drove down a quiet palm-lined residential street in Fort Lauderdale. On a large corner lot at the end of the block stood a modest, but well-groomed house. Johnny Rodriguez could certainly afford a more pretentious surrounding but his hard-knock upbringing in Mexico taught him to be more frugal, and besides he preferred to keep a low profile.

He parked in the driveway and walked past manicured shrubs to the arched entryway of the Spanish-style house. He knocked on the carved, heavy wooden door. A slight, gray-haired man whose mahogany skin matched the door opened it. His weathered face creased into a smile.

"Hello Senor Tony. Senor Juan is expecting you." The man stepped aside to let Tony in.

"Thanks, Alfonso." Tony stepped into the small, but tastefully decorated foyer. He followed Alfonso through the living area that was filled with heavy Moroccan furniture and complemented with classic Spanish sculpture and art. His shoes clicked noisily on the parquet floor in contrast to Alfonso's soft, padding slippers. They reached the rear of the room where Alfonso pushed open French doors that led out to a slate-tiled patio.

Federico sat under an umbrella at a glass-topped table. He was sipping a drink and talking on a cell phone. A beautiful brown-skinned woman sat next to him watching Johnny swim in the pool. She was dressed in a scanty two-piece swimsuit and looked like a cover model to Tony. As Tony approached, Federico snapped the phone shut.

"How ya doin', Tony?" The younger Rodriguez had barely a trace of an accent.

"Not so good Fred," said Tony.

"Hey, Johnny, Tony's here," Federico yelled to Johnny who had stopped swimming and was resting with his arms folded on the edge of the pool. Johnny nodded and pulled himself out of the pool. Fred turned back to Tony. "So what could be bothering you on a beautiful day like this?" He motioned to the sky and winked at the woman sitting next to him. "You remember Delores don't you?"

"Yeah," said Tony nodding to Delores who giggled. He had never seen her before.

"Shall I bring you something to drink, Senor Tony," Alfonso asked.

"No thanks."

Alfonso picked up a half-finished drink from an empty space at the table. "Will Senor Juan like another?" Alfonso asked Fred.

"Probably."

Alfonso bowed slightly and retreated to the house.

"Well at least sit down," said Fred.

Tony pulled out one of the heavy cast iron chairs and sat on the edge. Johnny walked up toweling himself off. His lean, bronzed body looked ten years younger than his fifty-two years would indicate. "Hello, Tony. What brings you to our humble abode?"

"I think you probably know, Johnny."

Johnny gave him a quizzical look. "Oh?"

"Yeah. Your boys made off with my money."

"Oh, that." Johnny shot a knowing look at Federico.

"Yeah. That."

Johnny had finished drying off and pulled out a chair for himself. "My understanding is that money doesn't belong to you."

Tony looked slightly flushed. "Is that what they told you?"

"No, that's what Max Burke told me."

"Well, that's bullshit."

Johnny raised an eyebrow. Tony didn't miss the sign. He took a breath and said, "Why didn't you tell me Burke was going to take my money?"

"You know Max happens to be a colleague of ours."

Tony ran his hand over his head. He looked at Fred who was idly rubbing Delores's back but obviously listening intently. He looked back at Johnny. "Yeah, well, the money thing is between me and Burke."

"It still is as far as I'm concerned," said Johnny. Then to Federico, "Did Alfonso take my drink?"

"He's bringing you another," said Federico.

Tony kept on. "So why are you letting him take my money?"

"I'm not actually. That's a deal between Sheldon and Vince and Max."

"But with your blessing. Those two wouldn't fart without your permission."

Delores giggled. Johnny smiled. "Perhaps," he said, "but this affair is really theirs."

"How so?"

Alfonso approached the table with Johnny's fresh drink.

"Thank you, Alfonso," said Johnny. "I'm sorry, Tony, did Alfonso offer you a drink?"

"No thanks." He waved off Alfonso a second time. "So explain to me how Sheldon and Vince get to play fast and loose with my money?"

Johnny nodded to Alfonso who retreated to the house again. "Max asked for the money you owed him and I told him I didn't have it … that Sheldon and Vince had it. He asked if he could make arrangements to retrieve it from them and I said I wouldn't interfere."

"Johnny, we had a deal …"

Johnny took a sip of his drink. "And I honored it. The money was given to Sheldon and Vince to give to you."

Tony was beginning to get the picture. Johnny would just as soon give Tony his money, but he also had an obligation to keep Burke happy. Burke owned dealerships in California that specialized in selling hot cars. There was a certain honor among thieves, but it all depended on the pecking order, and the timing. At the moment, Johnny needed Burke to distribute his product. Tony was just a peon.

"Oh, so you're playing Pontius Pilot … washing your hands of the situation?"

Johnny glared at Tony.

Tony chided himself for overplaying his hand. He sat back slowly and said, "I'm in a bad spot here, Johnny. I've put a lot of time and effort in on this deal and I've got a lot of expenses to cover."

"Perhaps your father will come to your assistance?"

Johnny knew perfectly well that Tony would not go to his father for help. That was what gave him the confidence to give Burke the green light to go after Tony's money. Mario Boccaccio was a made man in New York, but he had lost his patience with his youngest son. Tony was a continual disappointment; managing to screw up almost every task he was given.

Two years ago Tony crossed the line when he and his buddies robbed the courier of a rival family who was transporting a briefcase full of cash to Atlantic City. To keep the peace, Mario had to make good on the money and, to protect Tony, sent him to Miami in the care of his brother-in-law, Severino Sandrelli. Sevvy handled the Florida business interests for Mario. He also owned Paesano's, a popular restaurant. Sevvy didn't know what to do with Tony any more than Mario did, so he had him co-managing Paesano's with his daughter, Gina.

Everyone knew it was just a matter of time before Tony got into trouble again. He managed that by losing almost one and seventy-five thousand dollars in the casinos in the Bahamas and Puerto Rico, mostly money he had borrowed from Max Burke, a big car dealer in Miami.

Tony had met Burke while on an offshore gambling junket. Burke freely loaned the money to Tony because he was impressed by Tony's family connections and he thought Tony would be a good man to have in his debt. But it didn't work out that way.

Realizing that he was about to get stiffed, Burke introduced Tony to the Rodriguez brothers. He knew that Johnny and Federico might need some help getting a shipment of cars to California and that Tony still had some friends up north who would be willing to freelance. Tony could make some quick cash and start to pay off his debts. It looked like a good deal to Tony.

What Tony didn't know was that Burke didn't trust Tony and was planning all along to 'garnishee' Tony's wages. What he did know was that this would be the last straw if he had to ask his father or his uncle to help him out of this mess.

Tony ignored Johnny's comment. "Let me get one thing straight, Johnny. You're not going to interfere with

Sheldon's and Vince's deal with Burke, so you won't interfere with me if I get my money from them myself?"

Juan took another sip of his drink. He looked at the glass. "You really should try one of Alfonso's Mai Tais, they really are wonderful." Then he looked back at Tony. "As I said, that is between you and Mr. Burke"

Tony knew this was the best he was going to get.

3

"Hit me again, Levi."

The tall, thin bartender put his newspaper down, leaned his stool forward and reached over to the bottle of Glen Livet sitting on the bar. He started pouring the amber liquid into the glass of the man sitting across from him.

"Say when."

Tony, a full head shorter than Levi but more than his equal in weight, waved when the glass was a third full. Levi stopped pouring and grabbed the pitcher of water that was next to the bottle. He added another third to Tony's glass.

"What time is it?" said Tony.

Levi looked at his watch. "Just about two-thirty." The man nodded and picked up his glass to take a drink. Levi noticed sweat stains blossoming out under the arms of Tony's shirt.

The front door of the restaurant opened. Tony put down his glass and turned to look across the barroom into the empty restaurant. Dust motes swam in the sunlight that streamed in and framed a feminine silhouette in the doorway.

A woman, thirty-five, attractive with long auburn tresses and an olive complexion stepped inside, took off her sunglasses and closed the door. She walked across the restaurant; her flowered dress brushing the dining tables as she neatly sidestepped them. As she approached the bar, Tony turned back to his drink.

"Jesus, Tony. You into the sauce already?"

Tony took a long swallow. "What the hell is it to you, Gina?"

"You want something to drink?" asked the bartender.

"No thanks, Levi." Gina said. She set her purse on the bar, put in her sunglasses and pulled out a cigarette. "It's nothing to me, Tony. I just don't want the customers tripping over a drunk." She lit the cigarette and blew out a long stream of smoke. Levi pushed an ashtray across the bar toward her.

"I'm not any where near drunk. I'm just cooling off. It must be a hundred out there."

It was hot outside all right, Gina thought, but the air conditioning in the restaurant had the temperature around seventy. Too cool for her, yet she noticed beads of sweat on Tony's forehead.

"What are you doing here anyway? I thought you'd be out golfing with your new buddies," Gina said.

"Too damn hot for golf today. Besides them Mexicans don't golf anyway."

"You know, you're gonna get your ass in a wringer putting in with the Rodriquez brothers. Your father would bust a gasket if he knew."

"Why the hell should he care?"

"Because he doesn't want to have to bail your ass out again when you screw up."

"It's none of his goddamn business. He sent me down here to rot … baby sitting you and this goddamn restaurant."

Gina tapped her cigarette on the ashtray. "You know Levi, I believe I will have a Coke."

"Comin' right up," said Levi.

She took a long drag and blew the smoke in Tony's direction. "He sent you down here because he was tired of watching out for you."

Tony felt his face flush. "What time is it, Levi?" Tony asked.

Levi put a glass of Coke in front of Gina. "Two forty."

"I don't have time to bullshit with you right now, Gina." Tony turned back to his drink.

"What crazy scheme are you into now?"

"Whatever it is, I've got a hell of a better chance of making some money than this black hole."

"Paesano's might do a little better if you paid as much attention to it as you do to the Rodriquez brothers. And you sure as hell might live longer. Daddy doesn't want to have to scrape your carcass up and send it back to your father."

"Your father doesn't care if this dump turns a nickel. He just wants to keep you occupied and have a place to ..."

Gina cut him off by glancing at the bartender who was reading the newspaper.

Tony laughed. "You think Levi doesn't know what goes on around here. You know it all, don't you pal?"

Levi shrugged, "I don't know nothin', Mr. Boccaccio."

The door to the restaurant opened and all three looked across the empty room as a rotund man dressed in a print shirt, shorts and running shoes walked in. As he came closer his pocked marked face and ponytail came into focus.

"Hey, Marvin," said Tony.

"Oh shit, it's Marvin Seguin," mumbled Gina. She swung around to face the bar.

Marvin was an employee of Severino Sandrelli. Marvin met Tony when he was visiting one winter. They hit it off right away. They both had a predilection for partying and they often got together when Tony would come down to Florida over Christmas or on spring break. Their escapades were epic and the source of many barroom stories ever since.

Marvin slapped Tony on the back. "Wassup, paesan?" Then he leaned toward Gina. "How are you, my little cannoli?"

"Just great, Marvin," Gina said without looking at him.

"When are you going out with me?"

"I think I'm free on the 12th of never."

Marvin ignored her remark and turned back to Tony. "So what's so hot that you drag me out of bed so early?"

"Early? It's almost three o'clock, you reprobate."

"Hey when you're wheelin' and dealin' till dawn, three o'clock is early." He winked at Levi. "Am I right?"

"I wouldn't know nothin' 'bout that," said Levi. "What'll you have to drink?"

"How about a Bud, eh?"

Levi reached around behind him and pulled the beer out of the cooler. "Glass?"

"Naw. Bottle's good."

"It's too crowded here. Grab your beer and step into my office." Tony picked up his drink and steered Marvin to a booth in the back of the bar.

"Don't leave without saying goodbye," Marvin said over his shoulder to Gina.

"Wouldn't think of it," said Gina. She picked up her Coke and walked back into the restaurant. "I'll be in back, Levi."

Levi saluted and went back to his newspaper.

"So what's up?" asked Marvin, as he squeezed into the narrow wooden bench seat.

"I'm in a jam, buddy," said Tony.

"So when aren't you in a jam?"

"No, this one's serious. I was doing a job for the Rodriguez bros …"

Marvin stopped in the middle of lighting a cigarette. "The Rodriguez bros … are you nuts?"

"This was air tight … a little job that was going to net me a hundred and fifty large."

"You didn't have to cap somebody, did you?"

"Hell no … nothin' like that. Just help them move some cars out to the west coast. Give me one of those nails, will ya?"

Marvin offered Tony a cigarette. "And they were going to pay you one fifty for that?"

"Yep."

"Sounds sweet. What's the problem?"

"That fucking mick, Max Burke took my money."

"You're mixed up with Burke too? You sure keep some crazy-assed company." Marvin shook his head. "Why would the Rodriguez boys give him your money?"

"'Cause he told them I owed it to him."

"So? What's that to them?"

"The whole thing was a set up. Johnny Rodriguez and Burke are in bed together … he dumps their cars on the market in Los Angeles."

"Oh yeah, that's right, Burke is in the car biz."

"So he sets me up with this job and then tells Johnny that I owe him all this money and they fuckin' give it to him."

"Did you owe it to him?"

"That's not the point. I did the job and it's my money."

"So how much did you owe him?"

"I dunno. Maybe a buck twenty-five … maybe more."

"That's a pretty big tab. How'd you manage that?"

Tony smiled. "I dropped about hundred in the casinos, maybe twenty on partying. The rest I spent foolishly."

"Burke loaned you that much … without collateral?"

"He thought he was greasing the skids to get in good with my old man."

"And you let him think that?"

"Hey, if he wanted to lend it to me, who am I to say no?"

"But you had to know the party was going to end sooner or later. And Burke is no one to screw with."

"I need your help to get that money back."

"My help? You're playing out of my league … what the hell can I do?"

"Those two idiots, Vince and Sheldon are taking my money to Burke in California."

"Vince Jackson and Sheldon Isaacs? Man this just keeps getting better and better."

"I want you to help me track those assholes down and get my money back."

"Listen Tony, you're a pal and all, and I'd like to help you, but I sure as hell ain't going to California to get my ass kicked by those two crazy bastards."

"You don't have to go to California."

"But you just said they were in California."

"I said they were taking the money to California. They're driving there."

"Driving? What're they? Nuts?"

"Sheldon bought this huge bus and they're driving the damn thing to California. He thinks he's John Madden or something … he doesn't want to fly anymore."

"You mean an RV?"

"Yeah, whatever."

"When'd they leave?"

"This morning. I talked to them around noon and they were only in Orlando … I figure they can't be making good time in that monster truck. We could catch them before they leave the state."

"I hate to be the one to burst your bubble, bunky, but those things can make pretty good time. They could be in Tallahassee by now."

"No shit?"

"No shit."

"Well, how am I gonna catch those bastards?"

Marvin scratched his head. "Hell, I don't know."

"Come on, Marv, you know you're way around down here … there's gotta be a short cut or something."

Marvin pounded the table. "Hey, I got an idea."

"What? Wadda ya got?"

"I know this guy … a pilot … he made a few runs for me back in the nineties … you know what I mean?"

"Yeah, so?"

"Now he does charters out of some flee-bitten airport up by Hialeah. Maybe you could get this guy to fly you to Pensacola or something."

"Fly? Really?"

"Sure, why not? You could get in front of the boys and be waiting for them."

Tony crushed out the cigarette and thought about Marvin's suggestion.

"You know, you might have something there. What's the guy's name?"

"Mickey Soto. I don't have his number."

"What's the name of this airport?"

"I donno … it's one of them little joints … you can look it up."

"You're a big damn help. Mickey what?

"Soto … he's a good guy. Tell him you're a friend of mine. He'll take care of you."

"You're coming with me, right."

"Hell no I ain't going."

"Come on man, I'm gonna need some help."

"I'm not getting mixed up in this. Besides, I got shit I gotta do."

"What's more important than helping your buddy?"

"Hey, I got my own problems … anyway, I ain't going up in one of those little bug smashers."

"I'll remember this, you welcher. You say his name is Soto?"

"Mickey Soto … good guy."

Tony took a drink. "You really think this guy could help me?"

"Sure, why not."

Tony slid out of his seat and walked over to the bar. "Levi, hand me the phone book, will ya?"

4

"Damn it, Mickey, I'm dropping too fast!"

"Relax, Sara ... you're doing fine. Just pull the nose up a little and level off at 1200."

As the Piper Cherokee slowly regained a nose up attitude, the hot, noonday sun poured into the cockpit. Mickey Soto looked over at the student pilot. From her death grip on the control wheel, he followed the tension up her bear arms past her shapely breasts to her pursed lips and the furrowed brow peaking through blond tresses. Mickey sighed and shook his head slightly.

"Okay, Okay, you're doing great ... put in a notch of flaps and turn to 274."

Her perfume overpowered the smell of stale sweat, oil and deteriorating vinyl of the cockpit.   "Good, good, Sara ... you're doing great. Keep the nose up ... great ... now put in another notch of flaps."

"Shit, Mickey ... the speed is dropping too fast."

"You're okay ... now, just push the nose down a little and turn to final."

"I can't do this, Mickey ... I'm losing altitude too fast."

"Okay, okay ... I've got it ... let go," Mickey said.

The airplane greased onto the runway and taxied to the tarmac. As the plane swung into position in front of the fixed-base operation of his employer, Hayes Flying Services, Mickey shut it down and turned to Sara who was holding her face in her hands.

"You're doing fine, Sara. It's not easy. Everyone struggles with landings at first."

Sara turned her moist eyes toward Mickey. His rugged looks were not exactly handsome and he was much older than the men she usually dated, but he was funny and charming and his deep-set gray eyes had a worldliness that she had found immediately attractive.

"I'm an idiot, Mickey. I'm never going to get this."

Mickey took off his cap and ran his hand through graying, wavy hair. "You're not an idiot, Sara. You're good at this. It just takes time to get the feel of it, that's all."

"But after 35 hours? How many landings have I botched?"

Mickey winced. She was right, after 35 hours most of his students were well on their way to getting their tickets. Sara was struggling, but he didn't want to lose her. She smelled great, she certainly wasn't hard on the eyes, and, most of all, he needed the money. He put his cap back on and adjusted the bill.

"Look, maybe you're not as far along as you'd like to be, but you're improving. You're S-turns were perfect today."

"But those are easy compared to landing ... and I haven't done a good one yet."

"It just takes time ... you'll get it." Mickey unlocked the door and pushed it open, letting fresh air flood the cockpit. "Come on, kiddo. I'll buy you a cup of coffee."

Mickey stepped out onto the wing and turned to help Sara out. She lost her balance briefly and fell against him. He wasn't sure if it was on purpose or not ... he wasn't totally unaware that she was attracted to him, but he knew that letting it go any further would be a huge mistake. He grabbed her elbow and shoulder and in helping her regain her balance pushed her away slightly.

"Easy. Let me get down and I'll help you off."

The line boy, Jeff, had pulled up with the fuel truck and was watching closely as Mickey helped Sara down. "How was it up there today?" he said, hoping to get Sara's attention.

Mickey frowned at the way Jeff was leering at Sara. "Great, Jeff. Just take care of the fuel, okay?"

"Yeah, right, Mickey." He turned to retrieve the hose from the truck. It pissed him off that Sara completely ignored him in Mickey's presence, even though Mickey was twice her age. He thought Mickey was a burned-out lecher.

"Hey, I had one guy who didn't solo until he had 90 hours! And he wasn't bad," Mickey lied. He was desperately trying to cheer Sara up.

Sara took a sip from her coffee and looked at Mickey across the desk. She was beginning to take the hint that he wasn't interested in her beyond flying, and she sure as hell was just about out of patience with trying to master that skill. "Thanks, Mickey. But I don't think I'll ever get the hang of landing. Maybe I should just find a new hobby."

Sara's confidence was shot and Mickey was running out of ideas. Thankfully, white-haired Betty Armstead poked her head into the little office that he called home. She looked briefly at Sara and then winked almost imperceptibly at Mickey.

"Telephone, Mickey ... line 3."

Betty had been Glenn Hayes secretary, office manager, and troubleshooter for almost 40 years. For all intensive purposes, she ran the joint. She was brusque, abrasive and immensely efficient. All new pilots and instructors had to withstand her hazing before they were accepted into Betty's inner circle. After five years, Betty was just beginning to see Mickey as something resembling a human being.

Mickey was irritated at Betty's insinuation, but he was grateful for the interruption and the chance to think of something to turn Sara around. "Thanks, Betty," he said. Then, turning to Sara, "Do you mind?"

Sara shook her head. "No, go ahead."

Mickey picked up the telephone and punched the blinking light. "Soto, here."

"Mickey Soto?" said a voice with a Brooklyn accent on the other end.

"That's me. What can I do for you?" Mickey watched Sara as she blew on her coffee and gazed around the room at the airplane pictures and certificates and ratings that Mickey had acquired during his twenty-year flying career.

"You're a pilot, right?"

"Yep. You interested in some lessons?"

"Hell no," said the voice. "How long would it take to get to Pensacola?"

"Pensacola, Florida?

"No. Pensacola Alaska. Where the hell else?"

"You're looking for a charter?"

"I'm looking to get to Pensacola. You do that?"

"Sometimes. Who am I speaking to?"

"Boccaccio, Tony Boccaccio."

Mickey scratched his head. Why did that name sound familiar? "You know, Mr. ... ah ..."

"Boccaccio ... but call me Tony."

"You know, Tony, that a charter to Pensacola would be pretty expensive ... probably more than you'd pay to fly commercial."

"How much would it cost?"

Mickey did a quick calculation in his head. "I don't know … maybe around six, eight hundred dollars."

"Jesus, that's a lot of cabbage. How long would it take to get to there?"

"I don't no ... I'm guessing ... around two and a half, maybe three hours ... depending on the weather."

"Wow ... what the hell are you flying? A biplane?"

Mickey gritted his teeth. *Don't piss off the customer*. "Look, Tony, I've got to be honest. You'd be much better off going commercial. I can give you the number of a good travel agent."

"Six hundred, eh?"

"Roughly."

"Just a sec."

Mickey heard Tony talking to somebody, but it was garbled. Sara was starting to get up leave. Mickey held up his finger to indicate that he was almost done. She sat back down and folded her arms.

Tony was back on the line. "Okay, okay, I can do that." When can we go?"

"When do you need to go?"

"Right now."

"Now?"

"Yeah, this afternoon."

"Wow, I don't think I can ..."

"I really need to go today. If you can't do it I'll find somebody else."

Mickey hadn't had a charter in over a month and expenses were piling up. If Tony was willing to pay he wasn't about to let him get away. "No, no. Today's fine."

"That's good, when can we go?"

"It'll take me a couple of hours to clear the deck and get the plane ready to go. That okay?"

"Can't you make it sooner? I could be there in 30 minutes."

"Make it an hour .... that's the best I can do."

"All right ... an hour it is."

"Ah, Tony, one more thing. How long are you going to be in Pensacola?"

"I don't know? What? Maybe a couple of hours or so."

"Because I'm going to need fifty bucks an hour for idle time?" Mickey winced when he said it. He would be grateful just for the flight time charge.

"Fifty bucks an hour?"

"Yes, sitting around in Pensacola would be taking me away from generating other revenue."

"How about twenty-five?" said Tony.

Mickey didn't hesitate. "Okay, twenty-five."

"Okay, I can do that too."

Sara's patience had run out. She got up to leave, mouthing, "I'll see you later."

"Just a minute, Tony." Mickey put his hand over the phone. "I'm sorry, Sara, but this guy is hot to go to Pensacola.

"I understand, Mickey. I'll call you sometime."

"Don't forget to see Betty to set up a lesson for next week."

"Yeah, sure." She turned and walked out the door.

"Shit," Mickey said as he put the phone back to his ear.

"What?"

"Oh, no ... not you, Tony. "Do you mind me asking how you heard about me?"

"Marvin Seguin gave me your name."

"Marvin Seguin?"

"Yeah, he says he's a friend of yours"

"Oh, yeah, Marvin. I was just curious."

"In fact, he's sitting right here … you want to say 'hi' to him?"

The last person Mickey wanted to talk to was Marvin Sequin. "No, that's okay. Just say hello for me. See you in an hour then? You know how to get here?"

"Yep, got it covered. I'll be there by four o'clock." The line went dead.

All the bells and whistles were going off. But then he was broke, as usual, and couldn't afford to turn down a paying customer, even if Marvin Seguin was involved.

From his youngest days in Michigan, Mickey had wanted to fly. His parents encouraged his desire and sent him to Western Michigan University to pursue a degree in aviation. After graduating, he followed the usual path, providing instruction at little GA airports and building hours until he had enough to qualify for a right seat with one of the major carriers.

Then he met Sharon. She was beautiful and fun and expensive, not the kind of woman who would tolerate the meager wages of a fledgling pilot for long. But he was in love, so he nosed around for a way to make some fast money and found out that a guy in Florida was looking for a pilot to make a couple of runs to Mexico. It was risky and meant the end of his aviation career if he got caught, but the money was great. Marvin Seguin was the guy. He was the go between of a Columbian cartel and the guy who, at the time, oversaw the distribution of cocaine in south Florida.

Mickey made five runs for the cartel, each one more profitable than the last, but each one more dangerous. He netted $25,000 on the last run but came so close to getting caught that he'd had enough. He had enough money to buy an airplane and start a little charter service. He called Glenn Hayes, one of his instructors from Western who had bought a small airport in Dade County, just north of Hialeah. Glenn was happy to let Mickey work there, instructing and scratching for any charters he could find. So he brought Sharon down and they were married.

At first it was all peaches and cream. Mickey bought *Songbird*, an immaculate 1969 Piper PA-30B Twin Comanche, for $80,000 and still had enough money to keep the party rolling with Sharon. They bought a house in Hollywood and Mickey established himself at Hayes airport, flying charters around Florida.

But the charters were too few and far between and Mickey just didn't bring in enough to pay all the bills that Sharon racked up. The creditors started closing in and Mickey chose to sell the house rather than *Songbird* and that was the end of he and Sharon. She got what was left from the house proceeds and Mickey got *Songbird*. Although he was sorry to see Sharon leave, he loved the pristine little twin and felt that he had gotten the better the deal.

He didn't mind teaching, but charters paid better and he much preferred flying *Songbird* to the high-hour, student-weary airplanes of Glenn's rental fleet, so he wasn't too picky when they came up. He thought something didn't smell right about this thing, but if Tony Boccaccio was desperate to go to Pensacola, far be it from him to deny him passage.

Tony clicked his phone shut. "It's all set."

"So what are going to do if you catch up to them?" asked Marvin.

"I don't know. I'll think of something."

"You packin'?"

"Not right this second. I got a nine mil out in the car."

"Well, you better have it when you come up against those two."

"Yeah, I know. What about bringing it on the airplane?"

Marvin smiled. "That's the beauty of flying with Mickey Soto. He ain't gonna ask."

"You got the G on you?" asked Tony.

"Hell no. "I don't walk around with that kind of money."

"How fast can you get it? I gotta be there by four."

"My house is in the direction of the airport, you can follow me and pick it up on your way."

"Tell me again how to get there."

"Jesus. I'd have to tell you how to find your ass. Get me a piece of paper and a pen and I'll draw you a map."

Tony slid out of the seat, grabbed the phone book and took it back to Levi. "Hey, you got some paper and something to write with?"

"Sure thing." Levi reached under the bar, pulled out a pad of paper and a pen and slid it across the bar just as Gina walked up.

"Did we get that case Dom Perignon in?" she asked Levi.

"I'll go check."

As Tony reached for the paper and pen, Gina said, "So what are you two losers plotting?"

"I don't have time for this right now, Gina."

"I just want to know when I'll be needed to pull your ass out of the fire."

"Just tend to the Champaign will ya?" Tony turned to walk back to the booth.

"Only trying to help."

Tony flipped her the bird over his shoulder.

"Be nice. You don't want to piss off your only friend."

5

Mickey walked down the hallway from his office and passed through the pilot's lounge, a small room that consisted of a long folding table surrounded by ancient vinyl chairs. The walls were decorated with pictures of airplanes, charts and, covering one whole wall by itself, a giant aviation map of the U.S. that was published fifty years ago, when Hayes first opened. The opposite wall was mostly glass and looked out onto the tarmac and runway. The room smelled of stale coffee and the remnants of thousands of cigarettes.

Several of the old guard, some pilots who had been flying out of Hayes since it opened and some who had long since stopped flying, sat around the table watching flight operations through the window to critique landings and take offs, and telling the same jokes and stories they'd been telling as least as long as Mickey had been there.

"Hey, Mick, you teaching that young thing how to use your stick," said Stan, one of the older heads who held court daily in the lounge. The rest of the guys laughed.

"You jealous, Stan?" Mickey jabbed back. That made the guys laugh harder.

Mickey walked into the customer service area of the little building. Betty was sitting behind the glass counter, speaking into the radio microphone to some unsuspecting student from a near-by airport.

"We don't allow 'touch-n-goes' here. Please remember that in the future," she said harshly.

"Roger that," came the meek electronic reply.

Betty put down the mike. "Putz," she said, shaking her head disapprovingly.

"Did Sara make an appointment for a lesson next week?" Mickey asked Betty.

"No. She just paid for today and left."

"Damn it." Mickey spun the appointment book around and looked it over. "Betty, I've got a charter coming in today that I have to take. Can you see if Carl will take Mr. Raimus at 5:00 ... look's like he's got an open spot."

"How long will you be gone?"

"I should be back by midnight."

"Midnight? Where are you going?"

"Pensacola."

"That should be a good one."

"Yeah, I can sure use it."

"Who is paying you to go to Pensacola?"

"Some guy ... will you just see if Carl will do that for me?

"Must be some rich guy, eh?"

"I guess. Where's Jeff?"

Betty pointed out the window at the figure on the tarmac fueling a Cessna 152.

"Can you reach Carl, please?"

Betty picked up the mike, "Cherokee 367, Hayes Unicom," Mickey heard her say as he walked outside to see Jeff.

Jeff was cleaning *Songbird's* windshield and Mickey was just finishing the pre-flight when a late model Cadillac, covered with dust, pulled into the parking lot opposite the tarmac. A short, stocky man got out, adjusted his sunglasses and briefly followed the flight of a Piper Cherokee as it lifted off from the end of runway 04 before walking quickly toward the tarmac.

Mickey wiped his hands on the paper towel he had used to check the oil, stuffed the wad in his jacket pocket, and walked across the tarmac toward the man.

"Tony?" he shouted.

"You the pilot?" Tony shouted back.

"Yep."

The two met halfway between the parking lot and the airplane. Mickey stuck out his hand. "Nice to meet you."

Tony grabbed Mickey's hand and pumped it a couple of the times. "Sure. We ready to go?" He was looking around Mickey at *Songbird* behind him.

Tony's stocky frame was a full head shorter than Mickey and he looked a lot younger than he sounded on the phone. Mickey guessed mid-thirties. He had an olive complexion and his dark, pre-maturely balding hair was slicked back. Mickey couldn't see his eyes through the dark glasses but he noted the diamond pinky ring on Tony's hand and the gold chain glinting out from the undone top two buttons of a silk Hawaiian-print shirt. Tony's alligator shoes and silk sport coat looked expensive too. Mickey was a little taken aback by Tony's abruptness, but then he was used to being the hired hand.

"Just about. Mickey looked down at the ground. "Ah, look Tony ... I ... ah ... I don't want to seem crass about this, but, ah ..."

"You're wondering about the money? Don't worry, got it right here."

Mickey nodded. "Well, I hate to be a jerk about this, but I've been doing this a long time and sometimes ... well, sometimes people have promised things they don't always mean to keep ... you understand? You mind if I get half up front?"

"Yeah, yeah ... whatever." Tony reached into his jacket pocket and pulled out a money clip of $100 bills. He quickly peeled off three and handed them to Mickey. "Here ya go, pal."

Mickey took the proffered money. "It's probably going to be closer to eight hundred ... I hope you're not offended."

Tony looked a Mickey for a moment. Then he peeled off another bill and gave it to Mickey.

"You want a receipt?" asked Mickey.

"Hell, no." Tony stuffed the money clip back into his jacket. "Can we go now?"

"I might suggest that you use the facilities before we go ... it'll be a long stretch before we'll have access to any, and you don't want to use the pilot relief tube if you don't have to ... trust me on that."

"Yeah, sure, good idea," said Tony, looking at *Songbird*. "Guess there ain't no shithouse on that thing, eh?"

"Afraid not."

"So, where ... ?" said Tony, looking around.

"Just inside there," said Mickey pointing to the front door of the FBO. "Oh, you got any luggage or anything?"

"No."

Mickey shrugged. "Okay. Just come out to the airplane when you're ready."

Mickey watched Tony walk away for few seconds. He shrugged and walked to the plane.

"That your fare?" Jeff asked. He was noting on a clipboard the fuel that *Songbird* had taken on.

"Yep."

"Weird little guy."

"Maybe."

Songbird idled easily along the taxiway toward the active runway. The small window vent was open and Mickey had Tony holding the door open a few inches until they were ready to take off, but the afternoon sun still made the cockpit downright hot.

"Doesn't this thing have any air conditioning?" said Tony.

Mickey looked over at Tony. He pointed to the headset in Tony's lap. He had tried to get Tony to put it on before they left the tarmac, but Tony didn't want to. There was no mistaking Tony's lips mouthing, "What the hell," as he pulled on the set.

Mickey spoke into his microphone. "Can you hear me, okay?"

"Sure thing, Ace," said Tony.

"It's Mickey, okay?"

"Sure, whatever. Why don't you have AC in this thing? It's like a furnace in here?"

"Sorry, Tony, that's a luxury that I can't afford. Besides, AC robs too much horsepower from a plane this size. Why don't you take off your jacket?"

Tony would have loved to take off his jacket, but he was conscious of the Barretta nine-millimeter he had in the pocket. "That's okay."

Mickey shrugged. "Your call. Shut the door, will you?" He flipped the little vent window shut on his side, checked the lock on the door, then swung *Songbird* onto the runway and advanced the throttles. The little twin surged forward, gathering speed rapidly. At seventy miles an hour he gave the yoke a gentle pull and they were flying. He retracted the gear and held the speed at eighty to maintain the best rate of climb.

Mickey reached up to make sure the vent above Tony's head was fully open. As they rose, the air from outside was noticeably cooler and heat in the cabin was beginning to dissipate. "Thank God," said Tony as the cool air washed over him. "That's a lot of money to pay and not have any damn air conditioning."

"Sorry."

Mickey leveled off at 4,000 feet and banked around to course three-one-two. He pointed the panel-mounted GPS that displayed their course over Florida. "See that line? That's our flight path. You can follow our progress along that."

Tony looked at the GPS and could barely discern any movement over the map display. He noticed their ground speed at one hundred fifty eight miles per hour.

"Damn, can't this thing go any faster?"

"We're fighting a headwind."

"Huh?"

"We'll pick up a few miles per hour on the return ... when the wind is on our tail."

"What the hell?"

Mickey changed the subject. "So why are you going to Pensacola?"

"I just gotta catch up to my buddies ... they accidentally took off with something that belongs to me."

Oh, oh, thought Mickey. "Must be pretty important for you to go to all this trouble."

"You might say that."

"Do they know you're coming?"

"Oh, sure, sure."

Tony turned and looked intently out the window. After a few minutes had passed he asked, "What lake is that?"

"Okeechobee."

Tony pulled a road map out of his jacket pocket and opened it up, practically knocking Mickey's headset off in the process.

"Sorry, pal."

Mickey smiled thinly.

Tony managed to the fold the map to the area he wanted to see. "Shouldn't Lake Okeechobee be on our left?"

"No." Mickey pointed to the GPS display. "See? That's Okeechobee, off to the right."

Tony looked at the GPS and then he looked at his map again. Suddenly it dawned on him that they were flying direct to Pensacola, as the crow flies, not as a car would traverse the distance.

"We're not going to be following I75 at all?"

"We'll cross over seventy-five near Bradenton, but then we don't see any roads at all until we get to Pensacola."

Tony looked at his map again. "You mean we're going over water?"

"Fastest way. I assumed you were in a hurry."

Tony rubbed his temples. "Well, shit. That's no good at all."

"What? You wanted to sight see?"

"No. Well, yeah. Yeah, I want to sight see."

"What did you want to see?"

"I was hoping to see seventy-five up past Orlando."

"You got some kind of fascination with highways?"

"What do you care? I'm paying you."

"Well, that's the thing. If I follow the highways it's going to cost more."

"How much more?"

"I don't know, it will maybe add an hour, maybe more … maybe another couple hundred bucks."

"Two hundred? Shit that's almost a grand to go for a ride in this flying sweat box."

"Hey, I told you that flying commercial would be cheaper."

"All right, all right, I'll pay you. Just follow the roads, will ya?"

"You're the boss. I'll have to cancel my IFR flight plan."

"Whatever. And don't fly so friggin' high. I can't see nothin' from up here."

Mickey looked over at Tony. "Tony, I need to know. What's this all about?"

Tony looked at Mickey but Mickey couldn't see his eyes behind his sunglasses. "I told you, I'm just catching up to my buddies."

"I thought they were in Pensacola?"

"They're on their way to Pensacola."

"You said they knew you were coming."

"They do."

"So why are we chasing them down the highway?"

"They're in a hurry. I told them I'd meet them somewhere along the way so they wouldn't have to wait for me."

"Tony, I was born at night … but it wasn't last night. What the hell is going on?"

Tony pulled down his sunglasses so Mickey could see his eyes. "You think there's something going here?"

"Yeah. Yeah I do."

Tony smiled. "Marvin said you were a savvy guy."

"You said Marvin gave you my name."

"Yeah, he did … I asked him for a pilot who wasn't opposed to … well … who was flexible."

That sonofabitch, Marvin, Mickey thought. "And he gave you my name?"

"Yeah, he did."

"Well I have no idea why. I barely know the guy."

"Let's just say that I know you made a few runs for Marvin … from Mexico."

"I have no idea what you're talking about."

"Bullshit. Marvin told me that you flew some product from Juarez to Miami for him … and it wasn't chili peppers."

"Okay, maybe I made a couple of runs for Marvin back in the old days … but I had no idea what the cargo was."

Tony looked at him. Mickey's face reddened. "Okay, so I knew it probably wasn't legal ... but I didn't know exactly what it was."

"Whatever you say, Ace."

"Besides, that was a long time ago. I don't do shit like that anymore."

"Well, I'm not asking you to. Just do like I say and follow the damn highway, will ya?"

"What do we do if you spot them?"

Tony hadn't thought that through very clearly. "I'm not sure. I'll think of something."

"You know, we can't just meet up a truck stop."

"I know. I said I'd think of something."

"So you're just going to meet up with your buddies and then we're on our way back to Miami?"

"After I meet with my buddies we can head back to Miami."

"Really?"

"Really.

Well, that's a positive, thought Mickey. He called Miami control to cancel the IRF flight plan he had filed. From here on they would be flying VFR. He altered to course three-four-oh, reduced power and eased Songbird down to 1500 feet.

They were just passing over highway 80 when Mickey said, "If we follow this course, we'll intercept seventy-five just north of Tampa. Will that work?"

Tony looked at his map. "Yeah." He looked out at the miles of forest and swamp broken only by an occasional small town. "How long you figure it'll take to get there?"

Mickey looked at the GPS. "Looks like about forty-five minutes."

Tony checked his watch. "That makes it about five-thirty."

"That'd be about right."

"What's that give us what, another couple of hours of daylight?"

"Maybe a little more."

"Good."

6

Tony had lapsed into silence as Mickey threaded *Songbird* up through a corridor between the Lake Placid MOA and huge Tampa Class B airspace. North of Tampa, I75 ran slightly north by north east, so on their current course they would converge with the highway just south of the intersection with Florida's Turnpike. Roads and traffic below continued to multiply steadily as they approached the congestion of central Florida, making it difficult to identify individual highways. Mickey kept a close eye on the GPS and I75 appeared on the screen just as they crossed Highway 301. He looked through the windshield and could just make out the super highway just left of the nose.

"There it is, Tony."

Tony sat up and looked out the windshield. "Where?"

"There … just off to the left."

Tony strained to see. He could just make out a thin ribbon of concrete with cars and trucks crawling along. To the right he could see another highway. "What's that?"

"That should be Florida's Turnpike. See where it intersects with 75 just ahead?"

Tony could see where the two great highways merged in a tangle of on and off ramps. There were thousands of cars in his view, and even at 1500 feet it was hard to distinguish one from another. "Can you get down any lower?"

Mickey wasn't crazy about being this low over so much humanity. He pulled out the Tampa chart he had stashed in the door panel pocket and gave it a quick scan for radio towers or other man-made obstructions. None appeared in their direct path, so he chopped the power slightly and let the airplane slowly sink. He leveled off at a thousand feet.

"Lower," said Tony.

Mickey looked over at him. "That's as low as I'm going."

"All right, all right. Just keep following the highway."

"Why don't you tell me what their car looks like? I can help look."

"You just fly this crate. I'll look, okay?"

"You're the boss."

They flew on for a few more minutes, tracking the highway now just to the east so Tony could see better.

"What is it you're looking for?" Mickey asked again.

Tony looked at him. He realized that it made sense to have Mickey help. There was a lot of traffic down there.

"It's one of those big damn buses. You know ... the kind people vacation in."

"An RV?"

"Yeah, I guess that's what it is."

Mickey looked down. There were a few recreational vehicles in view, but nowhere near as many as there would have been a month ago when the snowbirds were in full flight back north. "You're lucky that it is late in the season, otherwise the road would be packed with 'em. What kind is it?"

"Now how the hell would I know that?"

"It's going to be pretty hard to spot something if you don't know what it looks like."

"I know what it looks like. It's a big damn bus."

Mickey pointed to a fifth wheel being hauled by a pick-up truck. "Like that?"

"No, like that damn thing over there." Tony pointed to a class A motor home in the southbound lanes.

"Okay. What color is it?"

"I don't know … maybe a light brown with strips of black in it."

"That helps. How do you know it'd be around here?"

"Because I talked to the guy who is driving it this morning and they were in Orlando. I figured they'd be at least this far by now."

"Why don't you call again and ask where they are now?"

Tony shook his head like that was the stupidest idea he'd heard in a while. Then it dawned on him that it wasn't such a stupid idea. He pulled out his cell phone.

"Will this thing work up here?"

"Sure … it's not exactly legal to use while airborne, but it'll work."

Tony punched up Vince's number.

A sleepy voice answered. "Yeah?"

"Vince, it's me, Tony."

"Yeah, I saw that. Waddaya want?"

"Where the hell are you?"

"Tony, we've been over that …"

"No, I mean, exactly where are you right now?"

"Shit, I don't know." Vince yelled to Sheldon. "Hey, where the fuck are …" Then to Tony,   "Why do you want to know?"

"Just curious."

"Well it's none of your …"

"About eighty miles from Tallahassee." Tony heard Sheldon yell in the background.

"Goddamn it, Shelly," Vince said.

Sheldon yelled back, "Did you not just ask where we were?"

"Yeah … never mind," Vince yelled back. Then to Tony, "Do you have anything important that you need, Tony?"

"Yeah, when do I get my fucking …" Tony became aware of Mickey and stopped in mid-sentence, but Vince knew what he meant.

"We've been over that too. I gotta go."

The line went dead. Tony snapped the phone shut and looked at his road map.

"How long would it take us to get to Tallahassee?

"That where they are?"

"No, but they are a lot further up the road than I thought they'd be."

Mickey was starting the get the picture. He didn't think Tony's friends were all that anxious to meet up with Tony. He should've known better than take a charter recommended by Marvin Sequin. But he was in it now. Best just to follow orders and get this charter over as painlessly as possible. He punched up the Tallahassee airport in the GPS.

"About forty-five minutes."

Tony consulted his map again. He held it up and pointed to a spot near Greenville. "Can you intercept highway 10 right about here?"

Mickey looked at the map. "Sure."

"Then let's do it."

Mickey climbed to 2500 feet and set the new course.

"Give me a heads up when we get there, Ace, will ya?"

"It's Mickey."

"Whatever."

"Ten coming up on the nose," said Mickey.

Tony had been studying his map intently; he barely looked out the window. "All right. Can you drop down again?"

Mickey pulled back on the throttle and let Songbird settle at a thousand feet before he reestablished cruise. He banked to the left so they were paralleling the highway that was just to the north. Eastbound traffic was heavy as commuters from Tallahassee made their way home, but westbound traffic was fairly light.

"How's this," said Mickey.

"It'll do."

They flew along for a few minutes. There were a lot of trucks but few RVs. Suddenly Mickey called out. "Hey, isn't that a brown and black RV?"

"Where?"

"About two-o'clock."

"What?"

Mickey pointed. "Right there."

"I can't tell. Can you get in a little closer?"

Mickey banked Songbird a little more toward the highway and dropped another hundred feet.

Tony got excited. "Damn, that looks like it."

"So now what?"

"I don't know. Can you put down somewhere up ahead?"

"What? By the highway?"

"Yeah."

"No. No I can't do that, Tony."

"Goddamn it. Then where?"

Mickey punched up the closest airport on the GPS. "Looks like there's a little GA airport about fifteen miles from here."

"Where exactly?"

Mickey pointed to a spot on Tony's map just ahead and to the north of their current position. "Right about there."

"Can I get a car there?"

"A rental? I doubt it. That's just a little airport."

"Well, hell, that won't do me no good."

"Sometimes the FBO will have a courtesy car that you can use."

"What's an FBO?"

"Fix-base operation. It's where you get fuel and stuff."

"You think they'll have a car there?"

"I don't know for sure. Some places do."

"Can you check?"

Mickey checked the GPS display for the radio frequency. "Meadville Unicom, Comanche 5831."

There was no reply. "Meadville Unicom, Comanche 5831," Mickey said again.

A static riddled reply came over the headset. "Aircraft calling Meadville. This is Agcat 4576. Duke ain't at the Unicom right now. He's out cutting the infield."

Mickey pressed the switch. "Thanks, Agcat."

Tony looked puzzled.

"Sounds like some local crop duster. He just told me that the airport manger isn't manning the radio. "

"No one is minding the store?"

"That's the way it is at small airports. You're pretty much on your own."

"Does the guy know if there is car around?"

Mickey keyed the mike. "Agcat, Comanche three-one. Is there a courtesy car available at Meadville?"

Another static reply. "Duke used to have an old truck he'd loan out. Don't know if it is still running."

"Thanks, Agcat." Mickey turned to Tony. "Probably a fifty-fifty chance we get something that rolls."

"Good enough. Let's go for it."

Mickey keyed the mike. "Agcat, what's the active at Meadville?"

"Two-eight."

"Thanks. Meadville traffic, Comanche 5831 five miles to the southeast, inbound for two-eight."

7

Five minutes later *Songbird* eased onto the runway at Meadville. As they rolled out they passed a man astride a rusty Ford 8N tractor mowing the space between the runway and the taxiway. He took off his greasy ball cap and waved it as they went by. He pointed to a clump of buildings a quarter mile off.

"Must be Duke," said Mickey.

"That hayseed runs this joint?"

"Probably the owner."

Mickey pulled off the active and onto the taxiway. They bounced along the rough pavement to the tarmac in front of the buildings where an assortment of aircraft sat in a row. Mickey pulled into a slot between a Cessna 180 and weathered Mooney.

He shut down the engines and reached over Tony to open the door. The steamy Florida afternoon rolled in. Tony undid his seatbelt and pulled himself up and out onto the wing.

"Jesus," he said trying to stretch out cramped limbs. "That ain't exactly first class, you know."

"Sorry," said Mickey as he waited for Tony to step down so he could exit the aircraft.

They stood in the hot, afternoon sun, listening the ticking and popping of the cooling engines. Off in the distance Duke was making his way toward them, mowing as he came.

"Listen, I don't think you should mention your business to that guy." Mickey nodded his head toward the man on tractor. "These country boys are pretty much suspicious of everything. He might want more answers than I do."

Tony nodded.

"Let's go inside," said Mickey.

He led the way across the Tarmac to an ancient clapboard two-story building. Tony followed him through a screen door into a small room that appeared to be the office. There was a counter over a glass case stocked with a couple of headsets, charts and training books. Behind the counter were a couple of desks, several filing cabinets and an old office chair. A radio and microphone sat amidst piles of papers. On the other desk a small tabletop fan rustled the papers as it strained to circulate air in the stuffy room.

On the back wall a water-cooler stood between two doors marked "Men" and "Women."

"Damn, I've got to piss like a racehorse," said Tony. He went into the men's room.

Mickey started to follow him in but stopped. It was obviously too small. He looked around and, seeing no one, shrugged and went into the women's room.

While Mickey was drying his hands, he heard the screen door slam. He opened the door and stepped back into the office where he came face to face with a giant of man, dressed in coveralls and grimy tee shirt. His bristled salt and pepper beard covered a creased and tanned face that appeared about sixty years old.

"Well, hey there," he said.

Mickey blushed, having just been caught coming out of the women's rest room. "Ah, hello," he stammered, "I … I …"

"Oh, don't worry about that. There's hardly more 'n one or two ladies a day use that thing anyway." He held out a hand. "I'm Duke."

Mickey shook his hand. "Nice to meet you Duke. I'm Mickey Soto."

"Nice airplane, Mickey. That, a '68 or '69 Comanche?"

"Sixty-nine."

"She's a cherry."

"Thanks."

Tony stepped back into the office and closed the men's room door behind him.

"Duke, this is Tony Boccaccio, my passenger," said Mickey.

"Nice to meet you, Tony. I'm Duke."

Tony shook his hand and nodded. "You run this joint?"

"Guess so."

"You got a car for rent?"

Mickey cut in, embarrassed by Tony's abruptness. "Ah, Duke, Tony and I are on our way to Pensacola. We thought we'd put down here to top off the tanks and maybe get some supper, if there is anything nearby."

Duke seemed unfazed. "Where you coming from?"

"Miami."

"Miami, eh? Why'd you put down here? Tallahassee is only another 40 miles or so. Probably get gas there cheaper, you know."

"We were hungry and I just didn't want to deal with Class B airspace. This just looked like a nice place to relax and stretch for a few minutes."

"Well, it is that. Far as food goes, there ain't much between here and Tallahassee. If you go right, toward Meadville, there's Etta's diner. Pretty good food there. If you go left, there are a couple of places by the highway that are okay."

"Do you happen to have a car we could use?"

Duke rubbed his chin. "I have a truck that I loan out from time to time. It's out in the hanger."

"That'd be great. How much you charge?"

"Oh, there's no charge … as long as you buy avgas."

"We're buying fuel, all right."

"Oh, and fill up the truck before you return it?"

"Not a problem."

Duke went behind the counter and opened a drawer in the desk under the radio. He pulled out a key ring and flipped it to Mickey. "I don't think there are any planes blocking the truck, but if there are just push 'em out of the way."

"Sure. Thanks."

"How long you think you'll be?"

Mickey looked at Tony. "I don't know …"

Tony finished for him. "Probably an hour or so."

"That'll probably get you into Pensacola after sunset. You know your way around?"

"Yes, I've been there several times."

"Then you know there's lots of restricted airspace, what with all the military around there."

"I know. And my GPS database is up to date."

"Good thing. You don't want that pretty airplane getting shot down."

"That'd ruin my day."

Duke chuckled briefly. "Well enjoy supper."

"Thanks. Oh, yeah, what time do you close up?"

"Hell, I'm here twenty-four-seven. I live in that mobile home behind the office."

Tony followed Mickey across the tarmac to the hanger.

"Maybe I should I wait here while you go take care of your business."

"After you told Duke how hungry we were? Might look kinda suspicious don't you think?"

"Is it?

"Naw, I just need to catch up to my buddies and get something from them."

"Look Tony, I'm just a pilot. I said I'd fly you to Pensacola because I thought that's where you were going.

Now I know there is more to this flight than meets the eye I just don't want to be any more involved than I am already."

"It's no big thing, Mickey. These guys just accidentally took off with something that belongs to me. I just need to get it back."

"I have a feeling they aren't too anxious to give it back to you."

"Of course they are. They're just in a hurry to get to California and they don't want to stop if they can help it."

"You sure about that?"

"Absolutely. Now come on, shake a leg. We gotta get going."

The door to the large hanger was open and they walked in among the half-dozen Cessnas and Pipers, a Pitts Special, and in the far corner, a gleaming KingAir C90. Parked on the side, behind a Cherokee 180, was an ancient and battered Ford pickup truck.

"That's it?" said Tony. "That's our ride?"

"Beggars can't be choosers. Help me push this Cherokee out of the way."

They maneuvered the Cherokee fifteen feet to the side, just providing enough room to pull the truck out of through the doors.

Mickey flipped Tony the keys. Tony flipped them back. "You're the pilot, you drive."

Mickey saw himself slowly slipping down the rabbit hole. "Yeah, sure."

They opened the doors and stared across the cab at each other. The floor was strewn with old coffee cups and crushed soda cans. Wadded up papers and cigarette packs covered the seats and there was a quarter inch of dust on the dash.

"What a shit hole," said Tony.

Mickey swept his arm over the seat to make room to sit. "Just hope that it starts."

Tony followed suit and the slamming doors echoed in the hanger. Mickey pumped the gas a couple of times and turned the key. The starter groaned for a second, then just clicked. They looked at each other.

Mickey pumped the gas again and turned the key. This time the starter caught and the engine fired. A cloud of white smoke filled the hanger.

"Jesus, get this thing out of here before we choke to death," said Tony.

Mickey put it in gear and carefully maneuvered past the Cherokee and out the door where the smoke dissipated into the atmosphere. He rolled down his window. "I think it needs a ring job," he said.

"Ring job? I think it should be blown up," said Tony.

"Like I said, beggars can't be choosers."

They pulled around the tarmac in front of the office. Duke was holding the hose from the fuel truck as he pumped gas into *Songbird*. He waved as they went by, oblivious to the cloud of smoke that trailed the pickup.

They drove around to the parking lot and then down the long driveway to the road that led back to the highway.

8

Ten minutes later they were sitting on the ramp to westbound I-10.

"You think they've gone by already?" asked Tony.

Mickey looked at his watch. "Unless they stopped along the way, they should've passed by here about ten or fifteen minutes ago. Can't you call them to find out exactly?"

"Yeah, sure, I'll call them. But let's get going."

Mickey put the truck in gear and accelerated down the ramp, merging easily with traffic as cars pulled into the left lane to avoid the cloud of smoke that followed them. Tony punched up Vince's number on his cell phone.

Vince answered. "What now?"

"Just wondering how it's going in that bus," said Tony.

"It's going fine. If you need anymore info, call Johnny, will you?"

"So where you at now?"

"I told you, Tony. Ain't none of your fucking business. Now unless you have something worthwhile to tell me, I gotta go."

Tony couldn't stand it any more. "You tell me where the fuck you are you goddamn thief. I want my money."

Oh shit, I knew it, thought Mickey.

"It ain't your money, asshole." Vince hung up.

Tony pounded the dash. "Shit, shit, shit."

"Look, Tony, this is not what I signed on for. How about I drive back to the airport and you take the truck and do whatever you have to do."

"How about you just shut the fuck up and drive the truck?"

Mickey was about to protest again, but when he looked over at Tony he was staring down the barrel of a gun.

"What, are you threatening me?"

"I'm telling you to drive this piece of shit … and a little faster, too."

"So you're going to shoot me if I don't."

"I might shoot you if you don't shut the fuck up."

"Then what?"

"Then it'd be a lot quieter and I could think."

Mickey didn't think Tony was really going to shoot him. For one thing he was currently doing seventy in traffic. For another, he didn't think that Tony wanted that kind of trouble. *But you never know.*

"Tony, how is shooting me going to solve your problem?"

Tony lowered the gun. "I don't have to shoot you. I know how you got the money to buy that airplane. I'll bet the DEA would be real interested in that information."

"Oh, that's how it's going to be?"

"I just need you to drive this truck right now."

"Okay, okay, I'll drive the damn truck. But that's all I'm doing. If we catch up to your friends you're on your own."

"Fine. Just catch them."

Mickey accelerated to eighty, the Ford protesting a little more with the increase in speed. "I think this is as fast as this bucket of bolts is going go," he said.

"Can't you get a little more out of it?"

"Not with these ball joints." Mickey had his hands full keeping the truck in one lane. "And look at the temperature gage."

Tony leaned over and saw the gage had risen to the red arc. "Goddamn it," he said.

They came up over a small rise and about a mile ahead the beige and black Winnebago came into view.

"There it is," shouted Tony.

They were gaining fast. Mickey working hard to keep the old truck under control as they weaved around the half-dozen cars that were in between them and the Winnebago. Within another mile they were 100 yards behind the big RV. The Ford was wobbling noticeably and Mickey watched the temperature gage creep further into the red.

"Pull along side."

"I'm not sure this thing is going to hold together."

"Just pull along side."

Mickey pulled into the left lane and within a couple of seconds they were even with the RV. He could not see the driver through the tinted window.

Brandishing his gun, Tony leaned out the window. "Pull over you sonofabitch," he yelled.

The RV was going about seventy so Mickey gratefully had to slow down to keep pace. But the temperature kept rising and the cloud of smoke following the truck was billowing now keeping the cars behind them at bay.

"Pull the fuck over," Tony yelled.

"I thought these were your friends," said Mickey.

"Shut up, will ya," Tony yelled back at him. Then to RV, "Pull over."

But the RV didn't budge.

Tony pulled his head in. "Get in front of him."

Mickey started to pull ahead, but the RV began to speed up too. He stepped harder on the accelerator. They were topping eighty and barely making progress on the Winnebago.

"Come on, will you get in front of him?"

"I'm trying but I don't thing the truck is going to make it."

"Keep your foot on it."

The speedometer crept up to eight-five and almost imperceptibly the Ford inched ahead of the RV. Another quarter-mile and they had the clearance to pull in front of it.

Mickey was easing the severely wobbling truck into the right lane when a loud bang came from the engine, which then seized up, causing the truck to decelerate rapidly. The driver of the RV reacted the only way he could, by standing on the brakes.

"Holy shit," yelled Mickey, but all he could do was watch helplessly as the RV loomed ever larger in the rearview mirror.

The two vehicles remained lockstep as they continued to slow, the larger one, nose-down, with clouds of smoke coming from the tires, just inches from the rear of the smaller one, smoke pouring from under the hood. Gradually the intricate dance came to an end as the RV managed to stop successfully, the Ford coasting another 100 yards up the road.

"Sweet Jesus," said Tony.

Mickey just sat with hands tightly gripping the steering wheel, watching a flock of birds wheeling in the sky over the trees.

Tony broke the reverie when he opened his door and jumped out. Mickey watched him run back to the RV, waving his gun at it like a hunter stalking a wounded beast. Cars were beginning to carefully pass in the left lane, the occupants gawking at the scene as they passed.

"Get out here," Tony yelled as he approached the RV.

He was surprised to see the door open and a balding, man wearing a golf shirt, Bermuda shorts, with socks and sandals emerge. He was holding his hands up.

"We don't want any trouble, mister," said the man.

"Who are you?" asked Tony.

"We called 911. The police will be here any minute."

"Police? Who the fuck are you?"

"What do you want from us?"

"Who are you?"

"P … Paul Harrington," the man stammered.

A female voice echoed from inside the RV, "What do they want, Paul?"

"Who is that?" asked Tony.

"My … my wife, Margaret."

"What do they want," repeated Margaret.

"Where're Vince and Sheldon?"

"Who?"

"Vince and Sheldon. Do I have to spell it for you?"

"I don't know who you are talking about."

"Paul, what do they want?" asked Margaret.

"I don't know," answered Paul.

"Tell her to get out here," said Tony.

"Look, mister, you can have whatever you want."

"I want her out here … now."

"Margaret, he says he wants you …"

"I heard what he said. What do they want?"

A curly-headed, middle-aged woman, came down the steps of the RV and out into the fading twilight. Folds of flesh protruded from a yellow tank top and filled a pair of blue shorts to capacity.

"We've called the police. They'll be here any minute," said Margaret.

"Who are you?" asked Tony.

"Margaret Harrington. Who are you?"

"Where are Vince and Sheldon?"

"How would I know? What do you want?" persisted Margaret.

"Is there anybody else in there?" Tony waved his gun at the RV.

"No. What do you want," persisted Margaret.

Tony pushed her aside and went up the steps of the RV. He gingerly peeked around the corner. An impeccably clean but empty living room was all he saw. He stepped further in, pointing his gun down the narrow room.

"What do you want?" said Margaret.

Tony ignored her and walked slowly past the galley down the hallway. He carefully opened the door to the tiny bathroom, stepped in and flung open the shower door. He retreated and continued into the bedroom. It too, was empty.

"Son of a bitch."

He walked quickly through the motor home and stepped out.

"You know the police will be here any minute," said Margaret.

"This thing belong to you?" asked Tony.

"Yes," said Paul.

"Damn. And you don't know where Vince and Sheldon are?"

"Who?" asked Paul.

"There're going to arrest you," said Margaret.

"You called the police?" asked Tony.

"Yes," said Margaret. "And they'll be here any second to arrest you."

"Damn," said Tony.

"Look mister, I don't know what you want, but …"

"How long ago?"

"How long ago, what?" asked Paul.

"How long ago did you call the police?"

"When you were trying to kill us back on the highway."

"Damn."

"Hey you were driving like a manic …"

"How much?"

"How much, what?

"How much do you want to keep your big traps shut?"

"What are you talking about?"

"If I give you five hundred dollars, will you forget about this?"

"Five hundred dollars? You damn near killed us and then you threaten us with a gun. Are you crazy?" said Margaret.

"Six hundred."

"Hey, you can't go threatening people like that and then expecting to buy your way out of it," said Margaret.

"Just a second." Tony turned and started to trot back toward the truck.

"What?" said Margaret.

"Don't move," Tony yelled over his shoulder.

Mickey had been watching the whole scene in the mirror. He saw Tony running up to the truck.

"We got a problem here," said Tony when he reached the driver's side window.

"Let me guess. Those aren't your friends."

"It looks like we pulled over the wrong damn bus."

"Oh, that's just fucking great."

"Look Ace, I need that $400 I gave you."

"What for?"

"Just give it to me, will ya?"

"Are you nuts?"

"Do you want to leave here in handcuffs?"

"What are you talking about?"

"Those Rubes called the heat. I'm going buy some cooperation."

Mickey pulled the money from his pocket and started to hand it to Tony. He pulled it back. "I know I'll never see this again."

"I'll double it. Just give it to me now."

"Yeah, sure." He handed the money to Tony.

Tony grabbed the bills and turned to head back to the Winnebago. He stopped and turned back to Mickey. "And if you're asked, these folks just pulled over to give us a hand with our truck."

He turned to go, stopped and turned back again. He handed Mickey his gun. "Oh, and do something with this will ya?"

9

"How about a thousand?" asked Tony as he trotted up to the Harringtons.

"Are you crazy?" said Margaret.

"A thousand?" asked Paul.

"Yeah. A thousand bucks, and all you have to do is tell the cops it was a mistake … that you thought it might be something serious, but when you pulled over you realized that we were just having a problem with our truck and needed help."

"We're not doing any such …"

"A thousand dollars?" asked Paul.

"Yep. A thousand bucks and we forget all about this little misunderstanding."

A county police car sped by in the eastbound lanes, lights flashing and siren blaring. It suddenly skidded to a stop a few hundred yards down the road and started to cross the median toward them.

Tony fanned out the bills. "It's all yours, just keep your trap shut about the gun and all."

Paul looked at the money. "Okay, you got a deal, mister."

"Paul!"

"Shut up, Margaret. A thousand dollars is a lot of money."

"Help me push the truck off the road," said Tony.

"Come on, Margaret, you can help."

"I'm not doing any such thing."

"Margaret. I told you to come." Paul grabbed her by the arm. "And don't you say a word about the gun to the police."

"Paul!"

"I mean it, Margaret."

The police car pulled up behind the Winnebago and two officers jumped out, pistols drawn. They walked forward, one on each side of the RV. When he spotted the Harrington's and Tony making their way to the truck the cop on the roadside of the RV yelled, "Everybody freeze."

The little group obliged. He gingerly approached them. "On the ground, now!"

"It's okay, officer. There's no problem here," said Tony.

"I said everyone on the ground, now!"

"Really, officer. It was just a misunderstanding."

The other cop hurried to his partner's side and yelled, "Down!"

Tony and Paul got down on the ground. Margaret stood defiantly.

"You too, lady."

Margaret did not budge.

"Ronnie, you check the van," said the first cop.

"You sure, Hank?"

"I got this. Check the van."

Ronnie went back to the RV. Hank spotted Mickey in the truck. "You, in the truck. Get out and get on the ground."

Mickey obeyed.

A second police car squealed to a stop behind the first. Two more officers emerged, weapons drawn, and ran up to the knot of people behind the pickup.

"What's going on?" said the officer in the lead.

"Don't know, Billy Ray. Just getting the measure of it," said Hank. "Delbert, why don't you go help Ronnie check out the RV?"

"Sure, Hank." Delbert retreated to the van.

"All right, what's going on here?" Hank asked no one in particular.

"I'll tell you what's going on …" said Margaret.

"It's all just a misunderstanding, officer," interrupted Paul from the ground. "These gentlemen passed us waving for help and we thought they were threatening us, but that wasn't the case."

"Who are you?" asked Hank.

"Paul Harrington. And that's my wife, Margaret."

"You the one who called 911?"

"Yes, but …"

"That your RV?"

"Yes."

"You got any ID?"

"Yes sir. It's in the Winnebago."

"Well get up and get it," said Hank. "You go with him, Billy Ray."

Paul got up and brushed himself off. "Come on, Margaret."

"She can stay here," said Billy Ray.

"But …"

"Hank won't hurt her. Come on." Billy Ray led Paul back to the van.

"Now why don't you tell me what happened here?" Hank asked Margaret.

Tony answered, "Like he said, officer, it was just a misunderstanding. My partner and I were …"

"I didn't ask you. I asked her. Who are you?"

Tony started to get up, "Tony, Tony Boccaccio."

"I didn't tell you to get up."

Tony got back down on the ground.

"You got any ID?"

"Yes, sir. In my wallet."

"Well get it out." Hank kept his gun trained on Tony while he reached into his pocket to retrieve his wallet.

"Officer, I …" said Margaret.

"I'll get back to you in a minute, ma'am."

Tony held up his driver's license to Hank.   Hank reached over and carefully grabbed it.

"Boccaccio, eh?" Hank mused on the name for a minute like it might mean something to him. "What do you do, Mr. Boccaccio?"

"I run a restaurant in Miami."

"But this is a New York license," he stated.

"I'm from there originally. I just haven't got around to getting it changed."

"How long you been here?"

"Two years."

"Two years? You operating a motor vehicle with this thing."

"Yes."

"Well, it isn't legal. You better get that thing changed."

"Yes, sir."

"You with this other guy?"

"Yes."

"You got any ID?" Hank said to Mickey.

Mickey pulled out his wallet, fished out the license and held it up. Hank stepped over to him and grabbed it. He looked it over.

"This your truck, Mr. Soto?"

"No, it belongs to the Meadville airport."

"Meadville airport? What are you doing with it?"

"I'm a commercial pilot and Mr. Boccaccio is my passenger. We just landed at Meadville to get gas and some food. Duke loaned us his truck."

"He did, eh?"

Ronnie and Delbert came up.

"Nobody else in the RV, Hank," said Ronnie.

"Thanks. Ronnie, will you go back to the squad car and call Duke at the Meadville airport. See if he loaned ..." he looked at the licenses in his hand, "... a Mr. Soto and Mr. Boccaccio his truck."

"You got it," said Ronnie and he started to head back to the car.

"Oh, and Ronnie, run these too?"

Ronnie came back and took the two licenses.

"Delbert, will you keep that traffic moving in the right lane?"

"You got it, Hank."

Delbert followed after Ronnie.

"You say you're a pilot, Mr. Soto?

"Yes."

"You got your pilot's license?" asked Hank.

"Right here." Mickey fished out his pilot's license and handed it to Hank.

"Officer, I …" said Margaret just as Billy Ray and Paul returned.

"Everything checks out, Hank," said Billy Ray.

"Now why don't you tell me what happened here," said Hank.

"Officer, these men …" started Margaret.

"Passed us back up the highway," finished Paul. "They were waving and gesturing to us and we misinterpreted their actions as threatening, but evidently they were having a mechanical problem and were just trying to get our attention to help."

"Somebody said something about being threatened by a gun," said Hank.

"Oh, no, officer. I just thought I saw a gun. That's why I panicked and called 911. But there was no gun."

"Either of you have a gun?" Hank asked Mickey and Tony.

"No, sir," said Tony.

"No," said Mickey.

"Well stand up and empty your pockets on the hood of the truck."

Mickey and Tony obliged.

"Now put your hands on the hood."

Hank ran his hand up and down their sides.

"There a gun in that truck."

Tony looked sideways at Mickey.

"No, sir," said Mickey.

"Billy, search the truck."

Tony raised his eyebrows. Mickey ignored him.

"Now why don't you tell me what happened?" asked Hank.

Tony answered, "We were on our way from Meadville when the truck started over heating. We didn't want to get stuck out in the middle of nowhere, so we pulled along side this RV and waved for help. When we got in front of them the engine seized up and these good people stopped to help."

"Where were you going?"

"We were looking for a restaurant," said Mickey.

"Why didn't you go to Etta's?"

"I don't know, I guess we were just looking for something ... you know, a little more upscale."

"Around here? There isn't anything like that until you get to Tallahassee."

"We just thought we'd take a look up the road."

Ronnie reappeared. "Duke says he loaned out his truck this afternoon."

"To these guys?"

"He couldn't remember their names, but they fit his description."

"Anything on the licenses?"

"No." Ronnie handed them back to Hank.

Billy Ray joined them from the other side of the truck. "It's clean, Hank. Well, it ain't clean, but there ain't no gun in there.

Tony looked at Mickey again. Mickey stared ahead.

Hank put his gun away and walked over to Harrington's who were now standing behind the pickup.

"You folks sure there was no problem here?"

Paul looked at Margaret. Margaret looked at the ground. "No, officer, he said, "It was all just a simple misunderstanding."

"That right, ma'am?"

Margaret continued to stare at the ground. "Yes, it was just a misunderstanding."

Hank gathered the other officers around. "What do you think?" he asked.

"Doesn't appear to be any foul play," said Billy Ray.

"No, it doesn't. But something just doesn't smell right," said Hank.

"What do you want to do?"

"Guess there's not much we can do."

He went back to Mickey and Tony. "Here." He handed them their licenses.

"Gather up your stuff and let's get this truck off the road."

10

Leaning against the front fender of the pickup, Mickey waved to the Harringtons as the Winnebago eased back on the freeway and passed by. Paul waved back but Margaret just leered at him.

Tony was rooting around in the bushes along side the road. "Where did you throw that thing?"

"You could have waited until the Harrington's were gone before you waded in there," Mickey yelled back. He walked over to where Tony was searching. "I told you, I heaved it in there at least fifty feet."

"Well, help me find it will you?"

"Why? So you can threaten me with it again?"

"Hey, I'm sorry about that. I was just stressed out at the moment. I wasn't going to shoot you."

"Maybe not, but I don't like having a gun pointed at me."

"I said I'm sorry. Come on, help me look. It's getting dark."

"I'm not going in that mosquito haven. Besides the tow truck is here."

Mickey walked back as a truck with the words 'Ralph's Auto Service, Meadville' written on the door pulled up behind the Ford. A portly black man wearing greasy dungarees, a work shirt with the sleeves cut off and cap displaying the logo for the Meadville Gun Club descended from the cab. He walked up to Mickey. The name 'Al' was stitched on his shirt.

"You the fellers that called for service?"

"That'd be us."

"What's the problem?"

"Engine seized. We're going to need a tow."

Al walked around to the front of the truck. "Say, isn't this Duke Hobb's truck?"

"Yes it is."

"He know you got it?"

"Yes he does. How about giving us a tow back to the airport."

"Sure. What's your partner doing over there?"

Mickey looked over at Tony who had worked his way deeper into the brush. "Oh, he lost his watch."

"In there?"

Jesus, that was lame. "He was taking a piss."

"And he lost his watch?"

"Don't ask me. Just get us out of here, okay."

"Sure." The driver walked back to his truck shaking his head.

Mickey watched him maneuver his rig around to hook up the Ford. Traffic was drifting over to the left lane to give the tow truck room. Mickey spotted a brown and black Winnebago approaching. As it passed, Mickey saw a black driver look over at the scene. He shrugged and walked back to the brush.

"Will you forget about the gun?"

"Are you fucking crazy," said Tony. "I'm not leaving a nine mil with my figure prints on it laying the bushes here."

Mickey had to admit he had a point. But then, that was Tony's problem. He waded in to the spot he remembered flinging it. A few minutes later he stepped on something hard and bent down to look at it. It was Tony's gun. He scuffed a small hole with his heel and pushed it in, then kicked dirt and grass over the top.

"Hey, you fellers riding back with me or you got some other plans?" Al stood by the side of the road wiping his hands on rag. The front end of the Ford was dangling beneath the crane off the rear of his truck.

"Come on, Tony. We gotta go," said Mickey.

Tony continued to kick around in the bushes. "Goddamn it, I gotta find it."

"It getting too dark and we're going to be left out here if we don't go now."

"Hey I gotta go," said Al.

"Hang on a second," said Mickey. He waded over to Tony. "Look, no one is ever going find that thing out here. Forget about it. I don't want to be walking back to the airport, okay?"

Tony stood up and looked at him. "Why'd you have to heave it in so deep?"

"Would you rather be trying to make bail at the county jail right now?"

"Of course not. But it's nerve-wracking knowing that it is laying out here somewhere … not to mention that it is an expensive little piece of hardware."

"Nobody is ever going to find it."

"You never know."

"Tell you what. You stay here and look for it. I'll meet you back in Miami and we can square things up." Mickey waded out of the bushes.

"Shit." Tony kicked at the shrubs and started after Mickey. "Wait up, Ace."

"It's Mickey."

"Whatever."

Al was sitting in the cab of his truck with the engine running. Mickey slid in next to him from the passenger side and Tony followed. Al waited for a break in traffic and eased the rig onto the highway.

"Jeez, now I really am hungry," said Tony. "Where's that restaurant the guy at the airport told us about?"

"Etta's?"

"That's it," said Mickey. "How far is that from the airport?"

"About half a mile."

"How late is it open?"

"Depends. She stays open as long as there is business, but if it's slow, she usually closes down around eight o'clock."

"What time is it now?" asked Tony.

Al looked at his watch. "Seven thirty-five."

"Can we make it?"

"I think so. Yours get broken?"

"My what?"

"Your watch."

"I don't have a watch."

"I thought that's what you were looking for in the bushes."

"What?"

Mickey nudged Tony.

"Oh, yeah. My watch. Too bad about that. Oh well, I've lost more expensive ones than that."

"I thought you found it."

Mickey nudged Tony again.

"Oh, yeah, yeah. I found it."

"But it don't work, eh?"

"Ah, no. No, it must've hit a rock or something."

"Must've been cheap."

"Yeah, it was cheap."

A cloud of dust drifted past the cab of Al's truck as it came to a stop in the dirt parking lot of Etta's Diner. Tony opened the door and jumped out. Mickey followed and shut the door.

"Tell Duke we'll be back there in about an hour or so," Mickey said through the open passenger window.

"Sure thing, mister." Al slipped the truck into drive and bounced back out onto the road.

The little café looked cheery and inviting in the surrounding gloom. It was past eight, but there were several cars in the parking lot, so the 'Open' sign in Etta's window was still lit. They walked across the dusty parking lot and stepped inside to a scene that confirmed the friendly exterior. A young family sat at one of the checkerboard tablecloth covered tables, an older couple at another. Two farmers sat at a Formica-topped counter sipping coffee.

A pert young, pony-tailed waitress was making her way to the family's table. She spotted Mickey and Tony and smiled. "Sit anywhere."

They picked a table near the door.

"I'll be right with you," said the waitress as she headed back to the kitchen. "Can I get you some coffee?"

"Sounds great," said Mickey.

"Sure, Sweetheart," said Tony.

Mickey pushed the cap back on his head and rubbed his temples. "Son of a bitch, what a day."

"Hey, it's been no picnic for me, Ace," said Tony.

"Mickey, okay?"

"Sure. So what now?"

"We get something to eat here, head back to the airport, and take off for Miami."

"Miami? There is no fucking way I'm going back to Miami without my money."

The older couple two tables away looked over at them.

"Will you keep it down," said Mickey. "This is a family place."

Tony lowered his voice and repeated, "There is no fucking way I'm going back to Miami without my money."

"So, that's what this is about. You're trying to steal money from some family?"

"No, I'm not trying to steal money from some fam …"

"Here you go." The waitress set down two porcelain cups. "You ready to order?"

Mickey looked at the glass case behind the counter that was filled with cakes, pies and rolls of all sorts. "You got any apple pie in there?"

"Best in the county."

"Great. I'll have a slice."

"Sure thing." She turned to Tony.

"I don't suppose you have any Rigatoni do you?"

"No, but Etta makes a mean Lasagna. I'm pretty sure there's still some left."

"I'll take an order of that, ah, what's your name?"

"Helen." She winked at Mickey and walked away.

Tony watched her head back to the kitchen. "Cute."

"So, you're not trying to rob some poor family. What the hell are you doing?" asked Mickey.

Tony turned back to Mickey. "I'm trying to get my fucking money back from some two-timing sonsabitches that stole from me, that's what I'm trying to do."

"Who?"

"Vince Jackson and Sheldon Isaacs."

"Who are they?"

"A couple of goons that work for the Rodriguez brothers."

"Never heard of them."

"Not surprising. They keep a pretty low profile. But if you live in south Florida and have anything to do with cars, they know who you are."

Mickey got the picture. "So, why would these guys steal your money?"

"Because they're a couple of goddamn thieves, that's why."

"How much did they take?"

"One-fifty."

"One hundred and fifty thousand?"

Tony nodded his head.

"That's a fair chunk of change."

Tony's voice started to rise. "You're goddamn right it is … and I want it back."

This time the farmers at the counter joined the older couple in looking a Tony.

"For Christ's sake, will you keep it down?" admonished Mickey.

Tony shrugged and brought his voice back down. "I can't help it. I just get so pissed when I think of those bastards driving down the road with my money."

"Where are they going?"

"California."

"California? Two guys who work for these Rodriguez brothers are driving a Winnebago to California?"

"Yeah. Sheldon don't like to fly."

Helen came up to the table with their orders. "Here you go." She set the plates down. "Can I get you anything else?"

"No thanks," said Mickey.

"Yeah. What time to you get off work, Helen?" asked Tony.

Mickey winced, but Helen wasn't fazed. She dealt with Tony's type twenty times a day. "Too late for you, Sweetie," she said and walked away.

A car pulling into the parking lot caught Mickey's attention. It parked and he saw Duke get out and walk up to the door.

"Oh shit," said Mickey. "I think we've got company."

The swung open and Duke ducked as he walked through the frame. One of the farmers at the counter swung around and shouted, "Hi ya, Duke."

Duke waved, "Hey, Ken. Hey, Ralph."

An elderly woman in an apron and hairnet stuck her head out of the kitchen order window. "Where ya been, Duke?"

"Been busy, Etta."

Duke spotted Mickey and Tony. He swung a chair around from one of the other tables and sat down with them.

"Al said you'd be here."

Mickey blushed. "We thought we'd build up our strength before we came to see you."

"Well, I knew ya'll weren't goin' nowhere, since I got your airplane. So what happened?"

Mickey cleared his throat. "Well, we had just passed a Winnebago and the engine seized up. We were damn lucky that motor home didn't slam into us."

"What were you doing out on the highway? I thought you were just going down the road for a bite to eat?"

"Well …"

Tony took over. "None of the restaurants appealed to me, Duke. I talked Mickey into heading down the road to see if we could spot something decent."

"I told you there wasn't much between here and Tallahassee."

"Well, I thought maybe we'd have a look around anyway."

Duke shook his head. He looked squarely at Mickey. "So how'd the police get involved?"

"Well …" Mickey started to answer.

"Funny thing about that, Duke. It appears that the couple in the RV thought we were threatening them somehow."

Duke kept his eyes on Mickey. "Were you?"

"Hell no. It was just a misunderstanding. We knew the truck was having a problem and I was waving at them, trying to get their attention to help us. We didn't want to get stranded out there."

"That so?" The question was directed at Mickey.

"Yep. That's pretty much how it was." Keeping his eyes on Duke, Mickey took a sip of his coffee.

Duke sat up and slapped his thighs. "So now we got the little problem of my busted truck."

"Yeah. Jeez. Sorry about that Duke. But it wasn't our fault. Damn thing just froze up on us," said Tony.

"Well, of course it did. That's a county truck. It ain't no highway truck. If I knew you were planning on zooming down a superhighway I wouldn't have never loaned it to you."

"What would you like us to do?" asked Mickey.

"It's going to cost me at least two grand to get that engine fixed. How about you give me half?"

"A thousand bucks. For that piece of shit?" said Tony.

"It's no show car, but it helps a lot of pilots get around while they are visiting us."

"I know, Duke, but Tony's right. A thousand is a lot of money. How about we cover the tow truck and give you a couple of hundred?"

Duke thought about that for a moment. "Five hundred. And you cover the tow." He pulled a receipt out of his shirt pocket. "Al charged me eighty to bring it home."

"All right," said Mickey. "Five-eighty. And then we're square?"

"Plus you owe me a hundred and sixty for fuel."

"One-sixty?"

"I told you, you could get gas cheaper in Tallahassee."

"That's seven-hundred and forty?"

"That'd be about right."

Mickey looked at Tony.

"Don't look at me, Ace. I gave you all I had."

"You take plastic?" Mickey asked Duke.

"Sure do."

"Well, give us a lift back to the airport and Mr. Boccaccio will pay you with his credit card."

"I don't have any fuckin' credit card."

"You don't have a credit card?" Even Duke was incredulous.

"Hell no. I deal strictly in cash."

"How about you?" Duke said to Mickey. "You got a credit card?"

"Well, yes, but …"

"Great," said Tony. "Let's go on back to the airport and Ace will settle up with you and we'll be on our way."

"Seven-hundred and forty dollars?" asked Mickey.

"That ought to do it," said Duke.

"But …"

Helen walked up to the table. "You want anything, Duke?"

"No, I was just leaving Helen."

"How about you fellas? You want anything else?"

"No, we're fine," said Mickey.

"Okay, well thank ya'all." Helen put the bill on the table.

Tony picked it up and handed it to Mickey. "Pay the tab and let's get out of here."

"You take plastic?" asked Mickey.

"Sure thing, Honey," said Helen.

11

"Just give us a few minutes, will ya Duke?" said Mickey.

"Sure." Duke went inside the airport office building.

Mickey watched the glow of Tony's cigarette as he flicked ashes on the tarmac. "You're already into me for eight hundred. I am not paying for Duke's truck. Or for the gas for that matter."

"I told you, I'll pay you back everything … double … as soon as I get my money."

"Tony, you're not getting your money back. Even if you caught up with those guys, you wouldn't be able to do anything."

"The hell I wouldn't. I'm getting my money back."

"How are you going to catch up to them? They could be anywhere between here and California."

"We'll find 'em."

"We?"

"Who else?"

"Hey, my role in this thing is done. I'm just trying to figure out how to get *Songbird* back to Miami."

"I told you, I'm not going back to Miami."

"Maybe you're not, but I am."

"You can't, Ace. You've got to help me. Whatever it costs, I'll pay you double."

"I don't have to do anything but go back to Miami."

"If it's a matter of money, I told you I'm going to …"

"It's not just the money. I don't want to have anything to do with this deal. We damn near got thrown in jail today. I'm done with that shit."

"Okay, okay, it got a little hairy today. But that's it. I won't ask you to do anything but fly me to a spot where I can hook with those guys. Then you're all done."

"Where? Where are you going to hook up with those guys?"

"I haven't figured that out yet … but I will."

"You don't have any idea where they are. And even if you caught up to them you wouldn't have any way of getting your money back. You don't even have a gun anymore … thank god."

"I don't need a gun to outsmart those two blockheads. I just need to catch up with them."

Mickey looked out at *Songbird,* barely visible in the dark, her spinners reflecting the light from the office windows. He could cut and run now and be out seven hundred and forty dollars, or he could hang in with this idiot on the remote chance that he'd get a sizeable chunk of change out of the deal. In the end, it seemed, greed always overruled common sense.

"What if you don't get your money back?"

"I will."

"Well, what if you don't. How do I get *my* money?"

"I don't welch on debts."

"What guarantee do I have?"

"You have my word. Ask anybody."

"You haven't exactly been truthful so far."

"Those were just details you didn't need to know about. When it comes to money I pay my way."

Mickey laughed.

"What's so funny? I don't welch on my debts."

"You may not be intending to screw me, Tony. But you don't have any money right now and from where I'm sitting the odds of you getting any seem pretty long."

"I will get my money."

"Okay, for the sake of argument, let's say I decide to go along with this. I'm still not putting out any more of my own money."

"Well, what the hell do you propose we do, Ace? We're stuck here in BFE with no money. I'm open to any ideas."

"Can't you get one of your people to give us a credit card number?"

"*My people* deal in cash. Come on, Ace. Just cover this tab and I will take care of you, I promise."

Mickey had to admit Tony seemed convinced that he would recover his money. Maybe he would, but Mickey was still pretty sure that he wouldn't see anything out it. But still there was an outside chance that he would. Well, at least they weren't in jail.

"I know I'll never see a dime out of this, but I guess there is no other way out of this mess."

Tony grinned. He stepped on his cigarette butt and slapped Mickey on the back. "Good boy. You won't regret it, I promise."

"Yeah, sure," said Mickey. "And pick that up, will ya?"

"Huh?"

Mickey pointed to the cigarette butt.

"Oh, yeah."

Mickey walked into the office. Duke was sitting at the desk, sifting through papers and waiting for them to make a decision.

"Here, you go, Duke." He handed Duke his credit card.

"I can't believe your charter doesn't have a credit card. Who doesn't have credit cards these days?"

Mickey didn't want Duke to think on that too much. "Yeah, funny thing. Anyway he's good for it."

Duke shrugged and ran it through the card reader.

"That's funny."

"What?" asked Mickey.

"It's not going through."

Oh, oh. "You sure? Try it again."

Duke ran the card again.

"Nope, it's coming back 'not approved'."

"Shit. I thought I had plenty of room on that thing."

"You got another card?"

"No. Try it one more time."

Duke did.

"Same thing."

"Let me call those idiots." Mickey went outside and pulled out his cell phone.

"What's up?" asked Tony.

"Card won't clear."

"Didn't you just use it to pay for dinner?"

"Yeah, seventeen dollars and forty-three cents. That probably put me over my limit."

"See? That's why I don't carry those things. They're goddamn worthless."

"I'm going to try to see if I can get an increase." Mickey punched in the telephone number from the back of the card and walked out toward *Songbird.*

"No luck," said Mickey.

"No luck?"

"Nope, bastards won't increase my credit."

"Oh, that's great. Now what the hell do we do?" asked Tony.

"I don't know. I'm fresh out of ideas."

Tony put his hands on his hips. "Shit."

"Sorry."

"Shit."

"If we don't have any money or credit we can't go any further. Hell, we can't even get back to Miami."

Tony pounded his fist into his palm. Then he pulled out his cell phone and punched up a number. "Marvin, It's me, Tony."

Oh, Christ. Mickey walked back out toward the airplane.
"Hey, I've got a little problem here."

Tony slammed the phone shut and Mickey wandered
back.

"Well?"

"That sleazy son of a bitch won't help."

That didn't surprise Mickey. "Now what?"

"I'm going to go talk to Duke."

"About what?"

"Don't worry, just let me handle this." Tony went inside
the office. He walked over to the counter and put his palms
on the counter. Duke looked up from his papers.

"Well?" said Duke.

"I've got a proposition for you."

"Yeah?"

"We're into you for what …? "

"Seven hundred and forty dollars." Duke finished the
statement.

"Seven hundred and change. I've got a Cadillac STS
with only ten thousand miles on it. Silver with gray leather
seats … all the bells and whistles. I'll sell you that thing for
twenty-five and you can turn around and sell it for thirty …
easy. You make a cool five grand. How does that sound?"

"I run an airport here. I'm not in the car business."

"I know that. But this is a great deal. You can't afford to
pass this up."

"Sure I can."

"Come on, Duke. I'm telling you, you can't lose. Five
thousand dollars. In your pocket. Guaranteed."

"Who am I going to sell a Cadillac to around here?"

"Just take it to Tallahassee. You'll have to beat the
buyers off with a stick."

"Sounds like a lot of trouble to me."

"It's no trouble. Take out an ad in the Tallahassee paper and people will flock out here to get their hands on it. At thirty K? Shit, I know I would."

"Then why do you want to sell it?"

"'Cause I'm in a bind here and I need the money now. Come on, Duke. You buy this car and you'll be doing us both a favor."

Duke rubbed his chin. "What kind of a car did you say?"

"A Cadillac STS."

Duke turned the computer on at the other desk and input the search information.

"How many miles?"

"Ten, maybe eleven thousand miles."

Duke looked at Tony. "You sure?"

"No more than eleven thousand."

Duke looked at the computer screen. "I'll give you fifteen thousand."

"Fifteen thousand? Come on, it's worth thirty-five."

"Thirty-two, according to the Blue Book."

Tony ran his hand through his hair. "Twenty. I'll give it to you for twenty thousand."

"Fifteen."

"You're killing me, Duke. We're talking about a beautiful automobile here. I can't let it go for fifteen thousand."

"Then I guess we've got nothing to talk about." Duke returned to his papers.

Tony walked around the office wringing his hands. "All right. All right. Fifteen thousand, but on one condition: you hold on to the car for a month and give me the right to buy it back for twenty thousand. How's that?"

Duke kept shuffling through papers. "I told you I'm not in the car business, and I damn sure ain't running a pawn shop. I'm sorry."

Tony pounded the counter. "All right, all right, fifteen thousand … no strings attached."

Duke stopped shuffling papers and looked at Tony. "Where is this car?"

"It's in Miami."

"Miami? I'm not buying a car that's in Miami."

"It's in Miami now, but I'll have it here by tomorrow."

"Okay. You bring it by tomorrow and if I like the way it looks, I'll give you fifteen thousand dollars for it."

"Can't you give me the money now? I guarantee the car will be here."

Duke laughed. "I may look like a rube … in fact I may even be one … but I sure as hell ain't that stupid. You show me the car … with the proper paperwork … and if it all checks out, I'll give you the money."

Tony had to admit Duke would have to be an imbecile to give him the money without the car. "Okay, you've got a deal. I'll have the car here tomorrow morning. But can you stake me some money for a motel room or something … on good faith?"

"You're already into me for seven hundred and forty."

Tony pulled off his ring. "Here, this is a fourteen karat gold ring with over 3 carats of diamonds … I paid eighteen hundred for it in New York. You hang on to this for the night."

"I told you. I'm not running a pawn shop here."

"Okay, I'll sell it to you for five hundred."

Duke held out is hand for the ring. He looked it over and went back to the computer. A few seconds later he said, "I'll give you a hundred for it."

"A hundred? Jesus, I thought you guys were honest out here."

"A hundred."

Tony held out his hand. "Make it twenties."

"All right, Ace, we're all set." Tony walked over to the bench in front of the office were Mickey was sitting. Tony sat down next to him. "I sold my car to Duke."

"You did what?"

"I sold him my car. Son of bitch drove a hard bargain, but we've got our seed money."

"You sold him your car?"

"Any port in a storm."

"How could you sell him your car? It's in Miami."

"Technically it's not a done deal until he sees the car. But it's clean. He'll like it."

"How is he going to see the car?"

"I'm going to get my cousin to bring here. If I can talk her into leaving tonight, she'll be here first thing in the morning."

"I can't believe you did that. He actually agreed to buy your car?"

"Sure did. I smooth talked him right in to it."

"So what do we do until morning?"

"There's a little mom and pop motel by the highway. Duke said he'd give us a ride there."

"How do we pay for that? I only have thirty-seven dollars left on my card."

"I sold Duke my ring." Tony held up his hand for Mickey to see. "I've got a hundred bucks … that should be enough for a room."

Mickey shook his head. "You are fucking amazing."

Tony wasn't sure if that was a complement or not. "I am not letting those sleazy bastards get a way with my money."

"Well, remember, I'm just the chauffeur. I'll take you on down the road, but that's it. I wait for you at the airport."

"Sure, Ace. No problem. You just get me in the vicinity of those assholes and I'll take care of the rest."

"And I get my share right off the top."

"Off the top. My word." Tony pulled out his phone. "I gotta call Gina."

Mickey stood up and walked away.

"Gina? How's the house tonight?"

"It's good, Tony. What's up? Gina asked suspiciously.

"I got a little problem here. I could use some help."

"Where's here?"

"Meadville."

"Where the hell is Meadville?"

"Near Tallahassee."

"Tallahassee? What are you doing there?"

"It's a long story. I just need your help right now."

Gina sighed. "What is it, Tony?"

"I need you do me a favor. Will you drive my car up here?"

"What?"

"Will you bring my car to me?"

"Your car? If your car is here, how did you get to Meadville?"

"I charted a plane."

"You're kidding."

"Nope. It was Marvin's idea."

"So that loser is in on this thing, too?"

"No. He just knew about the pilot." Gina would never help if she thought Marvin was involved.

"Why do you need your car?"

"It's a long story, but I sold it to the guy who runs the airport here."

"You sold it?"

"Like I said, it's a long story. Now I need it here right away."

"Are you crazy?"

"Gina, I don't have time to fuck around right now. Will you just help me out here?"

"Tony, I'm not driving your car to Meadville, or where ever the hell you are."

"You gotta help me out here, Gina."

"Why? What's going on?"

"You'll just get pissed if I tell you. Why can't you just help me out?"

"You're right, I probably will get pissed. But I'm not doing anything until I know what is going on."

Tony paused.

"You still there?" asked Gina.

"You know that I was doing a little side work with the Rodriguez brothers …"

"I knew it. I knew it. I told you that you would end up with your ass in a sling."

"Will you shut up and let me explain?"

Gina clenched her teeth. "Go on."

"Anyway, these two goons who work for them stole a hundred and fifty thousand from me and I'm trying to get it back."

"Where'd you get one-hundred and fifty thousand?"

"I told you. I was doing a job for Johnny Rodriguez."

"So, Johnny Rodriquez paid you one-hundred and fifty thousand dollars for … god knows what … and then two of his other bozos steal it from you?"

"That's right, but I'm going to get it back."

"Why don't you let Johnny handle this?"

"I told you, Gina, it's a long story."

"You're right. I don't want to know. So you're trying to track these guys down …"

"Vince Jackson and Sheldon Isaacs."

"So you're trying to track these guys down to get your money back?"

"That's about the size of it. And the trail is getting cold while we're chit-chatting on the phone. Are you going to help me or not?"

"How long are going to be there?"

"Until you get here. I need that car taco pronto."

"Tony, we've got a big weekend coming up. I couldn't leave here until Monday at the earliest."

"Monday? That's not gonna work, Gina. I need that car now."

"That's impossible. I can't leave this place tomorrow."

"I was kinda hoping you'd leave tonight. Then you'd be home by tomorrow."

"Tonight! Now I know you're crazy."

Tony decided it was time to play his trump card. "Gina, I've got a big problem here and you're the only one who can help me. Please. I need you to do this one thing for me. Your father would want you to." Tony hated to admit it, but he knew his Uncle expected Gina to look out for him. It killed him to use the ploy, but *any port in a storm*.

Gina sighed. "You are an asshole."

"I know it. But will you help me out here?"

"One problem, Tony. If I bring the car to you, how do I get back to Miami?"

Damn. He hadn't thought about that. "Can you get Levi to follow you up?"

"I don't know, maybe."

"Wait, I've got it. Why don't you come with me, then you can fly home?"

"Where are you going?"

"I'm not sure … Pensacola … maybe Mobile."

"Mobile?"

"It's not that far. You'll be home by tomorrow night. I guarantee it."

Gina didn't want to go ten miles with Tony, let alone all the way to Mobile. But there was one thing; she could keep an eye on him. Maybe keep him from going any further down this rabbit hole.

"Christ, Tony, I swear …"

"Then you'll do it?"

"Where is your goddamn car?"

"It's at Hayes airport … in Hialeah. There's an extra key in the office at the restaurant."

"You know, Tony, you're damn lucky that you're kin. Otherwise I wouldn't think twice about letting you stew in your own juices on this."

"I love you, Gina." Tony was spreading it on thick now."

"You've never loved anyone but yourself. You just love that fact that I'm stupid enough to help you."

"No, I mean it, Gina. You've always been like a sister to me."

"Okay, enough bullshit. I'll grab a couple of hours of sleep. After we close up tonight I'll have Levi take me to the airport."

"Fantastic. We'll be at this little motel right off the exit for Meadville … you can't miss it."

"I'll call you when I'm on the road." Gina hung up.

Mickey wandered back. "So, what's the deal?"

"She'll do it."

"Insanity runs in the family, eh?"

Tony ignored the jibe. "I gotta let Duke know we're ready to go."

"One thing, Tony."

Tony got up to go back in the office. "Yeah?"

"If your cousin is bringing your car here to sell to Duke, how is she going to get back to Miami?"

"She's coming with us."

"What?"

"Why? Is that going to cost extra?"

"No, but why would you want her to go on this goose chase?"

"You got another idea to get her home?"

"No, but …"

"Then she's coming with us."

12

Mickey watched the text crawl by at the bottom of the television screen as he idly stirred his coffee. Thankfully, the desk clerk had turned down the sound so he didn't have to listen to the carefully coiffed Barbie and Ken dolls read the sound bites. The motel was small, but clean and provided a continental breakfast in the tiny lobby.

He yawned broadly. They couldn't afford two rooms last night, so, to Mickey's horror, they had to share. There were two beds in the room, but Tony snored like a lumberjack so Mickey, anxious about the situation anyway, was lucky to get three hours of solid sleep. The shower this morning was life giving, but he sure would have appreciated clean clothes.

Tony sat next to him pouring over his road map. "So what's the plan?" Mickey asked.

"I'm trying to figure out how far those pinheads might have gotten by now."

"Well, say they average fifty miles an hour. If they drove all night that would put them, what … six hundred miles down the road?" Mickey took a bite of the bagel he had liberally covered with cream cheese.

"Six hundred from where?"

Mickey took a sip of coffee. "From here."

"But how do we know when they passed by here."

"I'm not sure, but I'm guessing it was around 7:00 last night."

"Now how the hell you know that?"

"Well, like I said, I'm not sure, but I saw a Winnebago just like the Harrington's go by while you were rooting around in the bushes looking for …" Mickey looked at the family at the next table; a young mother trying to get her four-year old to stop squirming and eat his cereal, the father was looking over his map and planning their day. "While you were busy."

"What! You saw those cocksuckers go by last night?"

The mother looked over at Tony and scowled. The father ignored them, hoping to avoid a confrontation.

"Keep it down will you?" Mickey nodded in the direction of the family.

"You saw those cocksuckers go by and didn't tell me?" said Tony in stage whisper that could be heard across the room. The mother jabbed her husband and said something to him. He glanced over his shoulder at Mickey and Tony and decided that breakfast was over.

"I don't know if it was them for sure, but I thought it might be." Mickey watched the man wipe the kid's face and gather up their belongings to leave. The woman looked perturbed.

"Why didn't you tell me?"

"What were you going to do? Run down the road after them?"

Tony conceded that Mickey had a point. "Still you should have told me."

"This is your business, Tony. I'm just a pilot. I just go where I'm hired to go." "Yeah, yeah. But in the interest of good customer service, if you see something that might be helpful you could let me know."

"Maybe."

"So you think you saw them go by last night?"

"I'm not sure. Is one of the guys black?"

"Yeah. Vince."

"I couldn't see anyone else, but the driver was black."

"That had to be them. Damn. I can't believe you didn't say anything." Tony sat back and rubbed his temples.

"Sorry."

"All right. So where do you think they are now?"

"Let me see." Mickey leaned in closer so he could read the map. "Well, if they made six hundred miles, that would put them around here." He pointed to a spot between Lafayette, Louisiana and Houston, Texas. "I wouldn't think they would have gotten much further."

"Holy shit. That's all the way to Texas. "

"Well that's just it. You don't really know how far they are."

"So the big issue is whether or not they drove all night or stopped somewhere?"

"If you knew that it would narrow it down somewhat."

Tony looked at the time on the television screen. Seven fifty-eight. He pulled out his cell phone and punched up a number.

"Vince, it's me, Tony."

"I know who it is. What do you want?" asked Vince.

"I didn't wake you up did I?"

"No you didn't. What the fuck do you want?"

"How'd you bastards sleep last night knowing you stole a hundred and fifty large from me?"

"I slept just fine, numbnuts. You'd have to ask Shelly about his night … he was the one driving. You've got five seconds to tell me what you want."

"I want my fucking money you sleazy sonof …" The line went dead. Tony flipped the phone shut and frowned. "I think they drove all night."

Mickey looked at the map. "That means they are at least as far as Lafayette."

"I told Gina that we wouldn't be going any farther than Mobile."

"Well, I can't imagine they aren't farther than that."

"That's going to be a problem."

"Not for me."

Tony looked at Mickey. "Maybe not, but I could use a little support on this."

"What can I do? I'm just the pilot remember?"

"You can keep your trap shut about how far these bastards might be."

"You're not going to tell her?"

"If she knows we're going to Lafayette, she'll make trouble."

"She won't be upset when we get there if she doesn't know?"

"I'll deal with her then. I just want to get the show on the road and if she thinks we're going beyond Mobile she won't want to go and then we'll have to screw around figuring out how to get her home."

"She's your relative."

"That's right. So just don't provide any unnecessary information when you meet her."

"Speaking of which … how far away is she? Thunderstorms tend to pop around here during the afternoon this time of year."

"I talked to her a half hour ago." He looked at the map. "She can't be more than twenty miles away."

Mickey stared across the parking lot of the motel. He could see the west- bound traffic on I10 as it whizzed past the off ramp. He held the cell phone close and stuck his finger in his other ear so he could hear over the traffic noise. "Hello, Betty?"

"Yeah, I saw your number on the caller ID. Where are you?" That was Betty; right to the point.

"Still in Florida ... at a motel near the Meadville airport."

"I thought you'd be back by now."

"Me too. I ran into some complications."

"Nothing serious, I hope."

"No, no, nothing like that. Just that my fare's business is taking longer than I thought."

"When are you coming back?"

"I'm not positive. Anybody trying reach me?"

"Glenn was asking for you. I told him you were on a charter. He wants to see you when you get back."

"Any idea what about?"

"How the hell would I know? Nobody tells me anything around here."

Mickey laughed. A fly didn't fart at Hayes airport with Betty knowing about it. "Well, tell him I should be back by tomorrow ... can't imagine this dragging on any longer."

"Can you check to see if I have any lessons today?"

"Just a second."

Tony walked up. "She should be here any minute," he said to Mickey.

"Good. I've ..."

Betty came back on the line. "You've got Tom Mathews at 2:00 and Donna Phelps at 4:00. You want me to cancel them?"

Damn it. They were both good students that he couldn't afford to lose.

"See if Carl can cover for me."

"He wasn't exactly thrilled about covering for you yesterday, you know."

"I know. But check with him anyway. If he won't then you'll have to cancel for me. There is no way I'll be back by this afternoon."

"Will do."

"Thanks, Betty, I owe you big time."

"That it?"

"That's it ... for now."

"Okay." Betty clicked off before Mickey could say goodbye.

Mickey was pouring another cup of coffee and Tony was staring out the window of the motel lobby when he saw the Cadillac pull into the parking lot.

"She's here."

Mickey looked around for a lid for his coffee. Tony went out to greet Gina.

He opened the passenger door. "It's about damn time."

Gina rolled her eyes. "You're welcome."

Tony slid in and shut the door. "No, I didn't mean it like that. I'm really grateful that you came. It's just that … well … I get anxious when I have to wait around."

Mickey came out of the lobby holding his coffee. He assumed he was relegated to the back so he opened the door and got in. Mickey stared at Gina's long brunet tresses, then he diverted his eyes when he realized she was looking at him in the rearview mirror.

"You must be the pilot."

He looked up. She had pulled her sunglasses down her nose so he could see a pair of dark brown eyes in the mirror. "Mickey Soto."

"Nice to meet you, Mickey. I'm Gina."

"Nice to meet you, too."

"So how'd you get dragged into this?"

"Will shut the fuck up and drive?" said Tony.

Gina ignored the comment and continued to look at Mickey in the mirror.

"I'm sorry," said Mickey, "This is Tony's show. I'm just the hired hand."

"Oh. Doing it for the money, eh?"

"That's about it."

Tony interrupted, "For Christ sake, Gina, will you leave the poor bastard alone and get going?"

Gina pushed her glasses back up and looked over at Tony so Mickey could see her profile for the first time. She looked to be in her mid-thirties, an olive complexion, long straight nose, and a wide mouth that was accentuated by deep red lipstick. "Keep your shirt on. I just want to know whose life you've managed to screw up this time."

"He's a big boy. He can take care of himself. Now will you please just get going?"

Gina glanced in the mirror at Mickey again. "You look like too nice of a guy to be mixed up with Tony," she said.

"Gina!"

"So where are we going?" she asked.

"It's just up the road a couple of miles." Tony pointed in the direction of the airport.

Gina slipped the car into gear and pulled out of the parking lot. "So what the hell is going on, Tony?"

"I told you all that last night. Vince Jackson and …"

"Yeah, you told me. They stole your money. What you didn't tell me is why."

"Because they are motherfucking thieves."

"Tony, there is more to this story. What is it?"

Tony looked over his shoulder at Mickey who was looking out the window, trying to act like he wasn't involved. He was listening intently.

Tony took a deep breath and let it out. "This guy, Max Burke …"

"Burke?" asked Gina.

"You know Burke?" said Tony.

"Everybody in south Florida knows Burke, you idiot. Don't tell me he's mixed up in this somehow."

"Turns out that I owe Burke a few bucks …"

"You owe Burke money?"

"A little, yeah."

"How much?"

"I don't know … maybe a hundred … a hundred and ten."

"Thousand?"

"Yeah."

"You owe Burke over a hundred thousand dollars?"

Mickey quit pretending that he wasn't listening from the back seat. He leaned forward to better hear.

"Yeah, so what?" said Tony.

"Keep going," said Gina.

"So Burke sets this deal up where I do a job for the Rodriguez brothers and he talks them into giving him my money … all of it … way more than I ever owed him."

"How much?"

"A hundred and fifty thousand."

Gina whistled. "So why are you out here chasing after these guys …?"

"Vince Jackson and Shelly Isaacs."

"Why are you chasing after them?"

"Because Johnny gave them my money and let them set up the deal with Burke. That way he could pretend he didn't have nothin' to do with it … keep his rep and all."

"This is really confusing, Tony. Why aren't you after Burke?

They were approaching the driveway to the airport. "Right up here, Gina." Tony pointed to the turn.

"So why are you still chasing after these Vince and Shelly characters?"

"They are taking the money to California to give to Burke. He's out there setting up things to help …" Tony remembered Mickey sitting in the back seat. "He's there on business."

Gina slid the Caddy into a parking spot. "And these to characters are driving across the country with 'your' money?"

"Exactly."

"And you think you can overtake them and get your money back."

"Absolutely."

"You're nuts." Gina turned of the ignition and got out.

Before Tony could follow, Mickey said, "Tony, this is a lot more complicated then you let on yesterday. I think this is the end of the line for me," said Mickey.

"Don't start with me, Ace."

"Why don't you and your cousin go after them in your car. I'll find someone to loan me some money to get *Songbird* back to Miami and …"

"I sold this car to Duke, remember?"

"Not yet."

Gina stood in front of the car smoking a cigarette. She looked at Tony through the windshield. Tony held up a finger to signal *just a moment*. "I can't catch up to Vince and Sheldon in a car. I need your airplane and I sure as hell can't fly it. You don't have to worry, I'm not going to involve you in anything. All you have to do is just fly me down the road. That's no big deal, right?"

"If that's all it is, no. But so far it's been a clusterfuck."

"It got a little hairy yesterday, but it won't happen again, I promise. Come on, Ace, there's going to be a nice payday in this for you."

"I don't trust you."

Tony held his hand over his heart. "I swear."

"You'll pay double my going rate whether you get your money back or not?"

"And I'll give you half up front … as soon as I do this deal with Duke."

"Half up front?"

"Yes."

"And I don't get involved in any funny business?"

"Promise."

Mickey got out of the car. Tony smiled and followed him. "Atta boy, Ace."

"It's Mickey."

"Right, Mickey."

"You mind if I smoke?" asked Gina.

"No, that's okay," said Mickey. He watched people strolling down the street of the little country town through the back window of the Cadillac. Gina rolled down the other window and lit a cigarette. They were waiting outside the bank while Tony and Duke were inside concluding their deal.

Just to make conversation, Gina asked, "How long have you been a pilot?"

Mickey rolled down his window to help with the ventilation. "Twenty-five years. Twenty as a professional."

She turned to look at him. "Wow, that's a long time."

"Yep."

"You must like it."

"I do. But then I don't know anything else."

"Tony said you know Marvin Seguin."

"Yes."

"He's a friend of yours?"

"No, just an acquaintance."

That's a plus, thought Gina. "What do you think about this hair-brained scheme of Tony's?"

"Not much."

"But you're going along with it?"

Mickey looked out the window. "I got sucked into this thing. I thought I was taking a normal charter to Pensacola and the next thing I know I'm chasing a motor home down I10."

"Chasing a motor home?"

"Tony didn't tell you that part?"

"No, he didn't."

"Well, it's probably not my place to say anything."

"Just tell me what happened."

What difference does it make? Thought Mickey. "We spotted an RV on the highway just like the one this Vince and Sheldon are supposedly driving …"

"They're in an RV?"

"I guess one of them doesn't like to fly, so they are driving an RV to California."

"This just keeps getting weirder. Go on."

"Anyway, we spot this thing, so I put down at the airport here and Duke loans us his truck and the next thing I know we are hot on the trail of the RV when the truck seizes up and the damn RV almost crashes into us."

"Oh, jeez."

"It turns out that the RV belongs to some retired couple. They got scared when they saw Tony waving a gun at them, so they called the police."

"A gun? You're kidding."

"No. It was a big freakin' scene."

"I can imagine. How'd you get out of that?"

"Tony paid the couple a thousand bucks to tell the police that it was all a big mistake."

Gina laughed. "That guy is amazing."

"I didn't think so yesterday."

"No, I don't imagine that you did. How is it that you're still here?"

"Same reason that I got involved in the first place … I need the money."

"And Tony promised to pay you when he gets his money back?"

"He said he'd pay me double my rate, and give me half as soon as he gets the money from Duke for his car."

"You think it's worth it?"

"I sure do need the money. What's your excuse?"

"Why am I going along with this, you mean?"

"Yes."

Gina stubbed out the cigarette in the ashtray. "He's my cousin and my father expects me keep an eye on him."

"Does that mean doing crazy stuff like helping him chase down a couple of goons?"

"No, but in spite of the fact that Tony is a nimrod, I do care about him and I do worry about him. I'm hoping I can talk him out of this and get him back to Miami in one piece."

"Good luck with that. He's seems pretty determined to catch up to those guys."

"I know. But maybe I can talk some sense into him. At least I can try to keep him from getting killed."

"Well, that's your business. All I know is that I'm taking him to the next stop … somewhere down the road … and then I just wait for him. Whatever he does after that is his business. When he returns, I'll take him back to Miami."

"How'd you get involved in the scene yesterday?"

"I didn't know what was going on yesterday."

Tony and Duke emerged from the bank. "Here they come," said Gina. "Does Duke know what is going on?"

"No, he just thinks we're continuing on our way to Pensacola."

Duke started for the back, but Tony stopped him and directed him toward the driver's seat. "It's all yours now," said Tony.

"No, that okay. I'll wait until we get back to the airport."

Gina sighed and got out and walked around the car. "No it's yours, Duke. You drive."

Duke smiled and took the keys from her.

"So you did it?" Gina said to Tony.

"Yep, all set." Tony smiled and opened the rear door for her. Mickey slid over so she could get in.

"We got time for some lunch," said Gina. "I'm famished."

"We gotta get going," said Tony. He shut her door and got in the front.

"I'm not going anywhere until I get some food. How about you, Mickey?"

"Might be a good idea. Who knows when we'll get the next chance?"

"We can stop at Etta's on the way back to the airport," said Duke.

"You got time?" asked Tony.

"Yeah. Besides, I can show off my new car."

13

As they walked across the tarmac toward *Songbird,* Tony peeled ten, one-hundred dollar bills from the wad of money in his hand and offered them to Mickey. "Here you go, Ace."

Mickey took the money. "Thanks."

"Thought that might grease the wheels."

Mickey didn't want to admit it, but it did.

Tony peeled a few more bills from the roll and stuffed them in his pocket. He offered the rest of the roll to Gina. "Can you hang on to this for me?"

"You want me to keep that?"

"It's too big for my pocket ... can you keep it in your purse?"

Gina took the money. "I guess I can do that."

"Just don't lose your purse, okay?"

They arrived at the airplane and Mickey helped Gina up on the wing. "You can stretch out in the backseat. Maybe get some sleep," he said.

"I doubt it," said Gina. She opened the door and eased into the back.

Mickey followed her in and slid into the left-hand seat. Tony got in last. Sitting in the morning sun made the cockpit stuffy.

"Don't shut the …"

"I know the drill," said Tony and he held the door open.

"Here," said Mickey handing Gina a headset. "You'll want to use this so we can talk in flight. It gets a little noisy up there."

"Thanks," she said.

Tony's headset hung over the right control column. "It's a pain in the ass," he said.

Mickey went through the preflight checklist and fired up the two Lycoming IO 320's, pushed the throttles forward just enough to start *Songbird* rolling. Duke stood in front of the FBO office and waved as they went by. Mickey returned a *thumbs-up* signal.

A few minutes later they lifted off runway two-seven and *Songbird* quickly gained altitude. They had determined that there was no point in following the highway all the way to Mobile, so Mickey filed an IFR plan direct to Mobile to save time and make it easier to get around the various military MOAs and class B airspace around Pensacola. So far the weather was holding, but thunderheads would probably start popping up in the afternoon.

Once leveled out at five thousand feet on cruise, Mickey relaxed and took in the scenery of the Florida panhandle. This was a side of Florida that was more in tune with the rural south than the congested, hard-partying central and south areas. As they passed by Tallahassee he could see the immense Apalachicola National Forest.

"Nice country around here," he said.

Tony was busy studying his map. Gina, gazing out the rear windows said, "Yes, it is."

"You ever fly in a light airplane before?" asked Mickey.

"A few times."

"So it doesn't bother you?"

"No. I actually enjoy it. You can really see things down low that you don't experience on an airliner."

"That's true."

"How come you don't fly for an airline?"

"It's tough to break into. Anyway, I like flying for myself."

"You make a living doing it?"

Mickey smiled. "More or less."

"Is this your airplane?"

"Yes."

"It's very nice."

"Thanks. It's my pride and joy."

"How long will it take to get to Mobile?"

Mickey looked at the GPS. "Just over an hour."

Tony broke in, "We should start following the highway before we get to Mobile."

"Okay, I'll cancel our flight plan when we're well past Pensacola. Then we'll descend and start following the highway."

Tony had been dozing when he heard Mickey talking to the air traffic control center to cancel their flight plan. He sat up with a jerk and ran his hand over his face. He looked back at Gina. She had taken off her headset, curled up in the back seat and was sleeping soundly.

"Where are we?" asked Tony.

"About fifteen miles east of Mobile." He pointed out to the southwest. "That's Loxley over there." Then he pointed to the northwest. "The highway is right over there."

He put *Songbird* into a slow descent. The differential in pressure on her eardrums woke up Gina. She sat up and put on her headset. "Where are we?" she asked.

Tony answered. "Just east of Mobile. We're heading down to follow the highway from here on."

They flew at a thousand feet just to the south of the highway. Crossing the causeway over Mobile Bay, the highway swings to the southwest, allowing Mickey to stay under the outer ring of Mobile Regional airport and still pass well to the north of the small, downtown airport.

They spotted several motor homes, but none of them were the correct color scheme. "It's like finding a needle in a haystack," said Mickey.

"You're never going to find them," said Gina.

"You're probably right, Gina. At least not here."

"What do you mean?"

Tony held up his map so she could see it over his shoulder. "I think they are much farther down the road. Probably more like here." He pointed to Baton Rouge.

"Baton Rouge!"

"More than likely."

"That's another … what … two hundred miles?"

Mickey checked the GPS. "More like one-fifty … direct."

"You told me that we were just going to Mobile … and then back home."

"That's what I thought at the time."

"What do you mean 'at the time'?"

"When I talked to you last night I thought we might catch them in Mobile. But I found out this morning that they drove all night. At least I'm pretty sure they drove all night. Anyway, that would put them well past Mobile, maybe as far a Lafayette."

"Tony, they could be in Timbuktu for all you know. There is no way you're going to find these guys, let alone get your money back. Just forget about it will you?"

"I'm not going to forget about it. They've got my money and I'm going to get it back."

"I just don't see how that's possible." Gina sat back. "Now, you told me that we were going to Mobile and then back to Miami. We're in Mobile. You can't find these guys. It's time to turn around and go home, right Mickey?"

"Leave me out of this," said Mickey.

"I'm not going back without my money, Gina," said Tony.

When Tony got like this, Gina knew it was pointless to argue. "If you're not ready to throw in the towel, then what is your plan? You could be following this highway to hell and back and never find those guys."

"I'm working on it."

"Somebody must know where they are."

"I've tried to worm it out of Vince. He won't tell me shit."

"Of course he's not going to tell you. But he might tell me."

"You? Why would he tell you?"

"Because I could make him an offer he couldn't refuse."

"What are you talking about?"

"I can make a call from here, can't I?" Gina said to Mickey.

"Technically yes. Legally no. But then I've broken a dozen FAA rules on this flight anyway, one more isn't going to make a lot of difference," Mickey answered.

"Give me Vince's number," she said Tony.

Tony punched it up on his cell phone and handed it to her. She added the number into her own phone and handed Tony's phone back to him. "What's Vince's last name?"

"Jackson."

Gina held up her hand for quiet. "Vince Jackson, please."

On the other end of the line Vince said, "Yeah. Who's this?"

"This is Gina Sandrelli. You may have heard of my father."

"Sandrelli? Sevvy Sandrelli?"

"Yes."

"Your father?"

"Yes.

"Well, well, Gina. Why would you be calling me?"

"I like a man who gets to the point … so will I. I've heard you're good at what you do and my father is looking for some help with some … collections shall we say."

"Look lady, I don't know what you're talking about."

"Then I must have the wrong Vince Jackson. I heard he was a tough guy who liked to make money."

"How much money?"

"Are you interested in the job?"

"Maybe. How much money are we talking about?"

Gina paused for a second. "Two grand."

"Yeah? For what?"

"Just to lean on a guy who owes my father some money."

"Who?"

"Marvin Seguin."

"Marvin Seguin owes your father money and he wants me to lean on him? Doesn't he have his own muscle?"

"Of course, but he's always looking for new talent and you came highly recommended."

"By who?"

"Johnny Rodriguez."

"Johnny told your father about me?"

"He said you were one of the best."

"Johnny said that?"

The hook was set. "He did. Are you interested?"

"I might be. But there is a little problem. I'm out of town and don't expect to be back for a couple of weeks."

"Really? Where are you?"

"I'm in New Orleans right now, but I'm on my way to Los Angeles."

"Two weeks, eh?"

"At least."

"That might be a problem. I'll have to talk to my father and get back to you."

"All right. If he is still interested let me know."

Then Gina said in her most seductive voice. "How do you like New Orleans?"

"It's a gas."

"Are you there long?"

"Just overnight. We stopped here on our way to California."

"Really? You're driving to California?"

"Yeah. In one of those RVs."

"You drove an RV into New Orleans."

"Not exactly. We stopped at this motel and RV park thing just off the highway. We're taking a cab into town. Probably hit the French Quarter and Harrah's."

"I love that place. You'll have fun."

"I'll bet it would be a lot more fun if you were here. You sound like a fun loving girl."

"I am, Vince. I hope you can take the job so I can meet you."

"Me too."

"Well, listen, I'll go talk to my father and let you know."

"Okay, baby. Later."

Gina flicked the phone shut. "You guys are all the same. A little female flattery and you'll say anything."

"Did you say New Orleans?" Tony asked.

Sheldon came out of the Winnebago's small bathroom. "Who was that?"

Vince stuck his phone in his pocket, sat back on the coach. "Some broad."

"What'd she want?"

Vince wasn't sure how much to tell Sheldon. He was a friend and colleague but this was a cutthroat business and they didn't have to know everything about each other. "She said she wanted to meet me."

"How'd she get your number?"

"I guess she got it from Johnny."

"Johnny is fixing you up with broads now?"

"You jealous?"

Before Sheldon could answer his phone rang. He looked at the number. "That's probably our ride. You ready."

"Let's go."

They emerged from the RV and walked the short distance to the front of the motel/RV park where a taxi waited to take them into New Orleans. They passed rigs of every conceivable size shape and people of the same description sitting at picnic tables or relaxing in lawn chairs. Most people watched them walk by with curiosity on their faces. What were two guys like them doing in a place like this? What exactly was their story?

"This place is a hoot," said Vince.

"Well, you wanted to stop in New Orleans and I sure as hell wasn't driving that bus downtown."

"I wish I coulda got a picture of you trying to park that thing."

"You know we could forget about this and head on down the road."

Vince stifled a laugh. "No, no you did fine."

Mickey decided to avoid the huge Class B Louis Armstrong International Airport and instead elected the smaller Class D airport on the banks of Pontchartrain. He joined the traffic pattern for runway 18 Right and followed a Cherokee 180 on down. He continued to follow the Cherokee 180 on the taxiway to one of the local FBO buildings. A line boy was present to direct *Songbird* into the parking space next to the Cherokee.

They all piled out and stretched. "Nice airplane, mister," said the line boy.

"Thanks," replied Mickey.

"You gassing up?"

"Yes.

"Let them know inside and they'll waive the landing fee."

"Okay. I don't know how long we'll be here though."

"There is a tie-down fee if you stay overnight."

"I don't think we'll be here that long."

They went inside the air-conditioned FBO office facility that also included a well-appointed pilot lounge. Gina and Tony headed straight for the restrooms. Mickey spoke to the young woman who manned the desk.

"Welcome to New Orleans," she said in that distinctive accent. "Are you getting fuel?"

"Yes. It's that red and white Twin Comanche," said Mickey.

"Bobby will take care of you. How long are you here for?"

"I'm not sure. It depends how long my passenger needs to conduct his business. I'm guessing a few hours."

"Well you're welcome to relax in the lounge. It's not quite as luxurious as it will be when our new facility is complete, but there is a television and reading material available and computers with Internet access."

Mickey looked around. "This looks fine."

"We've come a long way. You should've seen us a couple of years ago."

"I'll bet."

"Are you going to need transportation?"

"Probably. What's available?"

"We have a crew car available for pilots but it is only for local use. If you need more flexible transportation, I can arrange for a taxi or rental car."

"Thanks. I'll have to talk to my passengers."

"Take your time."

He went into the restroom. Tony was drying his hands. "What's your plan?" he asked.

"Gina said they were staying at a motel and RV park just off the highway'. I'm going to try to find that, I guess."

"There is Internet access here. My suggestion is to start there."

"I wouldn't have a clue how to go about doing that."

"How about Gina? Is she Internet savvy?"

"Probably."

"I'll find out what is required to get on."

Mickey got a password for the computer and Gina started helping Tony search for RV parks.

Mickey stood near by. "Oh, by the way, it's going to be $278.76 for the fuel," he said.

"What?" Tony turned to look at him.

"I need $278.76 for fuel."

"$278 dollars! What is that thing? A Saturn Rocket?"

"Avgas is expensive and we're burning seventeen gallons an hour."

"Holy shit!"

Mickey didn't respond.

"All right." He took a wad of money from his pocket and handed Mickey three, one-hundred dollar bills. "Bring me the change, Ace."

Mickey tossed the change on the table. "Here you are."

Tony didn't take his eyes off the screen.

"So what have you found?" asked Mickey.

"There are only three places near New Orleans that fit the description that Gina heard. He nodded toward the screen. I'm going to start with this one." Tony picked up his cell phone and punched in the number of the RV park.

Gina stood up and walked outside to smoke a cigarette. Mickey followed her. The sun was low in the sky and big thunderheads were building on the horizon.

"That could be a problem for us when we leave," said Mickey.

Gina lit her cigarette. Blowing smoke out she said, "The weather?"

"Yeah."

"How long do you think it will be before it becomes a issue?"

Mickey gazed at the sky. "A couple of hours. Maybe more, maybe less."

"He's not going to let go of this thing, you know."

"No, I don't think so."

"He is such an idiot."

"You'd know best."

"Seems like he's always involved in some hair-brained scheme that inevitably goes bad. One time, about fifteen years ago, he was visiting over Christmas and he meets a guy who is trying to smuggle cocaine in from the Bahamas. Tony offers to bring the stuff in for a piece of the action, so he borrows a cigarette boat from a friend and takes off for the islands. On the way back he runs out of gas. A Coast Guard patrol boat spots him and comes to the rescue. Of course Tony is loaded with contraband, so he throws it all overboard. The Guard rescues him, but he is out a quarter of a million dollars in product. His father and my father had to get involved and got the guy to settle for the wholesale price. That was typical.

"He got into some kind of trouble up north a couple of years ago. His father didn't know what to do with him so he sent him to Miami. My father didn't know what to do with him either so he asked me if I would keep him busy at the restaurant."

"You own a restaurant?"

"My father does. I just run it for him."

"What's the name of it?"

"Paesano's."

"Oh sure, I've heard of that. Tony works there?"

"He's the 'co-manager'. Mostly he just hangs out in the bar and drinks with customers. I knew it was only a matter of time before he got bored and found some trouble to get into." Gina put her cigarette in the ashtray by the door. "The amazing thing is that as much of a putz as he is, I really do like the guy. We used to have a lot of fun when we were kids."

"You have an interesting family."

She looked at him. "You don't know the half of it."

"It's probably better that way."

Mickey followed Gina back in. Tony was still engrossed with the computer and barely noticed them walk up.

"Well?" asked Gina.

"How do I get the directions to this place?" said Tony.

"They *are* there?" asked Mickey.

Tony looked up. "Damn right. I've got those bastards."

Gina sighed. "Here we go."

"Just help me find this place, okay?"

"Let me see." Gina sat down beside him and took over the mouse. A map soon popped up on the screen. "Here it is."

"Can I get a copy of that?" asked Tony.

"Yeah, just print it out," said Mickey.

Gina sent the document to the central printer. Mickey retrieved it. Handing it to Tony he asked, "How are you going to get there? You gonna want a rental car or taxi?"

"Taxi."

"Okay, I'll have the girl arrange for one."

The girl from the desk walked into the lounge. "Mr. Soto, you're taxi is here."

"Thank you," said Mickey.

"So we're agreed," said Gina. "If you come back empty handed we forget this thing and head back to Miami."

"Yeah, yeah." Tony got up to leave.

"How long do you think you'll be gone?" asked Mickey.

"I don't know. Two, three hours at the most I suppose. I'll call you if it looks like it's going to be much more than that." Tony walked out.

"I have a feeling we may be here for a while."

"You're probably right."

"You hungry?" Mickey asked Gina.

"Starved."

"I'll see if there is something nearby."

14

"Will there be anything else, sir?" asked the waiter.

"How about a glass of Port for desert?" said Sheldon.

"A particular brand?"

"How about a Taylor Fladgate?"

"Very good, sir." He turned to Vince. "And for you?"

"That sounds good. Whatever he is having."

"Very good." He backed away from the table.

"That is the best damn meal I've had since I was in New York last year," said Sheldon.

"You're mighty right, pard. They know how cook down here."

Sheldon sat back and wiped his mouth with his napkin. "So who is this broad that Johnny fixed you up with?"

"You're jealous, aren't you?"

"Just curious."

"Gina Sandrelli."

Sheldon sat forward. "Who?"

"Gina Sandrelli."

"Not Severino Sandrelli's daughter?"

"As a matter of fact, yes, she is."

"Are telling me that Severino Sandrelli's daughter wants a date with you?"

"Well, not exactly. She said her father wanted me to do a job for him."

"Why the hell didn't you tell me this before?"

"'Cause I didn't think it was any of your goddamn business, that's why."

"Do you know who Severino Sandrelli is?"

"Of course I do."

"Then you know he's Tony Boccaccio's uncle?"

"What?"

"You don't suppose there's a connection here, do you?"

"Oh shit."

"What exactly did she want?"

"She said that her father wanted me to lean on Marvin Seguin."

"Marvin Seguin! He's a friend of Boccaccio's. How did she get your number?"

"She said Johnny recommended me to Sandrelli."

"And you believed her? You knucklehead." Sheldon pulled out his cell phone. "I'll be back in a minute." He left the table.

The waiter returned to the table with the wine. "Will there be anything else?" Vince sat there dumbfounded. The waiter retreated discretely.

———————————————————————

Sheldon sat down heavily. "Johnny never gave Sandrelli your name. In fact he hasn't talked to him years."

Vince stared at his wine glass. "What an idiot."

"Yes, you are. What in god's name would lead you to believe that Johnny Rodriguez would give Severino Sandrelli your name for a job?"

"I don't know, she sounded so sincere."

"Ah, the operative word, *she*. What did you tell her?"

"I told her I was out of town for a couple of weeks. She said she'd talk to her father and get back to me."

"By any chance, you didn't happen to tell her where you were, did you?"

Vince replayed the conversation in his head. "Come to think of it, I think I did mention that I was in New Orleans …"

Sheldon signaled the waiter who quickly walked over to the table.

"Can we have our check please?"

———————————————————————

The taxi pulled in the parking lot of the Cajun Manor Motel and RV Park. The motel portion was a two-story building of 50 units. Behind the motel was a large open area with 75 motor home sites.

"This is it." said the driver. He handed the map back to Tony.

"Great."

"You want me to wait for you?"

"Ah, yeah. Yeah, wait for me, will you?" Tony handed him a hundred dollar bill. "Hang on to that until I get back."

"You got it."

Tony got out and went in to the reception desk.

A pleasant looking man of about sixty, potbelly and thinning hair, greeted him from behind the desk. "Can I help you?"

"Yeah. I'm looking for Sheldon Isaacs. I believe he has his motor home parked here."

"You must be the fella that called."

"Yep. That'd be me."

"You're a friend of Mr. Isaac's?"

"Business associate."

"Oh I see." He looked down at his computer screen and hit a few keys. "He's in site 41B."

"Great, thanks."

"No problem. You can just walk through the courtyard here, follow the walkway and it will take you right into the RV park."

"Thanks."

Tony followed the man's directions and was soon walking down a row of motor homes. Trying not to raise any suspicion, he smiled and waved to people who where sitting outside their rigs or fussing with adjustments or packing, but they couldn't help notice the short man with the slicked back hair, Hawaiian print shirt, dark slacks and alligator shoes. He didn't look like them.

He found site 41B. Tony couldn't believe his luck: the black and tan striped Winnebago sat dark in the humid evening. It was backed into a site against a stand of trees. Next door, light flowed from every window of a big Pace Arrow. He could see a woman preparing a meal while her husband watched TV. The site on the far side was empty, but there was another rig just past that, but it too stood darkened. He stood to the side for a long while surveying the scene. A couple strolled by.

Tony took the initiative. "Nice night."

"Beautiful," said the woman.

"Looks like storms later," said the man.

"No worry's in these things, eh?" said Tony.

"Guess not," said the man. They strolled on.

Tony ventured up to the door of the Winnebago and rapped on the window. After a couple of minutes, he rapped again. Satisfied that no one was there, he looked around for a rock. He couldn't find one suitable, but there was a garbage can across the street that was sitting on a pad of bricks. He walked over, kicked one loose and took it back. He stood in front of the door and hefted the brick. It was too quiet to smash the window.

But again his luck held. A big rig was pulling out and bumping slowly down the unpaved street. It was making a huge racket, but Tony figured there was enough noise to cover the breaking of glass. As it passed, he raised the brick and quickly smashed the window. The woman in the Pace Arrow next door looked up, but seeing the motor home pass by she went back to her cooking.

Tony tapped a few shards out of the bottom of the window. Again the woman looked up, but soon went back to her task. Tony reached through the window and, straining with all his might reached the latch. The door popped open.

He went up the steps and pulled the door shut behind him. It was as dark inside, but enough light came in through the window so he could see a flashlight mounted on the wall behind the door. He pulled it down and, keeping it pointed at the floor, turned it on. He looked out to see if anyone noticed. So far, nothing.

He worked his way through the living room, pulling all the shades down as he went. He made his way through the galley and into the short hall separating the living quarters from the bath and sleeping area. He passed a closet, opened it and shined the light in. A couple of expensive leather jackets and several silk shirts were hanging from the rack. A couple pairs of shoes were on the floor. That was all.

He made his way into the bedroom. Thankfully the shades were already down, so he quickly played the light around the room. A closet lined the back wall. He slid open a door and rooted around the clothes and shoes. He shined the light up and saw a Miami Dolphins gym bag. He pulled it down and zipped it open. There were 30 neatly wrapped bundles of hundred dollar bills. Each bundle marked $5000.

When the taxi pulled into the motel parking lot, the headlights played on the other taxi that was sitting next to the curb near the front door. Vince and Sheldon looked at each other.

"This is good, thanks," said Sheldon. He handed the man a pair of twenties. "Keep the change."

"Thank you," said the driver in a thick Hindu accent.

They got out and walked over to the other cab. The motor was running, the driver's head tilted back with his hat pulled down over his eyes. Vince rapped on the window.

The man sat up with a start. He rolled down the window a crack. "Yeah?"

"You waiting on a fare?"

"Yeah."

Vince held his hand out. "He about this high, a little chubby, dark hair?"

"Yeah."

"Thanks."

"Sure 'ting."

Vince turned to Sheldon. "He's here."

They walking into the lobby and as they passed the desk, the clerk said, "Oh, Mr. Isaacs. I didn't know you were out."

"Just out for dinner," said Sheldon.

"A man came in looking for you. I sent him on back to the park. I hope that's not a problem."

"No, that's fine. He's a friend of ours. Thanks."

They walked through the courtyard and into the RV park. As they approached 41B, the Winnebago looked dark. They stopped and watched for a while. Then they saw it; a glimmer of light through the bedroom window.

"You packing?" whispered Sheldon.

"No. I didn't think we'd get into the casino."

"Well he probably is."

"Don't worry. Got it covered."

Vince pulled the keys out of his pocket and walked quietly over to the motor home. He slipped the key in the lock of the exterior storage compartment, turned it until it unlatched and carefully lifted the door. He waved to Sheldon to come over.

"Hold this up," he whispered. Sheldon grabbed the door.

Vince reached in and felt around until he found a small suitcase. He slowly zipped it open and felt around the interior until he pulled out a Glock 17. He held it up for Sheldon to see. Sheldon nodded and lowered the door.

They inched down the side of the motor home to the door. Vince pointed to the broken window.

"That son of bitch," murmured Sheldon.

The door was unlatched. Vince pulled it open and motioned for Sheldon to stay were he was. Vince was an athlete and could move gracefully. Sheldon lacked such capabilities.

Vince went up the steps and into the living area. He could plainly see the flashlight flicking around the back bedroom. Gently and slowly he picked his way to the back. As he got closer he could see Tony holding the Miami Dolphin gym bag open and shining the flashlight inside. He felt around the corner for the light switch and flicked it on.

"Looking for something?"

Tony dropped the bag and the flashlight. He looked up at Vince holding the Glock on him.

"Goddamn, Vince. You scared the living shit out of me."

"Come on in, Shelly," Vince yelled. "We've got company."

15

"You were hungry," said Mickey.

Gina nodded as she finished chewing the last bite of her hamburger. "Mmmhum," she mumbled.

Mickey held up a French fry. "Food is pretty good here." He popped it in his mouth.

Gina wiped her mouth. "Not fancy but filling." She took a drink of her milk shake.

"I wish we had more time to go downtown. We probably could have found a nicer place."

"This was just fine. I was almost too hungry to appreciate fine dining."

"I hear you." Mickey took a sip of coke. "You're not from Florida originally are you?"

"No. I was born in New York, but moved down here when I was in grade school."

"I thought I detected an slight Bronx twang in there. How'd you end up in Miami?"

"Family business."

"Oh."

"You know my father and Tony's father are brothers?"

"I sorta figured that out."

"They are … how shall I say … entrepreneurs?"

"I figured that out too."

"Anyway, my father was dispatched by Uncle Mario to oversee their operations in south Florida."

"You like Florida?"

"Yes. It's pretty much in my blood now. I graduated from the University of Miami with a degree in business administration and have been running the restaurant for my father ever since."

"No family of your own?"

"No. It's hard to meet suitable guys 'outside the business' … and the ones inside the business are usually jerks. I came close to getting married a few years ago, but he turned out to be an asshole."

"Was he inside or outside?"

"He was a guy I knew in school. His family had money and they would never accept a girl with my background. He ended up with some country club bimbo his family fixed him up with."

"No other serious brushes?"

"Oh, there have been a couple that I've flirted with, but they fell apart for one reason or another. What about you?"

"I was married but it didn't last."

"What happened?"

"Let's just say that she was looking for a high roller and I didn't exactly fit the bill."

"Any children?"

"Thankfully no."

"So now you're just foot loose and fancy free? Flying around the country and having fun."

"Not exactly. Most of my time is spent giving lessons. I don't get that many charters and when I do it is usually local. Rarely outside of Florida."

"Tony told me you've done things a little more exciting than that."

Mickey flushed. "We all have indiscretions in our past."

Gina smiled. "Far be it from me to hold you accountable."

"Thanks. Speaking of Tony, I wonder how he is making out. Think he's back yet."

"I hope so. Otherwise it can't be good."

"I've only got the crew car for an hour, so we'd better head back to the airport anyway."

Mickey woke with start. He had fallen asleep in one of the overstuffed chairs in the pilot's lounge, which was now empty except for Gina who was curled up on the adjacent sofa. Mickey looked at the clock on the wall. It was five-thirty in the morning. He went to the rest room and splashed some water on his face. He walked outside and watched the airport waking up under a beautiful sunrise. Thunderstorms had rolled through during the night and air was fresh and clean. But no Tony.

He went back inside and walked over to the desk. A new girl was sorting through papers. "Any messages for me?" he asked.

"I'm sorry, what was your name?"

"Soto. Mickey Soto."

She checked. "No, Mr. Soto. Nothing."

He walked back to the lounge. Gina had not moved. He sat down at a computer and checked his emails. There was a note from Sara. She'd decided to quit flying and was learning how to golf. *Great*, thought Mickey. *She'll probably meet some country club hot shot and get herself a big fat diamond.*

"Been up long?"

He looked up at Gina. Her hair was tousled and clothes rumbled, but she looked strangely attractive. "Just a few minutes. Glad you were able to get some sleep."

"Thunderstorms kept me awake for awhile, but the last time I looked at the clock it was one-thirty, so I guess I got a few hours. Any word from our boy?"

"Nothing."

Gina frowned. "Not good."

"No. What do you suggest we do?"

"I'm going to use the john. See if you can find the number of that RV park."

A few minutes later Gina returned from the restroom. She looked refreshed and her hair was combed. Mickey pointed to the computer screen. "I think that's it," he said.

"Yes, that's it."

"What were the names of those guys?"

"There's a Vince somebody … I can't remember the other guy."

"Sheldon. Sheldon Isaacs." She pulled her phone out of her purse and entered the number of the RV park.

"Hello. I'm wondering if you have a Sheldon Isaacs registered there," she said.

A woman's voice on the other end said, "Just a minute, I'll check."

Gina pulled a cigarette out of her purse, and then realizing she couldn't smoke where she was, she put it back. The woman came back on the line. "There was a Mr. Isaacs registered here yesterday, but it appears that he left during the night."

"Oh shit."

"I'm sorry?"

"Are you sure about that?"

"According to the information I have here, he checked out at 10:08 last night."

"Thank you." Gina snapped her phone shut.

"This is bad, Mickey." Gina looked genuinely worried. "Isaacs pulled out last night."

Mickey didn't know what to say. If Tony wasn't back and the people he was after left last night, he didn't need to be a genius to put two and two together.

"What do you think we should do?" asked Gina.

He didn't want to do anything other than fly back to Miami, but he could see that Gina was distraught. "I know it looks bad, Gina, but don't jump to conclusions. Maybe he got his money back and went downtown to celebrate."

Gina looked at him. "You don't think he'd call and let us know?"

"You never know. He might have been swept up in the moment …"

"Something's happened, I just know it."

"Well, don't automatically think the worst."

"It's hard not to."

"I know. But there is every possibility that he's just been waylaid. Maybe we should just sit tight for a while and see if he checks in."

She put her hand on Mickey's shoulder. She was touched by the way he was trying to make her feel better. "You're right. We'll sit tight for a while."

"Yes. We'll get some breakfast and see what develops this morning."

"Okay."

"And I'd like to get some clean clothes … I've been living in these for two days."

"Good idea. Maybe after we eat and clean up we'll be able to think more clearly. You said there were showers here?"

"Yes."

They had breakfast in the same diner that they had dinner the night before, which was located across from a mall. Mickey picked up some socks and underwear and a couple of shirts. Gina also bought underwear and found some Levis, a top and a sweater. They were able to shower at the airport, and, feeling a hundred percent better, Mickey walked out of the FBO facility to check in with Hayes.

"Hi, Betty, it's Mickey."

"Hey there was a guy named Mickey who used to work here."

"Funny. Listen I've got a problem …"

"Yes, you certainly do. You had a lesson with Mr. Mead this morning and you're supposed to fly a carton of special computer parts to that circuit board manufacturer in Tampa this afternoon."

"Damn. I totally forgot about Mr. Mead. Is he angry?"

"He's a nice guy, but he's getting close to his FAA exam and didn't want to miss any flying time. Glenn took him. He wants to talk to you."

"Okay."

Mickey watched a Gulfstream taxi by. He sure could use one of those right now.

"Hello, Mickey?"

"Hi, Glenn. Gee, I'm really sorry about Mr. Mead …"

"What's going on?" Glenn knew that Mickey was no boy scout. He was worried that Mickey might be mixed up in something.

"Nothing. I just took a charter the other day that has turned into something of a nightmare. My passenger is trying to straighten out his business and we ended flying all the way to New Orleans."

"New Orleans?"

"Yeah. We got in last night and he asked me to wait while he concluded his business and … well … I'm still waiting."

"What kind of business is it?"

Mickey wasn't quite prepared for that. "Um, well, I'm not sure exactly. I think it might have … have something to do with real estate."

"Really?"

"I don't know for sure. He doesn't really talk much."

"When are you coming back?"

"I was hoping to be back this afternoon so I could take that charter to Tampa, but that's just not going to happen."

"I'll call Taylor Wayne … he is usually available on fairly short notice."

"Thanks, Glenn. And thanks for taking care of Mr. Mead."

"That's okay, but don't make a habit out of it. You know I want to help you Mickey, but I'm trying to run a business here and it is tough enough without having my pilots MIA."

"I know, I know. I really feel shitty about this."

"So I can look for you tomorrow?"

"Technically, tomorrow is my day off, but I feel like I owe you …"

"Don't worry about it. Go ahead and take tomorrow off. I'll see you on Monday."

"You're a prince, Glenn."

"Are you sure everything is okay?"

"Yeah, sure." Mickey didn't really sound as convincing as he'd have liked.

"You call me if you run into any more problems."

"Absolutely."

16

Tony tried to open his eyes but the sun was too bright. A shadow passed over his face and he was able to blink a couple of times.

"You okay, mister?"

Tony blinked some more. He looked up and could see the outline of a head. He moved his mouth to speak but nothing came out.

"Here."

The outline of an arm appeared and it was holding something.

"Wha …" Tony rasped. "What?"

"Here have some water." It was the voice of a young boy.

A hand slipped under his back and tried to pull him up. Tony helped by rolling on his side and raising himself onto his elbow.

A canteen was being waved in front of his face. "Drink some of this mister."

Tony took the canteen and poured some water on his face. It felt delicious. He poured some more then opened his mouth and poured some in. It was too fast and he choked a little.

"Take it easy. There's plenty."

With considerable effort, Tony managed to sit up. All around was a rolling terrain of scrub brush and cactus. The boy who had given him water was squatting next to him. He was no more than fourteen, obviously of Hispanic decent, dressed in dungarees, boots, a T-shirt that had a faded AC/DC logo on the front. A beat-up straw cowboy hat was pushed back on his head. A few feet behind him stood a chestnut horse, its head bowed low to casually munch on the sparse grass and brush.

Tony blinked in the blazing sunlight. "Where … where am I."

"Val Verde County."

"Where the hell is Val Verde County?"

"Texas. Where else?"

"Texas? You're shitting me."

"No, mister, I'm not shitting you. You're in Texas."

"How the fu … how did I get here?"

"I sure as hell don't know. I just found you here. Must've been one hellava party."

Tony looked down at himself. He was dressed only in his boxer shorts and under shirt. His legs and arms were sunburned. His head pounded and his mouth was still filled with cotton. Gingerly, he touched a sizeable lump on the side of his head. It hurt like hell.

"Yeah. Must've been."

Slowly, bits and pieces of the night before began to assemble in the pocked marked field of his brain. He remembered searching the motor home and finding the bag filled with packs of hundred. Suddenly the light in the room went on and Vince was standing there holding a gun on him. He dropped the flashlight and the bag.

"Looking for something?" Vince said.

"Goddamn, Vince. You scared the living shit out of me."

"Come on in, Shelly," Vince yelled. "We've got company."

Vince walked around the bed toward Tony. Holding the gun steady on Tony motioned for him to pick up the bag.

Tony slowly bent down and picked it up Vince grabbed it from him. He turned it upside down, dumping the contents on the bed. "You looking for that?"

"Yeah, dipshit, as a matter of fact I am." It must've been the wrong answer because in the blink of an eye, Vince swung his gun at Tony and everything went black.

When he came to he was laying on the floor of the galley. Vince dragged him to his feet and shoved him into the dining nook. Sheldon was sitting at the table across from him. He shook his head. "Tony, I knew you liked us, but I didn't think you'd follow us all the way to New Orleans just to party with us."

"You know goddamn well why I'm here."

"Oh, the money."

"Yeah, the money."

Tony rubbed the side of his head. He felt nauseous. "Jesus, Vince. Why the hell did you have to do that?"

"Because you weren't invited here, then you go and be a smart ass."

"I thought you could take a joke."

"Now you know better."

"So what are we going to do with you now?" asked Sheldon.

"Give me my money and let me go."

Vince slapped Tony across the face.

"Oww. Goddamn it, will you cut that out?" yelled Tony.

"I told you not to be a smart ass."

"You know Vince, we're not being very hospitable," said Sheldon. "Grab that bottle of scotch from the cupboard and offer Tony a drink."

"Unh?" said Vince.

"Make it the Johnny Walker, not the Glen Livet. We're good hosts, but not that good." Sheldon motioned toward the cupboard.

Vince grinned. He grabbed the bottle and a glass. He set them down in front of Tony.

"Poor your self a drink, Tony."

"Go fuck yourself."

Vince slapped Tony again. "Do it."

"Oww. Goddamn it, I'm telling you, Vince …"

Vince slid into the seat next to Sheldon and laid his gun on the table. "Telling me what?"

"Come on, Tony," said Sheldon. "This is New Orleans. Have a drink."

Tony poured some scotch in his glass and took a drink.

"Oh, Tony, you can do better than that." Sheldon reached over filled the glass with scotch. "Have a real drink."

Tony took another sip. Vince picked up the gun and pointed at Tony's forehead. "I said drink up, asshole."

Tony choked down a large swallow.

"That's a good boy," said Sheldon.

"Gee, I hate to drink alone. Aren't you boys going to join me?"

"We'd love to, Tony. But it's not a good idea to drink and drive. You enjoy yourself."

"Are we going somewhere?"

"Yes. We're all going to take a little ride." Sheldon slid the gun over in front of him. "Vince, will you dispatch Tony's taxi. Then settle up with the front desk."

Vince got up to leave. "You gonna be all right, Shelly?"

Sheldon wasn't known for his violent tendencies, but he had a mean streak. Besides, Tony wasn't exactly a threat either. "We'll be fine, Vince. You go ahead."

"Bring back the change, Vince. I gave that guy a hundred bucks to wait for me," said Tony.

Vince flipped him the bird and walked out.

"How'd you get here?"

Tony looked at him. "Taxi."

"To New Orleans?"

Tony suddenly realized that it was best that Sheldon not know about the charter flight here and Gina and Mickey waiting for him at the airport. "Oh, no. I took a flight to New Orleans … and took a cab here."

"Where's your cousin, Gina?"

"Gina?"

"You don't think I'm stupid do you?"

"I better not answer that. You've got the gun."

"I know Gina tipped you off that we were in New Orleans."

"She did?"

"Yes, she did. Where is she?"

"In Miami last I checked."

"She's not waiting for you?"

"Hell no. You don't think I'd bring her along, do you?"

Sheldon didn't think so. "Have another drink," said Sheldon.

Tony contemplated making a play for the gun, but Sheldon must have anticipated that because he picked it up and held it loosely pointed in Tony's direction.

Tony took a drink. "Why are you doing this, Sheldon?"

"Doing what?"

"Stealing my money."

"Burke convinced us that it wasn't your money."

"How? How could he do that? You know I did the job. The money belonged to me."

"According to Burke, you were working for him. He set it up so you could work off your debts."

"That's crazy. Even if that were true, I didn't owe him anywhere near that much."

"He said the rest was the vig."

"The vig? That's a lot of goddamn interest even for Burke."

"I didn't set the prices."

"That's ridiculous and you know it."

"That's between you and Burke. All I know is that we're getting a nice finder's fee for making the delivery."

"You're a goddamn crook, Sheldon."

"Now that isn't nice, Tony. But I'll forgive you. Now drink up."

By the time Vince returned Tony had his elbows on the table and was holding his head in his hands. He was humming the tune 'Yellow Bird.'

Vince laughed. "He can't hold his liquor."

"No, but he's a party animal. Get us unhooked and let's get this show on the road," said Sheldon.

Vince started to walk out and stopped. "Oh yeah. I just got a call from Burke."

"Everything okay?"

"Fine. But there's been a slight change in plans. He wants to meet us in Vegas."

"We weren't planning to go to Vegas."

"Well, that's what he wants to do. He said it wasn't all that far off our route."

"Shit. I don't want to go to Vegas."

"Why not? It'll be fun. Especially since our stay here got cut short."

"Does Johnny know about Vegas?"

"Burke said he did."

"We'd better check anyway. Johnny's expecting us to be in San Bernardino by Tuesday." Sheldon suddenly remembered Tony. He looked at him for signs of comprehension, but Tony was mumbling, "Yellow bird, up high in banana tree …"

"Okay. Let's get going. We've got a lot of ground to cover tonight."

"What about him?" Vince nodded at Tony.

"We'll find him a nice comfortable place where he can relax until we're done with Burke."

"What's your name?" Tony asked the boy.

"Clayton Morales. But everyone calls me Paco."

"You wouldn't happen to have a phone, would you Paco?"

"Nope. Wouldn't do no good anyway. You can't get a signal out here. You're not from around here are you?"

"Whatever gave you that clue?"

Paco missed the sarcasm. "Just a hunch. How'd you get out here?"

"I'm not one hundred percent certain about that myself."

"Did your car break down or something?"

"No. I guess I was traveling with some friends and they must have stopped around here and I got lost."

"You guess?"

"Well, like you said, it was a hell of a party." Tony decided to change the subject. "So, where the hell is 'out here'?"

"I told you, mister. Val Verde County."

"Yeah. You said that. Where is Val Verde County?

"Texas."

"You said that, too. The only thing I know about Texas is the Dallas Cowboys. I don't suppose we're anywhere around Dallas?"

"Oh, no. We're in southwest Texas. About forty miles north of Del Rio."

"Well, that helps. How far from Dallas is that?"

"I don't know exactly. Ain't ever been there. But it's a long way."

"How big is this Del Rio?"

"Don't rightly know, but it's big. My pop works for the railroad there."

"They got a railroad, eh?"

"Yep. It's a big town."

"How far is that?"

"About twenty-five miles."

"I don't suppose you'd help me get there?"

"I'd like to, mister, but I'm on my way home."

"Where's home?"

"About three miles." Paco pointed down a dusty two-track. "Over that rise."

"Who's at home?"

"My mom and little sister, Rachel."

"Would they be freaked out if you brought a stranger back with you?"

"Probably, but I guess I can't leave you out here."

"I appreciate that, Paco." Tony attempted to get to his feet, but sat back down heavily. "How about a hand here?"

Paco stood, grabbed Tony's arm and pulled. Between the two of them they managed to get Tony on his feet. Tony tried to take a step but the rocky surface was too tough on his bare feet. "How we gonna do this?"

"Stay there." Paco walked over to the horse, grabbed the reigns and pulled it over to Tony, who stumbled backward as the big animal approached. "This is Rio. He won't hurt you."

"I'm not used to being around anything bigger than a dog … and I'm not overly fond of them."

"Well, you sure as hell can't walk … not with out shoes. So if you want to get to my house you're gonna have to get on Rio."

"You're the boss."

Paco helped Tony put his foot in the stirrup and, with great difficulty, managed to get him to throw his other leg over the saddle. Once ensconced in the saddle, Tony's knee touched something furry. He looked down and saw two rabbits hanging from the horn.

"What the …"

"That's supper, mister. That's what I was doing out here in the first place." Paco patted the .22 rifle in the saddle scabbard. "Good thing for you, too. Otherwise you could've been out here for a long time before someone came down this road."

"Yeah, good thing."

Paco patted Tony on the knee. "You're gonna have to slid back so I can get up."

Tony followed the instructions and eased himself behind the saddle. Paco deftly pulled himself onto Rio. He grabbed Tony's hands and placed them around his stomach. With gentle dig of his heals he started Rio moving.

"Shit." Tony bounced insecurely on Rio's back, his bare legs dangling loosely. He clung tighter to Paco.

"Don't worry mister, I'll take it easy."

"You can call me Tony," he said through gritted teeth.

"Okay, Tony."

Rio walked slowly down the road cut through the arid vastness. The sun beat down mercilessly on Tony's back, reddening his neck and shoulders. He buried his head in Paco's back, drifting into sleep. When he did his hands slipped away. Paco grabbed them and pulled them up around his stomach causing Tony to wake up. This cycle continued several times, until eventually Paco said, "We're here."

"Huh?" Tony raised his head and looked around. They were making their way down a dusty driveway, at the end of which stood a doublewide trailer sitting on a foundation of cement blocks. A large, covered, wood porch extended nearly down one whole side of the home. The fenced-in yard was covered with scrubby grass that mostly grew in patches. On the side was clothesline, which was hung with sheets and towels that were billowing in the wind. Behind the house stood a large poll-barn, and various farm implements were scattered around. Two goats and several sheep looked up from munching the sparse grass as they passed by. A big German Sheppard raced around the side of the house barking madly.

"Oh, shit." Tony pulled his legs up as the dog approached.

"Hey, Wally," said Paco as he slipped down out of the saddle. He grabbed Wally by the collar before he could jump up on Tony.

"This here's Tony. You be nice to him." Wally calmed down, but he kept his eyes riveted on Tony.

"You sure that hound is safe?"

"He won't hurt you … not as long as I'm here."

"That's reassuring." Tony slid forward so he was in the saddle and could put his foot in the stirrup. Paco let go of Wally and reached up to help Tony get down. Wally immediately started sniffing around Tony's bare legs, which made him feel very vulnerable.

"Try petting him," said Paco.

Tony held out his hand, but Wally growled slightly. Tony pulled his hand away.

"Wally!" Paco yelled. He patted the dog on the nose. "He'll warm up to you eventually. You just gotta let him get to know you."

"Hopefully, I won't be here long enough for that to happen."

A short, rotund woman, wearing a housedress, stepped out onto the porch. "Paco, who's that with you?"

"A friend, mom."

"Oh?" She stepped down off the porch and walked over to them. She had a pleasant, brown face, with sparkling black eyes; her dark hair pulled back into a ponytail was streaked with gray. She eyed Tony suspiciously. "Why is your friend dressed like that?" Her speech was laced with a Spanish accent.

"I found him like this … out by Eagle Flats." Paco pointed to the north.

"Really?"

"I know this must seem strange, ma'am, but that's the truth. Paco found me out there just like this." Tony held his hands up.

"What's your name?"

"Oh, I'm sorry. Tony. Tony Boccaccio."

"You're not from around here are you Mr. Boc … Boc …"

"Just call me Tony. And no. I'm from Miami, Florida."

"You're a long way from home."

"Don't I know it? Thank god Paco happened along. Who knows how long I would have been out there."

"How did you get out *there*?"

"Like I told Paco, I was traveling with some friends and they stopped somewhere around here and I got lost."

"Got lost?"

"Well, to tell the truth, ma'am, we had been drinking a little and I don't exactly remember what happened. All I know is that I woke up on the ground out there and Paco was standing over me. He offered me water and brought me here."

She beamed. "Paco is a good boy." Paco blushed. She said, "You go take care of Rio. I'll deal with Mr. …"

"Tony."

"…with Tony.

Paco started to walk the horse away, and then he stopped. "Oh, I almost forgot." He grabbed the rabbits off the saddle and handed them to his mother. "Supper."

She took the rabbits like Paco was handing her a bag from the supermarket. "You go on." Paco walked away with Rio and Wally bounded after him. Then to Tony, "You come with me." She turned and walked back toward the house, motioning for Tony to follow. She went up the steps and set the rabbits on the porch.

Tony hobbled across the rough ground and up the steps. "All I need is a telephone and I can have someone pick me up."

"You need to get some clothes on first."

"Yeah, that might be good." He followed her into the house.

They stepped into the living room, which was surprisingly roomy and the conditioned air was cool and dry. The sparse furniture was old but the room looked clean and neat. The walls were decorated with Hispanic and religious art. A picture of the Virgin Mary dominated the far wall.

"Wait here." The woman disappeared into a room.

She reappeared a few minutes later holding a pile of clothes. "Here are some old things of Raymond's that I was going to give to the mission. He is about your size. I think they might fit you." She handed them to Tony.

"Raymond?"

"My husband. He's at work right now, but he'll be home this evening." She looked directly at Tony to make sure he understood.

"Thank you, ma'am."

"My name is Florenza. You call me Flo."

"Thank you, Flo."

"The bathroom is at the end of the hall on the right." She pointed. "You can clean up in there."

Tony started to walk down the hall.

"Just a minute." Flo went into the kitchen. She returned a minute later and handed Tony a bottle of lotion. "That is very good for sunburn."

"Thank you, Flo." Tony headed down the hall.

17

Gina put her hand over the phone. "It's Tony." Mickey looked up from the computer. Gina put the phone back to her ear. "Where are you?"

"Some place in Texas, near … what's the name of that town again, Flo?" Tony sat at the Morales kitchen table watching Flo making a rabbit stew.

Flo looked at Tony. He looked ridiculous in Raymond's Levis and plaid shirt. Although close in size, Raymond was slightly bigger and had about 20 pounds on Tony so the clothes hung loosely on him. "Del Rio.

"Yeah, that's it. Del Rio."

Gina covered the phone again. "He's in Texas … some place called Del Rio."

"What?" said Tony.

"I was just telling Mickey where you are."

"Well, when you figure it out, let me know."

"Mickey is checking now. Who's Flo?"

"Her son saved my life. I'm sitting at her kitchen table right now."

"What happened?"

"I'm not 100 percent sure myself, but I'll tell you all about it when you come and get me."

"Did you see Vince and Sheldon?"

"Yes, as a matter of fact I did."

"Did you get your money?"

"No."

"Somehow I didn't think you would."

"They even took the few hundred bucks I had in my pocket from selling the Caddy."

"Got it," said Mickey.

"Hold on a second, Tony," said Gina. She leaned over Mickey's shoulder to the map he had pulled up. He pointed to Del Rio. "I see it. You're about 150 miles west of San Antonio."

"Oh, that helps," said Tony. "How long will it take you to get here?"

"Just a second." Gina held her hand over the phone. "He wants us to come and get him."

"I figured," said Mickey.

"Tell Mickey not to worry about the money," said Tony.

Gina put the phone back to her ear. "What did you say?"

"I said tell Mickey not to worry about the money. I'll take care of him."

"You tell him." Gina handed the phone to Mickey.

"Listen, Tony, I'm not worried about the money anymore … I'm worried about my job."

"Ace! How are you?" said Tony.

"I was doing pretty well until I took your charter. There is no way that I can pick you up in Texas and make it back to Miami by tomorrow morning."

"Probably not, because I want you to take me to Las Vegas."

Mickey looked at Gina. "Las Vegas?" Gina rolled her eyes. "I'm not taking you to Las Vegas."

"I told you … I'll make it worth your while."

"Can't you just catch a commercial flight?"

"I don't have any money ... and besides, I'm in the wilderness ... I'm not sure they have even seen an airplane around here." Flo glanced at him. "No offense, Flo."

"What happened to the money from the Caddy?" said Mickey.

"Sheldon and Vince have it … along with my clothes."
"What?"

"I need you to come and get me. Whatever I promised you before, add another thousand bucks."

"Tony, this is getting out of hand. My job is in jeopardy."

"Oh come on, you're having the time of your life. You know this beats the shit out of nursing wannabe pilots about the skies over your airport."

"Students pay the bills."

"We're talking about some serious money here, Ace. If you help me get my money back, you're in for a bonus."

There it was again. The carrot dangling so greed could bat at it. "How much of a bonus?"

"How's ten percent sound?"

"Ten percent?"

"That's a cool fifteen grand. That's a lot of training flights."

"Plus expenses?"

"Absolutely. So how long will it take you get here?"

Mickey poured over the charts. He found a small, private airstrip just northeast of Del Rio that turned out to belong to neighbor of the Morales's. A direct flight to the airstrip was over 500 miles, but there was a huge Air Force base directly in their path, and at the altitude they flew they would have to vector around it, which would add at least 150 miles and another hour. Then there was the weather. A strong line of thunderstorms was working its way across New Mexico and if it rolled into Texas ahead of them it was going to be difficult to pick a way around it.

Flo Morales called the owner of the airstrip and arranged for *Songbird* to land there. Her husband, Raymond, would pick them up at 7:00 pm and Mickey could get some sleep so they could leave for Vegas the next morning. At 900 miles, that would be an all day flight. Then he'd need one or maybe even two days to get home.

Glenn was not happy about Mickey missing more time at the airport. Fortunately, Taylor Wayne was available to pick up the slack, but Mickey was worried about that. Taylor wanted more time instructing and he might pick up students, and maybe some charters, that ordinarily would go to Mickey.

He cursed himself for going through with this. It was all about the money, there was no mistake about that, but there was something else too. Gina was genuinely concerned about Tony and he just couldn't bring himself to abandon her. It wasn't that she couldn't take care of herself; she was tough and no nonsense. But she had a softness and vulnerability that made her attractive too. Mickey liked her.

When Raymond Morales pulled into the driveway that evening, Flo was out of the house in flash and waiting for him before he got out of the dusty pick-up truck.

"Raymond," she said as he stepped out of the truck.

He stopped in his tracks. Flo only called him Raymond when something was going on. "Yes?" he said suspiciously.

"We have a guest."

"Oh?"

"A stranger. Your son found him in the brush."

"He did?"

"Yes. He was bruised and sunburned and, other than the fact that he was dressed only in his underwear, he was okay."

Raymond's focus narrowed. "His underwear?"

"I had to loan him some of your old clothes."

"How did he get there … dressed only in his underwear?"

"He claims he was traveling with some friends and there had been drinking and he got lost from them."

"That's it?"

"That's all he saying. I think there is more to the story, but he either doesn't know, or he isn't saying. Anyway, he seems like a nice enough person."

"Is he from around here?"

"Definitely not."

"What's his name?"

"Tony Bocca … Bocca something or other."

"Where is this *Tony*? I'd like to meet him."

"He's in the living room watching TV."

Flo led the way into the house. There sitting in Raymond's favorite chair and drinking a Pepsi sat a short, pudgy man with slicked-back hair, wearing his old Levis and a faded checked shirt that were obviously too large for him. He was watching an afternoon court series where two parties go before a celebrity judge who entertains by acting surprised and outraged by the ridiculousness of the claims of the plaintiff and defendant.

Tony looked up from the television. "Hi, Flo. This must be Raymond."

"Ray, this Tony Bocca … Bocca …"

"Tony Boccaccio, but just call me Tony." He stood up, grabbed Ray's hand and pumped.

Ray stood there, shaking Tony's hand and staring at him blankly.

"You got a marvelous family here, Ray."

Ray recovered his hand. "Thank you."

"That boy of yours … well, let's just say I'd be scorpion food by now if he hadn't rescued me. And Flo, what a women. She takes me in, gets me cleaned up and puts some clothes on my back." Tony looked at the shirtsleeves that hung to his knuckles. "Of course they could use a little tailoring, but who's complaining, right?"

"I'm glad they were able to help you. Have you been able to find your friends?"

"Not the ones that I came here with. Those bastards wouldn't wait for their own mothers … no offense, Flo. But I did hook up with some other friends who are coming to pick me up."

"Tony's friends are coming by airplane," interjected Flo.

"Airplane?"

"Yeah, I flew to New Orleans with them where I met up with these other friends of mine and I took off with them in an RV."

"RV?"

"You know, one of those giant buses that you can live in."

"Yes, I know. And they drove you to Texas?"

"Yeah, we were on our way to Las Vegas."

"And you got separated from them?"

"Damnedest thing. We were drinking and they stopped so I could take a piss … sorry Flo … and I must've wandered off into the brush and passed out."

"And they left you?"

"Nice guys, eh?"

"But, Tony, this isn't on the way to Las Vegas."

"No?"

"No, this is quite a ways south of the highway to Las Vegas."

"Gee, I wonder what the hell we were doing around here. Well, like I said, we were drinking … who knows?"

Raymond looked at him suspiciously.

"Anyway," Tony continued. "I got a hold of my other friends … the ones in the airplane … and they are coming to pick me up."

"I called Mr. Bromly and asked if Tony's friends could land their plane there," said Flo.

Raymond looked at her. "You asked Alton Bromly if someone could use his airstrip." Alton Bromly was a wealthy rancher who looked with distain on his poorer neighbors, most of whom wouldn't piss on him if he was on fire. The last time Ray Morales had any contact with Bromly was several years ago when some of Ray's sheep had escaped the yard and wandered onto Bromly's ranch ten miles away. Bromly threatened to keep them and have them slaughtered if it happened again.

"Yes. You need to pick them up at seven o'clock."

"I do?"

"You don't mind, do you, Ray?" asked Tony. "I'll pay you for the gas and your time."

"I suppose I don't have a lot of choice, do I?"

"Why don't you sit and talk with Tony while I get supper ready. I'll get you a beer," Flo said to her husband.

Ray nodded. "Good idea." He sat down on the couch as she retreated to the kitchen.

Tony started to sit back down and stopped. "Oh, hey, this is your chair isn't it?"

"No, that's fine. You sit down."

Tony sat back down. A thunderbolt resonated in the distance. "I saw thunderstorm warnings on the television this afternoon."

"Yes."

"I hope that is not a problem for my friends."

"You said they were coming from New Orleans?"

"Yep. We started in Miami and ended up there. Then I ran into these other friends and, well, you know what happened."

"Not really."

Tony cleared his throat. "I've never been to Texas before. Interesting country."

"Where are you from?"

"New York originally. But I've lived in Miami for the past few years."

"Never been there."

"It's a great place, but not like New York. I miss the action there."

"I've never been there either."

"Never been to New York?" Tony was astonished.

Flo walked back in. "Supper will be ready in half an hour," said Flo as she handed Tony and Ray each a beer.

"Thanks, Flo. Your wife is a peach," said Tony.

The storm continued to build. Ray kept trying to pierce Tony's veil of secrecy but Tony kept him off balance with outrageous stories of life in New York and Miami, portraying a life style that was so far from his own; a lifestyle that Ray had only seen in movies. In the end he had to admit that Tony was a funny guy.

Mickey advanced the throttles, making sure the two Lycomings were fully up to speed before he released the brakes and the little twin bolted down the runway. As soon as *Songbird* was ready to fly, he gently pulled back on the column and they were climbing smartly. Runway 36 took them directly out over Lake Pontchartrain and he wanted as much altitude as they could get before they were looking down at water. He banked to the west and climbed to 5000 feet and settled into the long cruise across Louisiana and Texas.

The complex of bayous slowly gave way to the sun-dappled Gulf of Mexico coast. Gina squinted into the afternoon sun. "At least it is beautiful weather for flying."

"It is now," said Mickey. "I'm not so sure how it will be later this afternoon."

An hour and forty-five minutes into the flight the vast Houston metro passed to the north. Mickey called for weather report. Gina heard the bad news along with him; there was a solid wall of thunderheads from Eagle Pass to San Angelo. Pilot reports were coming in that it was a bad one and everyone was either hunkering down somewhere to ride out the storm or beating a hasty retreat to the east.

They droned on westward and watched the sky grow more dark and foreboding. Mickey saw the lighten strikes beginning to show up on the storm scope. "This is not good," he said.

"What are we going to do?" asked Gina

"I'm not sure, but I don't think we're going to be able to get through that mess."

As they droned on toward the darkening sky, turbulents increased and the ride got bumpier. Finally, he radioed for vectors around the thunderstorms. The nearest break in the wall was south of Eagle Pass, so Mickey turned south, flying along the face of the mounting wall to the west. The storms were approaching faster than Mickey anticipated and soon rain from the leading edge was pelting the windshield. *Songbird* was starting to buck like a wild horse. Lighting strikes were showing up all around on the storm scope. Occasionally one was close enough to hear the thunder.

"We're not going to make it around this. We're going to have to put down some where." He punched up the nearest airports on the GPS. "It looks like our best bet is Laredo."

"How far is that?"

"About 25 miles. We should be there in 10 minutes."

"You know best. I can tell you that this is not making me comfortable."

The weather kept closing in. Mickey called Houston Center and arranged for a straight in approach to Laredo. There was no other traffic in the area, evidently no else was foolish enough to be up. With visibility down to a few hundred feet, Mickey kept *Songbird* on the glide path as best he could. He nervously watched the altimeter unwind and when it reached 800 feet he began to see glimpses of the airport just ahead. At 700 he had the runway in sight and lined up. Still *Songbird* bucked in the turbulent air. Mickey's big concern right now was wind shear, that deadliest phenomenon that occurred in and around thunderstorms. A sudden blast of wind generated by the storm that could flip the airplane in a heartbeat.

Concentrating fully, Mickey kept up the dance on the rudder pedals to keep the little twin lined up with the centerline. As they crossed the end of the runway he reduced power almost to idle, but kept a little on to help them fly straight and level. That meant they were coming in a little hot, but the 8,000-foot runway was more than enough to keep them out of trouble. At last they heard the chirp of the landing gear meeting the runway and soon they were rolling out. They passed three runway exits before they were taxing slow enough to turn off. When they finally did, Mickey let out a big sigh.

"You were a little tense there," said Gina.

Mickey pushed his hat back. "Landing is tough enough without the added bonus of a thunderstorm."

Mickey called the tower and asked for a progressive taxi to the general aviation fixed base operation. As soon as *Songbird* shut down on the tarmac, Mickey reached in the back and retrieved his leather jacket. He handed it to Gina. "This might come in handy." He reached over her and pushed open the door and rain started pouring in. Gina put the jacket over her head and pulled herself up and out onto the wing. She carefully stepped down onto the pavement. Mickey was close behind.

A fuel truck pulled up. The driver, a teenager wearing a rain poncho, got out and approached them. "Heard you on the radio, sir," said the driver. "It's going to get worse. Thought I'd help you tie it down."

Mickey looked at the wings shaking in the wind. "Good idea."

"The lady can wait in the truck."

Gina took off the jacket and handed to Mickey. "Here. You're going to need this more than I am."

Mickey nodded and slipped on the jacket. Gina ran for the truck. The driver and Mickey quickly tied down the airplane and got into the truck, Gina sandwiched in between.

"I'll give you a ride to the office."

"Thanks." Mickey wiped the rain off his face.

"Kinda rough up there right now," said the boy.

"You could say that," said Gina.

"I don't think we got down any too soon," said Mickey.

Mickey pushed back from the computer and looked up at Gina. "Doesn't look good. These storms are backed all the way into New Mexico. I think we're stuck here for the night."

Lighting lit up the room. A tremendous thunderbolt followed. Gina winced. "I better call Tony. Then I should call the restaurant and tell them I'll be gone for at least another day."

"More like two … maybe three if you go to Vegas with us."

"Damn. I suppose you're right."

"I'll go check on accommodations for the night."

Gina nodded and flipped open her phone. She accessed the number Tony had given them.

A man with a Spanish accent answered. "Hello?"

"Hello. I'm looking for Tony Boccaccio."

"Just a moment." Gina heard him yell, "Tony! It is for you."

She heard some noise in the background, then, "Gina?"

"Tony, we've got a problem."

"You haven't crashed somewhere have you?"

"No, thank god. But we were forced down by the weather."

"Shit. When will you be here? We were just getting ready to drive to the airstrip."

A lightening strike was so close that the thunder was instantaneous. "I don't know what it's like where you are, but it's like the seventh circle of hell around here."

"Where is that?"

"Laredo."

"Does me no good at all. How far away is that?"

"Mickey tells me it's about 150 miles."

"You're that close and can't make it, eh?"

"No way. What's it like there?"

"Well, it is a little stormy."

"A little?"

"Okay, it's raining like a cow pissing on flat rock and the wind is howling like a banshee … but other than that it's fine."

"We're going to have to ride this thing out here. Mickey needs to get … we both need to get a decent night's sleep anyway."

"When can I look for you?"

"I don't know. We'll call you in the morning."

"What time?"

"I don't know. Seven o'clock, okay?"

"I guess that's it, then?"

"That's it. I'll talk to you then." Gina flipped the phone shut just as Mickey walked up.

"There's a motel about a mile from here. They have a restaurant there too. The FBO offered their crew car but I sent for a cab. Some other helpless pilot might fly in here yet tonight and need transportation."

"Sounds good. I'm exhausted."

Tony put down the phone and walked back into the living room. "Looks like my friends can't make it. The storm has them pinned down in some place called Laredo. They won't be able to make it here until tomorrow morning at the earliest."

"So, you're staying with us," said Ray.

"You sure?"

"Sure I'm sure. You're staying."

"I'm not sure when they will be here tomorrow."

"Don't worry about it. I'm off tomorrow anyway."

"Damn, that's mighty kind of you."

"That's the way we are around here. We take care of strangers. Come on, let's eat.

18

A thunderclap shook the house. "Holy Madre," said Raymond.

"No offense there Ray, but these things don't have the greatest reputation for safety."

"Don't worry, Tony. We have been through many storms out here."

"It only takes one. Seems like every time there is a news report about a tornado they are showing footage of some trailer park that has been leveled."

"This is not a trailer, Tony. It is a modular house. And it is very well built."

"If you say so, Ray. Would you mind giving me another piece of that cornbread, Paco?" He held out his plate to Paco. "I can't believe how good this stew is, Flo. I never had rabbit before."

Paco and his younger sister, Ellie, sat in amazement watching their dinner guest. His Bronx accent, brusque manner and ill-fitting clothes were strange enough, but what really struck them was the way their father and mother seemed to tolerate his overly familiar approach. Most strangers in their world spoke in polite monotones; 'yes sir', 'no ma'am', 'thank you kindly' was likely all you'd hear. But Tony, who hadn't known them for more than a few hours, was talking like he knew them intimately.

Tony washed down his last bite of cornbread with a swig of Dos Equis. "Flo, that's the best rabbit stew I ever ate. Of course, it's the only rabbit stew I ever ate."

Flo smiled. "Thank you, Tony."

"I'm going to a rancher's meeting tonight," said Raymond.

Flo frowned. "You're not going out in this storm are you?"

"How's a little rain going to make a difference?"

"What about Tony?"

"Tony's going with me."

"What?" said Tony.

"We're going to a rancher's meeting."

"Don't you think I might be a little out of place?"

"Not at all. We do a little business and then we have a few drinks and a have some fun."

"You sure that I wouldn't stick out like a sore thumb."

"Of course you will. But that's okay. They're good guys and if you're with me you'll be all right."

Tony looked at Flo. She was gently shaking her head no. He looked at Paco and Ellie. They just sat and stared at him with wide eyes. *What the hell.* "Sure I'll go with you Ray."

"Great. Paco, you and Ellie help your mother clean up." Paco nodded.

"Come on, Tony."

Tony followed Ray out of the kitchen into a vestibule that led out to the back. Ray grabbed a poncho off a hook and handed to Tony. "Here, you'll need this."

Tony took it and watched Ray grab another one and put it over his head. Tony followed him out the door. The thunder and lightening had finally subsided but it was still raining hard. Ray started to dash across the yard to his truck. He stopped and turned to look at Tony who was standing under the overhang of the back door. "You coming?" he asked.

Tony looked at the poncho in his hand like it was the most ridiculous thing he had ever seen. He shrugged his shoulders. *What the hell.* He slipped on the poncho and followed after Ray. Wally came running after them, barking wildly.

"Oh shit," said Tony as he moved behind Ray.

"Wally! Stop it," yelled Ray.

Then Paco appeared. He too was wearing a poncho. Wally ran in circles, splashing in the puddles of rain, happy to have his favorite people near by.

"Paco, I thought I told you to help your mother."

"Ellie's helping her. I want to go with you, pop."

"You're mother would have my hide."

"She doesn't care."

"Yes she does. I'm not taking you tonight. Maybe sometime when your mother is visiting Tia Maria. Now go feed Wally."

"Come on, pop …"

"Not tonight, Paco. Now get out of here."

Paco shrugged. "Come on, Wally." The dog eagerly followed him.

"Thank god that hound is gone," said Tony.

"You don't like dogs?" asked Ray.

"Not ones that look like they'd like to have me for dinner."

"Wally is harmless."

"That's what they all say."

Harlan's Corners consisted of three buildings: a Chevron gas station, Harlan's Feed & Grain, and Sonny's Cantina. The cantina was a Victorian house from the turn of the twentieth century. The brick exterior was thick with countless coats of paint, of which the current color appeared to be a washed-out beige under the vapor lights that surrounded it. The entrance was on the side of the building, up a couple of broken cement steps. Just inside the door was a pool table and the two men playing stopped and looked up a Ray and Tony as they entered and shook off the rain.

"Hey, Henry, Bill," said Ray.

"How's it, Ray?" said Henry, a burly man with a three-day growth and wearing greasy Houston Astros cap. The other man just nodded.

"Good, good. The boys here?"

Henry poked his thumb in the direction of a second room, separated from the first by a large archway. "Not too many showed up tonight."

"Not surprised. Real gully-washer tonight."

"Yep," said Henry as leaned back over his shot.

They walked past the bar, through the archway into the other room, which was set up more like a restaurant than a bar. Several tables were shoved together, enough to accommodate 16 or 20 people, but only six seats were filled. All were middle-aged on up, grizzled hard-looking men who worked outdoors. Most had a beer or a drink of some sort parked in front of them. They all looked up when Ray and Tony walked up.

"How's it, Ray?" two of them said almost simultaneously.

"Good, good. What's going on?"

"Not much. Don't have enough for quorum tonight so we're just chewing the rag. Who's your friend?" The speaker, a thin cowboy, mid-forties, hat pushed back on his curly head, sat at the head of the table.

"Oh, this is Tony."

"Hi, Tony," said the cowboy. "I'm Angelo. This is Leonard, Cyril, Mark, Sid, and Ted." Each man around the table nodded and said hello to Tony as he was introduced. Tony said hello back to each one.

"How do you know Ray?" asked Angelo.

"We just met today."

"Paco found Ray out by Devil's Ridge this morning. Wearing nothing but his skivvies."

"Really?"

"Yeah, but it's kind of a long story …," said Tony.

"Sounds like an interesting one." Angelo waved to a pair of empty chairs. "Why don't you sit down and tell us. I'm getting tired of hearing the same bullshit I hear every week anyway."

They sat down, ordered beers from the waitress who followed them to the table, and Tony proceeded to tell them about how he ended up in Ray's company.

"No shit? And these were your friends?" said Angelo after Tony finished telling them his story. He seemed to speak for the others who just sat staring at Tony.

"More like acquaintances. I knew them in Miami."

"I guess I've been that drunk," said Leonard, a round-faced man with salt and pepper hair pouring out from under a faded Carhartt cap.

They all laughed at that.

"You may get that drunk tonight, Lenny," said Cyril, a white haired man sitting next to Leonard.

That seemed to break the ice. The men relaxed, ordered more drinks and went on with the idle chat and good-natured bantering that was typical of a rancher's meeting. By nine o'clock Mark, Sid and Ted had left and Cyril was getting up to go.

"Can you give me a ride, Cyril?" asked Leonard.

"You still don't have your license?" asked Cyril.

"Hell no. I've got another two months to go before I can even apply for a reinstatement."

"How'd you get here?"

"Carl dropped me off on the way home from work."

"You've been here since this afternoon?"

"Yeah."

"Come on, then, I'm getting your ass home."

Cyril and Leonard brushed past the waitress as they left.

"See you Lenny, Cyril," she said. "You boys leaving too?" she asked.

"One more round, Tammy," said Angelo.

Tammy looked at Ray. "You too?"

Ray looked at his watched. "Yeah, sure. Another round for me and my friend."

"You got it."

After Tammy retreated to the bar in the other room, Angelo leaned forward. "Got some matches going on over a Pablo's tonight. I'm thinkin' about headin' over there. You interested, Ray?"

"Hell no. Flo would kick my ass if she knew I went to a cockfight. She hates those things."

"What did you have to do? Check your balls with Flo before you left tonight?" said Angelo.

"Did you say 'cockfight'?" asked Tony.

"Yeah, why?" said Ray.

"Really? You're going to a cockfight, Angelo?"

"If I can talk your friend into going."

"Come on, Ray. That sounds like fun."

"I dunno, it's getting late …"

"Hey, aren't cockfights illegal?" asked Tony.

Angelo smiled. "Yes, they are."

Tony slapped Ray on the back. "Well, hell, then, let's go."

They followed Angelo to a ranch about five miles down the road. The rain had subsided, but lighten flashes still filled the sky to the east followed by distant rumbles of thunder. The yard of the ranch was filled with pick-ups and SUV's of all sorts. Ray pulled into a spot next to Angelo. The two-story clapboard house was dark. But Tony could see light streaming out of the wide-open doors of a barn in the back. Men, dressed mostly in denim, and cowboy boots, many wearing rain ponchos, were walking up and down the muddy path leading to the barn.

"This looks like quite a hoedown," said Tony as they joined Angelo standing next to his truck.

"It is," said Angelo.

They walked toward the barn. Ray and Angelo said hello to several of the men they passed on the path. Most said hello back. Some just nodded. Several stopped and stared at Tony as he passed.

"Friendly crowd," said Tony. "You sure I should be here?"

"You'll be fine. Just stick with me," said Ray.

"Like white on rice, pal."

They stepped inside the barn. It was much larger than the building behind Ray's house. More of a traditional barn with animal stalls and bails of hay stacked to one side. Farm equipment hung from the walls. In the center was a circular arena, about ten feet in diameter and surrounded by a fence of chicken wire about three feet high. Men were milling about everywhere, talking and smoking.

They worked their way over to a table where several men were handling birds. One of them, a small, wiry man with a weathered face was holding a smoky gray bird with iridescent blue-black tail feathers. "Javier," Angelo yelled.

Javier looked up. He smiled when he recognized Angelo. "Amigo."

"You brought Tornado."

"He is going to make me some money tonight. Who is this?"

"This is Ray's friend, Tony."

Holding his bird with both hands, Javier could only nod at Tony. "Nice to meet you."

"Nice bird," said Tony.

"You know fighting birds?" asked Javier.

"Not really. What are those?" Tony pointed to a velvet lined jewel box on the table that contained an assortment of shiny, precision stainless steel knifes.

"These are gaffs."

"Those look deadly."

"They are."

"Javier pays top dollar for his blades," said Angelo.

Tony watched Javier select a knife and gird it to the bird's own blunted spur, lashing it with surgical precision with what appeared to be catgut, taking care not to slash himself with the razor-sharp blade. Then Javier and another man holding a rust-colored bird made their way to the arena, which was now surrounded by at least four rows of men.

Calmed by their handlers' deliberate caresses and soothed by words muttered in low voices, the high-strung and excitable birds were quiet while the referee measured and verified each contestant's fighting equipment. Men surrounding the arena sized up the two combatants, deciding the odds for the match, and began to make bets.

Satisfied the warriors met the qualifications, the referee signals the fight is about to commence. The handlers begin to arouse their birds, swinging them back and forth, and building up energy. The excitement grows and the men who had been quietly wagering begin shouting to place last second bets.

At the referee's signal, Javier and the other man position their birds about a foot away from a line drawn in the dirt. At first, the warriors advance slowly, sizing up the competition, daring the other to strike first. The fight begins to resemble a boxer's pattern of jab and parry, searching for the opponent's vulnerable zone. Then, in a fraction of the time devoted to its preliminary ceremony and ritual, there is a flurry of feathers and just as suddenly, the birds are separated. They are resuscitated, repositioned and encouraged to go at it once again. The pattern is repeated several times until the gray bird finally surrenders, unwilling to fight anymore.

Javier gathered up Tornado and made his way through the crowd. His face flushed as boos and catcalls reverberated in the barn, the spectators disappointed with the meek showing of Javier's bird.

"That's it?" asked Tony.

"That's it," said Angelo.

"How many of these matches will they hold?"

"Depends on how many birds there are. Sometimes they will go all night."

Javier joined them, holding Tornado.

"Looks like you have dinner for tomorrow," said Angelo.

"I don't understand." Javier shook his head. "I thought he was primed and ready to kick some ass tonight."

"Did you give him some Viagra?"

Before Javier could answer, he was distracted by a commotion at the front door.

"It's a raid!" somebody yelled from nearby.

Tony looked toward the door. "What the f ..."

Ray grabbed him by the arm. "Cops. Let's go."

Men started pouring out the doors. "Stay with the crowd," yelled Angelo.

But a logjam at the door kept the crowd from moving. Ray pulled Tony toward a side entrance. "Let's go this way."

Angelo shouted again. "Stay with the crowd ... they can't get us all." Ray ignored him and kept pulling Tony toward the side door.

They stepped out into the damp air and almost into the arms of a huge Texas Ranger. "Where you boys goin'?"

"We were just leaving, officer," said Ray. "We didn't know what was going on here.

"Right. Come with me."

Ray looked at Tony. "I knew I shouldn't have come."

"Dean, come over here." Another cop was scuffling with some cowboys near a pickup.

"You boys wait here." Dean hurried off to help his colleague.

"Let's get out of here," whispered Tony.

"But …," Ray stammered.

"Come on." This time Tony grabbed Ray.

"Hey!" Dean shouted at them.

Without looking back, Tony pulled Ray into a thicket that ran down the side of the barn.

Dean shook a fist at them and turned back to help the other cop.

Tony stood hunched over, his hands on his knees. "You guys sure know how to have fun."

"I knew I shouldn't have come." Ray was hunched next to Tony behind a row of bushes.

"So they can arrest us for just being here?" said Tony.

"No. They can only arrest the guys who have a chicken in the ring … and those who are actually gambling."

"So what's the big deal?"

"The rest they try to detain to get names and addresses for witnesses … and to keep track of who is going to these things. Flo would be very angry with me if she knew I was here."

"No shit?"

"No shit."

They both peeked up over the top of the bushes and surveyed the scene. Several police cars were scattered around, lights flashing. Flashlights were streaming this way and that, bouncing off men who were scattering in all directions, splashing through puddles. Trucks were trying to get out of the parking lot, but a police car at the entrance blocked them. Two cops were escorting a handcuffed Javier out the front, one of them holding a small cage with Tornado inside.

"Now what?" asked Tony.

"I can't leave here without my truck," said Ray.

"Where is it?"

Ray pointed. His truck was near the entrance, but was pinned, front-end first, against a cottonwood tree by a rusty Ford Bronco that had backed in after it.

"Isn't your truck a four-wheel drive?" asked Tony.

"Yeah, so?"

"Give me your keys."

"What do you think you're going to do?"

"I'm going to get your truck. Just give me the keys."

Ray shrugged and handed the keys to Tony. "Meet me along the fence by the road … but on this side of the fence."

"You sure about this?"

"This is an area of expertise for me, Ray. Trust me. Now meet me by the fence." Tony pointed to a spot by the fence about 100 yards down from the entrance, away from the house. He slipped out from behind the bushes and started picking his way through the trucks and SUV's that were parked half-hazardly around the yard. Ducking occasionally when a flashlight beam would swing by.

He got to the cottonwood tree and looked around it. Three cops were standing in front of the Bronco, stopping trucks that were trying to get out. Others were starting to leak out across the front yard of the house toward a gate on the far side of the house, but a police car had pulled up to block that entrance as well.

Tony crept around the tree and made his way to the driver's side of Ray's truck. He unlocked the door and pulled it open just enough to get inside. Keeping his head down, he started the truck. He peeked up over the seat. The cop standing in front of the Bronco looked around. He must have heard the engine start but, in all the commotion, could not determine where it came from.

Making sure the four-wheel drive was engaged, Tony slipped the truck into gear and nudged the truck backward until the rear bumper of the truck was touching the rear bumper of the Bronco. He floored it and the Bronco began sliding forward on the wet grass.

The cop looked around. He spotted the Bronco sliding toward him. "Hey, what hell …?"

Tony moved the Bronco about six feet then threw the truck into 'drive'. Grass and gravel bounced off the Bronco and made the cop duck. He turned the wheel hard to the right. The back end spun around, spraying debris everywhere. Before he hit the fence, he turned hard to the left and floored it again. There was just enough room between the tree and the fence to slip through and Tony made it with inches to spare.

He looked in the rear view mirror to see the cop regain his footing and start to run after him. He saw Ray running toward the fence 75 yards away. The truck covered the distance in a heartbeat and Tony slammed on the brakes. Ray jumped in and Tony jammed it back into gear. The cop was almost on them, but dove for cover when the wheels started spewing more mud and gravel. Another 100 yards down the fence and Tony flicked on the lights.

"Just keep running the fence line," yelled Ray. "There's another gate about a quarter mile up.

Concentrating on driving, Tony grinned. "You got it."

They bounced along the ground, running over low shrubs and through larger ones until they reached an opening in the fence. Tony hit the brakes and spun the car to the right. The wheels squealed when they hit the pavement. He jerked the truck to the left and fishtailed down the road. Ray looked over his shoulder at the scene behind them. Red and blue lights were everywhere and white flashlight beams careened amidst them, but no headlights were following them.

"Madre de Dios," said Ray.

Tony laughed.

"Where did you learn to drive like that, Tony?"

"I told you this was an area of expertise."

"What about Angelo?"

"Angelo's a big boy, Ray, he can take care of himself. If we went back there now then we'd all be in the soup. You don't want Flo coming to bail your ass out of jail do you?"

"No."

"Well, then, let's just keep booking."

It was just before midnight when Tony pulled into Ray's driveway. The house was dark. "Pull around to the back," said Ray. The truck splashed through big puddles. "Shsssssh."

"I'm driving as quiet as I can." Tony drove up to the barn and stopped. He turned the truck off and handed the keys to Ray. "That was fun."

"Come on into the barn. Let's have a drink."

"Now you're talking."

Tony followed Ray into the barn and Ray flicked on the lights. It was about 25 by 20 feet and filled to the rafters with farm equipment. Wally came running up, barking wildly.

"Jesus," said Tony.

"Be quiet," said Ray in hoarse whisper. Wally ran in a circle in front of Ray. He grabbed the dog by the head and looked him in the eyes. "Calm down." Wally whimpered, but his tail wagged so hard it was banging a garbage can. "Calm down, Wally," whispered Ray. Wally finally lay down at Ray's feet.

"What is it with these damn dogs?" said Tony.

"He's a good dog, but he's Paco's. He doesn't obey me so well." Ray went over to a shelf that was filled with paint cans. He moved a few cans and pulled out a bottle of tequila. He took a drink from the bottle and offered it to Tony.

Tony took a step toward Ray and stopped when Wally made a rumbling growl in his throat. Tony looked down at the dog. "What?"

"Wally. Stop it," said Ray.

The dog stopped, but Tony kept his eyes on him as he backed toward Ray. He took the bottle from Ray, tipped it toward Wally, and took a long pull. He lowered the bottle and flapped his arm. "Damn."

"Good, eh?"

"Yeah." He took another pull. As he lowered the bottle he gestured to a tall safe in the corner. "What's that?"

"Oh, that's my gun safe."

"Oh yeah? What kind of guns do you have?"

"Come on, I'll show you."

They walked over to the safe; Wally sprang up and followed them, keeping a wary eye on Tony. Ray opened the safe, reached in and pulled out a Browning 12 gauge shotgun and handed it to Tony.

Tony set the bottle on top of the safe and took the Browning. "Nice gun."

"You know about guns, Tony?"

"A little."

"Are you a hunter?"

"Not really."

Ray looked at Tony. He took the shotgun back from him a replaced it in the safe.

"What else do you have in there?" asked Tony.

Ray pulled out a lever action Marlin 30/30 and handed to Tony.

Tony held the gun up and worked the lever. "Damn, this is like something from a cowboy movie."

"Great for deer hunting."

"You got anything … you know … smaller in there?"

"You mean a handgun?"

"Yeah."

Ray reached up to the top shelf and pulled down a replica 1873 Colt Single Action .45 caliber revolver. "This is my target toy." He handed it to Tony.

"Wow. This really *is* from a damn cowboy movie." Tony held the revolver up and sighted along the barrel. "Jeez, this thing is heavy as a rock."

"It kicks like a mule, too."

"How do you shoot the damn thing?"

"It's a single action revolver."

"What's that mean?"

Ray held out his hand for the gun. Tony handed it to him. "You have to pull back the hammer like this." He cocked the hammer. "Then you pull the trigger." He pointed the gun at the ground and pulled the trigger. Then he handed it back to Tony.

"Oh yeah. Just like the gunfighters." Tony cocked it and pulled the trigger. "You just use this for target practice?"

"Mostly. I take it with me when I'm hunting … for snakes and things."

"You interested in selling it?"

"Selling it?"

"Yeah. I'd like to buy it."

"I don't think so."

"What'd you pay for this?"

Ray rubbed his chin. "I think it was 350 dollars."

"I'll give you 500 for it. What do you think about that?"

"500 dollars?"

"Cash."

"What would you want a gun like this for?"

"I just like the way it looks."

"You could get your own from any dealer for three or four hundred."

"I know. I just don't like shopping. How about it?"

Ray took off his cap and rubbed his head. "I don't know, Tony …"

"Come on, Ray. You can get a new one and still have 150 left over. How can you beat that?"

"I can't. I just don't think it's a good idea to sell you a gun. There are rules about that kind of thing and I'm not a licensened dealer …"

"License, schmicense. Who's gonna know?"

"What are you going to do with it?"

"I'll probably just hang it on the wall in my den. It'll be a souvenir of my visit here with you."

"Souvenir?"

"Sure. A little memento of you and your family … you guys have been great to me."

"Well …"

Tony hefted the gun. "500 dollars, Ray."

"I sure could use a little extra cash right now."

"Sure you could."

"All right. I'll sell it to you."

"Oh, have you got any ammunition for it?"

"I thought you just wanted to hang it in your den?"

"You know I'm going to want to try it out … at least once."

Ray reached up on the shelf and pulled down a box of cartridges. He opened the box. "Looks like there are about a dozen bullets here. I'll throw them in."

"Thanks, that's great." Tony took the box and stuffed it in his shirt pocket. "Oh, and one more thing." Tony smiled sheepishly. "I can't give you the money until tomorrow."

Ray cocked his head. "Oh?"

"Yeah. I guess I lost my wallet. I'll have to get the money when my friends come to pick me tomorrow."

Ray looked at his own clothes draped over Tony. "Oh, yeah, that's right. You were in your skivvies when Paco found you."

"So I'll give you the money tomorrow?"

"Sure. Okay."

Tony grabbed the bottle off the safe and handed it to Ray. "We'll drink on it."

19

"Tony, telephone."

Tony opened his eyes and was staring at a pair of hairy legs. He followed the legs up, past the boxer shorts and T-shirt to the unshaven face of Ray Morales. "Huh?"

"A telephone call for you, I think it is your friends."

Tony looked around the room. The morning sun was blazing through the windows. The picture of the Virgin Mary smiled down on him. Slowly, he gained enough consciousness to become aware that he was lying on the couch in the Morales's living room. He sat up and rubbed his face. His tongue was thick and his head was pounding again. "Two nights in a row. Jesus. I just can't do that anymore."

"Flo was plenty pissed at me, too."

Tony stood up shakily. He was in his skivvies again, his borrowed clothes draped over the end of the couch. He pulled the pants on and followed Ray into to the kitchen. Flo was making coffee. "Good morning, Flo."

Flo nodded without looking at him.

"See, I told you she was pissed," said Ray.

Tony grinned in sympathy. He picked up the phone. "Yeah?"

"How'd your evening go?" asked Gina.

"You wouldn't believe me if I told you."

"That was quite a storm, eh?"

"That was just the half of it."

"How's the weather there now?" asked Gina.

Tony squinted through the kitchen window. Billowy cumulus clouds drifted in a cobalt blue sky. "Looks fine."

"That's good. We should be there around 9:00."

"Just a second." Tony put his hand over the phone. "They will be here at 9:00. Is that okay for you?"

Ray sat at the kitchen table. "That's fine."

"Yeah, that's good, Gina."

"Okay, we'll see you then."

"Great." Tony hung up the phone.

"What time is it?" asked Tony.

Ray looked up at the clock over the sink. "7:15."

"Is that enough time for a cup of coffee and a shower?"

Ray nodded.

"That okay with you, Flo?"

Flo wiped her hands on her apron. "You boys will do what ever you want anyway."

Tony cringed. "Ooo, she is pissed, Ray. Don't be mad at Ray, Flo … he was just being a good host … showing me around."

"I'll get over it," said Flo.

Mickey looked up from his eggs when Gina sat back down in the booth. "Everything okay?"

"He sounded hung over."

"Is he going to be able to make it to the strip?"

"That's what he said."

Mickey took a sip of his coffee. A decent night's sleep and hot shower had done wonders for his disposition, but he was still questioning his sanity. "Did you check in with the restaurant?"

"I called Levi last night. He said we had a banner weekend but he managed to keep everything going smoothly. I could tell he was upset that I wasn't there."

"Are you sure you want to go through with this?"

"No. But, I don't feel like I have a choice. Tony is way out on limb and I just can't let him fall without at least trying to save him. What about you?"

"I must be out of my goddamn mind."

Gina reached across the table and put her hand on Mickey's arm. "Well, I appreciate you hanging in. Hopefully once we get to Vegas we can reel Tony in and go home."

"I sure as hell hope so, but it sure would be nice if he got the money."

Gina pulled her arm away. "You don't think he has a chance of that do you?"

"If he doesn't I'm going to be out a bundle."

"I'll make sure your expenses are covered."

Mickey realized how mercenary he was sounding. He wished he had not made such a big issue about the money. "It's not your problem."

"No. But Tony is. I don't want you to get hurt because he is such a moron."

"Neither should you. I knew when I took this charter that something wasn't right, but I let my greed overrule my brain … as usual."

"I'm really sorry about that."

"Like I said, it's not your fault." Mickey reached for the check.

Gina grabbed it first. "Time for me to start picking up expenses." She reached into her purse and pulled out a credit card.

Mickey stared at the card.

"What's the matter? Is your manhood threatened when a lady picks up the check?"

Mickey blushed. "No."

"What is it?"

"You have a credit card."

"Of course I do. Why?"

"It's just that … well, Tony said his people 'didn't carry credit cards.'"

"Tony watches too many gangster movies."

"I hope you're not still mad at me," said Tony.

"She is, but she'll get over it," said Ray through the window of the truck.

Flo gave Tony a hug. "He's right. But you take care, Tony."

At first Tony's arms hung loosely by his side, then he slowly raised them and patted Flo on the back. "Thanks for all your help."

"You're welcome." Flo let go and back away. "I hope you find whatever it is that you're looking for."

"Me too." Tony opened the door of the truck and slid into the front seat next to Paco.

Ray turned the truck around and started down the driveway. Tony waved at Flo who was now standing on the porch of the house.

"Great wife you have there, Ray."

"Yes, she is."

They drove the ten miles to Bromly's ranch and pulled up to the main gate to a speaker mounted on a pole. Ray leaned out of the window and pressed the speaker button. "This is Ray Morales. My wife talked to someone yesterday about meeting an airplane at your airstrip."

A voice crackled back from the box. "Follow the driveway for a mile. At the t-intersection, turn to the right and follow the road to the strip."

A few seconds later the gate began to slide open and Ray drove down an asphalt road lined with cottonwood trees. Beyond the trees to the left was a manicured lawn. To the right was a fenced pasture where horses grazed.

"The Bromly ranch is the biggest spread in the county," said Ray.

"Really?" Tony gazed at the vast open spaces beyond the trees.

"Yep. The Bromly's have been here since the 1880's.
They think everyone else who lives around here is a
newcomer. But my people have been here a whole lot
longer than that … they just didn't think to buy up every
acre they could get their hands on. Of course they couldn't
have even if they wanted to. But we think this place is as
much ours as it is the Bromly's, right Paco?" Ray slapped
Paco on the knee.

Ray turned at the intersection and followed the road
over pastureland that eventually ended and gave way to
scrubby brush land. The road itself turned to gravel and
ended after another half-mile at a large pole barn that served
as a hanger and 3000- foot asphalt runway. A barbed-wire
fence, meant to keep livestock from wandering onto the
runway, surrounded the entire airstrip. Ray parked at an
opening in the fence that was closed by an un-locked chain-
link gate.   The wind moaned over the open land, stirring up
dust devils here and there.

They went inside the gate and walked around the
hanger, which was secured by a metal locked door.   A
security camera stared down blankly at them from the roof
of the building. There didn't appear to be anyone around.
They walked back to the truck and waited.

Paco stopped throwing stones at a fence post and
pointed toward the south. "There it is!"

Tony squinted in the bright sunlight. He could just
make out a speck in the crystal blue sky. "Maybe."

Ray, leaning up against the fender of the truck next to
Tony, shaded his eyes and looked in the direction that Paco
was pointing. "The boy has eyes like a hawk."

Soon enough the dot on the horizon grew and they
could hear the sound of the twin Lycomings as *Songbird*
banked onto the downwind. They watched the airplane

circle the strip, turn onto final and descend to the far end of runway. A puff of white smoke appeared as the tires touched the asphalt; a moment later they heard the audible chirp. As *Songbird* rolled out, Tony entered the gate and walked toward the hanger. The plane met them there, swinging around so it was pointed back down the runway. The props rapidly came to a stop and the door popped open.

Gina stepped out onto the wing as Tony walked up. "It's about freaking time."

"Hey, nice to see you too." Gina stepped down off the wing onto the ground. She looked at his puffy, red face, a visible lump still on the side of his head, the oversized, used clothes hanging loosely from his body. "You look like hell."

"Not surprising, since I think I was there."

Mickey stepped out onto the wing.

"Ace! You made it."

"Not exactly Dallas/Fort Worth International." Mickey stepped down onto the ground. Then, he too noticed Tony's appearance. "You join a rodeo?"

"Don't start, Ace." Then Tony turned to Gina. "You still have that money from the Caddy, right?"

Gina rolled her eyes. "Oh, oh."

Tony nodded toward Ray still leaning on his truck. "You see that guy standing over there?"

"Yeah?"

"I owe him 500 dollars."

"And I should care because …"

"Because I need 500 dollars of the money I gave you to hold for me."

"It's your money." Gina opened her purse and pulled out the money.

Tony took the money. He waved to Mickey. "Come on, I want you two to meet the people who rescued me from purgatory."

They walked over to Ray. Paco had resumed throwing stones at the fence post and continued to do so, ignoring the adults.

"Ray, I want you to meet some friends of mine."

Ray stood up and wiped his hands on his jeans.

"This is my cousin, Gina."

"Hello." Ray offered his hand.

Gina shook it. "Nice to meet you, Ray."

"And this is Ace."

"Mickey Soto," Mickey corrected Tony as he shook Ray's hand.

"And that's Paco, my savior."

Paco stopped throwing stones. "Hi."

"If Paco hadn't found me out in the brush yesterday, I'd be coyote food by now."

"You poor folks got stuck with this loser?" said Gina.

"Tony is a funny guy," said Ray.

"He is that."

Tony put his arm around Ray and directed him to the rear of the truck. "Step into my office."

Gina and Mickey were left to watch Paco resume throwing stones. Mickey picked up a stone and tossed it at the fence post, missing by several feet. "So, Paco, you found Tony?"

"Yes," said Paco between throws.

"Where was that?"

Paco stopped and pointed to the north. "Out there."

"He was by himself?"

"He was laying on the ground … didn't have on nothin' but his underwear."

"No kidding?"

"Nope."

"What were you doing out there?"

"Hunting rabbits."

"How did you get Tony out?"

"On Rios."

"Your horse?"

"Yep." Paco started throwing stones again.

"You brought Tony out of the desert on horseback?"

"Yep."

Mickey laughed. "I sure as hell wish I could have seen that."

Tony and Ray came back from the rear of the truck. Tony was carrying a paper grocery bag. "Well, we better get going," he said. "Ray, if you're ever in Miami, you stop at Paesano's and you'll get a full course dinner on me."

Ray shook Tony's hand. "I'll do that."

Tony walked over to Paco and held out a piece of paper. "And Paco, if you ever need anything, you give ol' Tony a call. I don't have my phone right now, but I will."

Paco stopped throwing and took the paper. "Thanks, Tony." He stuffed the paper into his pocket and started throwing again.

Tony turned to Gina and Mickey. "All right then, let's hit it."

20

A few cows turned to look as *Songbird* gathered speed and lifted off the runway. But when the little airplane was out of sight and the dust settled they went back to their idle grazing.

Gaining altitude quickly, Mickey looked down at the vast Texas landscape. The air was severe clear, the kind that often comes in the west on the backside of a cold front, like the one that spawned the storms of the previous night. Of course, he had seen scenes like these in the past, but on those runs he was always too nervous to enjoy them.

"All right, Tony, tell me what the hell happened," said Gina.

There was no response. Mickey looked over at Gina and pointed to her headset, then jerked his thumb toward the back. Gina turned in her seat and tapped Tony on the knee, startling him from his reverie looking out the window. She pointed to her headset. Tony sighed and put his on.

"What happened back there in New Orleans?" she asked.

"It's a long story," said Tony.

"We've got plenty of time."

"All right. I went to that place we found on the Internet, and sure enough, those sonsabitches were there … well, that stupid RV was there … they weren't. So I went in …"

"How'd you get in?"

"I didn't have a key, so I used a rock. Anyway, I'm looking around in there and I'll be damned if I didn't find the money."

"You found it?"

"Sure did, except that at that moment Vince shows up and gets the drop on me."

"Vince surprised you?"

"That's what I said. So the sonofabitch cold cocks me and the next thing I know I'm sitting at the table across from his asshole partner …"

"Sheldon?"

"Yeah, Sheldon. They decide to get me drunk … I guess so I'll pass out and they can do their thing."

"You're kidding?"

"Nope. The next thing I know I wake up in the middle of the desert and that kid, Paco is standing over me."

"Wait. You're drinking in New Orleans and then you wake up in a desert in Texas?"'

"That's what I'm telling you."

"You don't remember anything from New Orleans until you wake up in Texas?"

"Well, that's not completely true. They think I'm gone, but I hear them talking about meeting Burke in Vegas."

"You're sure you heard that?"

"Absolutely. I was pretty drunk by then but I definitely heard that, but that was about the last thing I heard, 'cause the next thing I know I'm in my underwear on the back of Paco's horse getting baked by the sun. But thank god the kid found me."

Gina laughed.

"You think it's funny that I almost died in the middle of the godforsaken desert?"

"No, but the image of you in your underwear on the back of a horse is." Gina forced herself to get serious again. "So Paco takes you to his house. What happened then?"

"Flo …"

"His mother?"

"Yeah. Flo let's me clean up and gives me some of Ray's old clothes. That's about when I called you."

"So you think Vince and Sheldon are in Vegas?"

"Probably, by now."

"And you think you can still get your money?"

"Damn straight. And now I'm really pissed because they took everything … my clothes, wallet, phone, and, what really pisses me off, the money I still had in my pocket from selling the Caddy. Oh, I'm getting my money back all right … and I'm gonna make those bastards pay for it."

"I thought we were just going after the money … no funny stuff," said Mickey.

"Don't worry, it won't involve you."

"You mean like I haven't been involved so far."

"You just get me to Vegas and you'll get your share."

"I'd rather not do any jail time for it … if I can help it."

"Nothing is going to happen to you, I swear."

The terrain rose quickly, easily getting high enough to require oxygen. Songbird was not pressurized so they had to wear masks. Mickey put his on and showed Gina and Tony what to do. Gina put a mask on, but Tony declined and fell asleep in the back.

After a stop at a small airport in the White Mountains of Arizona to top off the gas and stretch their legs, they continued on to Las Vegas. It was almost four in the afternoon when Mickey received clearance to land at North Las Vegas Airport, a general aviation reliever to the busier and more congested McCarran International.

When Songbird touched down, Tony lurched up in his seat. "What the hell ..."

"We're in Las Vegas," Mickey said.

Tony rubbed his temples. "Jesus, I've got the mother of all headaches.

Mickey turned the plane onto the taxiway. "I'm not surprised. There isn't a lot of oxygen at 12,000 feet."

"Damn. You got any aspirin, Gina?"

"I think so."

Songbird cleared the active runway and Mickey followed taxi instructions to the General Aviation FBO.   A fuel truck was waiting and the driver provided hand signals to a parking space in front of a large hanger. Mickey shut down the engines and popped open the door so Gina could exit. He followed her out onto the wing, and, after she stepped down, helped Tony unfold from the back.

"Damn," he said as his stiff muscles reacted to the movement. "Give me a minute here."

"Fill it up?" asked the driver.

"That'd be great." Mickey helped Tony climb down to the tarmac. Which way to the john?"

The driver pointed to two-story building next to the hanger. "Right in there … you can't miss it."

"Goddamn, I can hardly move my legs," said Tony. "Where's that aspirin, Gina?"

Gina handed him a couple of pills. "I'll see you inside, I need to use the little girl's room … right now."

"I'm right behind you," said Mickey.

"Oh, Gina, I need to use your phone," said Tony.

Gina handed him the phone. "I'll meet you inside."

Gina was sitting at a table in the pilot's briefing room, drinking a coke, and Tony was lying on the couch, rubbing his temples, when Mickey walked in.

"Gina, would you mind paying for the gas? I don't want to use the last of my cash if I can help it." Mickey asked.

Gina pulled the wad of bills from her purse. "How much is it?"

"280 dollars."

She peeled off the money and handed it Mickey. "Keep the change."

Mickey walked off to pay the bill.

"You're pretty generous with my money," said Tony.

"Somebody has to take care of the help."

Tony looked at the clock on the wall. "Lou should be here any minute." He had called Louis Martin, a friend from New York. When Mario sent Tony to Florida, Lou went to Vegas and got a job dealing blackjack on the strip. He worked at several casinos, ending up at the MGM Grand, where he eventually worked his way up to pit boss. Lou said he'd be glad to pick them up at the airport and take them to the Vegas Express, a casino that considered Tony a high roller and always made sure he was well compensated.

Another fifteen minutes had passed and Lou had still not shown. "Gina, give me your phone. I'm going to call that idiot."

Tony punched in a number. "Where the hell are you?" Then, after a pause, "What do you mean? We're at the terminal now." Another pause. "What terminal? How the fuck do I know? The terminal at the airport."

Tony looked at Mickey. "What the hell terminal is this?"

"This is the Air Aviation FBO."

To the phone Tony said, "It's ...," then to Mickey, "What the hell did you say?"

"Air Aviation, on the west side of the airport. He is at North Las Vegas, right?"

"He says it's Air Aviation at North Las Vegas, I guess it's the place where the little airplanes go." Then, after a pause, Tony said, "Here you talk to the man." He handed the phone to Mickey.

"Hello?" said Mickey.

A male voice on the other end asked, "Who is this?"

"This is Mickey Soto. I'm the pilot."

"So where is this Air place?"

"On the west side of North Las Vegas Airport. Where are you?"

"The terminal. I've been driving around here for an hour. Just passed the arrival area for the 10th time."

"The arrival area? What airport are you at?"

"Waddaya mean what airport? *The* airport."

"I think you must be at McCarran …"

"Yeah, that's it."

"We're at North Las Vegas … it's about six or seven miles north of McCarran."

"You're kidding? I didn't know there was another airport."

"Yeah, it's a small GA airport …"

"GA?"

"General Aviation … the little planes."

"Oh. Shit."

"Is that out of the way for you, because we can always get a cab …"

"Oh, for crissakes, put Tony back on."

Mickey handed the phone back to Tony.

"Hurry up, will ya," Tony demanded. Then, "Yeah, yeah, we'll be watching for you." He snapped the phone shut. "Jesus. What a moron."

"Who was that?" asked Mickey.

"Louie Martin."

"Who is he?"

"A friend."

"Does he know what is going on?"

"Do you?"

"Good point."

Twenty minutes later they were standing in front of the FBO when a black Lexus pulled up. Tony stepped off the curb and opened the passenger door.

"It's about damn time," he said as he slid in and shut the door.

Mickey and Gina got in the back.

"Hey, you said to pick you up at the airport. So I went to the airport," said Lou.

"How the hell did I know there was more than one airport?"

Lou looked at Tony. "So, what the hell are you made up for?"

"You don't want to know. Just get me to the hotel so I can get some real clothes."

"They might not let you in."

"Very funny." Tony held up the paper bag wrapped handgun he had purchased from Ray. "Where can I put this?"

"What is it?"

Ray opened the bag so Lou could see inside. "Goddamn it, Tony. You haven't been here more than ten seconds and you're already getting me into trouble."

"What? You're telling me you're not packing?"

"Hell no. I don't get involved in that kind of shit anymore. I've got a regular job now and I don't want to mess it up, okay?"

"Don't worry about it, you pansy." Tony opened the glove box and stuffed the bag inside. "Just hang on to that for me."

Lou sighed and looked over the back seat. "You must be Gina."

Gina noticed that Lou's hairline was similar to Tony's, except that he had light-brown hair. His face was long and thin and bushy eyebrows hooded his dark brown eyes. "Yes, nice to meet you." She extended her hand between the seats.

Lou took it and pumped it a couple of times.

"You remember my cousin, Gina, don't you?" Tony asked.

"I've heard you mention her, but we never actually met," said Lou.

"Really?"

"Really."

"You've been in Florida with me."

"Yes, but I never meet Gina. Believe me, I'd remember."

"Hell, you can't even remember your own name, you loser."

Lou shifted his gaze to Mickey. "You must be Mickey."

"Yep," he said.

"Okay, everybody knows everybody. Now, will you shut the hell up and drive?" said Tony.

"Keep your shirt on." Lou slipped the car into gear and pulled out onto Rancho Drive. "You know you might have given me just a little warning that you were coming to Vegas," he said.

"I didn't know I coming myself until yesterday," said Tony.

"Why didn't you call me then?"

"I don't have my phone and couldn't get your number until today."

"Where's your phone?"

"Same place as my clothes."

"And where are they?"

"It's a long story, buddy. I'll tell it to you over dinner."

21

Sporting a theme of mid twentieth-century train travel, the Vegas Station was one of the newest casinos on the strip. Approaching from the strip, the façade resembled Grand Central Station in New York, complete with sculptures of Minerva, Hercules, and Mercury. Lou pulled into the lobby area and a valet, dressed as a porter, was immediately at the door.

Lou got out and handed the boy five dollars. "Park it somewhere close, okay."

"Yes, sir." He opened the rear door for Mickey.

Another valet opened the doors for Tony and Gina. "Are you staying, sir?"

"Yes."

"Can I help you with your luggage?"

"I don't have any."

The boy was unfazed. "What about the lady?"

"She doesn't have any either."

"Okay. The front desk is just inside."

Gina, Mickey and Lou followed Tony inside the huge lobby. It was created in the style of the main concourse of Grand Central Station, albeit to a smaller scale, it still conveyed the cavernous space of the original. Below a vaulted ceiling painted as an evening sky, was the front desk, which resembled the main information booth of the original, including the giant four-faced clock. The exterior wall even featured huge, arched Tiffany glass windows.

Behind the desk, a woman, dressed in a white shirt and bowtie, black coat, and green eyeshade looked up from her computer screen and scanned the group as they approached. She appeared slightly surprised when Tony stepped up to the desk, but then, *this is Vegas*, she thought. "Can I help you?"

"A suite for Boccaccio."

"Just a moment, sir." She looked back down at a computer screen and started banging the keyboard while Tony drummed his fingers on the counter impatiently.

"Could you spell that, sir?"

Tony stopped drumming his fingers and spelled his name slowly and loudly, like he was talking to the village idiot.

"I'm sorry, sir, I don't see a reservation here."

"Of course not ... I didn't make one."

"Then we might have a problem, sir," the woman said nervously. "All the suites are occupied."

"Listen, lady, you call your manager and tell him Mr. Boccaccio is here and you'll be surprised how fast a a suite opens up." Tony said matter-of-factly.

The woman picked up the phone and punched a number. "I'm sorry to bother you, sir, but there is a Mr. Boccaccio here and he is looking for a suite and I'm showing that all the suites are booked." After a few seconds, she said, "Yes, sir," and put down the phone. "I'm so sorry Mr. Boccaccio, I didn't realize that a penthouse suite had been vacated this morning." The woman started tapping the keyboard.

Tony turned to Lou. "Amazing, isn't it?"

"You know the manager here?" said Lou.

"Oh, yeah, I know him.

"Tony!" Boomed a voice from behind them.

They all turned and a tall man, with a handsome, tanned face, dark wavy hair, and dressed in a tailored, pin-stripped suit approached from across the main concourse. "So good to see you again." His voice dripped with a mellow southern accent.

Alton Smith was the general manager of the Vegas Station. He had begun his career in an Atlantic City casino, where he had gotten to know Tony well. Alton liked Tony, even though he was a small fish, as high rollers went, and provided him with many of the perks that were reserved for the really big spenders. Of course, it didn't hurt that Alton also knew who Tony's father was. Two years ago Alton was tagged to run the new casino in Vegas and he brought his whales with him. When the casino opened he flew most of them in to sample the destination. Since then, Tony had been there several times, liberally spending money he had borrowed from Burke, and working his way up the high roller list.

Alton held out his hand, seemingly not noticing Tony's ridiculous garb. "How long are you staying with us this time?"

Tony shook his hand, "Not long, Alton. Maybe a day or two." He looked down at his clothes. "Sorry about the dress …"

"Hadn't noticed," Alton lied.

"Can you help me get some decent threads here?"

"Tony, you know your credit is always good here. Just get whatever you need and charge it to the hotel." Alton looked around at the group.

"Oh, this is Gina, my cousin from Miami."

Alton shook her hand. "Pleased to meet you, Gina."

"Nice joint you got here," she said.

"Thank you. We try."

Tony nodded toward Mickey. "This is Ace … I mean Mickey. He's the pilot who flew us here."

Alton seemed a little surprised that a hired hand would be with Tony, but he shook Mickey's hand anyway. "Hello, Mickey."

Mickey just nodded.

"And this is Lou. He's a dealer over at MGM," said Tony.

"Pit boss," corrected Lou.

Alton smiled. "Ah, bringing in the competition, eh?"

"Oh, I won't be staying," said Lou.

"Well, any friend of Tony's is a friend of ours." Alton turned to the woman behind the desk. "Make sure you take good care of Tony and his friends, Teresa."

"Yes, sir, Mr. Smith. We will."

Alton turned back to Tony. "Well, I've got to get back to running 'this joint'. If you need anything, Tony, anything at all, don't hesitate to let me know."

"Thanks, Alton. I will."

Smiling to the rest of the group, he said, "And nice to meet you all. I hope you enjoy your stay."

"We will," said Gina.

Alton turned and walked back across the concourse.

"Great guy," said Tony.

"I'll have someone take your things up to your suite, Mr. Boccaccio." Teresa's tone had become much more conciliatory.

"Won't be necessary. We don't have any bags."

"Reuben will show you to your room anyway."

The suite vaguely resembled a luxury train compartment, but considerably larger. Art deco wall sconces graced mahogany paneled walls, as did paintings of bucolic landscapes. The furniture was also in a clean, art deco design, as well as the other decorations scattered around the room. There was a fully stocked bar at one end of the room that featured a wine cooler, refrigerator, dishwasher and even a cigar humidor. A huge, flat screen TV dominated one wall. The floor-to-ceiling windows on the outer wall provided a panoramic view of Las Vegas.

Gina went to check the bedrooms at the far end of the room. Lou looked in a second bedroom at the opposite end.

Mickey stood by the large picture windows and looked out onto the Strip. "Impressive," he said.

"Can I do anything else for you, sir?" Reuben said in a thick Hispanic accent.

"Do the windows open?"

"No, sir."

"Too bad." Mickey gazed out the window. Directly below he could see the pool, surrounded by guests basking in the sun underneath a sprinkling of gently swaying palms.

"Will that be all, sir?"

"I guess so."

"Very good." Reuben backed slowly toward the door.

Tony stood behind the bar pouring a drink. "Take care of the man, will you?"

"Oh ... yeah .... thank you." Mickey gave Reuben two dollars.

Reuben starred at the money for a couple of seconds, then turned and left the room.

Lou returned from the bedroom. "Damn. You should see the bathroom in there. The bathtub could hold six people. You've got some serious comps here, Tony."

Tony held up his drink and inspected it. "You ought to get something for dropping a hundred grand in a casino."

Lou plopped down on the couch. "So now what?"

Tony took a drink. "As soon as I get some new threads, you are going to help me find Vince and Sheldon."

"You said they are traveling in an RV?"

"Yeah. They gotta be staying at some RV park around here."

"Tony, there are only about a thousand RV parks in Vegas."

"No shit?"

"No shit."

"Well, they're going to hook up with Burke. If he is in town somebody must have seen him around."

"Burke?"

"Max Burke ... I told you about him."

"The guy who set you up?"

"Yeah ... Burke. He's supposed to meet those guys here. If we can find him, maybe we can find them."

"How do you know they haven't hooked up and moved on already?"

"I don't for sure. But I don't think Vince and Sheldon have been here that long. In fact, I'm not positive they have even arrived yet."

"How do we find Burke?"

"We ask around. He's a big name in Florida, somebody around here must know who he is."

Gina walked in from the other bedroom. "That'll be my room," she said.

Tony ignored her. "Can you start making some calls?" he asked Lou.

"Yeah, I'll check around. But I've gotta work tonight."

"How late do you work?"

"I'll be done by midnight."

"Okay. I'll check things out on my end and I'll call you around twelve fifteen. In the meantime, you call me if you hear anything."

Lou got up to leave. "You got it."

As soon as the door shut after Lou, Mickey sat in his spot on the couch. "So what do we do while you're on your quest?"

"Nothing." Tony took the last swallow of his drink. "I told you that I wouldn't involve you in this, so you and Gina just enjoy the Strip and I'll let you know when it's time to go."

"Can you give me a clue?"

"Tomorrow. The next day at the latest."

"And if you don't get your money?" Gina sat in the chair next to the couch.

"I'll get it. But first I have to get some clothes."

"I'll go with you," said Mickey. "I could use some new underwear and maybe a clean shirt."

"Me too," said Gina.

Tony was on the phone and Mickey was drinking a beer and watching the Florida Marlins play the Dodgers. Mickey tried not to notice Gina in her new summer dress, but she looked like a million dollars and he couldn't help staring. "You look great," he said.

"Thanks. You look refreshed, too."

A shower, new kakis and a polo shirt did wonders. "I'm almost feeling human,"

"Who's winning?"

"Dodgers. Eight to three. Bottom of the seventh. Not looking good for us."

"It may not be our year."

"There's still plenty of time left to turn it around."

Tony hung up the phone. "Damn." He was dressed in a new silk Hawaiian print shirt, black slacks and black loafers.

"No luck, eh?" said Gina.

"Not so far. Seems a lot of people know who Burke is all right, but no one seems to have seen him around. I think I'll just start cruising the Strip … see what I can see."

"How about some dinner? I'm starving."

"Why don't you and Ace grab some dinner … and maybe catch a show or something … just charge it to the room. I'll get some room service."

"You sure you don't want to go?"

"No. I want to make some calls anyway. Which reminds me, can I borrow your cell phone again?"

"Why do you want my phone?"

"I might need to make a call while I'm out and I don't have mine, remember?"

"What about me? I might have to make a call, too. You know?"

"You can use Ace's phone … you have a phone, right, Ace?"

Mickey had been listening to the conversation with interest. He was surprised to find himself glad that Tony wouldn't be having dinner with them. "Yeah, sure, I have a phone."

"Well, there you go. How about it, Gina?"

Gina looked at Mickey, still pretending to watch the game. She reached for her purse. "Okay." She handed the phone to Tony. "Don't lose it."

"Thanks." Tony slipped the phone in his pocket. "Oh, do you have Ace's number in your phone."

"I don't think so."

Tony handed the phone back to her. "Can you put it in? Just in case I need to reach you in a hurry?"

Gina took the phone. "In a hurry?"

"You just never know."

"What's your number, Mickey?"

Mickey gave her the number and she entered it in the directory. She handed the phone back to Tony.

"Thanks." Tony slipped the phone into his pocket. "Oh yeah, one more thing … give me a couple hundred bucks?"

"I thought you could get all the credit you need here."

"I can, but only for action here. I want to move around the Strip a little."

Gina opened her purse and pulled out the money. "Here," she sighed.

22

"What'll you have?" The waiter spoke with a pronounced Brooklyn accent.

"I'll have a vodka martini," said Gina.

"Any particular brand?"

"Stoli."

"Stolichnaya, right. And the gentleman?"

"Glen Livet, neat," said Mickey.

"How about Glen Fiddich?"

"Fine." The waiter retreated to the bar.

Mickey looked at the picture of the California Zephyr winding through the Rocky Mountains that took up almost the entire wall. "That thing is amazing."

Gina looked around the Station Lounge. A train whistle and a brass bell hung over the bar. Railroad signs dominated another wall. Pictures of trains of all sizes and descriptions were scattered through out. "This whole place is amazing. It's like a throwback to a railroad themed bar that you might have seen in the fifties."

"It's kind of neat, though."

"In a kitchy way." She started to light a cigarette. "Will this bother you?"

"No," Mickey lied.

She lit her cigarette. "What did you think of that show?"

"That was amazing too. I've seen those shows on television and was impressed, but seeing it in person is a whole other thing."

"Yes, it is. Where do they get those performers?"

"No idea. The contortionists are the ones that blow me away. How in the hell can they do that?"

"They must train for that from birth."

"Gina?" A deep voice boomed from across the room.

Gina looked around. "Oh shit," she said under her breath."

"Who is it?" asked Mickey.

Before she could answer, a tall, beefy man walked up to their table. Dressed in an opened collar shirt and sport coat, he was obviously in his forties, with wavy, salt and pepper hair, and a round, red-hued face that was still somewhat handsome. "What the hell are you doing here?"

"Just slumming, Barry. How about you?"

"I'm here on business, just stopped in for a nightcap. Sure never expected to see anyone I know." Donahue smiled.

Gina looked at him carefully. "We were at the show. This is my friend, Mickey Soto."

Mickey held out his hand. Donahue's huge hand enveloped it. "Barry Donahue, Mickey."

"Nice to meet you, Barry."

Donahue smiled. "I'd say the same, but I'd rather be sitting where you are, pal."

Mickey blushed. "Oh, we're not …"

"Just kidding, Mickey. Gina's a hell of a girl." He turned to Gina. "Seriously, what are you doing in town?"

"Just here for a little R & R. You know, get away from the restaurant business for a while."

"That doesn't sound like you, Gina. I could hardly pry you out of that place."

The waiter brought their drinks. "Can I get you something, sir?" he asked.

"You mind if I join you?" Donahue asked Gina.

"No, not at all."

"In that case, I'll have a Stoli on the rocks … with a twist," he said to the waiter as he pulled out a chair to sit down.

"Very good, sir."

"So, how's your father?" Donahue asked.

"He's good," said Gina. "He's pretty much retired now. Just fishes and plays golf."

"What about your cousin?"

"Tony? Oh, he's fine."

"That's not what I hear."

Gina snuffed out her cigarette. "Really? What do you hear?"

"I heard he got his tit in a wringer with Burke."

"I wouldn't know anything about that."

"Isn't he still at the restaurant?"

"Yes, but I hardly see him. He just comes around to glad-hand the customers every once in while. That's about all I have to do with him."

"He's not here, in Vegas with you is he?"

Thankfully, Donahue's attention was diverted when the waiter brought his drink. Gina breathed slowly and steadily until he left. "No, he's not," she said. "At least not that I'm aware of."

"That's good, 'cause Burke is in town and it probably wouldn't be too healthy for Tony to run into him."

"Like I said, it's none of my business."

Donahue turned to Mickey. "So what's your line, Mickey?"

"Aviation ... I'm a pilot."

"No shit? Who do you fly for?"

"Oh, I'm not with any of the big carriers ... I'm just a charter service."

"Flying taxi ... that it?"

"Yep, I guess that's as good a description as any."

"Where are you from?"

"Miami."

"You too? Must be one of those corporate jet jockeys."

"Nope ... just my own light twin."

"Really. You fly anywhere?"

"Mostly just around Florida."

"What are you doing all the way out here?"

"This is where my customer wanted to go."

"So, do you fly anywhere."

"Why? You looking to go somewhere?"

"You never know ... you got a card?"

Mickey started to reach for his wallet, then stopped. "It wouldn't do you any good. Like I said I'm based out of Miami."

"Hey, I'm from Miami, too. You never know ... I always like to keep track of people I meet."

Mickey looked at Donahue for a few seconds, then dug his wallet out and proffered a card. "What the hell ... you can always use it to pick your teeth."

Barry looked at the card. "What kind of plane do you have, Mickey."

"A Piper Twin Comanche."

"How big is that ... I mean how many people can you carry?"

Mickey took a sip off his drink. "Comfortably? Two or Three."

"Gee, that is small ... and you came all the way out here?"

"Yeah ... it's pretty unusual, but my passenger wanted privacy."

Donahue looked at Gina. "Who's your passenger?"

"I hired Mickey," said Gina.

Donahue feigned surprise. "Really? You flew all the way out here in Mickey's little airplane?"

"I just didn't feel like dealing with the hoopla of flying commercial. By the time you go through security and fool around, a small charter is just as fast."

"You might have something there. How long does it take to get here?"

"About eleven or twelve hours."

"Which is it? Eleven or twelve? Seem like you'd know that if you flew all the way here."

Mickey looked at Donahue. What was with this guy? He did some quick math in his head. "Eleven."

Donahue shook his head. "That's an awfully long time."

"It's a nice, relaxing flight. And, like I said, no airport hassles," said Gina.

Donahue winked at Mickey. "Hey, whatever blows your skirt up." He looked at Gina and smiled. "So how long are you in town for?"

"A couple of days. You know Vegas … two or three days and you've had your fill."

"I know what you mean. But I wish I had some time to play anyway."

"What business are you in, Barry?" asked Mickey.

"The car business. I run a dealership in Florida."

"Which one?" Mickey took a drink.

"East Florida Imports."

"Where is that?"

"We're in Fort Lauderdale."

"What brings you to Vegas?"

"I here with my boss."

"Who's that?"

"Max Burke"

Mickey choked slightly. "Max Burke?"

"He owns EFI. I just run the joint for him. You know him?"

"No. But I've heard of him."

"Yeah, everyone knows Burke." Donahue looked at his watch. "Speaking of which, I'm supposed to meet him at midnight. I'd better get going." He drained his drink and stood up. "You take care of this lady, Mickey."

"We're not …" Mickey stammered.

"And I hope to see you again … soon," Donahue squeezed Gina's shoulder. "You look fabulous."

"Goodbye, Barry. Maybe I'll see you in Miami sometime."

"Maybe." Donahue pointed his index at her. He turned and walked away.

"Who the hell was that?" asked Mickey.

"Like he said, Barry works for Max Burke. He might work out of the dealership in Fort Lauderdale, but he really spends most of his time doing Burke's bidding … and that includes finding people Burke wants found."

"How do you know him?"

"He used to frequent Paesano's … a couple of years ago he started hitting on me and we went out a few times. I didn't know who he was at the time, but it didn't really matter … he's not my type … nothing came of it."

"He sure seemed pretty interested in how you got here."

"I'm sure he probably thinks Tony is here."

"I got the impression that he thought something was up."

"I should let Tony know he was sniffing around. Can I use your phone?"

"Card?" asked the dealer.

"Huh?" Tony was idly playing blackjack while watching the people coming and going and waiting for Lou to get off work.

"Would you like a card, sir?"

Tony looked up at the dealer, a petite woman, plain face, brown hair pulled back in bun. He looked at his hand. Fourteen. The dealer showed a seven. "Ah, yeah, hit me."

The dealer turned over a king of hearts. "Bust." She picked up his last five-dollar chip.

"Just not my night." Tony got up from the table.

"Sorry, sir."

"You win some, you lose some."

"Goodnight, sir."

Tony walked to the lobby. He watched the living statues for a while, making faces and trying to make them smile. Gina's phone started ringing. He walked outside and flipped it open. "Yeah?"

"I just saw Barry Donahue," said Gina.

"You're kidding."

"No. Mickey and I were having a drink at the hotel and Barry walks up out of nowhere."

"Son of a bitch."

"He was pretty nosey, too. I'm pretty sure he suspects that you're in town."

"Well, that's too bad. Takes away the element of surprise."

"Are you going to abandon this hair brained scheme so we can go home?"

"Hell no. I'm getting my money … if I have to shoot Burke himself to get it."

"Don't be an idiot, Tony. It just not worth that kind of grief."

"Maybe not to you. But it's a matter of honor now. The line was crossed when those two yin-yangs dumped me in the desert to die."

Gina knew there was no point in pressing the issue. "It's your funeral. I just thought you like know that Donahue is in town."

"Of course he is. If Burke is in town then Donahue is too. Those two micks are like goddamn lovers."

"Well, don't do anything stupid. Barry Donahue is a tough SOB."

"Yeah, yeah. Don't worry. What'd you two do tonight?"

"We ate at a restaurant in the hotel and took in the show at the Mirage."

"Great. I'll meet you back at the hotel later tonight. If all goes well, we'll be leaving for home … and it might be in a hurry, so make sure Ace gets some sleep."

"Okay. You take care of yourself."

"No problem."

Tony walked back inside and stood near the statues when something caught his eye. Vince Jackson was coming through the lobby. He might have noticed Tony, but he had a woman on his arm and was talking to her intently. She was tall, taller than Vince, young and very beautiful. Tony moved around behind the statue to put it between him and Vince. Vince passed by and entered the casino floor. Tony followed, making sure there were plenty of people between them. Vince stopped at the fifty-dollar blackjack table and pulled out a chair for the woman. Then he sat down beside her. He gave the dealer a wad of hundreds. She counted out chips and handed him two stacks. He slid one stack over to the woman. She smiled and patted his arm.

Tony backed into a row of slot machines and sat down at one. Looking between two machines, he could just see Vince's left arm. He pulled out the phone and flipped it open. 12:10. He entered Lou's number.

"Yo."

Tony had to stick his finger in his ear to hear over the din of the casino. "Lou?"

"Yeah."

"It's me."

"I figured that."

"I'm at Caesar's Palace and I just ran into Vince Jackson."

"No shit?"

"No shit. He's with some broad. I need you to come over here right away."

"I just finished my shift. I can be there in twenty minutes or so."

"Can't you make it faster?"

"I'll do my best. Where will you be?"

Tony stood up and looked around. "I'm in a row of slots right across from the Wheel of Fortune … just inside from the lobby."

"I'll find you."

"Hurry the hell up, will you? I don't want to lose this guy."

"I'll hurry."

"You're bringing your car, right?"

"I was just going to walk over."

"Bring your car."

"Okay."

"Mister, are you playing that machine?"

Tony turned around. Even though he was sitting down, he was staring eyeball to eyeball with an elderly woman. "What?"

"Are you playing that machine?" Rheumy blue eyes stared unblinkingly at him through oversized glasses. Her snow-white hair was in a tight, curly ball around her head.

"What do you care?"

"If you're not, I'd like to play it."

"Lady, there's twenty empty machines in this row. Go find another one."

"I want to play that machine. If you're not playing it, will you please move?"

Tony reached into his pocket and pulled out a handful of loose change. But it was a dollar machine and he didn't have enough. "I'm waiting for someone to bring me some change."

"No you're not. You were just talking on the phone. I was watching you."

"Buzz off, lady."

She stalked away muttering to herself. Tony looked between the machines. He could still see Vince's arm. He looked at the phone. 12:20. *Damn, when is Lou going to get here?* He looked between the machines again.

"Sir, are you playing that machine?" asked a male voice.

"What the hell?" Tony turned around and there was the little old lady again, except this time she was accompanied by a security guard.

"If you're not playing the machine, I'll have to ask you to move," said the guard.

"Can't she find another machine?"

"I want to play this one," said the woman.

"I'm sorry sir." The guard was sympathetic but a paying customer always comes first.

"Oh, for Christ's sake." Tony got up to move.

"Thank you, sir," said the guard.

"Thank you, officer." The woman gave Tony a dirty look and took his place at the machine.

The guard nodded and walked away.

Tony walked around the end of the row and looked at the blackjack table. Vince and the woman were gone. He looked around anxiously. "Damn it," he muttered. He walked up and down the rows of gaming tables. Nothing. "Damn it," he kept repeating.

Then he heard a shriek and turned around. Standing at a craps table was the woman, clapping her hands and Vince was standing next to her, grinning and patting her on her back. Tony quickly stepped behind a column. He carefully peeked around and saw Vince looking around the casino. He pulled his head back just before Vince looked in his direction. He pulled out the phone. 12:35. *Where the hell is that asshole?*

The phone started ringing. It was Lou.

"Where the hell are you?" asked Tony.

"I'm standing by the slots. Where the hell are *you*?" replied Lou.

"Oh, yeah. I moved." Tony looked around. "I'm standing by a column at the end of a row of five-dollar machines. There's a big, neon sign over the row that says 'Dollar Frenzy'.

"I see it."

Tony saw Lou walking down the row of card tables. He waved. Lou nodded and flipped his phone shut. Tony did the same and pointed down the row of slots next to the column. Lou nodded again. Tony peeked around the column again and then followed Lou. They stopped mid-row, out of site of the craps table.

"What's going on?" asked Lou.

Tony pointed. "Vince and the broad are playing craps at a table just beyond that column."

"What are you going to do?"

"I'm going to follow that sleazy bastard back to his RV."

"What if he doesn't go there?"

Tony hadn't thought of that. "Well, he has to go sooner or later, don't you think?"

"How the hell would I know?"

"That's where the money is and he's going to have to give it to Burke."

"Maybe the other guy is doing that right now."

"Sheldon?"

"Whatever."

"Well, shit. I sure as hell hope not. Anyway, this is the best deal I've got so I'm going make a play on it."

"It's your gig. What do you want me to do?"

"Help me keep an eye on Vince."

"What if the money is already gone?"

"Then I'll make those sonsabitches pay somehow."

Lou shrugged. "Like I said, it's your gig."

"You don't know Vince do you?"

"Nope."

"Great. That'll be a help. He's the black dude with the open-collared blue shirt. The broad is wearing a gold, sequined dress … what there is of it … and has long, black hair. Go take a look."

Lou walked to the end of the row and peeked around the column and came back. "They're there."

"Good. Since Vince doesn't know who you are, go find a slot machine that you can see them from and keep an eye on them. Call me if they move."

"You got it."

Lou turned to go. Tony grabbed his arm. "Oh, can you loan me twenty-dollars?"

"Sure." Lou pulled out his wallet and handed Tony a twenty. He walked away.

Tony sat down at a machine. *Shit. What if Sheldon was doing the hand off to Burke right now?* There was nothing he could do about it. He would just have to play out the deal he had going right now. He got up and walked to the end of the row and looked around the column. Vince and the woman were still there. Lou was sitting a slot machine on the other side of the table, idly punching the button and keeping an eye on them. Tony retreated to the bar.

Tony could see Lou in the mirror behind the bar. He watched him open his phone and punch in numbers. Seconds later Gina's phone started ringing.

Tony picked the ringing phone up off the bar and flipped it open. "Yeah?"

"They're on the move."

"Where are you now?"

"They've been playing Caribbean poker for the past half-hour, but it looks like they ran out of chips. They're walking toward the lobby."

"Stay with them, I'll meet you in the lobby." He grabbed the change off the bar, drained his scotch and hurried out of the bar.

23

Lou was standing under the arch leading from the casino floor to the lobby when Tony arrived.

"Where are they?"

"Standing outside ... must be waiting for the valet to bring a car around."

"Where is your car?"

"In valet."

"Son of bitch! Go get it. I'll watch them."

"Don't worry. It's right out front. I know most of the valet guys here and told them to keep it handy."

"Go get it and as soon as they go, I'll meet you out front."

"You got it."

Lou took off and Tony watched Vince and the woman standing just outside the main doors. Vince was nuzzling the woman and she was laughing and playing coy. A powder-blue Chrysler Sebring convertible pulled up. The woman got into the driver's seat. Vince slid into the passenger side.

The Sebring pulled away and Lou's Lexus pulled up right behind. Tony ran out and jumped in. "Hit it," he said.

The Lexus's tires chirped slightly as Lou accelerated after the Sebring. They turned right onto Las Vegas Blvd. The woman was driving aggressively, changing lanes and weaving around traffic, but that was one thing that didn't bother Lou. He easily kept the Lexus two or three cars behind the Sebring. As they drove, Tony opened the glove box and pulled out the paper bag wrapped revolver.

"Oh, shit," said Lou.

Tony flipped open the gate and started shoving in bullets. "Don't worry about it."

"Hey, I work in this town. I can't get a parking ticket without the casino giving me the third degree."

"This isn't going to involve you."

"What are you talking about? I'm driving the goddamn car."

"Don't be a pussy, Lou."

The Sebring turned right on Blue Diamond Road. There was considerably less traffic, so Lou had to hang back a little more. A couple of miles further and the Sebring's brake lights went on and it made a left turn. As Lou approached the spot where the Sebring turned, Tony could see a sign for the Haven RV Resort.

"This must be it," said Tony.

Lou turned into the driveway just as the Sebring was pulling away from the guard shack.

"Go slow, Lou." Tony slipped the gun under the seat.

As Lou crept up to the gate, a guard, holding a clipboard stepped out and held up his hand.

"What do we do?" Lou asked.

"Just shut up and leave the talking to me."

The guard leaned toward the driver's window. "Can I help you?"

Tony leaned toward him. "We're visiting Sheldon Isaacs."

The guard looked at his board. "Is Mr. Isaacs expecting you?"

"Yes."

"What is your name?"

"Burke"

The guard looked at his board again. "Yes, Mr. Burke." He pulled a slip of paper from the clip and held it out. "Put this on your dashboard."

Lou stared straight ahead. Tony nudged him.

"Oh, yeah. Sure." Lou took the slip.

"Mr. Isaacs is in 631. Just drive straight to the end of this road, take a left and follow the signs. You can't miss it."

Tony waved to him. "Thanks."

The guard stepped back and waved. "Have a nice night, sir."

Tony nudged Lou again.

"Sure." Lou pulled ahead slowly. "Now what?"

"Just follow the man's directions, but go slow, I don't want to get there until Vince and the broad are inside. They are obviously expecting Burke, which is going to make this much easier."

Lou wove around the park. Except for the flicker of the occasional TV screen, most of the RV's were dark. A few had lights on and they could see people playing cards or talking. Here and there were people sitting outside, talking quietly or just enjoying the night air.

"There it is," said Tony as they approached site 631. Lights were on in the RV, but the drapes were all drawn. The Sebring was parked on the side.

"What do you want me to do?"

"Don't hesitate. Pull in … like you own the joint."

Lou pulled in next to the Sebring.

"Turn off the motor, but you stay in the car. Just be ready to get the hell out of here, taco pronto." Tony reached under the seat and grabbed the gun.

He got out of the car and approached the RV. Duct tape covered the window he had broken in New Orleans. He cocked the hammer of the Colt and held it up. He rapped on the door. He could hear movement and Sheldon saying, "That must be Burke."

The door opened and Tony leveled the Colt into Sheldon's surprised face. He put his free hand on Sheldon's chest and pushed, backing him into the RV. Vince was sitting at the kitchen table next to the woman who was in the process of pulling a bag of cocaine out of her purse. As Sheldon backed into the room Vince looked up.

"What the fu …" He started to get up, but he was on the inside, pinned against the wall by the woman and he couldn't move fast enough.

The woman shrieked. Tony pushed Sheldon into the kitchen and swung the Colt around to point at Vince. "Just sit down."

Vince slowly lowered himself back into his seat. "Well, well. Look who passed his desert survival training."

"You too, Sheldon. Sit down at the table."

Sheldon slid in to table across from Vince.

"Were the hell did you get that thing?" said Vince.

Tony waggled the Colt. "I acquired it during my survival training."

"You sure you know how to use it?"

"Wanna find out?"

"One of us might get to you before you can cock it again."

"That's possible Vince. I wonder which one it will be?"

"Shut up, Vince," said Sheldon.

Whimpering, the woman started to put the dope back into her purse. "This ain't my scene, Vince, I gotta go …"

Tony waved the gun in her direction. "Just stay where you are. And leave the dope where it is, but put your purse on the floor."

The woman just looked at him. Vince reached for the purse.

Tony pointed the gun between his eyes. "Let her do it."

Vince patted her hand. They had given Tony a bad time and he might just be pissed enough to do something crazy. "Do what he says, Dashanique."

With tears in her eyes, her hand trembling, Dashanique picked up the purse and dropped it on the floor.

"Good girl … what was it? Dasha …"

"Dashinique," said Vince.

"Good girl, Dashinique. You just relax and nothing will happen to you."

"I guess Donahue was right, Sheldon," said Vince.

"Barry Donahue?"

"He said he ran into Gina Sandrelli … that's your cousin right?"

Tony feigned surprise. "Gina's in town too?"

"Barry's not the brightest guy in the world, but he knew that if she was in town, you probably were too."

"Barry Donahue couldn't find his ass with both hands."

"Let me guess," said Sheldon. "Your cousin and her boyfriend picked you up in Texas and flew you here."

"Boyfriend?"

"The pilot."

"He's not her boyfriend."

"Now how would you know that?"

"Because I hired the guy."

"Ah, things are starting to clear up. That's how you caught up to us in New Orleans … you've been flying across the country."

"Except for a few hundred miles across Texas in an RV." Vince laughed at his own joke.

"But how did you make it out of the desert?" asked Sheldon.

Tony smiled. "Like Vince said … I passed my desert survival training."

"Somebody must've found you."

"What difference does it make? I'm here now."

"Just curious, that's all."

"I just want my money."

"You know where it is … go get it."

Tony suddenly realized a tactical error. He couldn't leave the room and it wasn't practical to try and herd everyone into the bedroom. He backed up to a row of switches on the wall next to the door.

"Does one of these turn on the outside light?"

"I don't know," said Sheldon. "Try it."

Tony tried the switch closest to the door. Miraculously, the exterior light went on. He flicked it on and off a couple of times.

"You've got somebody with you, eh?"

"I've got this place surrounded." Tony flicked the switched a couple more times.

"Somehow I doubt that."

"God damn it." Tony flicked the switch half a dozen times.

Finally, he heard a car door open and Lou say in a hoarse whisper, "You want me, Tony?"

Tony yelled out the door. "Yeah, damn it. Get in here."

Lou came up the steps. "What's going on?"

"I need you to get something from the bedroom."

Lou surveyed the scene. "Hey, I can't get involved in this."

"Go into the bedroom and look in the closet. You'll see a Miami Dolphin's bag. Grab it and bring it to me."

"Come on, Tony. The casino will fire my ass in a heartbeat if ..."

Tony gently pushed Lou toward the bedroom. "Just help me out here, will you?"

Lou edged toward the back of the RV. "This is nuts."

"Lou. Please. The bag." Tony pointed toward the bedroom.

"All right. All right." Lou walked down the hall and disappeared into the bedroom. "It's dark in here," he said.

"That's your backup?" said Vince.

Tony ignored the comment. He yelled down the hallway toward Lou. "There's a light switch next to the door."

The light in the bedroom went on. They could hear Lou rummaging around in the closet.

Dashanique whimpered. "I gotta go. Can I please go?"

"You just behave, honey, and you'll be out of here soon," said Tony.

"Yeah. Don't worry babe ... this idiot can't keep this up for long," said Vince.

"Will you shut up?" said Sheldon.

Lou appeared in the doorway of the bedroom. He held up the Dolphin's bag so Tony could see it. "Is this it?"

"That's it. Bring it here."

Lou came back in the kitchen.

"Open it up," said Tony.

Lou pulled the zipper and held open the bag so Tony could see inside.

Tony smiled when he saw the stacks of bills. "Good man. Now take it to the car and get back in here."

Lou closed the bag and left the RV.

"Do you really think you're going to get away with this?" asked Sheldon.

"Yeah, I do. And by the way, where's the rest of my stuff? My wallet, phone and the money you took out of my pocket?"

"Fuck you," said Vince.

Tony waved the Colt. "No, you're the one who's fucked. Where's my stuff?"

Sheldon nodded toward a drawer in the kitchen. "It's in there."

Tony moved to the drawer and slid it open. He reached in with his free hand and pulled out his wallet. "Where's my phone?"

"No idea."

Tony opened the wallet. "Hey, where's the money?"

Vince laughed. "Sorry about that, partner. I put it into some high risk investments at the casino and they went belly up."

Tony pointed the gun directly at Vince's head. "Oh yeah? Well, I know you'll make good on them, 'partner'."

Lou reappeared behind Tony. "Now what?"

"Look through those drawers and see if you can find some rope or something," said Tony.

Lou started going through the drawers. "Hey, look at this." He held up a Beretta 9 millimeter.

"It is loaded?" asked Tony.

Lou checked. "Looks like it."

Tony held out his free hand and Lou put the gun in it. Tony hefted it and flicked off the safety. "Now this decreases your odds even more, Vince."

"You'll fuck up sooner or later," said Vince.

"Vince," said Sheldon.

"What? I'm just stating the obvious."

"We don't have to worry about Tony screwing up. Burke will take care of this for us."

"I'm not worried about Burke," said Tony. "You're the ones who should be worried."

"He's not going to let you take his money," said Sheldon.

"It's my goddamn money."

"That's not the way he sees it."

"Well, Burke can pound sand up his ass."

"He'll be pounding sand up your ass when he catches you ... and he will catch you."

"We'll see."

"Here's some duct tape, Tony." Lou held up a roll of the silver tape.

"Set it on the counter," said Tony.

Lou put the tape down.

"Here, take this." Tony held the Beretta out to Lou.

"Oh, shit, I can't take that."

"Look you're already in this. Just help me finish this up so we can get the hell out of here."

Vince laughed. "Yeah, help your buddy so you both can get killed."

"Will you shut the fuck up?" said Sheldon.

Dashinique whimpered. Vince snorted.

Tony waved the Beretta. "Lou. Please."

Lou gingerly took the gun.

"Now hold it on that asshole." Tony waved the Colt toward Vince. "If he does anything funny, shoot him."

Lou nodded.

"Now Dashinique, I've got a little job for you."

She whimpered louder.

"Just help me out here, honey, and you can go, okay?"

She sniffed and nodded her head.

"Now slide out of there and come over here."

Dashinique looked over at Vince. He looked away.

"Just do what he says," said Sheldon.

She slid out of her seat and inched over toward Tony.

"Pick up that tape."

She did.

"Vince, you put your hands behind your back."

"Fuck you, dipshit."

"I'm not fucking around here. I will shoot your ass if you don't put your hands behind you."

Vince looked up at Tony. There was something in his eyes that put enough doubt in Vince to obey.

"Now, Dashinique, you wrap that tape around his wrists. Lou, you watch her ... make she does it good and tight."

After she had wrapped Vince's wrists with several layers of tape, Dashinique looked up. "What do I do with the roll?"

"Just rip it off, honey."

She tore off the tape.

"Now, Sheldon, it's your turn."

Sheldon slowly put his hands behind his back. "You do know that you're a dead man, don't you?"

"We've all got to die sometime," said Tony.

"Jesus, Tony ..." said Lou.

"Don't worry, Lou, nothing is going to happen. Dashinique, you know what to do."

Dashinique began to wrap Sheldon's wrists.

"Don't believe him, Lou," said Sheldon. "Do you know who Max Burke is?"

"No," said Lou.

"Well, you will."

"Tony, who is this *Burke*?"

"Just a guy. Besides, this is between me and him, so don't worry about it okay?"

"You better worry, Lou," said Sheldon. "And you better start soon ... Burke is on his way here."

"What?" said Lou.

"He should be here any minute."

Tony was pretty sure that Vince was right, that's why the guard had Burke's name on his clipboard. He decided it was best to just keep things moving. He waved the Colt at Vince. "Slide your ass out of there."

Vince slid out of the seat and stood up. Lou backed up a couple of steps when he saw how tall and powerfully built Vince was.

"Dashinique, pull off his shoes."

She kneeled in front of Vince and waited for him to lift his foot. He stood defiantly.

She looked up at Tony.

"Vince, you let her take your shoes off or so help me I'm going to blow your fucking kneecap off."

"Just do what he says, Vince," said Sheldon. "No sense in risking our asses ... Burke will take care of him."

Vince snorted and lifted a foot. Dashinique pulled off his shoe.

"Now the other one," said Tony.

When both shoes were off, he said, "Unbuckle his pants and pull them down."

She unbuckled Vince's pants and let them drop to the floor, exposing his red Jockey briefs.

Vince laughed. "And while you're down there, baby ..."

"You're doing fine, honey," said Tony. "You're almost done. Sheldon, your turn."

As soon as Sheldon was standing in his striped boxer shorts, Tony stood aside so Dashinique could pass. "You're all done, honey. You can go."

She looked at Tony and carefully inched toward the door.

"Don't forget your purse," said Tony.

She went around behind Vince and picked up her purse. She stood up and put her hand on his shoulder. "I'm sorry, baby, I'm just not up for this scene."

"Just get the fuck out of here," said Vince.

Watching Tony carefully, she made her way to the door.

"It's okay, you can go," he said.

Dashinique slipped out quickly. They heard the Sebring start up and gravel spay as she backed up rapidly onto the pavement. Then a chirp of the tires and car sped away.

"Now what, dipshit?" asked Vince.

"Now we all go for a little ride," said Tony. He backed up in to the cab and waved the Colt toward the door.

Sheldon nodded to Vince. Then he stepped out of his pants and walked toward the door.

"Help Mr. Jackson find his way to the door, Lou."

Lou, who had been standing behind Vince, poked him with the Beretta. "You too."

"You'll be sorry you helped this guy, you little prick," said Vince.

Tony followed Sheldon out the door then, keeping an eye on him, turned the Colt back toward the open door. "Come on, Vince."

With Lou behind and Tony holding the Colt on him from the front, Vince followed them out the door.

"Help them into the back seat," said Tony. "Vince first."

Lou prodded Vince toward the rear of the Lexus. Vince hobbled on the gravel in his stocking feet. Lou opened the door and waved the gun for him to get in. Vince stood for a few seconds and looked at him.

"You know," said Lou, "I didn't want to get involved in this, but now that I am ... well, you know, 'in for a penny, in for a pound. I won't hesitate to shoot your ass if you fuck with me."

Vince narrowed his gaze. The little guy was nervous, but there was something about him that made Vince think he might be as crazy as Tony. He sighed and turned and squatted down until his rear made contact with the seat.

"How about a hand here?" he said to Lou.

"I'm not that stupid. Just get your ass in there."

With considerable effort, Vince tucked his legs up and into the car.

"Now you, Sheldon," said Tony.

Lou sheparded Sheldon around to the other side and into the car. A light came on in the motor home across the street. Lou saw the face of an older woman looking out of the window directly at him. He looked over at Tony. "Now what?"

Tony looked over at the woman. "Don't worry about her." Then he looked back at the RV. "Just a minute, I forgot something." He turned to go back inside.

"Are you nuts?" Lou yelled in a horse whisper. "We've got to get the hell out of here."

"Just keep an eye on those two ... I'll be right back." Tony disappeared inside.

Lou opened the drivers door and slumped down on the seat, his feet still on the ground. "Shit."

"Feeling stressed, Lou?" Vince said with a sneer.

Lou rested the Beretta on the seat back. "Yeah. So just keep your trap shut and I won't blow your head off."

Vince laughed. "That'd get the neighbor's attention."

Sheldon sighed. "Goddamn it, Vince."

The passenger door opened and Tony got in. "Alright, let's get the hell out of here."

Lou started the car. "Where the hell did you go?"

Tony held up two wallets. "Just trying to recoup some of money."

"Hey, that's mine," yelled Vince.

Tony turned to rest the Colt on the seatback, aimed loosely between Vince and Sheldon.

"You boys comfortable?"

Vince squirmed to get his taped arms in better position. "If there is anything left after Burke gets done with you, you're all mine."

"I'm shaking, dipshit."

Lou backed out onto the pavement. "Where to?"

"Out to the highway."

24

Barry Donahue pulled off the highway onto the driveway of the Haven RV Resort. As he approached the entrance, a uniformed guard came out of the shack and held up his hand.

Donahue stopped and buzzed down the window of the Lincoln.

"Can I help you?" said the guard.

"We're here to see Sheldon Isaac's."

"Really? Mr. Isaac must be a popular fellow."

"Oh?"

"Can I ask your name?"

A voice from the passenger seat answered, "Burke."

The guard looked at his clipboard then he leaned and shined his flashlight on the passenger to get a better look. He saw a well-dressed man of about fifty, with a handsome face and carefully coiffed hair. "Burke? Are you sure?"

The man looked at him with piercing blue eyes. "Of course I'm sure, you idiot. Now get that thing out of my face before I come out there and shove it up your ass."

The guard stood up. He shined the flashlight on the clipboard. "I'm sorry, sir, but a Mr. Burke just went in to see Mr. Isaacs not thirty minutes ago."

"What?" said Donahue, squinting in the glare of a pair of headlights that approached the shack from inside the park. A black Lexus pulled up even with the Donahue's car and slowed to a stop to allow the exit gate to rise.

The guard shined his flashlight at Donahue. "Can I see some identification?"

"Get that thing out of my eyes." Donahue held his hand up and looked away, taking his gaze over to the Lexus. The driver looked nervous. Then he saw Sheldon Isaac staring back at him from the back seat. "What the fu ...?" The Lexus accelerated rapidly, smashing through the half-open wooden gate.

The guard whirled to watch the Lexus speed away. "Hey!"

"Goddamn it, Max, that was Sheldon in the back of that car," said Donahue.

"Are you sure?"

"It was him all right."

"Then get after them." said Burke. "They must have the money."

Donahue slammed the car in reverse and stepped on the accelerator.

"Hey!" The guard jumped out of the way as the car backed up.

Donahue spun the wheel and the Lincoln skidded around. Then he jammed it into drive and tires spun and hopped, gaining purchase on the asphalt. Without looking for traffic, he raced onto the highway. The taillights of the Lexus were already a quarter of a mile ahead.

"Don't lose them."

"You might as well kiss your ass goodbye," laughed Sheldon.

"Shut up," replied Tony.

"Holy shit, that was Burke?" asked Lou.

"Just drive." Tony didn't actually see Burke, but he saw Barry Donahue and he knew that Burke was in that car.

"We're screwed," said Lou.

"You sure as shit are," said Vince.

Tony watched the headlights of the Lincoln gain on them. "Come on Lou, put it in gear will you?"

Lou floored the accelerator and Tony's side pressed into the seat, the Colt bouncing against the seat back.

Vince leaned toward the window to get out the line of fire from the precariously waving gun. "Be careful with that, will you?"

Tony ignored him and watched the headlights of the Lincoln diminish slightly. "Faster, Lou. I think we're losing them."

The road curved to the left and Sheldon leaned into Vince. He could see the speedometer over Lou's shoulder, the needle hovering around 105. The road curved back to the right and both Sheldon and Vince leaned to the left.

As the Lexus crept up to 110, the Lincoln began to fall back; Donahue was having trouble keeping the pace. Tony had to admit, Lou was a pretty good driver. "Don't let up, Lou … we're losing them."

He turned to look out the windshield. The road seemed to stretch forever into the dark night. Tony knew that even though they were increasing the distance between them and the Lincoln, it would take a lot of miles to shake them completely. A sign for Red Rock Canyon flashed by. "Take the road to that canyon, Lou."

"What?"

"Up ahead ... there must be a cut off for Red Rock Canyon. Turn there."

"Where?"

The road came up quickly. "Right here."

Lou jammed on the brakes. He tried to turn but the Lexus was going too fast and the car drifted sideways past the intersection, smoke billowing from the tires.

Tony clung to the seatback while Sheldon and Vince bounced around the back. "Jesus, Lou!"

"How about a little more warning next time," said Lou.

Vince pushed Sheldon off him with his shoulder. "Yeah, Tony. That would be good."

The Lincoln's headlights came around the last curve behind them. "Go, Lou, go!" said Tony.

Lou hit the accelerator and the tires spun until they got a purchase on the concrete. Already pointing north, the Lexus quickly gained speed on the road toward Red Rock Canyon.

"Nice move, Parnelli," said Vince.

"Shut up, Vince," said Tony. But he was more interested in watching the intersection behind them to see if the Lincoln would follow.

"Did you see that?" said Burke

"Yeah, yeah, I saw it." Barry Donahue watched the taillights of the Lexus turn right off the highway. He started slowing down to turn after them well before the intersection.

"Jesus, Barry, you drive like an old lady."

"I'll be happy to pull over and let you drive, Max."

"Just stay with them, will you?"

"I'm doing my best." He pressed the accelerator and the Lincoln's tires squealed around the corner. "You sure your money is in that car?"

"Of course it is. Why else would they be trying to lose us?"

"You think that Tony is in there? I didn't recognize the driver."

"You said you thought he was in town."

"How the hell do you think he got out of Texas? I thought Sheldon and Vince fucked him up pretty good."

"Evidently not good enough."

"I guess we should have left earlier. I had a funny feeling that something was up after I ran into his cousin, Gina."

"If you had told me about that sooner, we would have."

"I just didn't think he'd be a problem … after Vince told us where they'd left him and all."

"Yeah, well, he got out of there somehow and now he's trying to make a break with my money."

"You sure he's got it with him? Maybe it's still at the RV."

"He's got it. Just stay with him, will you?"

They were climbing steadily up a narrow, winding road when Tony saw the headlights of the Lincoln round the corner behind them. "Damn it, they're still back there."

Vince laughed. "Burke isn't likely to let go of his money easily, numbnuts."

"It's my money and he's not going to get it back."

"Like hell he's not."

"Will you shut up, Vince?" said Sheldon.

"What? Tony thinks he's going to make off with Burke's money."

"Just shut the hell up, will you?"

They all bounced suddenly as the tires slipped off the pavement as Lou maneuvered the Lexus around a bend.

"Damn it, Lou."

"Hey, this road is screwed up."

"Just keep us on it, okay?" said Tony.

"I am. I am." The Lexus careened from side to side as Lou maneuvered it around each bend.

Tony watched intently as the headlights of the Lincoln appeared around the last bend about a half-mile behind. "Damn, they seem to be staying with us now."

"I'm going as fast as I can."

Suddenly a street sign appeared in the headlight's beam. "Turn here," said Tony.

Lou slammed on the brakes and spun the wheel to the left. The car drifted for a second, then the tires regained their contact with the pavement and they hurtled down a street that led into a neighborhood of houses perched on the desert hillside. There were around two curves and well into the neighborhood in a matter of seconds, but they had to slow down on the residential street and Tony thought he could see the glow of headlights behind them. "I think they made the turn back there, too."

The road split up ahead. "Which way?" asked Lou.

"Right. Stay to the right."

Lou swerved to the right and sped several blocks past houses that were mostly dark.

"Turn left at the next street."

Lou braked hard and the tires squealed as they turned down the road.

Tony spotted a cross street. "Turn right here," he barked.

Lou did as he said.

"Turn off the lights and pull in this driveway."

Lou pulled into the driveway on the side of a house that was dark.

"Kill the engine."

"Oh, a little hide and seek, eh?" said Vince. He started bouncing up and down in the seat causing the car to rock.

Tony leveled the Colt directly at him. "So help me, Vince I will blow your fucking brains out if you don't stop."

Sheldon leaned against him. "Stop it Vince."

Vince stopped and leaned forward trying to see Tony's eyes, but it was too dark.

Tony pulled the hammer back. "I'm not kidding, Vince."

"You'll wake up the whole neighborhood," said Vince.

"I don't care."

"Burke'll find you."

"Maybe … but you'll be dead."

Vince leaned back. "I guess 15k ain't worth dyin' for."

"No, it's not," agreed Sheldon.

Tony said nothing but slowly released the hammer.

"Oh shit, there they are," said Lou.

Tony watched the Lincoln speed through the intersection of the road they had just turned off.

"Now what?" asked Lou.

"Just sit tight."

Lou buzzed down the window and let in the cool desert night air. Except for an occasional dog barking, it was very quiet outside. "I don't hear anything."

"They must have slowed down," said Tony.

At that moment headlights illuminated the intersection of the next street over.

"Get down, Lou."

Lou leaned toward the center so he could just see out the window. A few seconds later, the Lincoln passed slowly through the intersection.

"Oh man …"

"Just be still." Tony had hunkered down too, but he kept a watch on Sheldon and Vince between the seat backs.

When the taillights of the Lincoln passed out of sight Lou breathed a sigh of relief. "Honest to god Tony, I'm with you for one day and I'm back in the shitter."

"He's a piece of work, isn't he?" said Vince.

Tony ignored the remark. Sheldon elbowed Vince and nodded at a flyer from Vegas Station on the floor. Vince nodded back. They all sat in silence for several minutes. Then an intersection two blocks away lit up, followed by the Lincoln passing through in the opposite direction.

"They're still roaming around looking for us," said Lou.

"The man wants his money," said Vince.

"Sit tight," said Tony.

A few minutes later they heard the roar of an engine and Tony watched the Lincoln race back through the intersection of the street they had turned off of originally. A house across the street lit up and he could see a man peering out of a window.

"Oh shit," said Lou.

Tony held his breath, half expecting to see lights appear in the windows of the house they were parked at. But nothing happened and a few minutes later the lights of house across the street went out. "Let's stay put for a few minutes, then retrace our route back out to the highway."

"I could've sworn I saw them turn into the neighborhood back there," said Donahue.

Burke cracked the window and lit a cigarette. He took a drag and let it out, the smoke streaming out the small opening. "Maybe they did. They must've slipped past us somehow and got back onto the highway."

The car sped past a sign marking the entrance for the Red Rock Canyon scenic drive. "I'm not seeing anything up ahead ... you think they might have turned in there?"

"Check it out."

Donahue slowed and turned off the highway. They passed a visitor center that appeared closed and came to a stop at a gate crossing the road into the canyon. The gate was made of a heavy wooden beam, about the size of a railroad tie and was secured to a thick pole cemented in the ground by a heavy chain and padlock. A metal sign, illuminated by the headlights, read, 'CLOSED AT DUSK'.

"Doesn't look like they came this way," said Donahue.

Burke let out a stream of smoke. "No shit."

"So now what?"

"Get back on the road. They've got to be up ahead there somewhere."

"Which way?" asked Lou.

Tony looked up and down the highway. There was no sign of the Lincoln in either direction.

"Okay, turn left."

Lou pulled out onto the highway.

"How far is it?"

"What?"

"That canyon."

"I don't know … maybe five or ten miles."

"Why are you going there?" asked Sheldon.

"You'll find out."

Sheldon's voice rose in nervous tension. "Now wait a minute, Tony. You can't kill us … we didn't harm you."

Tony laughed. "That's true. You just left me in the desert hoping Mother Nature would do the job."

"We gave you a chance."

"You backed the wrong horse, Sheldon."

"Come on, we were just doing a job."

"You knew the money was mine."

"Johnny didn't think so."

"Yeah, but you knew it was mine."

"Hey, Burke offered us 15k to help him get his money back. He seemed pretty sure it was his," added Vince.

"Whatever Burke told you, I did the job for you. You knew that. You pay the guy that provides the goods."

"Okay, maybe we were wrong. But it was just business. It wasn't personal," said Sheldon.

"It seemed pretty personal when I woke up in the middle of nowhere in nothin' but my skivvies."

"It was just a joke."

"How come you're not laughing now?"

They rode along in silence for several minutes until Tony spotted the sign marking the entrance into Red Rock Canyon. "Turn in there."

Lou turned off the highway and passed the visitor center. He stopped at the gate that crossed the road into the canyon. They stared at the 'CLOSED AT DUSK' sign for a long minute.

"Damn." Tony got out and walked up to the gate. He looked around. A car was parked outside the visitor center, but the building was completely dark and he could see no sign of life. He pulled back the hammer of the Colt and aimed it at the padlock. He took one last look around, and pulled the trigger.

There was a blinding flash and Tony staggered back. The sound was deafening. It echoed off the canyon walls for a full second. The chain hung limp. He'd missed the lock but the bullet had shattered one of the links. He slipped the loose chain off the flange that held the gate to the pole and swung it open. Grinning, he stood aside and waved to Lou like a matador.

Lou stopped inside the gate and Tony jumped in. "Damn, Ray was right, that thing kicks like a mule."

"It sure as hell was loud. Who's Ray?" asked Lou as he accelerated up the road.

"A friend."

"From Florida?"

"Texas."

Lou swerved around a curve. "I didn't know you knew anybody in Texas."

"I've got friends all over. Just keep your attention on the road okay."

"Come on Tony. It's not worth it." They had driven for several miles in silence and Vince could no longer stand it. His voice had none of the usual bravado.

"Why not?"

"Because ... well, because we were just jerking you around. We never intended to kill you."

"You seemed pretty surprised to see me back at the RV."

"That's because we were ... we thought you'd be stuck in Texas for a while."

"Stuck in the ground."

"No, really. We knew there were people around there ... we could see the lights from ranches all around."

"The nearest ranch was several miles from where you dropped me off ... I've got the saddle sores and sun burn to ..."

Tony was cut off abruptly by Lou's violent braking, causing everyone to lean forward. Tony just managed to put out an arm to keep from slamming into the dash board.

"What the hell ...?"

A pair of eyes illuminated by the headlights stared at them from the middle of the road. Tony could just make out the dark form of small, horse-like animal. "What the hell is that?"

Lou shook his head. "I dunno. Christ, it came out of nowhere."

The animal turned away and continued its trek across the road.

"It's a donkey," said Sheldon.

"A donkey? What the hell is a donkey doing out here?"

"Maybe he lives here?"

"I didn't know they had goddamn donkeys out here."

"There're a lot of things you don't know, Tony."

Tony raised the Colt and pointed it between the seats at Sheldon. "Yeah, well, I know one thing ... this is the end of the line for you."

"Oh, shit, Tony ... not in the car!" Lou's voice rose in alarm.

"Relax, will you?" Tony opened the door and got out of the car. He opened the back door. "Get out," he ordered Vince.

"Fuck you, Tony. You don't think I'm going to make this easy for you." Vince seemed to have regained his boldness.

"Have it your way." Tony cocked the hammer of the Colt.

"All right, all right," Vince's voice lost it edge again as he struggled to get out of the car. "Keep your shirt on."

"You too, Sheldon. Out."

Sheldon shrugged.

"Get that asshole out of the car, Lou."

Lou got out and opened the other back door.

Sheldon swung his legs around and looked up at Lou. "A little help?"

Lou grabbed his arm and pulled. Sheldon clipped the top of his head getting out of the car. "Oww," he yowled.

Tony herded Vince around the back of the car as Lou helped Sheldon to his feet. The desert air had cooled considerably raising goose bumps on Sheldon's bare legs.

"Now Tony, there's got be a way to negotiate with you." Sheldon's voice quivered with cold and fear.

"Actually, boys, the negotiating you have to do is not with me ... it's with Mother Nature."

Vince snorted. "What?"

"That's right, smartass. See if you can get the other ass ... the one that just crossed the road in front of us to help you out."

"You mean you're not going to ..."

"Not today, anyway. Can't make any claims about the future ... but today I'm showing you boys the same courtesy you showed me."

Vince looked around at the forbidding blackness of the desert night. A new type of fear crept into his voice. "You can't leave us out here ... it's the same as killing us."

"No it isn't, Vince. It's not the same at all."

"But we'll die out here."

Tony slammed the back door shut. "Maybe. But you might get lucky ... this is Vegas after all." He walked around to the other side of the car and slammed that door shut. "Get in, Lou."

"Lou, talk some sense into him," said Vince.

"It's not my show." Lou opened the driver's door and got in.

"Hey, at least untie our hands, Tony."

Tony looked across the roof at Vince. He could just barely make out the outline of his head in the starlight. "See if you can get that donkey to chew it off." Tony yanked open the passenger door. "See you later, boys."

He got in and slammed the door shut. "Let's go, Lou."

Lou slipped the car into gear. "Damn, you had me worried there for a minute, Tony."

Tony could see Sheldon's bare legs in the taillights as they pulled away. He smiled. "I'll bet you weren't half as worried as they were."

The Lincoln rounded a curve and suddenly a pair of taillights appeared up ahead. "That must be them," said Donahue.

But as they drew closer it became obvious that the lights belonged to a Ford SUV.

"Where'd that guy come from?"

Burke rubbed his temples. "Who the fuck knows?"

Beyond the SUV, the lights of Las Vegas shimmered in the valley that opened up before them.

"Damn, we're almost back into town and there's no sign of them. We must've passed them somewhere along the way."

"Maybe if you didn't drive with your foot on the brake we might have caught them."

"I did the best I could. I'm not a goddamn professional, you know."

"Neither are those knuckleheads."

"Well, they were doing pretty good. They were …"

"Shut up, Barry. Let's just get back to town."

Donahue cringed. He hated the way Burke chastised him, like he was the idiot son.

"I think we might pay a little visit to Tony's cousin," said Burke. "What did you say her name was?"

"Gina. Gina Sandrelli."

"Sevvy Sandrelli's daughter?

"Yeah."

Donahue accelerated around the Ford.

"Now you get aggressive."

Donahue swallowed. "I did my best …"

"Don't be so goddamn sensitive, Barry."

25

Gina flipped through the channels one more time, but nothing caught her attention. She flicked off the TV and lay back on the bed. She'd enjoyed the evening with Mickey. He wasn't exactly her type; he was quiet and introspective. But he was also different from the men she usually dated. He actually seemed to be interested in her. He asked her so many questions; where she came from, how she liked running a restaurant, what movies she liked … things that most men seemed too busy talking about the money they made, or were about to make, or the people they knew, to care about. Of course, she knew that Mickey was no choirboy. She knew he had a past and that he had gotten into this mess because of his own greed, but weren't we all tainted in that way? She sighed and closed her eyes.

She sat up. *What was that?* She must have fallen asleep because she couldn't get a handle on what had woken her up. Then she heard it again. Someone was pounding on the entry door.

What the hell? Still fully dressed, she stood up and went to the bedroom door. She heard the pounding again; three sharp blows.

She opened the bedroom door and saw Mickey walking across the living room toward the entry door. She shouted, "Don't open …," but it was too late.

The door flew open and Max Burke, a solid thirty pounds heavier than Mickey, easily brushed him aside and charged into the room. Before Mickey could recover, Barry Donahue following closely behind grabbed him by the shirt front and pinned him against the wall.

"Where is she?" Donahue demanded.

Mickey made an effort to pull Donahue's hands away, but he was too strong.

"Relax flyboy. Just tell me where she is and you won't get hurt."

"Let him go, Barry, I'm right here." Gina stood in her bedroom doorway.

Donahue looked over at Burke, who nodded his head slightly. He released his grip and Mickey quickly pushed him away.

"Keep your goddamn hands off me," Mickey said.

Donahue grabbed his shoulder and shoved him toward the sofa. "Sit down, tough guy."

Mickey shrugged Donahue's hand off his shoulder and stood defiantly.

"Sit down, Mickey. They aren't going to hurt me," said Gina.

Donahue smiled. "The lady's right, tough guy. But if you don't sit down I'm gonna hurt you."

Mickey brushed his shirtfront and slowly sat down. "What do you want?"

"We just want to have a little chat," said Burke. "You got anything to drink in the joint?"

Gina pointed to the bar.

"Why don't you sit down by your boyfriend?"

"Why don't you just tell us what you want?"

Burke made his way to the bar. "Come on, Gina. We're all friends here. I understand you and Barry go way back. Sit down and let's all have a drink. What'll you have?"

Gina walked slowly toward the sofa. Donahue smiled and gestured to a spot next to Mickey. She sat down, keeping her eyes on Donahue. "I should have known there would be trouble if you were around," she said to him.

Donahue feigned a wince. "That hurt, Gina. I thought we were friends."

"That shows how perceptive you are, Barry."

Opening cupboards behind the bar and ignoring the exchange between Gina and Donahue, Burke asked, "What'll your boyfriend have?"

"Nothing," said Mickey.

"You sure? There's lots of good booze here." Burke hefted a bottle of Absolute in his hand. "How about you, Gina?"

"Nothing."

Burke cracked open the bottle. "Well, this isn't going to be much of party. Where's the ice?"

"In the fridge," said Gina.

"Oh yeah, there it is." Burke bent down and opened the refrigerator below the bar. "How about you, Barry?"

"Is there a beer in there, boss?"

Burke pulled out a bottle of Harp Ale. "How about that? Right from the old country, too."

He set the beer on the counter and pulled out the ice tray. "So, where is Tony?" he asked casually.

"Who?" said Gina.

Burke tossed a couple of ice cubes into a glass and poured the vodka over them. "Your cousin, Tony."

"How would I know?"

"He's here in Vegas with you."

"He is?"

He put the ice tray away and opened the beer. "You sure you don't want a drink?"

"No."

"How about you … what's your name?"

"Mickey." Gina answered for him.

"How about you, Mickey?"

"No," said Mickey.

Holding his drink in one hand and the beer in the other, Burke walked over to the sofa. Looking down at Gina, he answered her question. "Yes, he is." He handed Donahue the beer and sat down in the chair opposite the sofa. Donahue remained standing.

"So, let's just quit the bullshit and you tell me where he is." Burke took a sip of the vodka.

"Even if I knew, why would I tell you?"

"Because you're smart. You know where this is going and you want to avoid all the heartache and pain that would ensue if you didn't."

Gina looked at Burke. He knew Tony was in town and he knew they were together. There was little point in denying that. But she had an out. She didn't know where Tony was. He had her cell phone and she could find out easily enough, but Burke couldn't know that. "Okay, he was here. But I have no idea where he is now."

Burke feigned hurt. "Oh, so you were lying about not knowing he was in Vegas?"

"I didn't lie."

"I suppose you could make a case for that ... you just 'pretended' not to know." Burke took another sip of his drink. "So are you 'pretending' not to know where he is now?"

"No. Mickey and I went to a show ... we ran into Barry after ... he can confirm that ... when we came back here, Tony was gone."

Burke looked at Donahue who nodded briefly.

"So, he *was* staying here?"

"Yes."

"And you have no idea where he went?"

"No."

"What about you, Mickey? You have any idea where Tony is?"

"No."

Burke sighed. "Well, hell. I thought we'd find Tony tonight and then be on our way. But I can see that this is going to be more complicated." He took another sip. "Do you know why I want to find him?"

Gina knew there was no reason to deny that. "I suppose it has something to do with the money he thinks you have taken from him."

"Taken from him? Is that what he told you?"

"In so many words."

"I got the little twerp a job so he could settle his rather large debt to me with grace. Then he gets the idea that the money from the job belongs to him. Can you believe that shit?"

"I don't know what to believe. I just know what he told me."

"Then you agree that money might actually be mine?"

"Look, Tony is my cousin and I love him dearly, but I also know what kind of a guy he is. The truth does not always come easily to him."

Burke laughed. "Tony wouldn't know the truth if it came up and bit him on the ass." Donahue laughed too. Mickey even smiled.

Gina sat stony-faced. "He's no saint. Are you?"

Burke stopped laughing. "Point taken. But, none-the-less, the money in question … one hundred and fifty large … is mine and your cousin has managed to take it from the delivery boys."

Gina and Mickey looked at one another. She looked back at Burke. "He did?"

"Yes, he did. And I take offense to that."

Mickey could not be silent any longer. "That seems to be a problem between you and Tony. What do you want with us?"

Burke looked at him intently. "That's right … ah …"

"Mickey."

"Right, Mickey. That's right, Mickey, it is between me and Tony. But I don't know where Tony is and that's why I need your help."

"Our help? Gina told you that she doesn't know where Tony is either."

"She did. And I believe her. But she … and you … are still going to help us locate him."

Mickey didn't like where this was heading. "How so?"

"Well, Gina is going to come with us now, and you're going to stay here to tell Tony … when he returns … that he either gives us back our money or he will not see his pretty cousin again."

Mickey stood up quickly. Just as quickly Donahue pushed him back in his seat. "I told you to relax, tough guy."

Mickey had been in a few scrapes in the past … sometimes they worked out in his favor, sometimes not … so he was no stranger to physical violence, but Donahue was a professional and he knew how that would work out. He straightened in his seat and regained his composure. "Tell your trained monkey here to keep his hands off me."

"He will, if you just do as he says and relax," said Burke.

"I'm not about to relax while you're threatening Gina."

Gina looked at him.

Burke smiled. "Very gentlemanly of you, but also futile."

Gina touched his arm. She knew what Donahue could do. "He's right, Mickey. You don't need to get involved."

Mickey looked at her. "You think I'm not involved now?"

She dropped her hand. "I know you mean well, but I can take care of myself."

"So, I'm supposed to sit here while these goons take you away." He shifted his gaze to Donahue.

"Friends, Mickey. We're all friends here," said Burke. "Why, Barry and Gina go way back, right Gina?"

"I know him."

Mickey shifted his gaze back to Burke. "I don't care if they were married. Why don't you just get the hell out of here?"

"We are leaving, but not without Gina."

Mickey looked back at Donahue and saw the barrel of a 9mm pointed at him.

"We're not fooling around here," continued Burke. "Gina is going with us. She'll be alright as long as Tony cooperates."

"Yeah, well, I know Tony and I don't like those odds."

"Then you'll have to be very persuasive, Mickey. I know you can be."

Gina touched his arm again. "It'll be alright. I can take care of myself."

Mickey looked at her. She smiled and looked reassuring. "Don't worry. I can handle these guys."

Mickey knew she was right. She probably had a much better chance getting through this if he just backed off and let her go. He looked back at Burke. "What assurance do I have that you're not going to hurt her?"

Burke looked back with steely eyes. "None, really. But you don't have any choice either." Then his face softened. "But we're not going hurt her, Mickey. All you have to do is tell Tony to call us and we'll work it out with him … Gina will be fine."

"You said that he had to return the money or he 'wouldn't see his pretty cousin alive'. Isn't that what you said?"

"Maybe I said that … but that was just for dramatic affect … just so you would know that we're not kidding around here. Really, if you just make sure Tony contacts us I'm sure that we will work something out."

Mickey didn't believe him. He knew that he was going to have to do more than just get Tony to contact Burke. He was going to have to convince him to give the money back to Burke. "You and I both know that's bullshit, but you've got me over a barrel right now. But so help me if you harm her in any way I'll be coming after you."

Donahue laughed. "I'd look forward to that, tough guy."

Mickey's face grew red.

Gina stood up to prevent any further escalation. "Let's go, Barry."

Burke stood up. "That's a good girl." He set his glass down on a table next to the chair. "Nice to meet you, Mickey. Thanks for the drink." He started for the door then stopped suddenly. He pulled a card out of his pocket and flicked it into Mickey's lap. "That's my cell number." Then he waved his hand toward the door. "After you, Gina."

Donahue set his beer bottle down and stepped to the side so they would not pass between he and Mickey, the gun remained pointed at him. "Just sit tight, tough guy."

Mickey squeezed his knees. "I'm telling you asshole …"

Gina interrupted. "Do you mind if I get my purse?"

Burke kept escorting her toward the door. "Anything you need, we'll get for you." He opened the door. "Come on, Barry."

"Better go. Your master is calling you."

Donahue smiled and backed toward the door. "I hope we get to meet again."

"We will."

Gina turned in the doorway. "Don't worry, Mickey. I'll be alright."

"I know you will."

26

The streaks of gray were beginning to glow in the eastern sky when Mickey heard voices outside the door. The lock mechanism cycled and the door opened. Tony and Lou walked in. Lou was carrying the Dolphins duffel bag and Tony had a wad of bills in his hand and both men were laughing.

Tony stopped when he saw Mickey standing by the window. "Damn, Ace, what are you doing up?"

"Where the hell have you been?"

Tony waved the bills in his hand. "Kicking ass and taking names, if it is any of your business. I just hit the Triple Diamond machine for …"

"Gina is gone."

"… eight hundred clams …"

"They took Gina."

"What did you say?"

"I said Gina is gone."

"What the hell are you talking about?"

"Your buddies … Barry Donahue and Max Burke kidnapped your cousin."

Tony looked at Lou who was still giggling. Then he looked back at Mickey. "Donahue and Burke were here?"

Lou stopped laughing. He set the bag down.

"Tony, they took Gina." Mickey sat down on the couch and stared out the window.

"Donahue and Burke have Gina?"

"Yes."

"Gina is not here."

"No, she's not here … go look if you want to."

"You're not joking are you?"

"No, Tony, I'm not joking."

"Holy shit."

"Hey, Tony …" said Lou.

"Not right now, Lou." Tony ran his hand over his head. "You were here?"

Mickey looked at Tony. "Yes."

"And you let them leave with Gina?"

"What the hell was I supposed to do? Donahue was holding a gun on me."

"Geez, Tony …" said Lou.

Tony ignored Lou. "Yeah, I guess you were in a bind."

"A bind? They took your cousin and it's your goddamn fault."

"My fault?"

"You know damn well it is."

"Hey, Tony …" said Lou.

Tony glanced at Lou. He had a worried look on his face. "Go fix yourself a drink, Lou."

"What does this mean, Tony?"

"Just go fix yourself a drink and let me think, will ya?"

"You know, I work in this town and …"

"Lou!"

Lou walked over to the bar, muttering as he went. "All right, all right, I'm just trying to protect my interests here."

Tony followed Mickey's gaze out of the window. For several seconds the only sound in the room was the noise Lou made rummaging around the bar.

Lou's voice broke the silence. "Hey, where are the glasses?"

Tony ignored Lou's inquiry and walked over to Gina's bedroom. He stood in the open door and looked around the empty room. A few items of clothing were scattered about and her purse sat on the rumpled but empty bed.

"Oh, here they are," said Lou.

Tony glanced at Lou behind the bar. Then he walked slowly back to the living room. He dropped the money on the table next the chair that Burke had occupied and sat down heavily. He leaned forward and put his elbows on his knees and put his face in his hands. "When were they here?" he asked through his fingers.

Mickey looked over at him. "A couple of hours ago."

Tony sat back and sighed. "So that was what? About 3:00?"

"Yeah."

"See, I was right, Lou. If we had come straight back here instead of playing the slots, we'd have run smack into Burke."

"You were playing the slots?"

"Yeah, I felt like celebrating."

"Celebrating?"

"Hell yeah. I got the drop on Vince and Sheldon and got my money back."

"Your money?"

"Yeah, why?"

"Because Burke evidently thinks it is his money and he wants it back. That's why he took Gina."

"He's holding Gina ransom?"

"He wants you to call him." Mickey flipped Burke's card at Tony. It fell on the floor.

Tony slammed his fist on the arm of the chair. "It's too bad she had to get mixed up in this."

"You're going to call him, right?"

"Damn it."

"What's the issue, Tony? Your cousin is in danger … you've got call these people."

Tony stood up and started pacing back and forth in front of the window. "I know, I know, it's just that …"

"What? It's just what?"

"I've gone through so much to get that money."

"So what? It's Gina we're talking about."

Holding a martini glass, Lou walked over from the bar and sat down in Tony's chair. "What are you going to do, Tony?"

"Shut up, Lou."

Lou shook his head. "Look man, this is way more than I bargained for …"

Tony stopped pacing. "Lou …"

"He's right," said Mickey. "This has gone too far."

"Damn it." Tony started pacing again.

"There is no issue here, Tony. You've just got to call and arrange to get Gina back."

"I know. I know. Just give me some time to think, okay?"

"What is there to think about?"

Tony stopped pacing again. "Will you both just shut up and give me a minute to think?"

Mickey stood up and faced Tony. "You've got five minutes, then you're calling."

Tony starred back. "It's five o'clock in the morning."

"You're afraid you're going to wake them up?"

"Well …"

Mickey bent down and picked up Burke's card from floor. He held it up for Tony to see. "Five minutes." He set it on the table, walked into his bedroom and shut the door.

Tony started pacing again. "Damn it."

"This is some heavy shit, Tony."

Tony stopped and looked out the window. "I know it, Lou."

"Maybe I should be going. I've to work this afternoon."

Tony turned and looked at him. "Just stay put, Lou. I may need some help here."

"Come on, Tony, my ass is hanging out here."

"Nothing is going to happen to you."

"That Burke guy seems to be pretty well connected around here …"

"Lou, nothing is going to happen. Just relax, will ya?"

"What are you going to do?"

"How the hell do I know?"

"You going to call Burke?"

Tony stared back out at the brightening skyline. "I don't know … yeah … I don't know … maybe."

"Mickey's going to be pissed if you don't."

"Mickey can pound sand up is ass. He doesn't call the shots around here."

"Yeah … sure. Who the fuck is he, eh?"

Mickey stared in the bathroom mirror at his bloodshot eyes as he idly dried his hands with a towel. *Shit. How could he have let those bastards leave with Gina?* He threw the towel on the counter top, walked to the bed, sat on the edge and lay back. He was exhausted but knew he couldn't sleep. He could hear Tony and Lou talking in the other room. *What if Tony refused to call Burke?*

He remembered the look on Gina's face just before she walked out the door. She told him she'd be all right, and he was sure she would be … for a while at least. But then what? If Tony wouldn't call, he'd go after Gina himself. He didn't have any idea how, but he'd figure something out.

He was suddenly aware of silence in the living room. He got up and went to the door. Nothing. He opened the door. Tony was standing by the window. He didn't see Lou.

"Tony are you going to …"

Tony turned and looked at him. He held up his hand. Mickey hadn't seen that he was holding a phone to his ear.

"Max, it's me, Tony. I need to talk to you as soon as possible, so call me at this number, okay?" Tony snapped the phone shut. "He didn't answer."

Mickey walked into the room. "That's weird. You'd think he'd be standing by to take your call. Where's Lou?"

Tony swung his thumb toward Gina's room. "In the john." He went back to the chair and sat down. "Did you honestly think I wasn't going to call?"

"I wasn't sure. And if you're honest, you weren't either."

Tony nodded toward the duffel bag. "There's a lot of cabbage in that bag, and I went through hell trying to get it."

"I know, but your cousin?"

"Don't lecture me about family. Gina is a peach … she has always looked out for me."

"So what's the dilemma?"

"I worked hard for that money and I'm not about to let that slimy mick steal it from me."

"You're not going to give it to him to get Gina back?"

"I didn't say that."

"But you're thinking it, aren't you?"

"I want to be smart about this. Every time I try to cut a deal on my own, something always fucks up. I'm tired of that shit."

"This is no time to be clever, Tony. Just give Burke his money …"

"My money."

"… *the* money … and get Gina back here."

Tony looked at him. "Why are you suddenly so interested in Gina's welfare?"

Mickey blushed slightly. "I'm not, it's just that …"

"You got a thing for my cousin?"

"No, I'm just concerned about her, that's all."

Tony smiled slightly. "You do, don't you? You've got a thing for Gina."

"No, I …"

Gina's phone rang.

Still looking at Mickey, Tony picked up the phone. "Well, I'll be damned." He flipped open the phone and held it to his ear. "Yeah?"

"Sorry I missed your call, Tony. The cell service on the highway is not all it's cracked up to be." Burke's voice was surprisingly friendly.

Tony stood up. "Look asshole, you had no right to get Gina involved in this."

"Whoa, there tough guy. Let's not go throwing around names we wouldn't use in person."

"I'd use it in person, asshole."

"Somehow I doubt that."

"Did you say you're on the highway?"

"Yeah."

"With Gina?"

"She's resting comfortably."

"Where are you taking her?"

"It'll cost you to find out."

"What do you mean?"

"You give me my money back and I'll tell you where Gina is."

"So, you're holding her for ransom?"

"If you want to get technical."

"And if I don't give you the money?"

"Let's not go there."

"You know who her father is?"

"Severino Sandrelli."

"You think he is going to stand for this?"

"Somehow I don't think you're going to involve him."

Tony pulled the phone away from his ear. He ran his hand over his hair. Burke was right, there was no way he was going tell his uncle that he was responsible for putting Gina in harm's way. "Damn it."

"What?" asked Mickey.

"Nothing." Tony put the phone back to his ear. "I knew you were a sleaze bag, Burke, but I didn't think you'd stoop to being a kidnapper."

"Yeah? Well, where are my delivery boys?"

"Vince and Sheldon?"

"Yeah. What about Vince and Sheldon? "

"That's different."

"It is, eh?"

"I'm not holding Vince and Sheldon.

"Oh? Where are they?"

"On a nature hike."

"Upright?"

"Last I saw them. Besides, that has nothing to do with Gina."

"What do you think Johnny Rodriquez will say about that?

"Johnny knows that money is mine … he knows I was after it."

"That's you're story."

"Look, cut the bullshit, Burke. How do I get Gina back?"

"That's better, Tony. I'll make it very easy. You bring the money to me I'll give you Gina."

"Where?"

"Newport Beach."

"I thought you said you'd make it easy."

"That's pretty easy."

"No it isn't. I'm in Las Vegas. You bring Gina back here."

"I don't like doing business in Vegas … it makes me feel anxious," said Burke.

"How do you propose I get to Newport Beach?" asked Tony.

"You've been traipsing across the country … surely another couple hundred miles can't be a big deal," said Burke.

"You bring Gina back here and I'll give you the money."

"You're not in a position to set the terms."

Tony held the phone down. "Son of a bitch."

"What is going on, Tony?" asked Mickey.

"Burke wants me to bring the money to Newport Beach."

"In California?"

"Yeah."

They could here a faint voice coming from the cell phone. Tony put the phone back to his ear. "Give me a second, will, ya?" He pulled the phone away again.

"Okay, we'll go," said Mickey.

"What are talking about … we?"

"We'll fly there and take Burke his money."

"We will?"

"Yes, Tony, we will. Just tell Burke we're coming."

Tony stared at Mickey for few seconds. Then he put the phone back to his ear. "All right, Max. How do we hook up?"

"You call me as soon as you're in town, and we'll make the arrangements." said Burke.

"Why can't we make them now?"

"You just call."

The line went dead. Tony snapped the phone shut. "Jesus, when is this nightmare going to end?"

Mickey was already spreading a map out on the coffee table.

Mickey pointed at the map. "It looks like the best bet would be to fly into Long Beach."

"What about Orange County? Isn't that closer to Newport Beach?"

"A little, maybe. But it's a big airport. I've been to Long Beach before and it is friendlier to GA aircraft."

"Long Beach, eh?"

"There is a decent FBO there called Long Beach Center."

Tony rubbed his chin. "You know that just might work out."

Mickey started toward the bedroom. "I'll get my stuff. Let's go."

Tony looked at the clock. "Hold on there, Ace."

Mickey stopped and looked at Tony. "What?"

"I need some time."

Lou walked back into the room. "What? What's going on?"

"Time for what?" said Mickey. "We're going to California to give Burke his money."

"I'm not going to California," said Lou.

"Will you shut up, Lou?" said Tony.

"I'm just saying that …"

Mickey interrupted Lou. "There's no reason to wait. Let's go."

Tony sighed. "Look, I'm exhausted. I need to grab a couple of hours of sleep."

"How the hell can you sleep now?"

"You look tired too, Ace. You can't fly without some rest."

"I can't sleep now. We've got to get going."

Tony stood up and started toward Gina's bedroom. "You do whatever you have to. I'm going to conk out for couple of hours."

"What about me?" asked Lou.

"You go home, Lou. I'll call you later."

"I'm telling you I'm not getting in any deeper."

"Don't worry, you're not getting in any deeper. We'll just need a ride to the airport. So go home. I'll call you later."

"I could use a little gas money."

Tony nodded toward the money on the table. "Take that, buddy. It's yours."

"You sure?"

"You've earned it. Take it."

Lou picked up the money. "Thanks." He headed toward the door.

"Tony …" said Mickey.

"Get some rest," said Tony. "We've got a big day ahead of us." He walked into Gina's bedroom and shut the door.

"See you later," said Lou.

Mickey watched the door shut behind Lou. "Yeah."

27

The desert sun had risen high enough over the adjacent hotel for its rays to hit Mickey squarely in the eyes. He blinked and rolled over on his side to avoid them. He opened his eyes again and saw a soft beige light laced with pencil thin shadows of dark. As his eyes slowly focused he realized he was staring at the raised stripes of the material on the back of the couch. He sat up quickly and looked around the empty room. He pulled his cell phone from his pocket and flipped it open. 11:00. *Damn it.* He must have dozed off shortly after Lou left.

He got up, crossed the room and looked in Gina's bedroom. Empty. "Tony," he yelled. No response. He went to other bedroom and looked in. It too was empty. He walked around the living room and looked at the vestiges of last night. The furniture was askew and throw pillows were on the floor. Two empty drink glasses sat on the table next to the chair that Burke and Tony had both occupied. He picked up the glasses and took them over to the bar. He set them on the counter next to a coffee machine. The thought of a cup of coffee was appealing, so he decided to prepare a pot. While the coffee brewed, he went into the bathroom and splashed some water on his face. He looked and felt like hell, so he decided to shave and take a quick shower.

Fifteen minutes later he was standing at the window in the living room sipping coffee. He watched the throngs of tourists walking along the strip far below. Tony had suspected that his anxiousness about Gina was driven by something more than just concern for her welfare. Perhaps he was right. Gina had world weariness that matched his own, but she was open and honest in a way that so many of the girls Mickey had dated since his divorce generally lacked. Of course, it didn't hurt that he found her physically attractive.

Where the hell is Tony? He flipped open his phone and then realized that Tony was carrying Gina's phone. He didn't have her number. He looked out the window and saw a Cessna flying high over the desert. He opened his phone, found the number for Hayes airport and made the call.

"Hayes airport."

"It's me, Betty."

"Who?"

"Mickey."

"Mickey who?"

"Come on, Betty, it hasn't been that long."

"There used to be a Mickey who worked here."

"I need to talk to Glenn."

"This better be good."

"Betty …"

"Okay, I'll get him."

Mickey watched the Cessna drone on to the west. Then he heard Glenn's voice.

"Where the hell are you?"

"I'm in Vegas."

"Vegas!"

"It's a long story, Glenn … I'll tell you all about it when I get back."

"When will that be?"

"I'm not sure anymore."

"Are you in some sort of trouble, Mickey?"

"No, nothing like that."

"Well, what's going on?"

"My charter just keeps asking me to go further … he's paying me well, so I do."

"He better be paying you better than well … you're missing a lot of flight lessons."

"Yeah, I'm really sorry about that …"

"Don't worry, Taylor is happy to pick up the slack."

I'll bet he is, thought Mickey. "Glenn, am I still going to have a job when I get back?"

"I don't know. When is that going to be?"

"I'm just not sure at the moment."

"You sure you're okay?"

"Sure I'm sure."

"Look, Mickey, you just finish up your charter and get back when you can … there will always be more students."

"Thanks, Glenn, I appreciate that."

"And Mickey …"

"Yeah?"

"You be careful, okay?"

"I promise, Glenn."

Mickey snapped the phone shut. He looked for the Cessna, but it was out of sight. He finished his coffee and suddenly realized that he was starving. He wrote a note to Tony that he was downstairs in the coffee shop having a bite to eat and would be back in half an hour … and not to go anywhere.

Mickey walked across the casino on his way back from the coffee shop. A few people were working the slots, but it was nowhere near as busy as it would be later in the afternoon. Many of the dealers at the table games stood idly, cards splayed showily on the felt before them as bait, hoping to snare a hapless gambler. One dealer was busily filling an empty shoe at a table occupied by a single player. Mickey stopped abruptly. The player was Tony.

Mickey grabbed him by the arm. "What the hell are you doing?"

Startled, Tony turned around. Seeing Mickey his face went from panic to anger. He shook Mickey's hand from his arm. "Jesus, Ace. You scared the shit out of me."

"Do you know it's almost noon?"

"So what? We're not in any hurry."

"We're not in any … Gina is at the mercy of those thugs, you idiot."

"Relax. Nothing is going to happen to her. Besides they're probably still on the road to LA."

"We should be there waiting for them."

"I told you, they're not going to hurt her. We'll leave in a while." Tony slid a stack of chips toward Mickey. "Here, sit down and play a few hands … on me."

"Are you playing, sir?" Mickey looked up at the dealer. The tag on her blouse read Mabel.

"He's playing, Mabel." Tony grabbed a couple of chips off the stack in front of Mickey and placed a bet for him. Then he grabbed a couple from his own pile and placed a bet for himself. "Sit down, Ace, you're making Mabel nervous."

Mabel looked at Mickey, but he remained standing. "We don't have time for Blackjack."

Mabel patted the table and dealt the cards from the shoe.

"Sure we do," said Tony. "I'm telling you there is no big hurry … sit down."

"Maybe you don't think so, but I do."

Tony looked at him and smiled. "That's right, your interest in Gina is more than passing, isn't it?"

Mickey blushed and looked away.

Tony slapped him on the arm. "Hey, I think it's great. Gina is a terrific woman."

Mickey turned and faced him again. "Then why aren't we going after her?"

"Card, sir?" interrupted Maple.

Tony looked at the cards. Mabel had dealt Mickey a five and a six. Tony had a queen and a four. The dealer showed a two. "Hey, you have a perfect hand to double down."

"What?" Mickey looked at the table. He looked up at Mabel and she smiled at him.

"It doesn't get better than that, Ace," said Tony.

Mickey took a couple of chips off the pile in front of him and placed them next to the bet.

Mabel dealt him a seven and turned to Tony. "Sir?"

Tony held up his hand. "I'm good."

Mabel flipped over her hole card. A ten. She dealt herself a three. Then a jack. "Dealer busts," she said.

Tony slapped Mickey on the arm again. "See that, Ace. We've got it going on. Sit down and let's play awhile."

"You go ahead. I'm going back up to the room to pack up." Mickey turned to go.

Mabel had paid off the bets and was waiting for Tony to place another. "Sir?"

Tony picked a couple of chips off his stack and flipped them to Mabel. "Here, dear, that's for you." He stuffed the rest of his chips in his pocket and stood up.

"Thank you, sir." Mabel put the chips in her tip box. "Good luck today."

"I'm going to need it."

Mickey stuffed the pack of underwear and the two extra t-shirts he had bought in the hotel into the laundry bag from the closet. He could hear Tony in the living room talking to Lou on the phone, trying to get him to drive them to the airport. Mickey went into the bathroom and grabbed his toothbrush, razor and shaving cream and stuffed them into the bag. He went into the bedroom and gave it one last look around. He walked into the living room just as Tony flipped the phone shut.

"Well?"

"He'll be here in fifteen minutes," said Tony.

"Good. Let's head down to the lobby, then."

Tony looked at the Dolphin's bag sitting on the bar. "You go on down and look for Lou. I'll there in a few minutes."

"Tony."

"What? I just have a couple of calls to make."

"Can't you make them on the way?"

"Can't you just go down and look for Lou? I said I'd be there."

Mickey gave Tony a long look. Then he grabbed his jacket off the back of the couch and walked out of the room.

As soon as the door shut, Tony flipped open the phone and punched up a number.

A familiar voice answered. "Ms. Sandrelli?"

"Levi, it's me, Tony."

"Oh, Mr. Boccaccio, I thought it was Ms. Sandrelli."

"I'm using her phone. Listen I need a favor Levi."

"Is Ms. Sandrelli around?"

"No, Levi, but I …"

"'Cause I need to talk her."

"I know, but …"

"Things are getting crazy around here and I need some help."

"I know, but …"

"She said she would only be gone for a couple of days, and now it's …"

"Levi, I need a favor."

"I'm sorry, it's just that I can't run this place all by myself."

"I know, and she'll be back to help soon, I promise. But I need you to do something for me right now."

"What do you need, Mr. Boccaccio?"

"I need a phone number."

"Who's?"

"Go back in the office and look in the middle drawer of my desk … you'll see a red phone book. Go get it and bring it back to the phone, okay?"

"All right, just a minute."

Tony walked to the bar and poured a drink. He took a sip and held it to his forehead until he heard Levi say, "I've got it. What do you need?"

"Great. Look up the number for Carl Fontaine."

Tony jotted down the number. "Thanks a million, Levi."

"When is Ms. Sandrelli coming back?"

"Soon, Levi."

"I hope so, 'cause I can't run this place all by myself."

"I know. Look I've got to go. Thanks, Levi."

"Can I talk to Ms. Sandrelli?"

"Not right now, Levi. I'll have her call you soon."

Tony flipped the phone shut. He took a long pull on the drink and punched up the number Levi had given him. A few seconds later, he said, "Carl. Hey this is Tony."

"Tony who?" said a voice on the other end.

"What do you mean Tony who? Tony Boccaccio, that's who."

"Yeah, I knew, I was just pulling your leg. How the hell are you?"

"I'm great. Listen, I need a favor."

"Oh, oh."

"Come on, Carl, don't start with me."

"Hey, I haven't heard from you in two years, and the first thing out of your mouth is 'I need a favor'."

"Carl, this serious. I really need your help."

"Is this a job?"

"No, no nothing like that … well, not exactly."

"Tony …"

"It's a long story, but I'm on my way to LA and I'll need some help when I get there."

"What kind of help?"

"I'm just making a delivery and I need some transportation."

"A delivery? How hot is it?"

"It's not hot … I can't explain it right now … it's part of that long story."

"It's always a story with you, Tony. Where are you now?"

"Vegas."

"Vegas? What the hell are doing there?"

"That's part of the story … I'll tell you all about it when I get there."

"You know, every time I get involved with you, something goes haywire."

"Yeah, I know, I know, there have been some fuck ups …"

"Fuck ups? That's putting it mildly."

"Are you going to help me or not?"

"What do you need?"

"To start with, how about a ride from the airport."

"LAX?"

"No, Long Beach."

"Long Beach. Hell, that's right next door."

"I know, that's why I thought you'd be able to help."

"When are you going to be here?"

"Sometime this afternoon."

"Can you be a little more specific?"

"No, I'm not traveling on a commercial airliner; I've chartered a small plane. But I do know that we'll be at the Long Beach Center."

"What's that?"

"It's an FBO."

"What?"

"Never mind. Just ask somebody at the airport where the Long Beach Center is."

"Jesus, Tony, you never call me unless you need something."

"So are you going to help me or not."

There was a long pause.

"Carl?"

"Yeah, yeah, I'll pick you up from the airport."

28

Mickey stood in the lobby watching people come and go. A black SUV pulled up immediately followed by a stretch limo. Two beefy guys, wearing black t-shirts and sporting a variety of tattoos on their arms, jumped out of the SUV and ran back to open the rear door of the limo. A twenty-something male, dressed in faded jeans, white t-shirt, gray sports jacket, hair studiously tousled, stepped out, followed by a dewy blonde girl, also in jeans, bare mid-rift showing beneath a form-fitting red blouse. The black t-shirted guys made a big show of clearing a path to the lobby, but oddly, only two or three people seemed to notice the young celebrities. As they approached the door, an elderly man and woman, dressed in matching yellow sweat suits, were just exiting. The black shirts nudged them aside to allow the young couple to pass through the door. The old man said, "Who the hell is that?" The woman just shrugged. They turned and went on their way.

Mickey didn't know either, but he stepped back to allow the entourage to pass as they made their way through the lobby. A few people stopped to stare, but most seemed to be more curious about the commotion than star watching. Mickey turned back to the driveway to watch for Lou's Lexus. He saw a cab pulled up and a handsome, athletic black man get out. He paid the driver and turned to look around the entrance. He, too, was dressed in jeans, loafers without socks, and a cotton shirt that hung loosely over his waist. He was wearing a baseball cap with a Miami Dolphins logo.

"Ace."

Mickey turned and saw Tony coming across the lobby carrying the Miami Dolphins duffle bag.

"Lou here yet?"

Mickey shook his head.

"Where the hell is that guy?" Tony looked through the tinted glass wall toward the entrance. "Holy shit."

"What?"

Tony turned and hustled back into the casino.

"Tony, where the hell are you going?"

Mickey looked back toward the entrance. The man from the taxi was coming through the door. He looked briefly at Mickey, and then walked on past headed toward the registration desk.

"What the hell?" Mickey followed Tony into the casino. He stood for a moment and looked around. Then he spotted Tony as he disappeared around a bank of nickel slots. Mickey turned down the aisle after him. Tony was at the end of the row, sitting in front of a machine, the bag sitting on his lap. He was leaning to one side and looking down the cross aisle.

Mickey walked quickly down the row of machines. "What the hell is going on?"

Tony almost fell off the seat. "Christ." He was holding his heart. "What the hell are you trying to do?"

"I'm trying to find out what is going on."

"That was Vince Jackson."

"Who?"

"The guy in the taxi."

Mickey nodded. "I figured it was someone you knew."

"How the hell did he get back here so soon?"

"What do you mean?"

"Last I saw him, he and Sheldon were chasing donkeys in the desert."

"What the hell are you talking about?"

Tony leaned out to look down the aisle and turned back to Mickey. "When I got my money back from those bastards," he patted the bag on his lap, "I left them in the desert to contemplate the misdeeds of their miserable lives."

"You left them in the desert?"

"Like they did to me, remember?"

"Last night?"

"No, last week."

"I mean, you left those guys out in the desert last night?"

"Yeah. I can't believe how fast they got back into town."

"Oh, this is just great."

Tony looked down the aisle again. "We gotta get the hell out of here … taco pronto." He pulled Gina's phone out of his pocket and looked at the time. "Vince doesn't know who you are … you go back to the lobby and watch for Lou. But be careful 'cause if Vince sees Lou's car he might recognize it."

"Oh, great. What then?"

"I don't know. Lou will be on his own, I guess."

"What about me?"

"Just get the hell out of there."

Mickey held his gaze on Tony for few seconds.

"What?"

"You're crazy, Tony."

Tony shrugged. "When Lou gets here, call me on Gina's phone … you got her number in your phone?"

"No."

Tony flipped the phone open. "What's your number?"

Mickey told him and Tony punched it in. Mickey's phone rang. He opened it and snapped it shut.

"There, you've got the number. Now call me as soon as Lou gets here."

"Okay." Mickey walked around Tony and turned down the aisle. He glanced back and saw Tony watching him from behind the slot machine. He shook his head and kept going.

Occupying the same spot in the lobby he had earlier, Mickey watched Vince walk back from the registration area, cross the lobby and stand by a bank of elevators. He glanced over at Mickey, so Mickey quickly turned and looked back at the entry. He was pretty sure that Vince had seen him looking at him, but he didn't want to look back again. He just pretended that he was casually watching people come and go.

He saw Lou's Lexus pull up to the entrance and almost simultaneously heard the bell of the elevator. He glanced at them long enough to see Vince walking through the elevator door. As soon as the door shut, he pulled out his phone and made the call to Tony.

"Yeah?"

"Lou's here."

"You see Vince?"

"He just got on an elevator."

"Really? I wonder how he found out which room we were in."

"You want to wait around to ask him?"

The phone went dead at the same time he saw Tony walking into the lobby.

"Where's Lou?"

Mickey nodded toward the entrance.

"Let's go, then."

Mickey followed Tony outside. Tony jumped into the front seat, Mickey the back.

"What the hell took you so long?" Tony demanded.

"You woke me out of a sound sleep … we were up all night, remember?"

"It's a good thing you didn't arrive any earlier," said Mickey.

"Why is that?" asked Lou.

"You would have run smack into that Vince Jackson guy."

Tony nodded. "Yeah, you're right."

"Vince Jackson?" asked Lou. "He was here."

"Is here," corrected Mickey.

"How the fu ..."

"I got no idea," said Tony. "I sure thought he and Sheldon would be chasing their asses around that desert for while."

Lou put the car in gear and pulled away. "Oh, this is great. Now I got those two goons to worry about."

"Don't worry, Lou. It's me they are going after."

"So what happens when they don't find you? They're gonna start looking for me."

"They got no idea who you are."

"What if they made my license plate when we dropped them off last night?"

"You think they got friends in the Nevada DMV?"

"They must have some friends around here," said Mickey. "They seem to have found you."

"Yeah, what about that, Tony?"

Tony stared straight ahead.

"I'm telling you, Tony, if those guys start nosing around my casino, I'm screwed."

"Lou, will you shut up?"

"What about that, Tony. What if they track me down at the ..."

"Lou."

Lou kept mumbling to himself as they eased out onto the highway.

Tony turned to look back at Mickey. "How long will it take us to get to LA?"

"I don't know ... probably an hour or so ... depending on the winds. No more than two."

Tony nodded, and then settled back in seat for the rest of the ride to the airport.

"Damn." Sheldon winced as he applied an antibiotic salve to the bottom of his foot. It was raw and still bleeding from the desert. The sun was coming up over Red Rock Canyon when an elderly couple touring the park spotted them walking down the road. The old man was shocked after Sheldon told him that they had been dropped off in that condition, but Sheldon convinced him that it was just a prank a friend had pulled.

"Some prank," the man had said.

"Yeah," Sheldon answered from the backseat. "Our buddy is going to get his when we get back to town."

Sitting next to him, Vince nodded his head. "That's right, we're gonna think of something really juicy to pull on ol' Tony."

"Well, maybe you ought to talk to the cops when we get back to the ranger station," said the man.

"Cops?" asked Sheldon.

"Yeah, I guess somebody shot the chain off the gate last night."

"Really?"

"You didn't notice?" said the man.

"Gee, the gate was open when we got here."

"I still think you should involve the police in this," said the man.

"Don't worry … what's your name?"

"Densmore … Roger Densmore. This is my wife, Alice."

Alice sat stonily in the passenger seat.

"Don't worry, Roger, I assure there is no reason to get the police into this."

Vince had a worried look on his face. Sheldon shook his head. "Don't worry," he mouthed.

The sun was already starting to broil the valley when they reached the exit of the park. A county police car parked in front. A ranger and a policeman were standing near the entry gate. The cop was writing something on a pad. He looked up when he heard the Densmore car at the exit, a few dozen yards away.

"There they are," said Roger. "You sure you don't want to talk to them?"

"No, no, will just ride along with you back to town," said Sheldon.

Alice looked over at Roger. He looked back at her and smiled. Then he looked at Sheldon through the rear view mirror. "Sure, sure," he said, "I know you want to get back to give the business to your buddy."

"You got it, Roger." Sheldon grinned back. "Say, what did you and Alice think of the Park, anyway?"

Roger pulled out onto the highway. "It's beautiful, don't you think, Alice?"

Alice nodded stiffly and stared out the windshield.

Sheldon turned to see the policeman looking at them, but another early morning visitor pulling up to the gate diverted his attention.

"Where to?" asked Roger as they rounded a bend.

The park disappeared behind them, and Sheldon turned back to the front. "Anywhere in town is fine."

"No, no. I can't drop you off just anywhere dressed like that."

Sheldon looked down at his bare legs. He was reluctant to let the Densmores know where they were staying, but Roger was right, they couldn't go anywhere like this without drawing a lot of attention. "Do you know where the Haven RV Resort is?"

"Are you kidding? That's where you're staying?"

"Yes."

"What a coincidence. That's where Alice and I park our RV." Roger reached over and slapped Alice on the leg. "Isn't that a hoot, Alice?"

Alice's face seemed to go a shade paler.

"Really?" said Sheldon.

"Hell yes. We rent a space year round but we don't stay all year."

"I'll be damned. Isn't that funny, Vince?"

Vince frowned. "Yeah, that's funny."

Sheldon and Roger chatted idly about Vegas on the ride back to town. Vince and Alice sat looking out the windows.

As they pulled off Blue Diamond road into the RV resort, the guard stepped out of his shack and approached the car. He smiled when Roger rolled down the window. "Oh, hi, Mr. Densmore."

"Hi, Phil," replied Roger.

Phil glanced at the back seat. "You got visitors?"

"Not exactly, Phil. This is Sheldon and Vince … they're staying here too?"

Phil didn't recognize them. "Really? What site."

Sheldon leaned forward. "631."

Phil looked down at his clipboard. "Mr. Isaacs?"

"Yep."

"Sorry I didn't recognize you, Mr. Isaacs."

"That's okay. We just got here a couple of days ago."

"Well, have a good day, folks." Phil stood back to allow the car to pass.

"See you later, Phil." Roger rolled up the window and drove into the park. He looked at Sheldon in the review mirror. "631 did you say?"

"That's it."

"Well, we're in 108 … in fact that's our place," said Roger.

Sheldon looked at the neatly kept trailer as they passed. "Very nice."

"Don't be strangers. Come on over and visit."

"I don't think we're going to be here much longer."

"When are you leaving?"

Sheldon looked at Vince. Vince shrugged. "Maybe today."

"Short visit, eh?"

"Just a stop on a road trip."

"Where are you headed?"

"LA."

"We'd much rather stay here than that beastly place, right Alice."

"Me too, Roger, but we've got business there," said Sheldon.

Roger pulled up to 631. "That's a nice rig. What happened to your door."

Sheldon looked at the duct tape that covered the window. "Got hit by a rock on the highway."

"Doesn't that just piss you off?"

"It sure does, Roger, it sure does."

Sheldon heard a dull thud, followed by, "Goddamnit." Vince had banged his elbow again in the tiny shower of the RV. "This fucking thing is like a phone booth," yelled Vince.

Sheldon picked up the phone that was sitting on the table in front of him. *No use putting it off any longer*, he thought. He punched up Burke's number.

"I wondered when you'd call," said the Burke on the other end.

"Who knew the guy was so resourceful?"

"He sure got the drop on you, didn't he?"

Sheldon blushed. "Look, Mr. Burke. I'm sorry. We just never expected to see the guy again."

"You should have made sure of that."

"We're not your hitters."

"No, I suppose not. But you lost my money, didn't you?"

Sheldon blushed again. "We're going to get it back."

"You're too late. I've already made arrangements for that."

"What?"

"I got tired of chasing Tony around the desert and decided to take a more direct approach."

"What are you talking about?"

"I've got the girl."

"What girl?"

"Tony's cousin, Gina?"

Sheldon tried to say something but couldn't.

"What's the matter, Sheldon, cat got your tongue?"

"How the hell did you do that?"

"What difference does that make? I've got her and Tony is bringing my money to me."

"Where?"

"You don't need to know."

"And Tony's coming to you?"

"What if we get to him first?"

"Forget about it. You'll just screw things up."

"Come on, Mr. Burke. We carried your money halfway across the country. You gotta give us a chance to fix this."

"Leave it alone, Sheldon. I've got it handled. I don't need you two idiots anymore."

"But …"

"I said forget about it."

Sheldon heard the line go dead. He still held the phone to his ear for a while before he snapped it shut and set it on the table.

―――――――――――――――――――――――――――――

"You talk to Burke?" Vince was buttoning his shirt when he came into the kitchen area of the RV.

Sheldon stared at the phone in front of him. "Yeah."

"Well, what'd he say?"

"He's got Gina."

"Who?"

"Tony's cousin, Gina. He's holding her for ransom."

"You're kidding." Vince smoothed out his shirt front.

Sheldon looked up at him. "Why don't you tuck your shirt in? You look like a slob."

"I'll wear my shirt any fucking way I please. What'd Burke say?"

"I told you, he's holding Gina."

"So what?"

"So, we're out of the loop. He's made a deal with Tony to bring him the money."

"Where?"

"He wouldn't say."

Vince slammed his fist on the counter top. "Son of a bitch. That means we don't get our 15k."

"That's exactly what it means."

"What if we get the money first?"

"Burke said to forget about it."

"Yeah, but what if we did? He's got no guarantee that Tony will deliver the money to him."

"He's got a pretty damn good guarantee. Tony's not going to risk his cousin for 150K."

"You don't know Tony."

"Well, Burke thinks he'll bring him the money and he told us to forget about it."

"There's no goddamn way I'm forgetting about it. That little bastard got the drop on us and I intend to make him pay."

"I'm telling you Burke will be pissed if we screw up his deal."

"He won't be pissed if he gets his money."

"Maybe not. But if the deal gets screwed up and he doesn't get his money … I'm telling you he'll be pissed and we'll be fucked."

"We'll get him his money."

Sheldon looked squarely at Vince. "You think so?"

"I know so." He sat down at the table across from Sheldon. "Look, we know Tony's probably staying at Vegas Station, and he's not likely to be in any big hurry … he thinks we're still wandering around the desert. I'll beat it over there and ambush him. He won't know what hit him."

"What if he's not there?"

"So what? We don't have the money now anyway. Besides, I'll track the bastard down."

"Vince, if you fuck this up you know it'll be our asses."

"I'm not going to fuck anything up. If I don't find him, then we're no worse off than we are now. If I do, I'll get the money, you can be sure of that."

Sheldon looked out the window.

"I'm telling you it'll work. I'll get the money. We'll take it to Burke and collect our 15K."

Sheldon looked back at Vince. He was dubious about Vince's plan, but he was mad enough at Tony to give it try. "All right. Go for it."

Vince grinned. "Damn straight. I'll get the sonofabitch. Call a taxi." He stood up and went back to the bedroom.

"You sure you can pull this off?"

"Absolutely," Vince yelled from the bedroom. "Hey, where's my hat?"

The phone Sheldon had set on the sink rang. He put down the tube of antibiotic salve and picked up the phone. "Yeah?"

"They're gone."

"How do you know?"

"Because I looked in their room, that's how."

"At Vegas Station?"

Vince sighed. "Yes, at Vegas Station."

"How'd you get in the room?"

"Because Dashanique's sister works the desk at the hotel."

"And she let you in?"

Vince sighed again. "She gave me a key."

Sheldon shook his head. "You got pull, that's all I can say."

"Yeah."

"How long ago did they leave?"

"Hard to tell, but it kinda looked like they had just left."

"What now?"

"I'm going to try to find that little twerp that was helping him."

"Lou?"

"Yeah, Lou."

"How are you going to find him?"

"Remember him saying something about working at a casino?"

"Vaguely."

"I'm pretty sure that's what he said. I'm going to cruise up and down the strip and see if I can find him."

"Seems like finding a needle in a haystack."

"Maybe, but I'm going to check around … maybe I'll get lucky."

29

Mickey watched the desert slip by below them. Mountains dotted the horizon and the sun reflected off the endless shades of brown that was the southwest. It reminded him of his trips across northern Mexico, but with sweating hands and a stomach in knots he never really appreciated the stark beauty. He wasn't all that much more relaxed now, but at least he didn't have to worry about dodging Customs and Immigration. He wasn't worried about Gina's safety, he knew Burke wouldn't hurt her now, but he wasn't too sure what would happen if Tony tried to get cute with this deal, and he was pretty sure Tony would try anything to keep his money.

He looked over at a sleeping Tony. He was envious because he hadn't got much sleep and the steady droning of *Songbird* across the vast open spaces made his eyelids heavy. But it was time to start planning for their descent into Long Beach and things would start to happen fast after that.

Tony woke up when he heard Mickey talking to the Los Angeles Control Center. He was still pissed that Mickey insisted on filing a flight plan before they took off from Las Vegas, but Mickey said that the LAX airspace was too big and there was too much traffic around LA to try to fly into Long Beach VFR. "How long till we land?" he asked.

Mickey held up a hand and then read back instructions from the controller. When he finished he looked at the GPS then over to Tony. "It looks like about forty-five minutes."

Tony nodded and looked out the window at the desert below.

"What are we going to do when we get there?" asked Mickey.

"I've got a buddy picking us up."

"You've got friends everywhere."

Tony looked at Mickey and smiled. "I'm a friendly guy."

"When do we meet with Burke?"

He looked back out the window. "You don't need to worry about that."

"I'm not worried … I just want to know."

"I'm supposed to call him when we get there."

"You're not going to do anything stupid are you? I mean, you're just going to give Burke his money, get Gina and get the hell out of there, right?"

"You got it."

"You're not bullshitting me here?"

Tony looked back at Mickey. "You really are worried about Gina, aren't you?"

Mickey blushed. "Of course, she's in danger."

Tony grinned and slapped him on the leg. "Well, don't worry, pal, you'll see your fair lady again."

"It's not that … it just …"

"What? Are you trying to tell me you don't have a thing for my cousin?"

Mickey didn't answer; he just busied himself with the approach to Long Beach.

"Hey, Lou, the dealer at table 12 wants you."

Lou looked up from the shift schedule. "Huh?"

"Roberto is trying to get your attention."

He looked over at the table and saw Roberto looking back at him. He put down the clipboard and walked over to the table.

"Yeah?"

"Guy wants to talk to you," said the dealer, pointing to one of the players at the table.

"How can I help you sir?" asked Lou.

Vince looked up. "Can you comp me a room?"

Lou blanched. "Uh, I … I …"

"Come on, I'm a high roller," said Vince.

"You … you should check with Player's Services."

"That's what I told him, Lou," said Roberto.

"I don't have time for that shit. I know you can help me."

"Uh, well …"

"Come on, Lou," said Vince.

Lou looked around. He tried to compose himself so Roberto wouldn't see him trembling. "Uh, can … can you step over here sir." He pointed to a spot between two empty tables. "Perhaps I can help you."

"That's more like it, Lou." Vince stood up.

Roberto wondered why Lou was sweating. "Everything okay, Lou?"

"Yeah, sure, fine." Lou walked over to the spot where Vince was already standing.

Vince looked around. "Nice place. I'll bet you like working here."

Lou grunted.

"What's the matter? You don't seem happy to see me."

"How … how'd you find …"

"It wasn't that hard."

"What do you want?"

"Don't worry, I just want to have a little chat with you."

"Chat?"

"Yeah. You tell me where Tony is and I won't create a scene here and blow the whistle on your … what should I call them … you're side jobs?"

Lou was trembling. "You're not going to …"

"Kick your ass? Naw. Not that I wouldn't like to, you little prick. But you tell me where Tony is and I'll show you what swell guy I can be. I can be very forgiving."

"But I don't know where he is."

"Lou, if you don't tell me, all hell is going to break loose here … I'll bet your bosses wouldn't be happy to know that you were involve with an armed kidnapping."

"Oh, Christ … don't …"

"And after they throw your ass out on the street, I'll be waiting to stomp it into the concrete."

"But I'm telling the truth, I don't know where he is."

"When did you last see him?"

"I drove him and that other guy … Mickey … to the airport."

"Now we're getting somewhere. Who's Mickey?"

"I don't know … he's just a pilot."

Vince nodded. "How long ago did you take them to the airport?"

"I don't know … a couple of hours ago, I guess."

"Around 1:00?"

"Yeah, around 1:00."

"Where were they going?"

"I think there're going to California."

Vince looked at Lou. "Where exactly?"

"I don't know."

The assistant pit boss had been watching and walked over. "Everything okay, Lou?"

Lou turned and looked at him. "Yeah, fine, Bill. I'm just having a chat with Mr., ah …"

"Jackson," said Vince.

"Mr. Jackson," repeated Lou. "Seems we know some of the same people."

"Isn't that a hoot?" said Vince.

"You're sure everything is okay?" Bill asked again.

"Yeah. Just review that shift schedule for me would you?"

"Sure."

Vince watched Bill walk away. "Nosey guy."

"He can smell trouble."

"There isn't any trouble here, Lou. Just help me track down Tony and I'll be on my way."

"I'm telling you, I don't know where he is."

"Do you want me to call Bill over here?"

"No, don't …"

"Then tell me where he is."

Lou looked around. Bill was holding the schedule clipboard in his hands but he was keeping an eye on them. He smiled and nodded at Bill. Bill nodded back and looked at the clipboard.

"You've got ten seconds here, Lou."

Lou rubbed his temples. He looked up and saw Bill staring at him. He smiled and nodded.

"Five seconds, Lou."

"Wait, wait …"

Vince held up a hand to get Bill's attention.

"Ok, ok, I'll tell you."

Vince lower is hand and smiled at Bill. "I'm listening."

"I'll have to call him."

"So, call."

Lou heard Tony's nasal Brooklyn accent. "Yeah, what's up, Lou?"

"Nothin', just wondered how you're doing."

"I'm doing fine, Lou. Why the hell should you care?"

Lou looked at Vince. "Hey, can't a friend ask how a friend is doing?"

"What do you want, Lou?" asked Tony.

"Nothin'. I just wanted to make sure you got to LA okay … those little planes are dangerous."

"We just landed, as a matter of fact."

"In LA?"

"Why are you so interested in where we are? Is somebody there with you?"

"No, no, I'm here by myself. I'm just worried about you flying in that little plane … them things are always winding up in trees and shit."

"I don't know what the hell you're talking about, Lou."

"I'm not talking about anything … I was just worried about you, that's all."

"You haven't run into Vince Jackson, have you?"

"Vince Jackson?"

"Yeah. I saw him sniffing around Vegas Station just before we left … remember? He didn't track you down did he?"

Lou tried to keep his constricted throat from choking off his words. "No, no. I haven't seen him. You sure that was him you saw?"

"Trust me, it was Vince Jackson."

"Well, I haven't seen him."

"You'd tell me if you had, right?"

"Sure. Sure, Tony, I'd tell you."

If you could, thought Tony. "Well, that sonofabitch is around, so you keep your eyes peeled."

"Oh, I will, Tony."

"So, is there anything else, Lou?"

"No, no." He looked at Vince. "Oh, how was it getting into LAX?"

"We didn't land at LAX, we landed at Long Beach."

"Long Beach?" He nodded at Vince. Vince smiled back. "Where in Long Beach?"

"At the airport, Lou. Where the hell do you think?"

"Oh, I didn't know they had an airport."

"Look, I'm hanging up, Lou. You call me if you see Vince Jackson."

"Absolutely." He looked at Vince's questioning look. "Ah, where are you going to be staying?"

"How the fuck do I know, Lou? We just got here. Besides, it doesn't make any difference … you got my cell number."

"Oh, yeah, right."

"Goodbye, Lou."

The line went dead. Lou snapped his phone shut.

"Long Beach, eh?" Vince looked hard at Lou.

"That's what he said."

"Okay, Lou. You did all right."

Lou smiled thinly.

Vince reached in his coat pocket and felt around. He found Dashanique's sister's card. "You got a pen?"

Lou pulled out a pen and handed it to him.

Vince scrawled a number on the back of the card. "You call me at this number if you hear anything from Tony." He held the card out to Lou.

As Lou reached for the card, Vince grabbed his wrist. "We're going to be coming back this way and if I find out that you heard from Tony and didn't let me know, I'm gonna bake your ass golden brown. You understand me, Lou?"

Lou pulled his arm back but he couldn't break Vince's grip.

"Do you understand me, Lou?"

"Yeah, yeah, I understand."

Vince let go of his wrist. Lou rubbed it with his other hand. Vince stuffed the card in his coat pocket. "Don't lose that number, Lou. I'll be expecting a call from you."

Lou nodded. He watched Vince walk away. He turned and saw Bill looking at him. He adjusted his coat and smiled as he walked over to him.

"What was that all about?" asked Bill.

"Nothin'. Just a guy who knows a friend of mine."

"He didn't look all that friendly to me."

Lou looked to where he'd last seen Vince, but he had disappeared into the crowd. "He was an asshole."

30

Tony looked at the phone for a moment and then he slipped it back into his pocket.

"What did he want?" asked Mickey as he turned Songbird off the active runway.

Tony rubbed his chin. "I'm not sure, but I think he was trying to tell me Vince Jackson was there."

"You think Jackson tracked him down?" Mickey looked down at the chart in lap trying to figure out which taxiway to take. He followed the one that led to the Long Beach Center FBO on the east side of the airport.

"I'd almost bet on it. Lou wouldn't call to check on my health."

"You think Lou will be okay?"

"I don't know, but if he sold me out, I'll kill him myself."

Mickey looked at Tony. "What do we do now?"

"We call Burke and make arrangements for the drop … what else?"

"I wasn't sure you were going to go through with it."

Tony looked at Mickey. "Ace, she's my cousin … I'm not going to jeopardize a family member."

"Glad to hear it."

Mickey pulled *Songbird* into the parking space indicated by the line boy. By the time he shut down the engines and avionics, Tony was already out and scrambling off the wing. Mickey pulled himself out of the cockpit and stood up on the wing and stretched in the warm sunshine.

"Top 'em off, mister?" asked the line boy.

Mickey looked at Tony. "Well?"

"We don't have time for that right now, Ace," said Tony.

The line boy looked at Tony, then back at Mickey.

Mickey shrugged. "Guess you better hold off for now."

"They'll hit you with a ramp fee if you don't buy any gas," said the boy.

Mickey looked at Tony. "He's right; we'll have to pay one way or another. Besides, it might be a good idea to have full tanks waiting for us."

Tony shook his head. "Jesus. All right, you do what you have to do. I'll call Burke."

"You gonna pay them inside?"

Tony sighed. "Yes, I'll pay them."

Mickey nodded to the boy. "Top 'em off." As the boy started the fueling process, he watched Tony walking toward the FBO, muttering as he went.

Mickey walked through the doors into the cool air of the FBO. He looked around but didn't see Tony. He walked up to the large glass counter, where a perky, young blond sat tapping on keyboard. Her nametag read, Emma.

"Hi, Emma. My passenger just came in here. Did you see where he went?"

"Oh yes, his friend was waiting for him. They're in the lounge."

"Where's the lounge?" he asked.

Emma pointed. "Right over there, sir."

He started to walk away.

"Oh, which plane are you with?" Emma called after him.

He turned and walked back to the desk. "The Twin Comanche."

"The one just being fueled?"

"Yeah."

"Will that be cash or credit, sir?"

"My passenger will take care of it."

Emma smiled. "Yes, sir."

Mickey nodded and walked toward the lounge. He still couldn't see Tony, but he could hear him. He walked in the direction of a chair that was facing away from him and found Tony sitting in it, his head well below the top of the back. He had the phone to his head and held up a finger to Mickey when he saw him. There was no one else around.

"I'll be there," Tony said into the phone.

Mickey watched furrows form on his brow.

"I said I'll be there and …" Tony's face grew redder.

"I'll be there, all right?" he repeated.

Tony snapped the phone shut. "Jesus Christ, what a suspicious bastard."

"Burke?"

"No, it was that asshole, Barry Donahue … his barking dog."

The name made Mickey's face flush. "I met him. So, what's the deal?"

"He wants to meet at 11:00 tonight."

"Why 11:00? Why not now?"

Tony looked up a Mickey. "How the fuck do I know? Maybe they're going bowling first … what difference does it make?"

Mickey ignored the sarcasm. "Okay, so when we take the money to his house tonight and …?"

"His boat."

"What?"

"He wants the meeting at his boat."

"His boat? Where is that?"

"He said it's docked at a marina … in Newport Bay."

"Newport Bay? That's crazy. Why can't we just meet him at his house?"

Before Tony could respond, a middle-aged man with wavy salt and pepper hair, gold rimmed amber sunglasses and a thin mustache approached them, wiping his hands on his pants and muttering, "I hate those damn dryers."

"Ace, this is Carl," said Tony.

Mickey held out is hand to Carl. "I'm Mickey Soto."

"I'd shake your hand but …" Carl held up his still moist hands.

"That's okay," said Mickey.

"You the guy flying this idiot around the country?"

"Yes."

"How'd you get mixed up with him?"

"Just lucky, I guess."

Carl laughed. "Funny guy, Tony."

"He's a riot," said Tony

"So what's up?" asked Carl.

"What do you say we get some food? I'm starving."

"Sure. I know a little place just a couple of miles from here. Let's go there and then you can tell me all about your business."

"Ah, before we go, you've got something to take care of at the desk."

"Huh?"

"The fuel tab, remember?"

"Oh, Jesus." Tony shook his head. "All right, come on, let's go pay the lady."

Emma was still tapping on the keyboard when Mickey, Tony and Carl approached the front desk. She stopped and looked up. "Yes, sir?" she asked.

"What's the tab for fuel on that Cherokee?" asked Mickey.

Emma tapped some keys and starred at the computer screen. "268 dollars and 57 cents," she said.

Tony shook his head. "Jesus, what does that thing take? Champaign?"

"Fuel is very expensive these days," said Emma.

"Does that cover the ramp fee?" asked Mickey.

"Yes, sir. We don't charge a ramp fee if you purchase fuel."

"And tie down?"

"How long will you be here?"

Mickey looked at Tony.

"I don't know," said Tony. "How late are you open?"

"We close at 11:00, but you can access your airplane any time. Are you leaving tonight?" asked Emma.

"It's possible."

"Do you have the code for the gate lock?"

"No," said Mickey.

Emma jotted some numbers on a piece of paper and handed them to Mickey. "This will be good until tomorrow. We change the code every couple of days."

Mickey glanced at the paper and nodded. "Thanks."

Tony pulled out a wad of bills and peeled off three hundreds. While Emma made the change, he asked, "Is there a decent hotel near by?"

"Yes, sir." She handed the change to Tony. Then she picked a sheet of paper off a stack next to her keyboard and handed that to Tony. "Here's a list."

Carl grabbed the list. "Screw that. You're staying with me."

"We just need some place to hole up for a few hours."

"So what? Save your money."

Tony nodded. "Okay."

"You can come too, doll."

Emma smiled politely. "Thanks, Carl, but I've got other plans."

"Carl?" said Tony. "You know this mug?"

"Emma and I got to know each other while I was waiting for you," said Carl.

"Jesus, you're still an operator, buddy."

"Emma's a sweet girl." Carl slapped the counter, startling Emma. "Anyway, you've got a standing offer, babe. You just call me if you get bored."

Emma smiled. "I'll remember, Carl."

Tony threw the Dolphin's bag in the trunk of the silver Lincoln. Mickey tossed his bag in after it. Tony jumped into the passenger seat, Mickey the backseat.

"Nice ride," said Carl

Carl started the car. "Thanks. It's about time you got out to my part of the country."

"Too goddamn many people out here."

"What? New York is a small town?" said Carl.

"I don't live in New York anymore. I live in Miami."

"Miami? No, shit. I thought only retired people lived in Miami."

"Remember, Gina, my cousin?" asked Tony.

Carl smiled. "Gina Sandrelli? Sure I remember her."

"Her old man has a restaurant down there and I'm running it for him."

"Severino Sandrelli?"

"Yeah."

"You're running a restaurant for Severino Sandrelli?"

"Why is that such a surprise?"

"You just don't seem like the type."

"Waddaya mean, 'the type?'"

"I don't mean that in a bad way … I just don't see you running a restaurant, that's all."

"Well, Gina helps … we sort of run the place together."

Watching the palm trees and endless strip malls pass by and idly listening to the conversation, Mickey snorted loudly.

Smiling, Carl looked in the mirror. "I guess you do know this guy."

"He doesn't know shit," said Tony.

"So, how is Gina these days?" asked Carl.

Tony let out a long breath. "That's why I'm here."

"Gina's in trouble?"

"Not exactly … but I've got a little problem on my hands."

Carl glanced over at Tony and tossed his head toward the back seat.

"He's okay. He knows what's going on."

Carl looked in the mirror again at Mickey. Then he shrugged his shoulders. "So, you gonna tell me?"

"Let's get some food and I'll tell you all about it."

31

Carl sat back and threw his napkin on the empty plate in front of him. "So, tell me more about this Burke guy."

"Burke." Tony pushed his own empty plate away. "That was a damn good Reuben. I wouldn't think you could get something like that out here."

"New York doesn't have a corner on the market of Jewish Delis," said Carl.

Tony looked around the bustling restaurant. "Who knew?"

"So, what about Burke?"

"He's a big noise in southeast Florida … everyone knows who he is. He owns a few car dealerships, but he's into all kinds of stuff. He specializes in moving hot metal. He has a deal with a couple of Mexicans … the Rodriquez brothers … they snatch the wheels and Burke moves them through his dealerships … he's got two or three out here."

"And you got sideways with this guy?"

"He loaned me some cash so now he thinks he owns me."

"Why don't you get your family involved? I know they could straighten the guy out."

"No fucking way, Carl. They don't need to know about this."

Carl nodded. "Yeah, I know. Your old man thinks you're enough of a …" Carl paused. "He's got enough of his own problems, right?"

Mickey held a French fry a few inches above a pool of ketchup on his plate, pausing to glance at Tony.

Tony's face glowed. "Yeah."

"So, what's your next move?" Carl said, hoping to cover his faux pas.

The color slowly returned to Tony's face. "I don't know … I haven't thought it all out yet."

Mickey dipped the French fry in the ketchup. "What's the big deal? You just give the money to Burke and Gina leaves with us."

"Nothing is ever as easy as it appears," said Tony.

Carl looked back and forth between Tony and Mickey. "I have to admit, it doesn't seem all that complicated, Tony."

"You don't know Burke."

"That's true, but if he gets his money …"

"It's not his fucking money."

Carl held his palms up. "If he gets *your* money why would he hold Gina any longer?"

"You just never know what that asshole might do," said Tony.

"You think he might pull something?"

"I just want to be prepared, that's all."

Carl nodded. "Yeah, I guess you can't walk into something like this with your eyes closed."

"Tony, you said there wouldn't be any funny business." Both heads turned to Mickey. "You said you'd hand the money over to Burke and we'd get Gina back."

Carl turned toward Tony, a puzzled look on his face.

Tony stood up. "Let's go outside and have a cigarette." He reached in his pocket and pulled out a wad of bills. He peeled two twenties off and tossed them on the table next to Mickey. "Take care of the bill, Ace."

"I don't smoke anymore," said Carl.

Tony glared at him.

"But a nail sounds good." He leaned over the table and grabbed the two twenties to hand back to Tony. "Here. You're my guests, it's my treat."

Tony grabbed the bills and threw them on the table again. "Hey, when you're working for me, I pick up the tabs."

"But I'm not …"

Tony cut Carl off. "Let's go."

Carl stood up slowly. "Sure."

"We'll be outside, Ace. Will you take care of the tab?"

Mickey's eye's narrowed. He nodded slowly.

Tony exhaled and watched as the smoke drifted away against the blue sky.

"Who the hell is that guy?"

Tony turned to Carl. "Who?"

"Your buddy in there."

"Ace? He's a guy I hired in Florida to help me chase down Vince and Sheldon."

"The guys who took your money."

"Yeah."

"So he's not in the business?"

Tony dropped the cigarette butt on the ground and stepped on it. "Hell no. He's just a pilot for hire."

"And he's talking to you like that?"

"We've been through a lot together."

"Still, that's a lot of crap from an employee."

Tony watched the traffic on the street in front of the restaurant. "He's got a stake in this now."

"What do you mean?"

"He has a thing for Gina."

"You're kidding?"

"No … and besides, we're sort of partners now."

"Partners?"

"He's been flying me all over the country."

"So what? He's a pilot … that's what he does."

"Yeah, I know, but it started out as just an overnight thing … it's gone a little beyond that … I guess I owe him something."

"Still, he sounds like an employee to me."

"Technically, I suppose."

"You really think he has the hots for your cousin?"

"I do."

Carl laughed. "Imagine, Severino Sandrelli's little princess falling for a flying taxi driver."

Tony looked at him. "What the fuck do you know, Carl?"

Carl stopped laughing.

Tony put his hand on Carl's shoulder. "Look, I'm a little stressed. I've been chasing my money all over the goddamn country, my cousin has been kidnapped, and I haven't had much sleep."

Carl smiled. "That's okay, pal. I'm sorry I got so nosey about your buddy. So, what do you want to do?"

"Is Swede still in town?"

"Far as I know. You thinking of bringing him in on this?"

"Might be a good idea to have a little insurance. Can you get a hold of him?"

Carl rubbed his chin. "Yeah, I suppose."

"Call him up and see if he's available tonight."

Mickey walked up and held out the change from the bill to Tony.

"No, you keep it, Ace. A tip," said Tony.

Mickey stuffed the money in his pocket.

"That's pretty short notice," said Carl.

"Carl, will you just call him?"

Carl pulled out his phone and flipped it open.

"Alone," Tony added.

"Oh, yeah, sure." He wandered off into the parking lot.

Mickey watched Carl walk away. "Call who?"

"An old friend."

"Does this have anything to do with getting Gina back?"

Tony lit another cigarette. "Will you just trust me on this?"

"I wish I could."

"I know what I'm doing, Ace."

Carl pulled the LS into the garage of a typical southern California, Spanish style ranch with an orange tiled roof. Tony got out and looked out at the similar houses that lined the street. "When did you move here?" he asked.

"You've never been here?"

"No."

"I guess it's been more than three years since you've been out here."

"I liked that apartment you had."

"They were converted to condos and I figured if I was going to buy something I'd rather it be a house."

"Damned middleclass of you."

"Hey, a guy has to settle down sooner or later."

"I'm sorry, Carl, this just isn't you."

Mickey ran his hand over the roof of a red Porsche 911 Cabriolet parked in the adjacent stall.

"What year is this?"

"'82. That's my baby."

Mickey looked in at the austere but purposeful interior with admiration. "I can see why."

"I can take you for a ride in it, if you want."

"Not right now, Carl," said Tony. "We got more important things to do."

"Yeah, sure." Carl popped the Lincoln's trunk. "Grab your stuff and come on inside."

"We're probably not going to be here long enough to need it," reminded Tony.

"Hey, you gotta have someplace to hang out … take a shower or whatever."

Tony shrugged.

Carl started to open the door and the nose of a big, black lab stuck out excitedly. "Get back, Butch."

"Oh shit, not a goddamn dog," said Tony.

"Butch wouldn't hurt a fly."

"I've heard that before."

"You afraid of dogs?"

"Hell no, I just don't like them sniffing my crotch."

"All right, I'll put him outside if it'll make you feel more comfortable." Carl pushed Butch back from the door. "Sorry, buddy, you're not wanted."

Tony stood in the doorway while Carl maneuvered Butch out the sliding glass back door. As soon as the door shut, Tony entered the house. He looked around at the plain kitchen, ignoring Butch bouncing off the glass door, barking wildly. Nothing looked out of place. "You live here alone?"

"Mostly." Carl grinned, assuming Tony would know what he meant.

"Looks pretty damn clean for a bachelor pad."

"I've got a house keeper that comes in once a week." Carl shook a fist at the back door. "Shut up, Butch." The dog stopped barked and looked in at him, his sad eyes pleading for a reprieve. "Come on, I'll show you where can stow your stuff."

Tony and Mickey followed Carl out of the kitchen, Butch whining and pawing at the door. They walked through the spare but neat living room and entered a hallway on the opposite end of the room. Half way down the hallway Carl stopped and pushed open the door to a bathroom. "Here's the can."

Tony looked in. The floor tiles were pink and white, a large mirror ran the length of Grecian-styled vanity, and the pink shower curtain was accented with the outline of porpoises. "You decorate this?"

"Hell, no. I just haven't gotten around to redoing it."

"How long did you say you lived here?"

"Three years."

Tony nodded. "No hurry, I guess."

Carl waved toward an open door at the end of the short hallway; an arm of the hallway branched off in two directions. "That's yours, Mickey."

Mickey looked in at the small bedroom with two twin beds. "It's fine." He walked in and threw his bag on a bed. "Mind if I use the bathroom?"

"That's what it's there for."

"Just make sure you leave the fan running. I'm going want to use it too, you know," said Tony.

Carl laughed and pointed to another room at the end of one hallway arm. "You're over here, Tony."

Tony followed Carl into a slightly larger bedroom, dominated by a king-sized bed and a gaudy oak dresser. "Haven't gotten around to decorating this room either, eh?"

"Well, actually, yes. This is my stuff."

Tony looked at Carl. "What the hell happened to you?"

Carl shrugged. "Like I said, a guy has to settle down sooner or later."

"Settling down is one thing, but this?"

Carl looked hurt. "What, you don't like it?"

Tony realized he was belittling Carl. "I'm kidding you, buddy. It's a swell joint. Thanks for letting us stay with you."

"You always took care of me when I was in New York."

Tony set the Dolphin's bag on dresser, walked over to the window and pulled the curtain aside to look out. "Well, I appreciate it Carl. What'd Swede say?"

"He's up for some action … said he was bored shitless. He's looking forward to hearing from you."

"Great." Tony watched a woman walking her dog while the dog squatted on Carl's front yard. "Have you still got that boat you took me out on the last time I was here?"

Carl grinned. "Damn, that was good time …"

"No shit … it took me a week to sober up." Tony watched the woman look around while the dog did his business. "You still got that boat?"

"Yeah. Why?"

"Where is it?"

"I still have that slip in Alamitos Bay."

Tony saw the woman put on a pair of plastic gloves, pick up the dog shit and put in a baggy. He shook his head. "How far is that from Newport Bay?"

Carl narrowed his eyes. "Why?"

Tony turned away from the window. "I want you and Swede to take the boat down there."

"I should have known there'd be a catch when you picked up the lunch tab." Carl sat on the bed. "Look, Tony, I'll pick up Swede for you, but then you're on your own."

"All I'm asking you to do is take Swede for a boat ride."

"It's always more complicated than you paint it, Tony."

Tony's face reddened slightly. "Well, this is different. I just need you to drive the boat down to Newport and back."

Carl sighed loudly. "Tony, Tony … why are you doing this to me?"

"Because I need help, and I'm not about to hand my money over to that goddamn mick."

"But what about your cousin?"

"She'll be fine. Look, are you going to help me out here or not?"

"This is starting to sound like one of your idiotic schemes."

"I don't need your shit right now … are you going to help me?"

Carl sighed again. "What exactly do you have in mind?"

"I haven't worked it all out just yet. Can you get the boat down there tonight?"

"Yeah. Who's paying for the gas?"

"I'll pay for the gas … will you do it?"

"Yeah, hell, I suppose I could do it."

"I knew I could count on you." Tony smiled. "Oh, and one more thing. Don't mention anything about this to Ace in there."

Carl squeezed his forehead. "I must be out of my fucking mind."

Emma looked up from her magazine to watch a man wearing a Miami Dolphin's cap approach the desk. "Can I help you?" she asked.

Vince flashed a smile at her. "A couple of friends of mine were supposed to fly into town today, but I haven't heard from them yet and was getting worried. You haven't seen them, by any chance, have you?"

"There's been several charters in here today … do you know what type of plane they are flying?"

"No, but one guy is sort of short, about forty, with balding, slicked back hair …"

Emma's face brightened, "Was the other guy taller, with long, wavy hair … kind of salt and pepper?"

"Yeah, that'd be him."

"They came in around noon."

"Which plane is theirs?"

Emma pointed toward the large window that looked out on the tarmac. "That red and white Twin Comanche."

Vince squinted at the airplanes silhouetted in the setting sun. "Which one is that?"

"That small, twin engine … second from the end of the row facing us."

Vince picked out *Songbird* nestled between a Gulfstream III and a King Air. "Oh yeah, that'd be it. They said something about flying in a Cessna."

Emma looked at Vince. "That's a Piper."

Vince laughed. "Cessna, Piper … they all look the same to me."

Emma smiled. "Most folks don't know the difference."

"You said they got here at noon … I wonder why I haven't heard from them. Do you know where they went?"

"I'm not sure." Her eyes narrowed slightly. "Can't you call them?"

Vince looked at the tag on Emma's blouse. "I lost my cell phone yesterday, Emma, and all my numbers were in it."

Emma's face softened. "I had that happen to me. That is so irritating."

"Makes me crazy." Vince rubbed his chin. "So, you don't know where they went?"

"No. But they left with Carl."

"Carl?"

"Their friend, Carl. He was waiting for them."

"Oh yeah, Carl. He's a friend of Tony's." Vince looked up at the ceiling as though thinking to himself. "What's Carl's last name?" He looked back at Emma. "You didn't happen to catch Carl's last name did you?"

Emma's smile faded. "No, I didn't."

"Did they happen to say how long they were staying?"

Emma looked at Vince suspiciously.

Vince quickly picked up the change in demeanor. "My wife insisted that Tony visit us while there're in town … you know, she wants to have a big dinner and all … but he wasn't very specific about his plans so I don't know what to tell her."

Emma's face softened a bit. "I understand. I don't think they were sure either … in fact I think they said they could be leaving tonight."

"Tonight?"

"That's what I heard."

"Boy, my wife will be disappointed if he doesn't make it for dinner … she's been planning for days."

"I can imagine."

"Well, thank you Emma." Vince flashed a toothy smile. "You've been very helpful."

"You're welcome." Emma watched Vince walk away.

Vince slipped into the passenger seat of the Winnebago.

"Well?" Sheldon asked

"Bingo."

"They came in here?"

Vince pointed through the fence to the red and white twin Cherokee parked on the tarmac. "That's their plane."

"Well that's good, because I'm getting tired muscling this rig around the goddamn airport. You sure it was them?"

"How many short, balding guys do you think landed here around noon?"

"Where'd they go?"

"Well, all I know is they left with some guy named Carl."

"Carl? Carl who?"

"Emma said he's a friend of Tony's."

"Emma?"

"The chick on the desk in there."

"But she didn't know his name?"

"No."

Sheldon slammed his hands on the steering wheel. "All right, let's start making some phone calls."

"What if Tony has already given the money to Burke?"

"We'll deal with that problem when we get our hands on the little creep."

32

The sun was already well below the horizon when *Permesso* left the calm water of Alamitos bay for the open ocean and a 20 knot southerly breeze. At 28 feet, Carl's Bayliner was big enough to travel comfortably down the coast, but not big enough to damp out the four-foot swells. Carl looked back at Swede Johansson. He was standing up and hanging tightly to the coaming, rocking back and forth as *Permesso* splashed through the waves and keeping his face into the cool, salt air.

"You getting a little green around gills?" Carl asked over the noise of wind and waves.

He heard the response in a barely audible Swedish accent. "Fuck you. Just drive this thing, okay?"

Sven was an ex-body builder who had made it all the way to the title of Mr. California. After his glory years he had a much-celebrated tryout with the LA Rams, but never grasped the game and failed miserably. He attempted boxing but was too slow. He got into pro wrestling but could never follow the scripts. Eddie Cohen, the Sandrelli lieutenant in charge of west coast operations, had been in the audience during a particularly embarrassing show in which Sven was suppose to lose, but ended with his opponent being carted off with a broken leg. Eddie approached Sven and offered him the opportunity to freelance as muscle for the Sandrelli's. His prospects ever shrinking, Sven accepted, reluctantly at first, but soon he discovered it was a skill for which he was imminently suited and he began to take on his assignments with great relish.

Carl watched Seal Beach Pier slip past on their port side. Beneath the glow of the lights, he could see fishermen lining the sides and people strolling along behind them. A restaurant perched precariously at the end of the pier was lit brightly and through the windows he could make out diners eating hamburgers and sipping malts. Along the south side of the pier, surfers were taking advantage of the evening break. He saw some pick up a wave and deftly weave around others still bobbing on their boards and then bail out just before the surf crashed into the massive pylons.

Once past Seal Beach, Carl settled *Permesso* into a southeasterly course about a half-mile off shore, close enough to see cars traveling up and down the Pacific Coast Highway. But it was hard to maintain a straight line in the swells and he wasn't able to make more than 10 knots. He looked at the clock on the dashboard. It would be close, but he still figured that they could make Newport by ten o'clock.

Swede was looking forward to some action, but Carl hoped it wouldn't come to that. If Tony had figured it right, in a couple of hours *Permesso* would be heading back north with the money on board and without Carl ever having to get off the boat. But the whole plan depended on Carl's memory of the marina in Newport Bay and a large dose of the principal ingredients of Tony's schemes: timing and luck.

The air coming off the ocean had cooled since sunset, but Tony didn't mind; he thought the salt air swirling around the cockpit of the Cabriolet was a refreshing change from the exhaust and industrial smells of Long Beach. It had been tough talking Carl into loaning him the Porsche, but Carl had to pick up Swede and he couldn't possibly fit in the little roadster. It was the first moment of relative enjoyment that Tony had experienced in a week. "I guess it's a California thing, but I have to admit that there's something to cruising on the PHC in a sports car with the top down."

Mickey watched the waves turning to white foam in the moonlight as they broke on the shore along an open stretch of highway. He hadn't said a word since they had left Carl's house.

"Come on, Ace, loosen up."

Mickey looked at Tony. "I'll relax when we have Gina back."

"Don't worry. You'll be enjoying a midnight snack with the girl."

Mickey turned back to the ocean. He watched the bouncing lights of a boat running on a parallel course just off shore.

***

The clock on the radio read 10:28 when the Porsche pulled off Bayside Drive into the well-lit parking lot of the marina in Newport Bay. Tony slid the roadster into a spot away from the few cars that were still in the lot and turned off the engine.

"We're early," said Mickey. "You think we can get this over with now?"

"We're supposed to wait in the car."

"I thought we were meeting on Burke's boat?"

"Donahue said to wait in the car in parking lot." Tony got out of the car.

"Where are you going?"

"Just going to have a cigarette and check things out."

Mickey started to get out of the car.

"Hold on, Ace."

Mickey sat back down. "Now what?"

"You need to stay here in case somebody shows up."

"What if you're not here?"

"I'll be back in couple of minutes … just relax, okay?"

"It's pretty hard to relax right now, okay?"

"It's a nice night. The car has a great radio. Enjoy yourself."

"You really are nuts, you know?"

"It's no big deal, Ace. Like you said, I'll just give Burke the money and we leave with Gina."

"Why don't I believe that?"

Tony started to walk away.

"Hey," Mickey shouted.

Tony stopped and turned around.

"The keys?"

"Oh yeah."

Tony walked to the edge of the parking lot overlooking the marina. He leaned on the fence next to a set of steps that led down to the several docks that jutted out from the break wall. Boats of every description bobbed gently in slips under lights that lined the docks. Most were dark, but a few were lit up and showed signs of life. He pulled out Gina's phone and punched up Carl's number.

"Yeah?"

"Where you at?" asked Tony.

"Just entering Newport Bay," Carl answered.

"Just now?"

"It was a tough slog getting down here."

Tony looked at the sky. The stars were twinkling brightly and while a breeze blew in off the ocean, it seemed calm enough. "Really?"

"Really. Are you at the marina?"

"Yeah."

"It's the one off Bayside Drive?"

"Yeah. Is Swede ready?"

Carl looked at the back deck. Swede had on a black jacket and stocking cap. He was checking over a 9mm

Berretta. "Yeah, he's ready. How will he know which boat is Burke's?"

"I'm not sure."

"Tony, are you kidding me?"

"There must be a hundred boats in the marina … how the hell can I tell which one is Burkes?"

"This is a hell of a time to think of that, Tony."

"I just never dreamed there'd be so goddamn many boats."

"Tony, this is Newport Bay."

"I know, but …"

"Jesus, if this is another one of your cluster-fucks, I'm turning this thing around right now and heading back to Long Beach."

"No, it'll be all right. Just dock your boat and tell Swede to watch the steps from the parking lot … when he sees somebody carrying a Miami Dolphin's bag, grab the bag and then get the fuck out of there."

"Are there any empty slips?"

"I can't tell from here." Tony peered out into the dark. "Well, yeah, I guess maybe I can see a couple."

"We're going to have to make this fast. If I pull into a slip that someone returns to, there'll be holy hell to pay."

"It'll be fast. What time is it now?"

"10:40."

"How soon will you be here?"

"I'm just rounding Balboa Island now."

"What does that mean?"

"I'll be there in five minutes."

Tony flipped the phone shut. He pulled out another cigarette and lit it. *God, I hope this doesn't get fucked up.*

Mickey watched Tony cross the parking lot toward the car. The radio clock said 10:52. He motioned to Tony to hurry.

"What's up?" said Tony when he reached the car.

"It's almost 11:00."

Tony slipped into the driver's seat. "We've got eight minutes yet."

"I just didn't want to be here by myself if they showed up, okay?"

"Relax, will you? You're making me nervous."

The clock read 11:09 when Mickey saw a flash of light from the fence gate where Tony had stood a few minutes earlier. He nudged Tony who was fiddling with the radio. "Is that them?"

Tony looked up. "Where?"

Mickey pointed to the gate. "Over there."

A light flashed again.

"Must be." Tony flicked the Porsche's lights on and off.

Mickey could see a man walk through the gate into the parking lot. His stomach clinched.

"Just don't do anything stupid," said Tony.

"That goes double for you."

The man slowly crossed the lot, passing in and out of the shadows as he walked underneath each yellow, overhead light. As he approached the car Mickey recognized Barry Donahue. He stopped several feet from the Porsche. At first Mickey thought the object hanging from his left hand was a gun, but he saw it was a flashlight.

Donahue shined the light into the car. "You brought the hero with you. You were supposed to be by yourself."

"Couldn't keep him away," said Tony.

"At least you're on time."

"What did you think?" said Tony.

"I didn't think you'd show at all."

"I sure as hell wouldn't be here if you didn't have something that was more valuable to me than money."

"I didn't know anything was."

"Just get Gina so we can get this over with, will you?"

Donahue smiled thinly. He held the flashlight toward the gate and flicked in on and off twice. Two people walked through the gate and began to cross the parking lot. Mickey could tell it was a man and a woman.

"It's Gina," Mickey whispered.

Tony nodded.

"So, the hero wants to rescue his damsel in distress, eh?" asked Donahue.

"No, he wants to pound your sorry ass into a sand hill."

Donahue walked around to the passenger side and leaned on the door with both hands. "Is that so, hero?"

Mickey held off the urge to whip the door open and slam Donahue in the nuts. He kept his gaze straight ahead.

"Not talking, eh?"

"Shut the fuck up, Donahue, before I turn this mad dog loose on you," said Tony.

"I wish you would, you little Guinea."

Burke and Gina walked up to the car. "Renewing old friendships, Barry?" "Yeah, I'd love to get closer to this guy." Donahue patted Mickey on the shoulder.

"Some other time." Burke stepped aside so Tony and Mickey could see Gina. She didn't look any worse for the wear. Her hair was pulled back in a ponytail and she was wearing khaki pants and a black long sleeve top, not the clothes she had been wearing when Mickey had last seen her. In the dim light, it was hard to tell where she was looking.

"See, we took good care of her."

"You all right, Babe," said Tony.

"I'll survive," said Gina.

Burke stepped back in front of her. "The money, Tony?"

Tony got out, walked behind the car, opened the trunk and pulled out the Dolphin's bag. He handed the bag to Burke. "You mean 'my' money."

"It could have been your money, my friend, if you settled your debts in a timely manner." Burke set the bag on the hood and zipped it open. Donahue leaned across the hood and shined the light in.

"It's all there," said Tony. "Well, almost, I've had to cover a few expenses along the way.

Donahue reached in the bag and pulled out the Colt revolver. "Hey, what's this?"

Tony reached for the gun, but Donahue pulled it away. "Hey, that's mine," said Tony.

Donahue stood back and held the gun up admiringly. "Where the hell did you get a horse pistol like this?"

"None of your goddamn business … just give it to me."

Donahue handed the gun to Burke. "Nice piece," said Burke. "Ought to be worth something, don't you think, Barry?"

"Sure, boss." Donahue shined the light in the bag again. He pulled out two wallets. "More goodies, boss."

"Those are mine."

Donahue flipped one of the wallets open and shined the light on it. "Vince Jackson, it says here." He opened the other wallet. "Sheldon Isaacs?"

"I took them fair and square," said Tony.

"I'll see that they get them back," said Burke. "Put 'em back, Barry."

Donahue tossed the wallets back in the back in the bag.

Burke put the gun back in the bag and zipped it shut. "If I can get anything for the gun, I'll take it off your tab."

"What tab?"

"You're into me for 175 large, remember?"

Tony pointed to the bag. "Well I think stealing this from me makes us even."

"You do, eh?"

"Yeah ... are we done here?" asked Tony.

"For the moment."

"Good." Tony got back in the car. "Come on, Gina. Let's get the hell out of here."

Gina walked around the car. When she passed Donahue, he grabbed her arm and said, "This doesn't mean we're finished, does it sweetheart?"

Gina jerked her arm away. "We were never started."

"Let's go, lady-killer," said Burke.

Donahue laughed. "I'll call you when I get back to Florida."

"I can't wait," said Gina.

Donahue backed away from the car. "I'll be looking you up too, hero."

Mickey opened the door and jumped out. Gina stepped in front of him. "Forget about that asshole," she said.

"Are you all right?" said Mickey through clenched teeth.

She smiled. "I'm fine. Let's just get out of here." She brushed past Mickey but paused for a second before getting into the car. She kissed him on the cheek. "Thank you."

Mickey wanted to hug her, but wasn't sure how she'd react. "Don't mention it."

She smiled again and slipped into the car. Mickey watched Burke and Donahue walk away until they were almost to the gate. Then he started to get into the car. "This is going to be a little tight."

Gina squeezed into the middle of the little roadster. "Nice car, who's is it?"

"A friend's," said Tony.

Mickey pressed in close to her and pulled the door shut. She smelled great, but felt even better. "Let's go, Tony."

Tony nodded but made no move to start the car. He watched Burke disappear through the gate behind Donahue. A gunshot split the air.

"What the hell was that?" asked Mickey.

Tony jumped out of the car and walked quickly toward the gate.

"What are you doing?" yelled Mickey.

Tony ignored him and kept walking to the gate.

"Oh shit, I was afraid of something like this."

"What the hell is that idiot doing?" asked Gina.

"I'm going to find out. You stay here." Mickey opened the door.

Gina grabbed his arm. "Donahue is an asshole, but he's a dangerous asshole."

Mickey pulled away and got out. "I'll be careful. You just wait here." He shut the door and trotted across the parking lot after Tony.

Standing at the gate, Tony looked down the steps and saw Swede struggling with Donahue. Burke dropped the Dolphin's bag, and jumped on Swede's back, choking him with the crook of his arm. The gun Swede had been holding in his right hand clattered to the ground. He reached up to loosen Burke's grip, but it was too late, he was already losing consciousness and began to slump.

Tony bolted down the steps and grabbed the bag and ran out on to one of the dock protruding into the bay.

"Goddamnit, Tony's got the bag," yelled Burke.

Donahue easily broke free of Swede's weakening left hand. He backed away and delivered and devastating kick to Swede's groin. Swede fell to his knees. Burke, still riding his back, came with him and flipped over his shoulder onto the ground. Donahue clinched his hands together and swung them at the side of Swede's head. The contact snapped his head oddly to the side and he fell forward with a great thud. Donahue began to brutally kick his fallen foe.

Burke rolled over and raised himself to all fours.

"Forget him. Get Tony."

Donahue stopped and looked around. "Where is he?"

33

Mickey reached the fence next to the gate and peered down. He heard shouting and in the glow of the dock lights he could see Tony running out on the dock, the Dolphin's bag clutched in his arms. Donahue was standing over a large man lying on the ground. Burke was on his hands and knees, yelling, "He's on the dock."

Mickey saw Tony stop and look around. He heard him yelling. "Carl, where the hell are you?" Mickey could not hear a response, but he heard Tony yell again, "Where?"

Mickey saw the running lights of a boat at the end of the dock flash on and off.

Tony started running again, but now Donahue was twenty feet behind him. Mickey saw the boat at the end of the dock pulling out of the slip. He heard Tony yelling, "Wait, you sonofabitch."

Tony reached the end of the dock and the boat kept backing away. Without hesitating Tony leaped into the water in the now vacant slip. Donahue reached the spot a second later, but Tony had grabbed the loose bowline and was being dragged out into Newport Bay.

The boat kept moving and by the time Burke reached the slip it was seventy yards out into the bay. It finally drifted to a stop and a figure leaned over the side, grabbed the bowline and pulled Tony to the boat. Tony handed the bag to him and splashed around to the stern, where he struggled up the ladder and flopped over the transom. The boat shifted in to forward and began to pull away.

Burke had managed to get to his feet and had followed Donahue out onto the dock. When he realized what was going on, he yelled, "Forget that asshole, get the broad."

Donahue turned and began sprinting back down the dock. "Oh, shit," said Mickey. He turned and ran back toward the car.

Gina saw him coming and slid over the center console and into the driver's seat. She started the Porsche and shifted it into gear just as Mickey arrived. "Where's Tony?" she shouted.

Mickey leaped over the passenger door, "Let's get the hell out of here."

Gina popped the clutch, the tires slipped for a second and caught. The roadster leaped forward, but Donahue had reached the parking lot and was running full-tilt for them. Gina swerved in his direction. Donahue, realizing what was happening, stopped abruptly and took a couple of steps backward, but it was too late. He dove forward just as the car reached him. He slammed into the hood and windshield. Gina slammed on the brakes and jammed the Porsche into reverse. Donahue slid off the hood and onto the pavement.

Burke appeared through gate and raised Swede's gun toward the car. A flash appeared and instantly a bullet hole appeared in the middle of the windshield.

"Oh shit," yelled Mickey.

Gina jammed the gearshift into first and the tires squealed loudly as she spun the wheel to the left. Mickey saw another muzzle flash and braced for impact, but nothing happened. He tried to hunch down, but the accelerating, swerving car pushed him back into the door. The Porsche flew over a speed bump spread across the entrance to the parking lot and drifted sideways onto the street.

By the time Mickey could get his breath, Gina had slammed the gear into third and they were doing 75 back toward the highway. "Jesus, where did you learn to drive like that?"

They were approaching a traffic light at the intersection of the Pacific Coast Highway and Gina relaxed her foot on the accelerator and pushed in the clutch, smoothly downshifting. "Are you all right?"

"I think so."

As they reached the intersection the light turned green and she accelerated into a left turn onto the highway. "What happened back there?"

"I was just going to ask you the same thing."

"Where's Tony?"

"Out to sea."

"What?"

Mickey explained what he had seen.

Gina slowed for a traffic light in Newport. "Boat? Whose boat?"

"I've got no idea."

"But he's okay?"

"I saw him flop over the side and boat pulled away out into the bay. That's when Donahue turned and ran for the parking lot." Mickey paused and looked at Gina. "You think he's dead?"

"Who?"

"Donahue. He didn't look to good last I saw him."

"I don't give a shit. He deserved it."

"Did he …" Mickey turned and looked ahead at the highway. "Did he bother you?"

Gina laughed. "He wished." Then she stopped laughing. "Not that he didn't try."

"You mean …"

"He had delusions that he could charm me into bed with him … that's all." Gina stopped for another light. She looked over at Mickey. "Why are you so interested?"

Mickey blushed. "I don't know … I just … I guess …"

She smiled and put her hand on his leg. "Thanks for caring."

His leg felt like a red-hot poker was touching it. Mickey picked her hand up and squeezed it. "I do, you know."

She pulled her hand away from his and caressed his cheek. A car horn honked behind them. The light had turned green. She shifted the car into gear and pulled smoothly away from the intersection. "Where to?"

"Back to Carl's, I guess. Maybe we'll hear from Tony."

"Carl? Carl Fontaine?"

"You're driving his car."

Gina laughed. "So he's the *friend*?"

"You know him?"

"When Tony's father was looking for a place to put him, he sent him out to LA for while, hoping he might look after family affairs. Tony hooked up with Carl Fontaine and, as usual, that was pretty much the end of Tony's attention to business. He spent most of the time on Carl's boat."

"Carl has a boat?"

"I've heard about some wild escapades on Carl's boat."

"I'll be dipped … that sonofabitch planned this all along."

She glanced over at Mickey. "You seemed surprised."

"I thought … I hoped he was just interested in getting you back."

"Oh, I'm sure he was, but money is just too strong of a lure to the guy."

"You're not disappointed?"

"Tony's family and I love him, but I know him too … he just can't help himself."

"Well, I'm pissed. He promised me there'd be no funny business."

"To Tony it wasn't funny business … it was business as usual."

Shivering in his wet clothes, Tony stood next to Carl as he carefully guided *Permesso* around the northern end of Balboa Island.

"What happened?" asked Carl.

"It all went to shit …"

"Yeah, I sorta noticed."

"… but I got the money. Why didn't you wait for me?"

"Tony, I didn't want to get involved in the first place … I sure as hell wasn't about to lose my boat."

"Well, thanks a hell of a lot … I damn near drowned back there."

"I stopped to pull you in."

"Like a goddamn fish, you bastard."

"What about Swede?" Carl asked.

"I don't know, he was on the ground when I saw him."

"I heard a shot … did he catch one?"

"I don't know."

"I hate to leave him."

"There's nothing we could've done."

"You could have just given Burke his money."

Tony ignored the remark. "Can't you go any faster?"

Carl peered out into the darkness ahead of the boat. "Too many things to run into around here … I can't go any faster until we get out of the bay."

Tony looked anxiously behind. "Well hurry it up, Burke is probably firing up his boat right now."

Carl nudged the throttle slightly to give Tony the sense of increased speed, but they stilled plowed ahead at a maddeningly slow pace. As Carl nosed *Permesso* into the channel that connected Newport Bay with the Pacific Ocean, Tony saw the running lights of another boat rounding Balboa Island, now about a mile behind them.

"Oh, shit, that's them," said Tony.

"I don't think they could have gotten underway that fast," Carl replied.

"Who the hell else would it be at this time?"

"Could be anybody … there are a million boats in this bay … lot's of people go fishing at night."

As *Permesso* advanced into the channel the other boat dropped from sight. Carl advanced the throttle and the stern squatted down as the propeller dug into the water. Tony started shivering violently.

"Why don't you go down below and dry off. You can probably find some dry clothes to put on," said Carl.

Tony looked around, but there was no sight of the other boat. "Yeah, I'm freezing my ass off."

He opened the hatch door and started down the steps, but stopped and went back to the stern to grab the Dolphin's bag.

"Don't take that thing down there, it's dripping wet," said Carl.

"I sure as hell ain't gonna leave it up here."

"Who the hell is gonna to take it?"

Tony stared at Carl.

"What? You think I'm gonna take it? I don't even know what it is. Besides, where the hell do you think I'd go?

Tony turned and walked down the stairs with the bag. He looked around the cramped cabin, then he put the dripping bag in the sink in the galley. He opened the door to the tiny head. "Jesus, how do you take a dump in here?" he said aloud. He grabbed a towel from the bar next to the miniature sink.

He shut the door, slung the towel over his shoulder and started rummaging through the various closets and cupboards in the cabin. Eventually he found one with some clothes. He pulled out a pair of slacks and a Hawaiian print shirt. *Probably one of mine*, he thought. Swaying precariously as the boat bounced through the swells, he slipped off his wet clothes, toweled off and pulled on the slacks and shirt.

The pants were a little big, but the shirt fit just fine. He looked at the belt on the pants lying on the floor. He shrugged, picked up the pants, pulled off the belt, dried it with the towel and threaded it through the loops of the too large slacks. He laid the towel on the table in galley, then picked up the wet pants again and emptied out the pockets onto the towel. He sat down on the bench seat and pawed through the pile.

He opened the roll of soggy bills and spread them out to dry. He emptied the contents of his wallet and spread everything out. He picked up Gina's cell phone and flipped it open. The screen was blank. He pressed the button to turn it on. Nothing. "Damn it."

He got up, went to the sink and opened the Dolphin's bag. He pulled out Vince and Sheldon's dripping wallets, laughed, and dropped them in the sink. Then he pulled out the Colt and set it on the counter. He turned the bag upside down and dumped all the stacks of bills in the sink.

He dropped the bag on the floor and went back to the closet to find something to replace it. He pawed through the clothes and found a small, green canvas National Car Rental bag.

He grabbed another towel from the head and spread it out next to the sink, and then he scooped all the stacks out of the sink and put them on the towel. He picked up each end of the towel and rolled the stacks back and forth, letting the towel soak up most of the moisture. He poured the contents of the towel into the National bag. He grabbed the wallets out of the sink and threw them in the bag. Then he toweled off the Colt, put it in the bag and zipped it shut. He opened a cupboard under the sink and stuffed in the bag.

He pawed through the closet again and found a jacket. He slipped it on and went back up on deck. Staring back into the darkness, he saw the running lights of several boats, but one caught his attention. It was far behind, but it appeared to be on a similar course as they were.

"How long have they been there?" he asked Carl.

"Who?"

"That boat back there?"

Carl stared into the darkness behind them. "Which one?"

Tony pointed. "That one."

Carl squinted. "How the hell would I know? I can barely see it. Anyway they don't seem to be gaining on us … probably just some fishermen."

"It's him, I know it is."

34

Burke stood over the big man and nudged him with his foot. "Get up."

Swede's eyes blinked and Burke kicked at him again, "I said, get up."

Swede just stared up at him. All he could see was the outline of a man framed in the overhead lights of the marina.

"Get the hell up."

Swede tried to roll up on one side, but the pain in his chest was too much and he rolled back on the ground.

Burke waved Swede's gun. "Get up or I'll finish you right here."

Swede saw the gun and moaned, "I think some ribs are broken."

"I'm not kidding, asshole. I'll finish you with your own gun if you don't get up right now."

Swede rolled up on to his elbow again. The pain was intense, but he gritted his teeth and managed to get to his knees. Blood dripped from his chin onto the ground. He touched his cheek and winced. He dabbed at his mouth with his sleeve and felt blood soak through to his arm.

Burke pushed him with his foot and he rocked back on his knees. "Get your ass up."

Swede struggled to his feet. Arms clutched around his throbbing torso, he swayed back and forth like a drunk.

"Up those stairs." Burke waved the gun at the half dozen stairs that led up to the parking lot.

Swede moaned and staggered forward. He clutched the stair railing to steady himself, but Burke pressed the gun into his back.

"Up."

Swede made his left foot reach up to the first step and pulled the rail with his arms to hoist his body up after it. He thought someone was holding a blowtorch to his chest. Burke kept pushing with the gun and step by agonizing step he made his way up to the parking lot.

"Over there."

In the dim glow of the parking lot lighting he could see a body lying on the ground about twenty yards away.

"Hurry up, before the cops get here."

Swede staggered over to the body. Donahue was face down, arms and legs splayed out. The right leg was cocked at an odd angle from the knee.

"Pick him up," said Burke.

Swede looked at him. He could barely carry his own weight. How the hell would he manage to pick up 200 pounds of dead weight? Burke pushed the gun into his back, causing a white wave of pain to wash over him. He steadied himself for a moment, then slowly bent down and rolled Donahue over on his back. He looked dead, but as Swede reached under his armpits and pulled him up, he heard Donahue wheeze.

"Come on, hurry the hell up."

Swede pulled again but the pain was too great. He was not able to lift Donahue off the ground. He stepped over Donahue and reached under his arms from behind. With maximum effort and bolts of pains searing through his chest, he could manage to drag Donahue backward.

"Jesus Christ, you big ape. Is that the best you can do?"

Swede stopped and looked up at Burke.

Burke waved the gun back toward the stairs. "Just keep pulling."

Slowly, Swede made his way to the stairs. Burke kept anxiously watching the street, expecting to see flashing lights at any moment. "Goddamn it. Hurry the hell up."

Dragging Donahue, the Swede backed his way down the stairs. Each time Donahue's feet bounced down to the next step, he heard a moan escape from the limp body.

At the bottom of the steps, Swede asked, "Where to?"

Burke waved the gun toward the dock that jutted out into the south side of the marina. "Out there."

Five minutes later they were standing next to Burke's 42-foot luxury cruiser, *Last Lap*. "Hoist him on board," demanded Burke.

Swede gritted his teeth and with all his strength, dragged Donahue onto the boat. Burke followed. He waved the gun to a ladder that led up to the flying bridge. "Up there."

Swede looked at Donahue's body on the deck and then at Burke.

"Leave him there," said Burke.

Swede shrugged and worked his way painfully up the ladder, Burke following close behind.

"Stop." Keeping the gun pointed at Swede, Burke made his way over to the cockpit and started the engines. He flipped up the seat and pulled out a roll of duct tape. He walked back over to Swede and before Swede could blink, bashed him in the side of the head with the gun. Swede went down in a heap.

Quickly, Burke rolled Swede face down, taped his hands behind his back and then his feet together. He cocked Swede's legs at the knees and secured his feet and hands together. He went back down the ladder to the main deck and looked at Donahue's limp body. He shook his head. "Jesus, Barry."

He jumped back over the side and loosened the fore and aft lines that secured the boat to the dock. He made his way back up to the cockpit on the flying bridge and slowly backed the boat out of the slip. His eyes were level with the parking lot and could see flashing red and blue lights bounce in the air as patrol cars flew over the speed bumps.

Swede moaned. Burke glanced over to make sure the big man was still secure, and then he shifted *Last Lap* into forward and motored slowly into the bay. Running without lights, he applied more power. He looked over his shoulder and saw lights play around the parking lot. When he saw two flashlights were moving toward the steps to the docks, he nudged the throttle still more. As *Last Lap* passed the bridge to Balboa Island she was finally out of sight from the marina.

Burke reduced power, but kept running without lights. Just able to make out the way ahead in the moonlight, he prayed they would not encounter another boat before exiting the bay. The clock on the dashboard read 11:34, still early enough for night fishermen to be heading out or daytime stragglers to be returning to port. Rounding the north end of Balboa he spotted a boat heading for the channel just a few hundred yards ahead. It couldn't be Tony, he thought, they had at least a fifteen-minute lead.

Maintaining the separation, he followed the other boat into the channel and out into the Pacific, where it picked up speed and headed due west. Bobbing in the ocean swells, Burke gazed around the horizon. Several boats were visible, but one on a northwest heading caught his attention. It was at least three or four miles away and seemed to be moving quickly. Instinctively, he set a northwest course, increased power and set the autopilot.

He made his way back down to the main deck. Donahue hadn't moved. Burke looked closer at his right leg and could see that it was obviously badly broken. He was going to need medical attention and if he regained consciousness he was going to be in a great deal of pain.

"Sorry, buddy," Burke muttered. He went below and found a medical kit containing a syringe of morphine. He grabbed a blanket and went back on deck, where he administered the morphine and covered Donahue with the blanket.

"That's the best I can do, Barry," he said. He went back up to the bridge. *Last Lap* wallowed nauseatingly in the following seas and Swede was moaning and beginning to move.

"You're not going to be sick are you?" asked Burke.

"Fuck you," was the muffled reply.

"What was that? I couldn't hear you."

"You heard me, prick," Swede answered more clearly.

Burke's left leg lashed out and caught Swede squarely in the side.

"Fuck you," wheezed Swede.

"You know you could go on cursing me and I could go on kicking you forever, but that wouldn't do either one of us any good. Why don't do tell me where Tony is going and I'll let you rest in peace."

"Fuck you," the reply.

Burke wound up to deliver another kick, but stopped when he saw Swede puke. "Goddamn, you *are* sick."

Swede moaned and puked.

"Hey, how about doing that over the side?" Burke pulled out a pocketknife and cut the strand of tape that secured Swede's feet to his hands. "There, get your fat ass up and put your head over the side."

Swede rolled on his side. Burke grabbed his arm and helped him to his knees, Swede obliging passively. In that position, his head could just make it over the railing, just in time for another round of heaving.

Burke backed away. "Nothing worse than being seasick, is there, asshole?" He was starting to feel a little nauseous himself, so he went to the cockpit and stuck his face into the breeze. He could still make out the boat he had seen earlier, but it seemed to be increasing the distance. He added a little more power.

He glanced over at Swede, who was still retching over the side. "Enjoying the ride?"

Swede said something, but it was inaudible over the engine and wind noises. Burke went closer so he could hear. "What was that?"

Swede fell backward. Lying face up on the deck, his face covered with spittle, he said, "I'll tell you whatever you want ... just get me off this thing."

"Well that's damned cooperative of you. Where is Tony going?"

Swede moaned, turned his head and retched again.

Burke went to the cockpit and reduced the speed to help quiet the action of the boat. He went back to stand over Swede. "He got on a boat ... where is that sonofabitch going?"

"A boat?" Swede moaned, his head rolling back and forth.

"Yeah."

"Must be Carl's."

"Carl? Carl who?"

"Carl Fontaine."

"Never heard of him."

"He's a friend of Tony's ... it was his boat."

"No shit ... I didn't know Tony had any friends. Where'd they go?"

"I guess they ..." Swede retched again. "I guess they are probably going back to Alamitos Bay."

"Alamitos?"

"That's were Carl keeps his boat, but I couldn't swear that's where they are going ... are you going to let me off this goddamn thing?"

"Sure, just as soon as we get to Alamitos Bay."

Swede moaned. "Oh Christ ... help me."

Burke leaned down and grabbed Swede's arm. "Sure." He helped Swede get to his knees and get his head over the side just before another round of uncontrollable retching.

Burke skipped quickly backward. He went back to the cockpit, yelling over his shoulder. "Bet you'll be ready for a nice, greasy hamburger when you get on shore." Laughing, he punched up Alamitos Bay on the GPS.

It was 12:45 when Gina turned into the driveway of Carl's house. "Carl lives here?"

"Pretty mundane for a gangster, eh?"

"Carl's no gangster … he's just one of Tony's idiot friends."

"Well, he plays the part anyway."

Gina laughed. "They all think they are a bunch of big shots." She turned off the motor and handed the keys to Mickey.

Mickey got out and looked at the front of the Porsche. There was a large dent in fender, the right headlight was cracked, and there was a bullet hole just above the tire. "Carl is going to be upset about that."

Gina ran her hand over the dent. "Screw him … that's what he gets for being friends with Tony."

As soon as Mickey opened the door of the house he could hear Butch whining and pawing at the back door.

"Whose dog?"

"Carl's … his name is Butch."

"A dog, too? This guy is a riot."

Gina followed Mickey into the kitchen. He went to the back door, slid it open and Butch came bounding in, running in circles around Mickey and Gina, sniffing and whining.

"Poor Butch," said Gina. "I wonder if he's been fed."

"I don't know. He seems hungry." Mickey bent over and began petting the dog. "You hungry, boy?" Butch put his paws on Mickey's thighs and licked his face. Mickey stood up and rummaged through the cupboards until he found some dog food. Seeing the bag sent Butch into a frenzy. "Guess so."

Mickey found the dog's dish in a corner of the kitchen entry. He poured some food into the dish and Butch buried his face into the food. Mickey picked up the water dish and took it to the sink.

"I think you've found a friend," said Gina.

Mickey filled the dish with fresh water. "I'm sure it's only the food." He set the water down next to Butch.

"Still, he seemed to like you."

"That's me ... dogs and babies."

Gina smiled. "Show me around."

They walked through the sparse living room. "Definitely a bachelor pad," said Gina.

"Wait until you see the bathroom." Mickey reached through the open door and flipped on the light.

Gina stuck her head in. "Oh my god."

"He claims it was that way when he bought the house a couple of years ago and he just hasn't gotten around to redecorating. Personally, I think he likes it."

"The pink shower curtain with the porpoises is a nice touch."

"Yeah, I thought so, too."

Mickey showed her the bedrooms. "Solid middle class, eh?"

"Who knew?" Gina followed Mickey back to the living room. He sat on the couch and she sat next to him, putting her elbow up on the back so she faced him. "Thank you."

"For what?"

"For being there. I wonder if Tony would have showed up if you weren't pushing him."

"Sure he would."

Gina smiled. "I love my cousin, but I know him, too."

"He's a little quirky."

"Quirky? That's being charitable."

"Okay, he's nuts ... but I'm learning to like the guy."

"That would put you in the minority ... but that's what I like about you."

"What?"

"You can find something worth liking in a guy like Tony."

Butch came bounding into the living room and started sniffing and licking around Mickey's legs.

"Butch seems to like you, too."

"He'd love the dog catcher if he fed him."

Mickey idly petted Butch, the dog's head resting on his knee. He looked at Gina. "Are you okay?"

"I'm fine."

"I mean ... after all you were kidnapped."

"Seriously, I'm fine. I couldn't go anywhere, but I wasn't abused." She waved her hand up and down her body. "See, I even got some new clothes out of the deal."

Mickey pulled his hand away from Butch, but the dog kept nuzzling his leg until he resumed petting. "Well, I was worried about you."

Gina put her hand on Mickey's shoulder. "That means a lot to me."

Mickey leaned over and kissed her gently. Butch whined and nuzzled his leg. Mickey pulled away from Gina. "Stop it, Butch." The dog cowered. "Just relax, will you?" The dog lay at his feet.

"I'm a complicated woman," said Gina.

"Name one who isn't."

"I mean, my family is ... out of the ordinary."

"I didn't just fall off the cabbage truck. I know about your family."

"Tony isn't really representative of what they are about, you know."

"I hope not."

"I mean, there are some … well, some … let's just say different views about getting along in the world."

"I'm not exactly a boy scout."

"I expect not … not if you've gone along with Tony."

"Let's just say I've pushed the envelope a little at times myself."

Gina smiled. "I'm shocked, Mickey."

Mickey blushed slightly. "What I'm trying to say is that I don't care about your family."

"But they might care about you."

"What do you mean?"

"It's usually frowned upon when I get involved with someone that is outside of the business."

"My past is not exactly lily white. Your secrets are safe with me."

"I know, it's just that …"

"This has nothing to do with your family, does it?"

"No, I suppose not."

"Is there someone else?"

"No, no. There's no one else."

"What then?"

Gina pulled her hand away from his shoulder. "I've been in relationships before. They just never seem to work out."

"You think I'll end up hurting you?"

"You're a great guy, Mickey, I know you'd be kind, but …"

"But you think … in the end … I'd walk out on you."

Gina looked down at her lap. "I've learned how to be alone. I think it's best that way."

"How about giving me a shot here? If I hurt you in any way, you can turn your family loose on me."

Gina looked back at him and laughed softly. "Don't think I wouldn't."

He brushed her cheek with his hand. "Seriously, I think I deserve a chance."

"Maybe." She leaned over and kissed him.

Mickey put his arms around her and kissed her back. Butch jumped up and began whining and nuzzling at their knees.

Gina smiled and pulled away. "I think he's feeling left out."

"Goddamn it, Butch, that's it." He stood up, grabbed the dog's collar and started to pull him into the kitchen.

"What are you doing?"

"I'm throwing this fleabag outside."

Gina stood up and pulled Mickey's hand away from Butch's collar. "No you aren't." She knelt down and petted the dog's head. Butch licked her face, his tail wagging wildly.

"I get it. The dog wins."

"For the moment." Gina stood. "Come on boy, let's see if there is any food in that kitchen. I'm starving." She went into the kitchen, the dog bounding after her.

35

Permesso's exhaust burbled gently as Carl eased the Bayliner into the slip in Alamitos Bay. Tony stood near the bow on the port side, holding a line. As soon as the gap of water narrowed to a foot, he jumped onto the dock, wobbled precariously, and eventually he regained his balance. He knelt down and wrapped the bowline around a dock cleat several times.

"Come back here and I'll toss you the stern line," said Carl.

"Christ," Tony muttered. He went to the end of the dock and grabbed the stern line that Carl tossed him and wrapped it around a dock cleat. He stood and shouted to Carl, "Hey toss me the bag."

"What?"

"The bag … that green bag near the hatch."

Carl looked around and spotted the green National Car bag that was sitting on the deck and tossed it over. Tony set the bag down, lit a cigarette and watched Carl shut down the boat and secured the hatches.

When he finished, Carl stepped off the boat and looked at the dock cleat that held the stern line. "What the hell is this?"

"What the hell is what?" asked Tony.

Carl knelt down to retie the line. "How long do you think this would have lasted?"

"Who do you think I am? Admiral Halsey?"

"Obviously not." Carl stood and walked to the bowline to retie it.

"Yeah, well, fuck you." Tony flicked his cigarette into the water.

"Hey, there's enough pollution in this bay. Do you mind?"

"What is it about owning a boat that turns people into such pricks?"

Carl ignored the remark and went to secure the lines on the starboard side.

Tony watched him anxiously. "You about done there, Captain Ahab?"

Carl finished securing the boat. "All right, let's go."

At the top of the steps that led from the marina to the parking lot Tony stopped and looked back out into the black ocean. Several boats were scattered across the horizon, but one in particular seemed to be moving steadily toward the bay. "Isn't that the same boat that we were watching out there?"

Carl peered into the darkness. "Hard to tell ... could be."

"Yeah, well I think it is. Let's get the hell out of here."

Mickey opened the milk jug and sniffed the contents. Satisfied that it was reasonably fresh, he poured the milk into a bowl filled with Raisin Bran that he had found in a cupboard. He put the milk back into the refrigerator and carried the bowl over to the kitchen table and sat down. "Better than nothing."

Gina nodded. She was chewing a bite of a bagel she had found, toasted, and spread with cream cheese. Butch, who was been sitting nearby, waiting for a crumb to hit the floor, jumped up and ran to the door. Almost instantaneously, the garage door began to open.

Mickey and Gina looked at one another. "Must be somebody with a door opener ... I hope it's Carl," said Mickey. He ran to the living room to look out the window.

He returned to the kitchen and passing by Gina on his was to the garage entry door said, "It's Carl's car."

Tony opened the door and light from the car pulling into the garage streamed in. The car stopped and the motor turned off. Carl emerged from the driver's side and Tony from the passenger's. He opened the rear door and pulled out the green bag. Carl went over to look at the Porsche.

"Surprised to see us?" asked Tony.

Standing in the doorway, Mickey answered, "You might say that."

"What the hell happened to my car?" cried Carl.

"What?" said Tony.

"My car … my car is fucking ruined."

Tony went over and looked at the damage. He looked up at Mickey, "What happened."

"What do you think?" said Mickey. "Donahue tried to get Gina."

"Really? What happened to him?"

"Gina hit him," said Mickey.

Tony laughed. "No shit? She hit the sonofabitch?"

"She had to."

"No doubt. It couldn't have happened to a nicer guy."

Carl looked on the verge of tears. "What about it Tony?"

"Big deal … a few dents. You can bump that out, no problem."

"What about this bullet hole?"

Tony looked back at Mickey.

"Burke took a few pot shots at us."

Tony ran a finger over the hole. "A little Bondo … it'll be as good as new."

"Goddamnit, Tony. You've ruined my car."

"Relax. I'll pay for it."

"You're goddamn right you'll pay for it."

"Don't be such an old woman." Tony walked to the door.

Carl traipsed after him. "Do you have any idea how much money I've put into that car?"

Mickey stood aside to let Tony and Carl enter.

"Well, it didn't exactly go down the way I'd planned, but the results were good." Tony held up the bag.

"Yeah, I wanted to talk to you about that," said Gina.

Tony turned and saw Gina sitting in the kitchen. "Another precinct heard from." Tony led the way into the kitchen and set the bag on the table. "You okay?"

"Yeah, thanks for asking."

"Hey, I made sure you were safe before I went after the money."

"What about my goddamn car, Tony?"

Tony sighed and turned to Carl. "I told you I'd take care of it … will you let it go?"

"I would have appreciated knowing what you were doing," said Mickey.

"I couldn't tell you, Ace; you'd have never gone along with it."

"You're damn right. What the hell were you thinking?"

Tony sat down at the table. "I got Gina back and I kept my money. What's wrong with that?"

"You could have gotten us all killed … that's what's wrong with it."

"Not to mention wrecking my car," added Carl.

Tony ignored Carl. "You both look healthy to me."

Mickey stood behind Gina. "Thanks to Gina's driving ability and the fact that Burke is a lousy shot."

Tony reached over and patted Gina's hand. "See, I knew you could handle it."

"Barry Donahue might not be doing so good," said Gina.

"That's what he gets for kidnapping you."

"Who was the guy laying on the ground by the dock?" asked Mickey.

Tony stopped laughing. "A friend of mine."

"You must be running out of friends. Is he dead?"

"I don't know."

"You mean you just left him there?"

"I had to … those two maniacs were trying to kill me."

"You could've just given them the money."

"That's what I said," chimed in Carl.

"They probably would have killed me anyway," said Tony.

"Yeah, well you deserved it," said Mickey.

"Burke wouldn't have killed you, Tony," said Gina. "He just wanted the money."

"You don't know that," said Tony. "Besides, I wasn't going to give that stupid mick my money."

"But you'd risk everyone around you for it?" said Mickey.

"What's the big fucking deal? You're both okay. I'm okay … and I've got my money."

"What about Swede?" asked Carl.

Tony looked down at the floor. "Yeah, well, I'm sorry about Swede … but he's a tough guy … he can take care of himself."

"That's the problem with you, Tony. Once you get what you need out of people, they are own their own." said Mickey.

"Hey, Swede knew what he was getting into … he lives for shit like that. Sometimes it just goes bad."

"I'm not just talking about Swede … I'm talking about Gina, Carl, me."

Tony stood up. "Hey, I don't have to listen to this shit." He grabbed the bag off the table and headed to the living room. He paused and turned in the doorway. "You are just a flying taxi driver I happened to hire … why the hell should I care what happens to you?"

"I'd say I've gone a little above and beyond the call of duty … wouldn't you?"

"Don't give me that crap … you could've left anytime you wanted … you stayed for the money, plain and simple."

Mickey flushed. "So I'm a mercenary. That doesn't mean I can be used."

"Sure it does. That's what mercenaries are for." Tony turned and walked away.

The kitchen was quiet until they heard a bedroom door slam. Mickey slumped down in the chair that Tony had occupied. Carl rummaged through the refrigerator and found a beer. He held it up to Mickey. "Want one?"

Mickey shook his head.

"Don't listen to that ingrate," said Gina.

"No, he's right … I did it for the money. In spite of my better instincts."

Carl sat down next to Gina and unscrewed the cap of the beer bottle. "Well, don't feel like the Lone Ranger. I knew this was a disaster in the making." He took a swig from the bottle. "Did I say no … like I wanted to?"

Gina laughed. "I guess we're all a bunch of idiots. I should have never left the restaurant in Miami, but Tony just has a way of talking people into things they don't want to do."

That broke the ice and they all laughed.

"He is a piece of work, though, isn't he?" said Mickey.

Carl nodded. "I could tell you stories …"

"I've known the guy all my life. There's nothing you could tell me that would surprise me," said Gina.

Carl looked at the remnants of Gina's bagel and Mickey's half eaten bowl of cereal. "You guys hungry?"

"Famished," said Gina.

"What do you have in mind?" asked Mickey.

"How about a pizza?"

Gina nodded. "Sounds great."

"You can get one delivered this late?" asked Mickey.

"No. But there is a store near by that makes pizza 24/7 … they don't deliver after midnight, so I'll just have to pick it up."

"If you're willing to go, I wouldn't turn it down."

"Hey, Tony," Carl yelled, "You want some pizza?"

"Fuck you," came a muffled reply.

"Guess not," said Carl. He stood up and grabbed a refrigerator magnet with a pizza store ad. "Pepperoni and mushrooms ok?"

"Sure," said Gina.

Mickey nodded.

Carl dialed the number on his cell phone and placed the order. "It'll be ready in 20 minutes."

36

Carl had related a story about one of Tony and his escapades aboard *Permesso* that had Mickey laughing and Gina shaking her head. "We were so drunk," Carl continued, "I don't know how the hell we ever found Alamitos Bay."

Carl looked up looked up at the clock above the sink. "Oh shit, I've got to go." He stood up abruptly and Butch stood with him. "I'll be back in a few minutes." Butch followed him to the door, his tail wagging excitedly. "You stay here, buddy." He pushed Butch back and went into the garage, shutting the door after him. Butch stood at the door until he heard the car back out and the garage door shut. Then he came back and sat at Gina's feet.

Gina patted his head. "You need to go out, boy?"

Butch's tail thumped on the floor. Gina stood and went to the back door. She slid the door open, but Butch did not go out. He stood in the open doorway and growled lowly.

"What wrong boy?" Gina peered out into the dark yard, but could see nothing. The dog stood rigid, growling louder.

"What's the matter with Butch?" asked Mickey.

"I don't know." Gina knelt next to the dog. "What is it, boy?" She stood and found a light switch next to the door and flipped it up. A porch light illuminated the brick patio immediately outside the door, but the yard beyond was still cloaked in darkness.

Burke suddenly appeared in the pool of light on the patio. Gina saw a gun in his right hand. "Hello, Gina. I …," before he could finish the sentence, Butch was out the door and on him, knocking him backward off the patio.

Mickey jumped up and ran to Gina's side. "What the hell?"

Burke rolled around the yard, Butch keeping him pinned. "Get this goddamn dog off me or I'll kill him."

Tony came running into the kitchen. "What's going on?"

"It's Burke," yelled Gina.

"Oh, Christ."

A shot rang out, but Butch persisted in keeping Burke on the ground.

"Oh, Christ," repeated Tony.

"He'll kill Butch," said Gina.

Mickey looked around the kitchen. Nothing caught his eye. Another shot rang out.

"We've got to do something," yelled Gina.

Mickey ran into the garage and reappeared with a baseball bat. He ran out into the yard and stood over the roiling mass of man and dog. "Look out, Butch." The dog paid no attention, so Mickey just swung the Louisville Slugger into the pile, making contact with Burke's right arm.

"Goddamn," yelled Burke. He rolled to his right, the gun dropping from his hand, and then he rolled completely onto his stomach.

Mickey seized the gun off the ground. "That's enough, Butch."

The dog stayed on Burke, biting at his head and neck.

"Butch," yelled Mickey, and reached for the dog's collar. With a yank, he managed to pull the dog off.

Barking loudly, Butch strained at his collar. "Give me a hand, here," yelled Mickey.

Gina ran out and grabbed onto Butch's collar. Between the two of them, they managed to get the dog away from Burke.

Butch was quivering and growling. "You got him?" asked Mickey.

"I've got him," said Gina.

Mickey slowly let go of the collar. "Get him back into the house."

The dog continued to strain at his collar, but had relaxed considerably. Gina ran her hand down his back. "You okay, boy?" Gina pulled Butch's collar and he responded. She backed him into the house.

Tony stepped aside to let them in. "Who knew a goddamn dog would save my ass?"

"Somehow I doubt that that was his intent," said Gina.

Tony stepped out onto the patio and went to Mickey's side. "Give me that thing."

Mickey looked at the gun in his hand. He handed it to Tony.

A light went on in the house immediately adjacent to Carl's backyard. Then an outdoor light went on at the house next to that one. Someone appeared at the window.

Tony hefted the gun and held it on Burke. "Get up you sonofabitch."

Burke rolled over onto his back, wincing and holding his right arm. "I'll kill you," he said to Mickey.

"You're gonna have to live through this first," said Tony. "Now get your ass up."

Burke sat up slowly. There were several abrasions on his hands and face, but surprisingly little blood. "Up until now it was only about the money, Tony. Now its personal."

"Yeah, well, it's still only about the money to me. Just get your ass up."

Burke struggled to his feet. He brushed off his clothes and ran his hand through his hair. "It's too bad that dog interfered. I was just going to get my money and leave. Now I'm going to have to hurt you, Tony."

"You're talking pretty big for the guy on the wrong end of the gun. And besides, it ain't your goddamn money."

Burke continued to brush his sleeve and pant legs. "I loaned that money to you."

"We had a deal and I was going to pay you back."

"With what? You wouldn't have had a dime if I hadn't set you up with Johnny Rodriguez."

Tony looked around. The lights had come on in a couple more houses. "I'm not talking about this anymore. Just get your ass in the house before the neighbors form a posse."

Tony stepped back so Burke could pass in front of him, and then followed closely behind.

"Now what?" Mickey was a step behind.

"The cops are probably on there way. We've got to get the hell out of here."

"So what? We're just private citizens minding our own business when an intruder invaded."

"You can stick around and answer questions if you want to … I'm getting the hell out."

"What about Carl?"

"Don't forget, your friend Carl," said Burke. "You'll have to screw him over just like you did your pal, Swede."

Tony stepped into the kitchen behind Burke. "Hold it right there, Burke. Sit down and put your hands on the table."

Butch began to snarl and whine. Gina held him back.

"Put the dog outside," said Tony. "Ace, see if you can find something to secure this asshole."

Mickey nodded and went out into the garage.

"Swede, eh? So, he's not dead?"

Burke laughed. "No, but he sure prayed for death out on that ocean."

"So, that was you behind us?"

"Swede was very cooperative once he realized you didn't give a shit about him."

"Where is he now?"

"Waiting for me on the boat, with his new friend, Barry Donahue."

Gina slid the door shut. "Barry's not …"

"Dead? Nah, but you sure fucked him up."

"He deliberately got in the way."

"He is one dedicated employee, I'll say that."

Mickey reappeared with a coil of rope and roll of duct tape.

"Use the tape," said Tony. "Put your hands behind your back."

Wincing, Burke slowly put his arms behind him and Mickey secured them with the duct tape.

The low wail of a siren caught Tony's attention.

"Oh shit, we've got to get out of here, now."

"How?" asked Mickey. "We can't fit four people in the Porsche?"

"We'll take the sedan."

"Carl took it to get some pizza."

"Pizza? Oh, for Christ's sake."

"The three of us could fit in the Porsche … we'll just leave him here."

Burke blanched. "Hey, you can't leave me here."

"Why not?" asked Tony.

"Hey, you got your money. Let me go and you can pay me back when you get around to it."

"Pay you back? You can pound sand up your ass … I had to chase you across the damn country to get my money back."

"All right, all right, let me go and I'll cut your debt in half."

"In half?"

Mickey cut in. "I hate to interrupt negotiations, but if we're going to beat the cops, we'd better hit it right now."

Tony and Burke looked at him. Then Tony turned back to Burke. "You're not in a position to negotiate."

"All right, all right. You get me back to my boat and we'll call it square."

Tony started pulling open drawers in search of a knife. He found one and held it to the tape on Burke's wrists. "All debts forgiven?"

"Yeah, yeah ... just cut the fucking tape, okay?"

Tony pushed the gun into Burke's back. "Remember, I've still got the gun ... don't fuck with me on this."

"Whatever ... let's go, okay?"

Tony slit the tape and Burke rubbed his arm. "Goddamn, did you have to break my arm?"

Tony turned to Mickey. "Did Carl take his phone with him?"

"I don't know," said Mickey.

"I think I saw him slip it in his pocket," said Gina.

Tony felt his pocket, then remembered that he had ruined Gina's phone. "You got your phone, Ace?"

"Yeah, but I don't have Carl's number."

"Damn," said Tony.

"Wait a second," said Mickey. He grabbed the number of the pizza store off the refrigerator.

Tony ran to the bedroom to retrieve the green bag. The police sirens growing louder, he looked out the bedroom window. Red and blue lights were bouncing off the houses as the cars approached. He ran back to the kitchen. "Too late. We've got to go out the back."

They piled out onto the patio, Butch snarling and nipping at Burke's Legs. "Get that mutt away from me."

No one paid any attention. Lights were on in houses on three sides, but the house to the west was dark. "That's our best bet," said Mickey, and led the group to a six-foot, wooden fence that separated the two yards. He helped Gina over the fence, Butch leaping up and down after her.

"You've got to stay there, boy," she said through the slats.

Burke struggled to hoist himself over but got stuck halfway over, his stomach resting on the top. Tony flipped his legs over and he landed with a thud.

Mickey helped Tony scramble over, handed him the gun, and reached to pat Butch. "You stay here, buddy." Then he pulled himself over,

Burke lay on his back. "Sonofabitch, I think you broke my other goddamn arm."

Mickey and Tony managed to get Burke on his feet. The house of the yard they were in remained dark, but the outside of Carl's house was ablaze with lights. Butch started barking.

"Sshhhuussh," hissed Mickey.

"That goddamn hound is going to draw attention back here," said Tony.

Butch barked some more and a light played around Carl's yard.

"This way." Mickey headed quickly away from the fence. The others followed and gathered behind him at a gate on the opposite side of the house. There was still no indication of life in the house, so he opened the gate and walked slowly down a driveway that ran along the side of the house, the rest in tow. He leaned around the corner of the house and pulled quickly back.

"What is it?" whispered Gina.

"There are two cop cars parked in front of Carl's and two cops are standing in the driveway."

"What are they doing?"

"Just standing there, talking." He looked at the four-foot high hedge running the length of the driveway down to the street. "We can probably make it to the street with out them seeing us if we stay down along that hedge."

"What then?" asked Tony.

"There's two big trees at the end ... they might block their line of sight and we can make it down the street."

"Let's go," said Tony.

One by one, they crouched down and made their way slowly along the hedge toward the street. They were almost halfway down the driveway when a light played across the lawn of the house immediately on their right. It was from a police car that was moving slowly down the street, shining a spotlight around the neighborhood. Mickey froze and the rest followed suit, but they were exposed and if the light hit them, they would surely be spotted. Miraculously, as the car passed, a big Aspen at the end of the driveway blocked the light and they fell in its shadow. The car passed without stopping.

Mickey let his breath out. "Jesus."

"Just keep moving," said Tony.

As Carl put the pizza on top of the car and fumbled for his car keys, he heard a voice say, "Hey, buddy."

He looked in the direction of the voice. It was the young clerk from the store. "Is your name Carl?"

"Who wants to know?"

"There's a telephone call for you."

"Telephone call?"

"Yeah. Inside. Someone called and asked if Carl was still there. He described someone who looked like you."

"Who is it?"

"Didn't say. Just said it was important."

There were only two people who knew where he was. "Okay, thanks." Carl followed the clerk back into the store.

The clerk went behind the counter and handed the phone to Carl. "Yeah?"

"It's me, Tony."

"How'd you know I was here?"

"How do you think? Look it doesn't matter … you can't go home … there're cops crawling all over your place."

"Cops? Where are you?"

"Down the street, dodging cop cars … I can see three cars in front of your place right now … it's lit up like Christmas."

"Oh Christ." Carl looked at the clerk who was pretending to be thumbing through a magazine but was listening intently. Carl turned around so his back was to the counter.

"You there?"

"Yeah. Tony, what the hell happened?"

"I don't want to get into all that right now. You just need to pick us up so we can get the hell out of here."

"Where are you exactly?"

"I don't know … about ten or fifteen houses away from yours."

"Which way?"

"Toward the boulevard."

"Can you make it across the boulevard without being spotted?"

Tony paused. "Yeah, I think so."

"There's a junior high school just on the other side … I'll meet you in the parking lot."

"How long?"

Carl turned to look at the clock on the wall behind the counter. The clerk turned and put his nose back into the magazine. "About 1:30."

"Okay."

Carl was about to hand the phone back to the clerk when he paused. "Tony, why didn't you call me on my cell?"

"I don't have one that works with your number on it."

"Oh, yeah. I'll see you in a few minutes."

Carl handed the phone to the clerk. "Thanks."

"Sounds like you got problems," said the clerk.

"Surprise birthday party … the birthday boy is getting suspicious."

The clerk looked up at the clock. "Yeah, sure." He watched Carl leave and get in his car. As the car pulled out of the parking lot, the pizza flew off the roof. "What a numbnut."

37

"What time did he say he'd be here?" asked Mickey.

Tony peeked around the eucalyptus tree they were huddled behind. "One-thirty."

Mickey flipped open his phone. "It's twenty to two."

"He'll be here … or I'll wring his goddamn neck."

Just as the words were out of his mouth, Carl's car pulled into the school parking lot. The little group ventured out from the behind the tree near the corner of the school building, quickly ran the short distance to the car and piled in.

"Let's get the hell out of here," said Tony from the passenger seat.

Carl glanced in the rearview mirror at Burke in the backseat with Mickey and Gina. He turned toward Tony. "Who is that?"

"Burke. Carl, there are cops all over the goddamn place. Will you just get the hell out of here?"

"Tony, what the hell is Burke doing in my car?"

"Carl."

"All right, all right."

Carl backed up the car and turned back toward the entrance. There was no traffic on the boulevard, so he pulled right out. No sooner were they motoring slowly down the road than a cop car passed by in the opposite direction. Carl watched in the rearview mirror as it turned onto his street.

"Tony, do you mind telling me what is going on?"

"Burke came to your house …"

"My house? Burke came to my house?"

"Your buddy, Swede, told me where you lived," said Burke from the backseat.

"Swede's okay?"

"More or less … he's on my boat."

"This is really getting bizarre."

"Will you shut up and just listen?" said Tony.

"Okay, okay. What happened?"

"Burke tried to get the money back, but Butch got to him first …"

Carl smiled, "Good ol' Butch."

"Are you gonna listen?"

"Yeah, yeah … go on."

"Anyway, Butch helped us get the jump on him and now he wants us to help him get back to his boat, so he's going to let go of my debt."

"No shit?"

"No shit. You just have to drop him off at his boat."

"Where's his boat?"

"Alamitos Bay," said Burke.

"So it was you following us?"

Carl shook his head. "Tony, why are the cops at my house?"

"Burke let loose a couple of shots while he was rolling around on the ground with Butch."

Carl blanched. "Tell me Butch is okay."

"He's fine. But the neighbors evidently got a little freaked and someone called the cops."

"Oh, shit."

"We barely got out the back. We jumped the fence into your neighbor's yard and managed to get down the street without being seen."

"So, what am I supposed to do about the cops?"

"Just tell 'em that someone tried to break into your house and Butch scared 'em off."

"You think they'll believe that shit?"

"What are they gonna do? You weren't there … you can prove that right?"

"I guess."

"So, what can they do?"

"I don't know … my record ain't exactly clean."

"If they give you any shit, you let me know … I'll make sure you have the best attorney."

"Oh, thanks a hell of a lot."

"Look, it just happened. You'll be all right."

"I'd be all right if I hadn't let you talk me into any of this crap. I shoulda known better."

"Hey, you were bored … you had fun … admit it."

"I ain't admittin' nothin'. Just do me a favor and the next time you're in town, don't call me, okay?"

"Suit yourself, grandma. Just take Burke back to his boat after you drop us at the airport."

Mickey watched the dash clock flip to 2:17 as they pulled into the parking lot for the Long Beach Center FBO. He felt the fatigue that had been seeping into his bones since he sat down in the car. "I'm thinking maybe we should get a room for the rest of the night … I don't think I'm up to flying anywhere right now."

"Hell no," said Tony. "We've got to leave town tonight."

"Why?"

"Because … well, because there are cops looking for us."

"They're not looking for us … they just want to know who fired a gun a Carl's house."

"Look, you don't have to fly all the way to Florida … just get us out of here. How about Vegas? That's only an hour or so … you can do that."

"I suppose … but don't press me to go farther once we're up there."

Tony smiled. "You're a good man, Ace. Go get that plane of yours ready, we'll be right behind you."

Mickey opened the door, but before he got out, Gina squeezed his hand. "Be careful," she said.

"You're coming too, right?"

"Yes."

Mickey took her hand in his, "Then I'll be all right." He got out and walked to the tarmac gate.

Tony turned to look at Burke. "So, we're straight now?"

Burke sighed. "Yes, Tony, we're straight. But like I said, stay out of my way from now on. I might not be so friendly next time our paths cross."

"I just want to make sure you're not going to send your goon squad after me."

"We made a deal," said Burke, "I won't come looking for you."

"Who's that?" asked Carl.

"Who's who?" said Tony.

"That guy coming toward the car … I think he's carrying a gun."

Tony turned to look out the window in time to see Vince Jackson sprinting toward the car. "Oh shit … where the hell did he come from? Hit it, Carl."

"What?"

"Go. Now."

Carl put the car in gear and stepped on the gas. Jackson leaped to his right to dodge the rapidly accelerating car. He held the gun up, but decided not to fire. Instead he turned and ran toward the gate.

Mickey opened his wallet and pulled out the slip of paper with the code number for the gate that Emma had given him. He held it up to see it better in the floodlight that hung from the side of the building. Then he heard Carl's car take off. He whirled around and saw Vince Jackson running toward him. With the gate on one side and the building on another he was trapped; there was nowhere to go. He fumbled with the paper and tried to punch in the code on the gate lock, but before he got two numbers in, Vince was on him.

"Going somewhere, flyboy?"

Mickey turned toward Vince. He was holding a gun in his right hand that was pointed at Mickey's heaving chest.

"You seem a little surprised," said Vince.

Mickey calmed his breathing enough to speak. "I guess I didn't expect to see you, Vince."

"You know who I am?"

"I saw you in Vegas."

Vince recalled the lobby at Vegas Station and smiled. "Too bad I didn't know who you where at the time … we might not be meeting like this."

"What do you want?"

"What the hell do you think?"

"I don't have your money."

"No shit. But your boss does."

"He's not my boss."

"He hired you, didn't he?"

"He's a paying passenger."

"Whatever. Now it'll be your job to convince him to give me the money."

"He's not going to give you the money."

"You better hope so."

As the Lexus sped through the FBO parking lot, Tony spotted the Winnebago parked along a fence. "Why didn't I see that earlier?" he said.

"You were too busy thinking about your money," said Burke, laughing.

"Tony, what the hell are you doing?" asked Gina.

"Trying to save our asses."

"Carl, turn this thing around," Gina demanded.

Carl glanced at Tony.

"Keep going," said Tony.

"Goddamn it, Tony," yelled Gina.

Tony turned to look at her. "We're not going back there."

The Lexus screeched to a stop at Lakewood Boulevard. "Which way," asked Carl.

"I don't care … just get the hell out of here."

Carl wheeled right and the tires chirped as the car accelerated.

"Wasn't that Vince Jackson?" asked Burke.

"You know him?"

"His partner, Sheldon Isaacs, tried to make a deal with me to return my money."

"When?"

"A couple of day's ago. I told them to pound sand … I already had it taken care of."

"So why are they still on the trail?"

"Must not like to take 'no' for an answer."

"They think they're still working for you?"

"Probably."

"So, if they find out that you're not after the money, they'd have no reason to keep Ace."

"I'm sure they'd still want their cut."

"How much was that?"

"Ten percent … for delivering the cash."

"They're doing all this for a lousy fifteen grand?"

"They're still on Johnny Rodriguez's payroll, so that's just bonus money."

Tony thought for a while. "So, if you gave them the fifteen grand, they'd let Ace go and it's all settled?"

"That's the way it looks."

"Will you play along?"

"You mean let them think they are still working for me?"

"Yeah, let them think they are delivering the money to you, so you give them the fifteen grand."

"Why should I do that?"

"Because we're friends now and friends help each other."

"We're not friends, Tony. We have a business arrangement."

"All right. What do you want?"

"I think ten percent would be appropriate."

Tony winced. "Now you want fifteen K too?"

"That's my price."

"Wouldn't it be thirteen-five?" asked Carl.

Carl looked at him. "What?"

"Well, if you give those guys fifteen, you only have 135 left, and ten percent of 135 is thirteen thousand, five-hundred."

"Say, that's right." Carl turned back to Burke. "How about it? Thirteen-five?"

"Fifteen."

"But, what about what Carl just said?"

Burke shook his head. "Fifteen."

"That's thirty G's I'd be out."

"You walk away debt free and a hundred thousand," said Gina. "Stop playing games."

Tony stared out the window for a few seconds, and then turned back to Burke. "Have you got any way of contacting those idiots?"

"I have Sheldon's number on my cell."

"Will you get him on the horn for me?"

"We have a deal?"

"Yeah, yeah … you bloodsucker."

Burke pulled out his phone and flipped it open. He scrolled through the incoming calls, found Sheldon's number and pressed the 'Talk' button.

"Burke?" said the voice on the other end.

"Yeah."

"I was just thinking about you. I can't believe you're calling."

"Why?"

"I've got your money."

"You have my money?"

"Well, almost."

"What does that mean?"

"I just need to contact that yin-yang, Tony Boccaccio … I've got something he wants, so I know he'll give me the money."

"How about I put him in on the phone with you?"

"What?"

Burke handed the phone to Tony.

"Sheldon, you idiot … what the hell are you doing?"

There was a pause on the other end. "Tony, what are you doing with Burke?"

"He's my guest."

There was another pause. Tony could hear muffled conversation, then, "You mean prisoner?"

"No, I mean guest."

"I'm a little confused here. Are you two working together now?"

"Of course not."

"Then what in the hell is going on?"

"Didn't you know? Max and I are friends now."

"That's bullshit."

"No it isn't … ask him." Tony handed the phone back to Burke.

"What do you want, Sheldon?"

"That asshole says you're friends now … that right?"

Burke took a deep breath. "Yeah."

"What the hell?"

"What does it matter to you?"

"It doesn't … it's just that, that …"

"You're worried that you won't get your cut now?"

There was a pause on the other end. "No, I'm not worried. I've got an insurance policy."

"Oh? What's that?"

"I've got the pilot."

"What does that have to do with me?"

There was another pause. "Put Tony on, will you?"

Burke handed the phone to Tony.

"Yeah?"

"Listen, asshole. You bring me the money or your buddy's flying days are over."

"So what?"

"He's your boy, isn't he?"

"He's just a hired hand."

Gina slapped Tony in the back of the head. Tony winced. "Just second," he said to Sheldon. Then he lowered the phone and turned around. "Gina, goddamn it … I'm trying to talk here."

"Tony, I'm telling you, if you don't turn this car around and give them whatever they want, so help me …"

"Look, let me handle this. I'll get Ace back okay. Will you trust me here?"

"No, just turn the car around."

Tony turned back to the front and held the phone to his ear. "Okay, you've got, Ace."

"You're telling me you don't care what happens to him?" asked Sheldon.

"What if I did?"

"You give us the money and we let him go," said Sheldon.

"What are you going to do with it then?"

"Then we give it to Burke."

"What if I just give it to him?"

Another pause. "Just bring me the money. I'll give it to Burke."

"That doesn't seem very efficient."

"Maybe not, but that's the way it is going down."

"All right. You still at the airport?"

"Hell no … too much security floating around there. We're …" Sheldon's voice trailed off but Tony could still hear him. "Where the hell are we, Vince?" Tony heard a muffled response, and then Sheldon was back on the phone. "We're in Seal Beach."

"Seal Beach? Where the hell is that?"

"I know where it is," said Carl.

"Never mind," said Tony. "We've got it covered. Where in Seal Beach?"

Another pause. "The pier."

"Let me get this straight. I bring the money to the Seal Beach Pier parking lot, you give it to Burke and you let Ace go?"

"Put Burke back on."

Tony handed the phone back to Burke.

"Yeah, Sheldon?"

"If we give you the money, we still get our fifteen large?"

"Sure."

"Okay, let me talk to Tony again."

Burke rolled his eyes and handed the phone back to Tony.

"Yeah?"

"All right, that's the deal. You bring the money here and we give you back your boy."

"Okay, we'll be there in …" Tony held the phone away from his ear. "How long will it take us to get there?" he asked Carl.

"About fifteen minutes."

"Twenty minutes," Tony said into the phone."

"All right." Sheldon clicked off.

38

As they motored through the quiet streets of Seal Beach, Tony turned to Burke. "You're not going to welch on this deal, are you?"

"What do you mean?"

"If I give the money to those bozos and they give it to you, you give it back to me, right?"

"Less thirty grand."

"Yeah, yeah."

"That's our deal."

"Here we are." Carl turned off Ocean Avenue into the city parking lot adjacent to the pier. The Winnebago was parked in a spot designated for buses. Lights were apparent in the windows. "This might not be the smartest place to meet."

"Let's just make this fast and get the hell out of here," said Tony. "Pop the trunk, Carl." He got out of the car, followed by Burke and Gina. "You wait here," he said to Gina.

"Why?"

"Because I don't want you getting all hysterical."

"Tony, don't be an idiot."

"Please, I'm asking you to stay here."

Gina sighed heavily and got back in the car. "He better not screw this up," she said to Carl.

Tony zipped open the National bag and pulled out the Colt. He tossed it into the trunk, zipped the bag shut and slammed the lid. He and Burke walked around to the other side of the RV and knocked on the door. Sheldon Isaacs opened it up.

Sheldon shook his head. "I can't believe it."

"What?" asked Burke.

"You and that dirt bag together."

"Fuck you," said Tony.

"Oh, no offense, Tony … it just strikes me as a little odd."

"Yeah? Well, so do you, fatso."

"No need to get personal." Sheldon backed up the steps. "Come on in."

Tony and Burke followed him inside the RV.

Burke looked around the interior. "You drove this thing across the country?"

"Yeah. It's a great way to travel."

Burke laughed. "If you're a truck driver, I guess."

Tony offered the bag to Sheldon. "Here you go, creep. Where's Ace?"

Sheldon took the bag and set it on the kitchen table. He zipped it open and looked inside. "Well, looky here." He pulled out his and Vince's wallets. "They feel a little damp."

"It's a long story," said Tony.

"I'll bet it is." Sheldon opened his wallet. "Hey, there was a couple hundred bucks in here …"

"Travel expenses."

Sheldon rifled through the wallet and saw that everything else was in place. He pulled out a couple of stacks of the money. "Hey, these are damp too."

"I told you, it's a long story."

Sheldon shrugged. "It'll still spend, I guess." He counted out fifteen thousand and laid the bills on the table. "Our commission, right Burke?"

"Sure."

Sheldon zipped up the bag and handed it to Burke. "Pleasure doing business, boss."

"Hey, aren't you forgetting something?" asked Tony.

"Oh yeah, your boy. He's out on the pier with Vince."

"The pier?"

"I figured that we might need a little distance … you know, in case things didn't go so smoothly."

"Yeah, well, you got your money. Bring Ace here."

Sheldon reached over and grabbed his cell phone off the kitchen counter. He flipped it open and punched in a number. "Bring flyboy back here." He flipped the phone shut and set it down. "He'll be here in a moment."

Tony got up. "Come on, Burke … it's a little crowded in here."

Burke got up. "See you around, Sheldon."

"Sure. Let me know when you have another run for us, boss."

Burke nodded. "Yeah, sure."

Tony grabbed the bag off the table. "See you, dipshit."

"You're letting that sleaze bag carry your money?" Sheldon asked Burke.

"Sure. It's his."

"What?"

"We made a deal," said Tony.

"You're telling me that the money isn't yours, Burke?"

Burke nodded. "That's right."

"Too bad, sucker," said Tony and he turned and started down the steps to exit the RV.

"Wait just a goddamn minute."

Tony halted in his tracks. "What now?"

"Let me get this straight, Burke. The money doesn't belong to you?"

"Nope."

"It's his?"

"Yep."

"Then you don't care if we take it from him?"

"Well …"

"What's to you?"

"Nothing, really."

Tony turned around. "Hey, wait a minute, Burke. Don't be giving this douche bag any ideas."

Sheldon continued as though Tony wasn't there. "If we take the money, you won't come after us?"

"Why should I? It's not my money." Burke paused for second. "Well, that is most of it … fifteen grand of it is mine."

"What do you mean?"

"Tony agreed to give me fifteen grand if …"

"Burke!" shouted Tony.

"Opps, guess I wasn't supposed to tell you that."

"You're saying that if you get your fifteen, you don't care what happens to the rest?"

"Burke!" repeated Tony.

"Did I say that?" said Burke.

"I just want to know that you won't come after us if we take the rest," said Sheldon.

"No … but I'd better get my fifteen."

Sheldon reached for his cell phone. Tony pushed Burke aside and swung the green bag so it hit Sheldon in the shoulder. The phone clattered on the floor. Sheldon dived for it and Tony dropped the bag and jumped on top of him.

Burke backed down the steps. "I'll let you ladies sort this out." He went outside and walked back around the rocking RV and got in the car.

"What's going on?" asked Gina.

"Cat fight."

"What are you talking about?"

"Tony and fat boy in there are wrestling over a cell phone."

"Burke, what is going on?"

"Sheldon decided that he wanted more money."

"Why?"

"Guess he figured Tony wasn't as big a threat as I was."

"He knows the money isn't yours?"

"I think so."

"You think so?"

"Okay, I know so."

"Burke, how would he know that unless you told him?"

"I might have let it slip."

"The deal was that Tony would give you fifteen grand if you played along with him."

"I did … more or less."

"Sounds like less to me." Gina opened the door to get out.

"I wouldn't go in there if I were you."

"Well, you're not." She got out and slammed the door shut.

Straddling Sheldon with his right arm around his neck, Tony braced his feet and pulled with all his might. For a pudgy, out-of-shape man, Sheldon put up a surprising resistance, but slowly he gave way and began to straighten up. Tony relaxed his left leg enough to kick the phone a couple of feet away. Sheldon tried to lunge for it again, pulling Tony with him, but before he could reach it, Tony's heel came down hard on it cracking the plastic case.

With all his might Sheldon stood up, causing Tony to be thrown backward into the kitchen table seat. Sheldon grabbed the phone, but as soon as he picked it up, the top broke away and the battery fell out. "Goddamn it," he shouted. He threw the remaining phone parts down turned to grab at the green bag, but Tony raised his foot and pressed it against his chest. Sheldon stumbled backward and Tony leaped up and ran down the steps and out the door, narrowly missing Gina.

Gina jumped back. "Tony!" she shouted.

She heard somebody shouting, "Hold him. Hold him." Gina turned to see Sheldon Isaacs charging down the steps.

He made a grab at the bag in Tony's hands, but Tony gripped the bag tightly.

"Piss on it," said Sheldon, and he turned and ran toward the pier.

"Gina, I told you to stay in the car," said Tony, panting heavily.

"Tony, what is going on?"

"Just get back to the car … now."

"I'm not going anywhere until you tell me where Mickey is."

"Vince has Mickey out on the pier and dipshit there is welching on the deal … he wants all the money, now."

Gina watched Sheldon jogging across the parking lot. "So they're holding Mickey until you give it at all to them?"

"Less the fifteen that they owe Burke."

Gina sighed. "Tony, give them the money."

"Are you nuts?" said Tony.

"Give them the goddamn money, Tony."

"I'm not giving them a goddamn thing."

"That's it." Gina delivered a lightening fast kick to Tony's groin.

Tony's breath came out in a wheeze and he doubled over in pain. Gina quickly wrenched the bag from his hand and took off in a sprint after Sheldon.

Burke and Carl watched Sheldon make his way across the parking lot. "You think Tony is okay?" asked Carl.

"Sheldon doesn't have the bag … Tony must've got the best of him."

"You think he's okay."

"Who cares?"

"What about Gina?"

"She's tough as nails … take my word for it."

They saw Gina flash past the car.

"Hey, wasn't she carrying that green bag?"

"Looked like it."

A few seconds later, Tony rounded the Winnebago. He was hunched over and holding his groin. He banged his hand on the trunk. "Open this up," he demanded.

Carl popped the trunk. Tony leaned in, fished around and found the Colt. He stood back and slammed the lid. He sucked in a breath and straightened as much as he could and staggered off after Gina.

"Oh, this has to be good," said Burke as he opened the door and got out.

"Hey, I'm not staying here," said Carl, and he got out too.

They quickly caught up to Tony who was bent over, but still moving forward. Walking along side, Burke put his hand on Tony's back. "You seem a little out of breath there, Killer," he said.

"Fuck you, you prick," Tony wheezed. "You were supposed to keep your mouth shut about our deal."

"Hey, I'm really sorry about that … it just slipped out."

"You okay, Tony?" asked Carl.

"I just got kicked in the nuts. No, I'm not okay, Carl."

Carl winced. "Jeez, that freekin' hurts, don't it?"

"Yes, Carl, it freekin' hurts."

"Can I do anything for you, Tony?"

"Just help me get out on that pier, will you?"

"Sure, Pal."

Sheldon had slowed to a walk and Gina was rapidly gaining on him, but he was already on the pier, and, although there were only a handful of other people still on it at this late hour, she was reluctant to shout out to him for fear of attracting too much attention. She kept moving, two or three people stopping to stare at her jog by, her shadow stretching before and after her as she passed under the light towers that illuminated the pier.

For the first hundred and fifty yards, the wooden structure passed benignly over beach sand. From there on, she was running over water, the wild Pacific surf licking hungrily at the huge wooden support pilings all the way out to the end, nearly 300 yards away. Halfway out on the pier she caught up to Sheldon. She could see Vince and Mickey coming from the other direction.

Vince noticed Gina coming up from behind Sheldon. "What's she doing here?"

"Huh?" Sheldon turned toward Gina. "What the …?"

Gina pushed passed Sheldon and ran up to Mickey.

"Hey!" yelled Vince.

Gina dropped the bag and threw her arms around Mickey. "Are you all right?"

Almost as surprised as Vince and Sheldon, Mickey fell back a step; then he put his arms around Gina. His cheeks glowing crimson, "Hi," he said.

Sheldon saw the bag at the feet of the embracing couple. "That for me?"

Gina pulled away from Mickey, but kept her gaze on him. She kicked the bag toward Sheldon. "Yeah."

Sheldon bent down to pick it up. "Glad somebody in your family has some brains." He zipped it open to look inside.

Gina ignored him and embraced Mickey again, this time kissing him full on the mouth. She pulled back and looked into his dazed eyes. "I was worried about you."

He smiled awkwardly. "Jeez, if I'd known I'd get this kind of response, I'd have put myself into harms way a lot sooner."

Sheldon zipped the bag shut. "Come on, Vince let's get the hell out of here."

"What about these two?"

"Let 'em get a hotel room."

"You sure?"

"Yeah, we don't need flyboy anymore."

Sheldon turned to start walking back toward the shore. "Have nice life," he said over his shoulder."

"Hey Sheldon, isn't that Tony coming toward us?" asked Vince.

"What?"

"There, just up ahead."

Sheldon squinted toward the pier entrance. He could just make out Tony, Carl and Burke as they passed under a light. Tony was still staggering slightly, but he could make out the Colt dangling from right hand.

"Oh, Christ," said Sheldon. "Back to the love birds ... quick." He turned toward Gina and Mickey. Vince followed; his hand on the butt of the Beretta tucked in his belt underneath the loose fitting shirt he was wearing.

Mickey was still holding Gina, her face pressed against his chest when he saw Sheldon and Vince coming back toward them. "Oh, oh."

Gina pulled away and turned to see them too. "Now what?"

"I don't know, but it can't be good."

Within seconds they were face to face with Sheldon and Vince.

"Take him in there." Sheldon nodded toward an opening in the low, wooden wall that separated the fishermen from the pier strollers.

Vince pulled out the Beretta from his under his shirt and gave Mickey a shove toward the opening. "In there, flyboy."

Gina kicked Vince in the shin. "Get your greasy hands off him."

Vince winced in pain. "Get this broad away from me."

With his free hand, Sheldon grabbed Gina by the arm and pulled her away. She whirled and kicked him in the shin.

"Ow! Goddamnit!" He let go and bent to rub his leg.

Gina turned back to Vince and Mickey, but they had already gone behind the wall, although she could still see their heads and shoulders. She charged toward the opening, but Vince held the Beretta to Mickey's head.

"Stay away, lady, I'm telling you."

She stopped in her tracks. "If you harm him, I'm going to rip your …"

"Gina!"

She turned and saw Tony, Carl and Burke not more than ten yards away. She froze in her tracks. "Go back, Tony," she said.

"Where's the money?" said Tony.

"Right here, dipshit," said Sheldon, holding up the green bag.

Tony raised the Colt. "Hand it over."

"If you try to take this, flyboy goes swimming with an ounce of lead in his head."

A young couple, walking arm in arm, were approaching from the end of the pier. They saw the scene in front of them and stopped.

Tony waved the Colt at them. "Get the hell out of here."

Without a word, they scurried by, and then broke out into a trot toward the shore.

"Great. Now the cops are probably going to show up," said Burke.

Tony ignored him. "Give me the bag, Sheldon."

"Tony, he's not kidding," said Gina. "They're going to kill Mickey if you don't get out of here."

Tony looked at Gina. Then he saw Mickey behind the wall and the Beretta that Vince was holding against him.

"Go on back," said Sheldon.

"Shut up and hand the bag over," said Tony.

"If you take the bag, your friend gets it."

"So what?"

"Tony!" yelled Gina.

"I'm not letting these assholes take my money."

Tears were streaming down Gina's face. "Stop it, Tony."

"You better listen to her, Tony," said Sheldon.

"You shut the fuck up," said Tony.

"Come on, Tony, it ain't worth getting someone killed over," said Carl.

"Who asked you?"

"You can stay if you want," Burke said to Carl. "I'm getting the hell out of here before the cops come." He turned to go, and then he stopped and turned back. "After you ladies finish sorting this out, someone owes me 15k."

"What?" asked Sheldon.

"I'll be sending someone to collect, so don't fuck with me," answered Burke. He turned to go.

"Hey, wait for me," said Carl, and he trotted after him.

"What's he talking about?"

"None of your goddamn business. Just hand me the bag," said Tony.

"You're buddy's gonna get it."

"Tony!" cried Gina. "What the hell are you doing? Can't you see they're going to kill Mickey?"

"They aren't going to do shit. There just a couple of scumbags who think they're gangsters."

Vince pressed the gun against Mickey's temple. "Now, Sheldon?"

"Tony, please …" sobbed Gina.

Tony looked to the sky. The moon had set earlier and there were a few clouds, but the overhead lights of the pier blotted out all but the brightest stars, so most of what he saw was just inky darkness. He could hear the waves crashing against the pilings below, creating a mild tremor that he could feel through the planking of the pier. No longer exerting any effort, and standing in the cool, salt air, his perspiration soaked shirt felt clammy against his skin and he shivered slightly. He shifted his gaze to Mickey. Mickey's neck was buried in the crook of Vince's left arm, his head tilted to the left, but he just stared back blankly. Tony lowered the Colt. "Oh, Christ," he said, almost inaudibly.

Sheldon let out a sigh. "First smart thing you've done today."

Gina ran to him and gave him a hug. "Thank you, Tony."

"I can't believe I'm doing this," said Tony.

"Now you and Gina go back to your car and leave," said Sheldon.

"What about Mickey?" asked Gina.

"He stays with us for a while."

"Why?"

"Because I don't trust Tony, that's why."

"Go on, Gina … I'll be okay," said Mickey.

Tony put his arm around her. "Come on, he'll be all right."

Gina looked at him. "You're sure?"

"We won't harm Mickey if your cousin keeps out of our way," said Sheldon.

"When will you let him go?"

"He'll call you when he's free."

"But …"

"Don't worry, Gina, they won't hurt him," said Tony.

Gina nodded. She walked over to the wall and looked at Mickey. "I'll be waiting."

Mickey smiled, "Can't wait."

39

Sara keyed the mike. "Hayes traffic, Piper one-four F, turning final."

The single engine Piper Cherokee leveled off after turning on its final approach and Sara pulled the flap lever to its full extension. Mickey looked over at Sara and saw a thin, blue vein pulsing in her temple. She was a model of concentration. He was just about to tell her to reduce the power when she reached over pulled the throttle back and the RPM's dropped. The nose dropped too, but Sara increased the back-pressure on the control wheel and the nose came back up. The descent of the airplane was steady and controlled, the numbers on the end of the runway fixed in the windscreen.

Mickey rubbed his hands on his thighs and stifled the urge to tell Sara what to do next. The low, chain-link fence at the boundary of the airport flashed by and runway numbers disappeared from view. The horizon dropped below the nose and the airplane seemed to hang, suspended in midway, and then the barely audible chirp of the main gear contacting the pavement reached Mickey's ears and he felt the Piper settle, the nose dropping quickly.

Sara reached down and released the flap lever. Mickey glanced at her and she was still concentrating, braking gently and keeping the airplane's nose gear tracking down the centerline, but a thin smile had formed on her face. As they approached the second runway turnoff, the airplane's speed had decreased enough to allow a smooth left turn.

Sara keyed the mike again. "Hayes traffic, Piper one-four F, clear of active." She guided the airplane onto the taxiway and followed it to the parking area in front of the FBO. She braked to a stop and pulled the throttle to idle.

"Don't shut it down," said Mickey.

Sara held her hand on the red mixture knob and looked over at Mickey. "What?"

Mickey opened the door and held it against the prop wash created by the idling engine. "I'm getting out and you're taking her around again."

"You're kidding."

"No, I'm not, Sara. You've nailed five landings in row. You're ready to solo."

"Oh, shit, Mickey. I'm not ready for this."

"Sure you are. Just do what you've been doing for the last three lessons and you'll be fine. I have all the confidence in the world in you." He unplugged his headset, pushed the door all the way open and stepped out onto the wing.

"But Mickey …," Sara yelled.

Mickey leaned down and looked at her. "I wouldn't send you if I didn't think you're ready. Trust me." He stood up, slammed the door shut and stepped down off the wing.

Sara looked pleadingly at him through the window. He smiled, gave her an 'OKAY' sign with his right hand and waved her away with his left. He stepped away from the airplane, almost backing into Jeff, who had been standing nearby watching.

"You think she's ready?" asked Jeff.

Without taking his eyes off Sara, Mickey said through a fixed smile, "I sure as hell hope so."

Sara waved and Mickey gave her a 'thumbs up'. The engine revved and the Piper began to roll forward. Mickey held his hat against the increased prop wash. "I sure as hell hope so," he repeated.

They both watched Sara steer the airplane onto the taxiway, heading on to the active end of the runway. When it had disappeared from view behind some hangers, Mickey turned to walk to the FBO. Jeff yelled after him. "Oh, I forgot to tell you … Gina is waiting in your office."

Mickey smiled and waved over his shoulder. He went into the FBO lobby and heard Betty talking to Sara on the radio.

"… wind one-seven-five at eight knots. The active is oh-four."

"Roger," replied Sara.

Betty looked up at Mickey. "Turning a pigeon loose, eh?"

Mickey held up crossed fingers. "Can you give me the handheld?"

Betty handed the portable radio to Mickey. "Gina's in your office."

"I heard." Mickey headed into the pilot's lounge, past the old guard, on his way to his office.

"Hey, Mickey, you lettin' that little filly solo?" asked Stan.

"She's ready."

"She'll need to be rubbed down after that ride."

"Maybe you can handle that, Stan."

The guys laughed at that. Mickey made his way to his office. The door was open and Gina was sitting at his desk, thumbing through an aviation magazine.

"Anything interesting?" Mickey asked.

Gina looked up. "This stuff is so boring." She tossed the magazine on the desk, stood up and brushed out the wrinkles in her sundress. She put her bare arms around his neck. "You're much more interesting."

She smelled of suntan lotion and perfume, a heady mixture to Mickey. "So are you, but I've got a solo bird up there and I have to monitor her." He held up the radio.

"You're no fun." She kissed him and then let him go. "I'll wait."

"You're leaving Tony in charge?"

"It's early. There aren't any customers yet, so he can't do much damage. He'll just be shooting the breeze with Levi."

Mickey turned on the radio and heard the end of Sara's announcement. "…affic departing oh-four, remaining in pattern."

"Oh, jeez, I better get out there," he said.

"Go on, do your duty."

"I don't care, there is no way you'd ever get me in one of those things," said Levi, squatting in front of the refrigerator to stock it with beer bottles.

Tony stopped doodling on a napkin and looked down at Levi from across the bar. "I'm telling you it's great. You can really see the landscape changing as you pass over it … not like being in a big jet where it all looks so abstract."

Levi kept putting bottles on the refrigerator shelves. "Those little airplanes are always ending up in trees. Besides, I can fly to LA to visit my brother in four hours … how long did it take you?"

"That's not the point. It's not about the destination, it's about the journey."

"How long?"

"Look, we were fighting headwinds …"

"What's that?"

Tony held the pen in the air to demonstrate his point. "It's when you are flying into the prevailing winds … it doesn't effect your airspeed, but is slows down your groundspeed."

"What the hell?"

Mickey had had to explain headwinds to Tony at least four times before he grasped the concept. Tony sighed and started doodling again. "It just takes longer to fly into the prevailing wind."

"So how long did it take you to get to LA?"

"I don't know … about a week or so."

Levi shut the refrigerator door and stood up. "A week? I could've driven out there faster than that." He bent down and picked up the empty beer case.

Tony stopped doodling again and put the pen down on the bar. "There were a lot of other factors … stops along the way. But that was the beauty of the thing … we could come and go as we pleased … we didn't have to go through the whole airport thing every time we wanted to stop somewhere."

"Still, a week seems like a hell of a long time." Levi turned to put the case on top of a pile of several others that he was stacking alongside.

"Coming back was a hell of a lot quicker. We made it in two days."

"That's better, but it still seems like a long time to me."

"Well, it is … but you should see some of the sights you can see flying low like that."

Levi turned back, put his hands on the edge of the bar and leaned into them. "Like what?"

Tony took a sip from the drink that was sitting in front of him and thought for a few seconds. Then he said, "Like the wide open spaces of the west. Like watching the landscape change from brown to green … when you get east of the Mississippi it's pretty much all trees down there."

"Sounds boring."

"It's not." Tony took another drink. "What am I arguing with you for? What the hell do you know?" He picked up the pen and started doodling again.

The phone behind the bar rang and Levi picked it up. "*Paesano's*." He listened for a second, and then said, "Yeah he's here." He held the phone out to Tony.

Tony took the phone. "Yeah?"

"I heard you were back in town," said a voice with Spanish accent.

"Johnny. Hey, I was going to call you …"

"When?" asked Johnny.

"Look, I'm still a little mad at you … you let those sleazebags, Vince and Sheldon, screw me out of my money."

"I told you, it wasn't my business … that was between you and Max."

"You caused me a lot of grief, Johnny."

"You might be happy to know that Mr. Jackson and Mr. Isaacs are no longer in my employ."

"Really."

"They've decided to go freelance."

"Yeah, now that they have a nice grubstake."

"But that's not why I called."

"Yeah?"

"I wanted to tell you that my shipment made it out to California with no problems … your drivers were great."

"No kidding? I guess, with all the excitement, I kinda forgot all about that."

"I've got another shipment coming up in a couple of weeks and I'd like to use your crew again."

"Really?" Tony looked at Levi, who shrugged and turned to busy himself behind the bar.

Christopher Hudson currently resides in a northern suburb of Detroit, Michigan. A former denizen of cubeville, he has written and produced many corporate videos and marketing projects. In addition to his previous novel, NORTHERN CROSS, he has written several short stories and screenplays.

NORTHERN CROSS (www.northerncrossonline.com)
See the video preview at:
www.blazingtrailers.com/show/51/

Made in the USA
Charleston, SC
23 November 2010